ANGEL

Barbara Taylor Bradford was born in Leeds, Yorkshire, and was a reporter for the *Yorkshire Evening Post* at sixteen. By the age of twenty she had graduated to Fleet Street as both editor and columnist. In 1979 she wrote her first novel, *A Woman of Substance*, and that enduring best-seller was followed by seven others: *Voice of the Heart, Hold the Dream, Act of Will, To Be the Best, The Women in his Life, Remember* and *Angel*. Six of her books have been made into television mini-series. Her novels have been published in 82 countries and 24 languages with 40 million copies in print. Barbara Taylor Bradford lives in New York City with her husband, film producer Robert Bradford.

D1323032

BARBARA TAYLOR BRADFORD

Angel

This edition published 1994 for The Boots company PLC
by special arrangement with
HarperCollins*Publishers*
77-85 Fulham Palace Road,
Hammersmith, London W6 8JB

Special overseas edition 1993

First published in Great Britain by
HarperCollins*Publishers* 1993

ISBN 0 583 31853 3

Set in Palatino

Printed in Great Britain

For my beloved husband Bob,
with whom I have always shared the
many-splendoured thing.

Contents

The angels keep their ancient places;—
Turn but a stone, and start a wing!
'Tis ye, 'tis your estrangèd faces,
That miss the many-splendoured thing.

Francis Thompson

PART ONE

Shining Stars

ONE

She stood near one of the huge stone pillars, a little to one side in the shadows, watching the fight.

The woman, whose name was Rosalind Madigan, was taut with nerves. Her hands were clenched at her sides and she held her breath; then her lips parted slightly in anticipation and anxiety surfaced in her eyes.

Metal struck metal as swords clashed.

The warriors battled on. They were fencing to the death; she knew there could be only one winner.

Brilliant light, penetrating the windows set high in the castle walls, glanced off their swift and lethal swords. Gavin, the smaller of the two, was slender, supple and fleet of foot. He went on the offensive, moving with great speed, his rapier thrusting forward dangerously. He drove his opponent back . . . farther back across the stone floor of the vast Great Hall. Suddenly he had the advantage.

James, the other knight, taller, broader, more cumbersome of body, was now pinioned in a corner, his back pressed close to the wall, a mixture of fury and fear blanching his face.

To the woman, it seemed that the fight would be over sooner than she had anticipated. It was perfectly obvious to her that Gavin was about to triumph. Then, much to her amazement, James managed, somehow, to shift his stance, ever so slightly but just enough to manoeuvre his bulk into a new position. Unexpectedly, he lunged forward purposefully, and she sucked in her breath. *He* now had the advantage.

Gavin, somewhat taken by surprise, was thrown into a defensive position. Surely this was not the way it was meant to be, she thought, and leaned forward, her eyes riveted on the two men.

Gavin moved backward swiftly, and with his usual dexterity, as nimble as a dancer, he parried James's thrusts with immense skill and strength.

James went on lunging after him, breathing heavily, brandishing his sword with equal expertise, but he was not quite as light on his feet as Gavin.

The two men were moving into the centre of the baronial hall, fencing feverishly. Attack. Parry. Attack. Parry. James had begun to pant excessively, his movements slowing. Gavin was gaining ground once more. He was on the offensive, in superb control, moving in for the kill.

James stumbled and went down, his sword clattering across the stone floor, out of reach.

In a flash Gavin was by his side, standing over James, the point of his sword resting close to the other knight's throat.

Their eyes locked in an intense and powerful gaze. Neither one could look away.

'Kill me then, and be done with it!' James cried out at last.

'I do not choose to soil my sword with your blood,' Gavin intoned coldly but in the softest of voices. 'Suffice it that I have won this last, and final, fight. Now it is truly finished between us. Be gone from these parts, return on fear of death.'

Taking several steps backward, he sheathed his sword in the scabbard that hung from the belt around his waist, walked across the floor and up the wide staircase without a backward glance. Only when he reached the top of the stairs did he briefly look down at James before disappearing into the shadows.

There was a moment of total silence.

Then the director's voice rang out. 'Cut! And print!' he shouted, adding jubilantly, 'And that's a wrap, guys!'

The actor called James scrambled to his feet; the director hurried across to confer with the cinematographer; everybody began talking at once, milling around the set, laughing, joking, slapping each other on the back.

Ignoring this sudden hullabaloo, Rosalind picked up her bag, hurried across the floor and up the staircase, seeking Gavin. He still stood in the shadows on the platform where the stairs ended. When she reached him she saw that he held his body rigidly; there was strain in his eyes and, underneath his make-up, gooseflesh speckled his face.

'You're hurting,' she said.

'A bit. I feel as if a steel hand is gripping the back of my skull. I need the collar, Rosie.'

15

Instantly, she pulled it out of her bag and helped him to put it around his neck. A week ago, on location in Yorkshire, Gavin had been thrown by his horse. He had sustained muscle and nerve damage to his neck and left shoulder, and had been in pain ever since.

As she fastened the collar he looked down at her gratefully and smiled, visibly relaxing now that the surgical collar was giving him support. He had discovered it helped him more than the pain-killers.

'I couldn't help worrying about you during the last scene,' Rosie said, and shook her head wonderingly. 'I don't know how you got through it.'

'That's the magic . . . the magic of the theatre, of acting. Once I started the scene, the adrenaline began to pump like crazy and the pain disappeared. At least, I was no longer aware of the pain. I was swept up in the role of Warwick. I was submerged in him. I'd become him. The role always takes over, I guess, and I'm oblivious to everything when I'm acting.'

'I know you are. Still, I did worry about you.' She gave him a small smile. 'After all these years, you'd think I'd know better, wouldn't you? And anyway, I've always said your concentration is one of the secrets of your success.' She took hold of his arm. 'But come on, let's go, Charlie's waiting with James, Aida and the crew.'

As Rosie and Gavin walked down the staircase a cheer went up and the crew began to applaud enthusiastically. They were well aware that the star of their movie had been in agony for days, and they admired Gavin Ambrose, not only for his talent as an actor, but for his stoicism after his injury and for his total dedication to the film. He was a true professional who had been determined to finish the picture on time, and the crew wanted to show their admiration and appreciation.

'You were great, Gavin, just great,' Charlie Blake, the director, said, grasping his hand when Gavin and Rosie reached the bottom of the stairs. 'And I have to tell you, I didn't think you'd get it in three takes.'

'Pity it wasn't in one,' Gavin replied dryly. 'But thanks, Charlie, and thanks for letting us keep the fight going the way you did. It worked this last time around, didn't it?'

'You bet it did! I'm not going to cut a single second of footage.'

'You're a real trouper, Gavin,' Aida Young, the producer, said, stepping forward, giving him a motherly hug, albeit very carefully because of his neck. 'They don't make them any better. You've got plenty of what it takes.'

'Thanks, Aida, that's a rare compliment indeed, coming from you.' Gavin glanced over at James Lane, who had just acted in the fight scene with him, and grinned. 'Congratulations, Jimbo.'

James grinned back. 'And congratulations to you, mate.'

'Thanks for making it easy,' Gavin went on. 'Fights are pretty tough to choreograph, and your timing couldn't have been better. In fact, it was perfect.'

'Let's face it, we're a couple of regular Errol Flynns,' James answered, winking at Gavin. 'It's a pity Kevin Costner just did that remake of *Robin Hood*, or we might have had a stab at it ourselves.'

Gavin laughed and nodded, and then noticing Aida's expression he exclaimed, 'Hey, don't look so worried, honey. My neck's okay, honest it is. I'm even going to make the wrap party later.'

'I'm glad, and that's lovely,' the producer said, then cautioned, 'but only if you're up to it.'

Gavin's eyes swept over the crew. 'Thanks,' he said with genuine sincerity. 'Thanks for everything, you've all been terrific, and we're gonna have a real celebration later today.'

'You bet we are, Gavin,' the gaffer answered, and the crew surged around him, to tell him what a great guy he was, the best in the business, and to shake his hand.

A short while later, Rosie and Gavin left the huge sound stage where the Great Hall of Middleham Castle had been re-created, and went out into the corridor behind the set.

Here it was a jumble of cables, and scaffolding rising to the ceiling, the latter built to hold the Klieg lights used to provide simulated sunshine outside the castle walls. Carefully, they picked their way through the maze of wires and equipment; for different reasons, they were both relieved the last scene had been shot, that the film was in the can. Silently, lost in their own thoughts, they headed for Gavin's quarters on the back lot.

'Are you really going to New York at the end of the week?' Gavin asked, hovering in the doorway of the bathroom which adjoined his dressing room, tightening the belt of his white terrycloth robe while staring at her intently.

Rosie looked up from her notebook, returning his long stare.

'Yes,' she said after a moment, and put the notebook back into her bag. 'I have a meeting with some Broadway producers. About a new musical. And I have to see Jan Sutton as well. She's thinking of putting on a revival of *My Fair Lady*.'

Gavin began to laugh. 'That wouldn't be very rewarding for *you*, would it?' he asked, moving swiftly across the floor as he spoke. 'After all, Cecil Beaton made an unforgettable statement with the costumes he designed for the original production. Everybody remembers them.'

'That's true, yes,' Rosie agreed. 'But, you know what, it could be very challenging. I wouldn't mind tackling it . . . we'll see what happens.' She shrugged, and went on quickly, 'I'm going to LA from New York. To see Garry Marshall. He wants me to do the clothes for his new movie –'

'Instead of the Broadway shows, or as well as?' Gavin interrupted.

'As well as.'

'Rosie, you're crazy! It's too much! You're killing yourself with work these days. Why, this year alone you've done two West End plays and my film, and let's face it, this one hasn't been easy. In fact, it's been very demanding, to say the least. Is it going to be the same again next year? Three or four projects? Enough's enough, for God's sake.'

'I need the money.'

'I'll give you as much as you want. Haven't I always told you, anything I have is yours.'

'Yes, and thank you, Gavin, you know how much I appreciate that. But it's not the same – what I mean is, money from you is not the same as the money I earn myself. Besides, it's not really for me. I need the extra money for my family.'

'They're not your family!' he shot back with uncharacteristic vehemence, and a look of irritation crossed his face.

Rosie gaped at him, taken by surprise, and bit back the words that had instantly sprung to her lips. She remained silent, baffled by the flash of anger, so transparent, the strong reaction, so unexpected.

Swinging around abruptly, Gavin seated himself in the chair facing the dressing table, reached for a jar of cold cream and a box of tissues, obviously intent on taking off his theatrical make-up.

'They *are* my family,' she said finally.

'*No*. We're your family. Me and Nell and Kevin!' he exclaimed, pushing the tissues and cream away with a sudden harsh movement of his hand.

Ignoring his impatience, she thought: And Mikey. He is family too, wherever he is. And Sunny. A faint shadow fell across her heart, and she sighed under her breath, thinking of them, concern surfacing.

A split-second later, pushing herself up from the sofa, Rosie walked over to Gavin and stood behind him, resting her hands on the back of his chair. Her burnished chestnut head hovered above his darker one, and her green gaze was questioning as it met and held his grey-blue eyes reflected in the mirror.

As if in answer to her unspoken question, he murmured in a gentler voice, 'We said we were a family, remember?' and then he lowered his eyes and focused on the photograph on the dressing table.

Rosie followed the direction of his glance, her own settling on the images in the silver frame. There they all were. She and Nell, Gavin, Kevin, Mikey and Sunny, arms looped, shining faces smiling, eyes bright with expectation and hope. It had been taken such a long time ago. They had been so young . . . and orphans, each one of them.

'We promised we'd always be there for one another, no matter what, Rosie. We said we were a family,' Gavin persisted. 'And we were. We are.'

'Yes,' she whispered, 'a family, Gavin.' She pushed back a sudden rush of sadness that threatened to overwhelm her . . . the tragedy was that they had all broken their promises to each other . . .

Gavin lifted his head, caught her eye in the mirror again, and his familiar crooked, and now famous, smile flashed endearingly, lighting up his face. 'If you're so hell-bent on killing yourself, then it had better be on one of *my* movies, where I can at least pick up the pieces, if needs be. How about it, will you do my next picture?'

Her serious expression dissolved, the solemnity in her eyes vanished, and she started to laugh. Then she exclaimed, 'It's a deal, Mr Ambrose. You've got yourself a deal!'

There was a sudden knocking on the door, and Will Brent came in. Will was from Wardrobe, and he said quickly, 'I came to help you get out of your costume, Gavin, but I see you've already done so. Sorry to be late.'

'No problem, Will, I've only taken off my doublet. Perhaps you'll help me with the rest of my stuff, especially these boots.' Gavin grinned at Will and stuck out a leg.

'Right away,' Will said, loping across the room.

'I'll see you at the wrap party,' Rosie murmured, kissed Gavin lightly on top of his head, and went over to the sofa to retrieve her bag.

'Remember what I said, Angel Face. You're on for my next picture,' Gavin called out before turning his attention to the surgical collar. Gingerly, he adjusted it on his neck, grimacing as he did.

TWO

A blast of cold air hit Rosie in the face as she stepped outside. Shivering, she pulled her jacket closer around her and looked up.

Above her the sky was bleak and unremitting, filled with clouds the colour of lead. Even though it was still afternoon it was already gloomy and growing darker, the kind of English winter's day to which she had grown accustomed of late.

There was a hint of drizzle in the wind, and she could not help wondering what the children of England would do if it rained after all.

Today was November the fifth. Bonfire Night, they called it. Aida had told her this over lunch last week, and the producer had recited the ancient verse, passed down over the centuries, which she had learned as a child: 'Please to remember the fifth of November, gunpowder, treason, and plot.' Bonfires would blaze throughout the British Isles tonight, effigies of Guy Fawkes would be tossed into the flames, fireworks exploded, and potatoes and chestnuts roasted in the fire, as was the tradition – providing it didn't rain, of course.

'All being well, we'll be wrapping the picture on the fifth,' Aida had said to her, over their snack in the studio restaurant last Tuesday. 'But I'm afraid we won't be allowed to have a bonfire. For security reasons, obviously. However, maybe we can come up with something appropriate – to celebrate Bonfire Night as well as the end of the film.'

She had not been able to determine exactly what Aida had meant by *appropriate*, but she and everyone else would soon know. The wrap party was scheduled to take place in a few hours.

Rosie glanced around as she hurried across the deserted back lot of Shepperton Studios, walking in the direction of her office in the production building.

She had been based here for the past nine months, and the territory had grown so familiar to her it now felt like home. Also, she had enjoyed working with Aida and the crew, who were all British, and with whom she had felt comfortable and at ease from the start.

Quite unexpectedly, it hit her how much she was going to miss Shepperton and everyone connected with the movie. That was not always the case; sometimes she was relieved and thankful when a film was finally in the can, so that she could make a fast escape, fleeing without looking back. But an enormous camaraderie between the cast, crew and production people had built up on *Kingmaker*, and over the long months of working together the feelings of closeness and intimacy had become more pronounced than ever. Perhaps that was because this particular production had been troubled right from the outset, and in consequence everyone had hung together to fight for it, determined to make it succeed. She was sure it would. In the picture business it was something of a given that a difficult film frequently turned out to be the best, once it was cut, edited and scored, and up there on the screen.

They had all worked incredibly hard, extending themselves beyond the call of duty, even when they were almost too exhausted to continue. Yet somehow they had. And Gavin, who had put his heart and soul into the role of Richard Neville, the Earl of Warwick, had given a stellar performance, an Oscar-winning performance. At least that was her opinion, but, no doubt about it, *she* was prejudiced.

Pushing open the double glass doors of the production building, Rosie went down the narrow corridor and into her office. After closing the door behind her she leaned against it for a moment, her eyes sweeping around the room, taking everything in: the drawings lining the walls, the racks of costumes, the huge table covered with research and the many and varied accessories she had designed.

During the nine months she had been camped here she had accumulated innumerable possessions, and it struck her that she was facing a great deal of packing in the next few days. It was a relief to know she had her two assistants, Val Horner and Fanny Leyland, to help catalogue her drawings, pack them along with the costumes she wanted to keep for her archive, and box up the books and photographs which had been used for research.

Her main sketches of the costumes for Gavin were

pinned on the long wall of the office, and now she walked over and stood looking at them, for a moment studying the designs intently, her head to one side. Then she nodded to herself.

Gavin was right, *Kingmaker* had been a very demanding film, not only because of its size, elaborateness and huge cast, but also because of the pomp and ceremony and other historical elements in the script, which she had had to take into consideration, and which had naturally influenced her designs. It had been quite a challenge. Nevertheless, she responded well to challenges; they seemed to bring out the best in her. And difficult and backbreaking though the work had been, she was gratified that she had had the opportunity to be part of a picture of such sweep, scope and magnitude.

Right from the beginning, when they had first gone into preproduction, she had been exhilarated about it, brimming with excitement and energy.

Her main focus had been on Gavin, who was cast in the leading role of Warwick. The Earl had been the most powerful man in England during the middle two decades of the fifteenth century. A Yorkshireman of Royal blood, descended from King Edward III, he was the premier Earl of England in his time, and one of the greatest magnates and warrior knights who had ever lived – truly the stuff of legend. It was Warwick who had put his cousin Edward Plantagenet on the throne of England during the civil war between the Royal Houses of York and Lancaster. Commonly known as the War of the Roses, so named because of the emblems of the white rose of York and the red

26

rose of Lancaster, Warwick had been a major player in that war. He had, in the end, been responsible for defeating the Lancastrians in several bloody battles, and had handed the realm to Edward of York, the legitimate heir.

Because Warwick was the power behind the throne and the chief adviser to his nineteen-year-old protégé, King Edward IV, his contemporaries had dubbed him the Kingmaker. This name had stuck over five centuries, hence the title of their movie. The screenplay, by Oscar-winning screenwriter Vivienne Citrine, focused on Warwick in 1461, when he was in his thirty-third year and at the height of his powers, the action continuing for two more years, with the film ending in 1463.

Rosie's main concern had been to create costumes for Gavin that were medieval in style, but which also suited him, flattered him, looked good on film, were comfortable to wear and move about in.

As always, her aim was to give the clothes genuine historical accuracy. It was her belief that costuming, like sets, must bring a period vividly to life on celluloid, and thus help to make the movie realistic and wholly believable. She was as renowned for her skill at doing this as she was for her immense talent, and it was one of the many secrets of her success as a theatrical designer. Rosalind Madigan's costumes had long been noted for their unique sense of period, whether it was a period from the past or of the present, and she also made certain they delineated the rank, class and nationality of the characters in a film or a play.

Her research for *Kingmaker* had been so extensive she realized at one point that she had done far more than she usually did, and than was necessary. But this was because of Gavin. The film was his idea, and his own personal project. He was one of the executive producers, and had even raised the money to finance it. Hollywood had wanted no part of it, despite the fact that Gavin was as big a star as Costner, Stallone and Schwarzenegger, and at the top of the box-office charts. In fact, Gavin had faced the same kind of situation Kevin Costner had when that actor had tried to get the Hollywood studios interested in *Dances with Wolves*. None of them had wanted to commit to it, and Costner had gone out and done it all himself, had raised the money required with the help of Jake Ebert, an independent producer based in Europe.

The actual concept for *Kingmaker* had been entirely Gavin's – *his vision* – and he had believed in it with such a fervour he had ignited everyone around him, filled them with his own brand of enthusiasm.

A history buff, and long intrigued by Warwick, he had been seized once more by the drama, excitement, achievement, glory and ultimate tragedy of the Earl's life when reading yet another biography of him. His imagination fired, and filled with inspiration, he had selected a few key years, when Warwick's star had been at its apex, and had developed his own story outline for the film. He had then hired Vivienne Citrine to write the screenplay. Together they had worked on it for over a year, until Gavin was satisfied it was as perfect as it could ever be, that it truly was a fine shooting script.

Rosie herself had been very taken with the project from its inception. Gavin had first discussed it with her when she had seen him in Beverly Hills late in 1988, and not unnaturally her excitement had known no bounds when he had finally managed to glue it all together last year.

Long before they had started preproduction in England, she had begun her research for the costumes, reading biographies of Warwick and Edward IV, as well as history books about England and France in the Middle Ages. She had studied the art and architecture of the period in order to have a total visual picture of the times, and once she was in London she had spent long hours in the historical costume departments of various museums.

When the assistant director, production designer, production manager, several other members of the unit and Gavin had left the studios to go scouting locations, she had gone with them.

They had first visited Middleham Castle on the Yorkshire moors, once the great Northern stronghold of Warwick, which still stood but had long been a desolated ruin, its broken towers and shattered chambers windswept and open to the elements. But Gavin had felt it was important to see the castle and the terrain where Warwick had grown up and had lived out a large portion of his life.

Together she and Gavin had walked through the vast empty space that had once been the Great Hall. It was roofless now, its walls crumbling into further decay. Under a sky of piercing blue, they had stepped across a stone-flagged floor partially grown-over with

29

grass and with tiny spring wildflowers sprouting up between the cracks. Despite its tumbledown appearance it had been impressive and had captured her imagination, and Gavin's also. Later they had driven over the sombre implacable moors where Warwick had fought some of his most decisive battles.

At the end of their trip they had travelled farther afield, had pushed on towards the East Coast. Gavin had wanted to visit York Minster, the magnificent Gothic cathedral in the ancient walled city of York. It was here that Warwick and Edward IV had once marched in soaring triumph and glory, moving across the plain of York on their caparisoned horses, at the head of their great armies, their silken armorial banners blowing in the wind, the two of them heroes to all of England – the valiant young King and the Kingmaker. To Rosie, this was one of the most colourful and effective ceremonial scenes in the script, and she had been excited about designing the costumes for it.

Between several more trips to Yorkshire, and many more hours spent cloistered in libraries and museums, she had eventually acquired enough knowledge to start all of her designs, confident that she knew more about medieval England than most people.

As it turned out, the only real problem Rosie encountered was the designing of the armour. Recalling the worry and anxiety of that now, she eyed the suit of armour standing in one corner of the room, and winced. She would never forget the terrible struggle she had had in creating the prototype.

There was one big battle scene in the script, which, despite the difficulty of shooting it and the costs involved, Gavin was determined to keep. And so she had had no alternative but to make a stab at designing the medieval armour plate.

In the end she had been able to overcome her many problems with it, but only because of Brian Ackland-Snow. Brian was their immensely talented production designer, another Oscar-winner – for the movie *A Room with a View* – who at the time had been in the process of bringing fifteenth-century England to life on the sound stages of Shepperton.

As far as Rosie was concerned, Brian was a genius, and she was well aware that she would be eternally in his debt. He had introduced her to a manufacturer of underwater diving suits who was able to copy her design for the suit of armour using a strong and rigid neoprene with a silver coating which cleverly simulated the iron used for armour in the Middle Ages. This synthetic rubber was light in weight and comfortable for the actors to wear, yet on film it looked exactly like the real thing.

Swinging around, Rosie walked over to the large table at the other end of the room, knowing she must assess the massive piles of research stacked there.

Immediately, she realized she would need as many as six large tea chests in which to pack everything. Apart from the books, sketches and photographs, there were swatches of specially-dyed fabrics, such as tweeds, wools and broadcloths; samples of suede and leather for boots, trousers, jerkins and doublets; pieces of fur, plus a vast array of velvets and silks.

Baskets and trays held a fantasy collection of brilliant, glittering costume jewellery – brooches, rings, necklaces, earrings, bracelets, fancy buttons, belts, scabbards and gilded-metal crowns. All the stuff of pomp and ceremony and majesty needed for an historical movie of this nature.

What a production it has been, she thought almost wonderingly – costly, elaborate and complicated beyond anything they had ever imagined at the outset. And it had been so fraught at times. Tempers had flared, angry words had been exchanged, and there had been a few temperamental scenes, quite apart from the genuinely serious problems they had had to contend with: bad weather and illnesses, to mention only two, which had caused delays and spiralling costs. On the other hand, filming had never been anything but thrilling, that really was the only word to use, and it had turned out to be the most splendid production, the likes of which she had never before worked on. And perhaps never would again.

Whenever she had been able to, she had gone with Gavin to see the rushes – the footage shot the day before and processed overnight in the lab. Every scene she had watched in the studio screening room had taken her breath away. The 'look' was there, vivid and visually arresting; the unfolding drama was spellbinding; the acting superb.

Gavin was forever worried about the film; they all were, in one way or another. But just a short while ago, as the last scene was shot and the movie wrapped, she had known deep in her bones that they really did have a winner. A sure thing. She was convinced that Gavin had made a movie that was of the same quality, calibre and importance as *The Lion in Winter*, and that it would win a clutch of Oscars.

Eventually, she roused herself from her meanderings about her work and the film, realizing how much she had to accomplish in the next three days.

And so she went and sat down at her desk in front of the window and, pulling the phone towards her, she dialled. The number rang and rang until finally it was picked up, and a familiar girlish voice said, 'Hello, Rosalind, sorry I took so long to answer. I was up on the ladder, putting your boxed files on the top shelf.'

'How did you know it was me?' Rosie asked, laughter echoing in her voice.

'Don't be so silly, Rosalind, nobody else phones me on this number, you know *that*.'

'Only too true. I'd forgotten for a minute. Anyway, Yvonne, how are you?'

'Fine, and so is everyone else. Collie and Lisette are out, though. Did you wish to speak to Collie?'

'Well, yes, I did, but it's okay, really it is. I was just touching base, and I wanted to tell you that I mailed two cheques last night. One each for you and Collie.'

'Thanks, Rosalind.'

'Listen, honey, I'm leaving for New York on Saturday and I –'

'You told me you were flying on Friday when we spoke the other day!' Yvonne exclaimed, her tone rising ever so slightly.

'I'd planned to, but there's a lot to pack up here, and so I've decided to take the plane on Saturday morning. Incidentally, I'll be sending quite a few boxes over to you, so just pile them up there in a corner of my studio when they come. I'll deal with them when I arrive.'

'When will that be?'

Recognizing the sudden plaintive note in the young woman's voice, and wishing to reassure her, Rosie said quickly, 'December. I'll be there in December. That's not so far away.'

'Do you promise?'

'I promise.'

'It's not the same here when you're away. And I miss you.'

'I know, and I miss you, too. But I'll be there soon.' There was a moment's hesitation on Rosie's part, and then she said, 'By the way, did Guy come back?'

'Yes. But he's not here. He went out with Collie and Lisette. And his father.'

This was so surprising to her, Rosie exclaimed, 'Where have they gone?'

'They went to see Kyra. It's her birthday.'

'*Oh.*' Rosie paused momentarily, then clearing her throat she continued, 'Give them my love, and lots of love to you, Yvonne. Thanks for looking after everything for me, I really appreciate it. I don't know what I'd do without you.'

'It's nothing. I enjoy it, Rosalind.'

They said their goodbyes, and Rosie put the receiver back in the cradle, sat staring into the distance, her mind focused on Guy. How curious it was that he had gone with the others to see Kyra. It was so out of character. But then rarely, if ever, did she understand *his* motivations. He was a mystery to her; she supposed he always had been, really. There was one thing she was certain of, though. His scrupulous politeness to Kyra was merely a mask he donned in order to conceal his bitter loathing of her. He was jealous, of course. She had detected that unfortunate emotion in him long ago. Jealous of Kyra, and of his father's friendship with the Russian woman and his deep affection for her.

Rosie sat back in her chair, glancing at the photograph of Guy, Lisette and Collie resting on the corner of the desk. She had taken it herself last summer, and there had been something so carefree and happy about that snap she had had it enlarged and framed. But their insouciant smiles hid turmoil and pain and unhappiness – at least these were the feelings lurking in Guy and Collie, she knew that far too well. Lisette was still too young, at the age of five, to have any knowledge of such painful things. Guy was a problem, there was no longer much doubt left in her mind about that. Not only to his father, but to everyone else, most especially her and Collie, whom he blamed, unreasonably, for most of his troubles.

'Out of sync,' was how Gavin described him. He had never liked Guy, and was fond of saying that he should have lived in the 1960s in Haight-Ashbury. 'That bum's an ageing hippie, out of place, and *way* out of his time frame,' he had said to her only the other day, an acerbic edge to his voice. There was a grain of truth in Gavin's remark; more than a grain, actually. But there was nothing she could do to change Guy; sometimes she thought he was on the road to self-destruction.

However, whatever Gavin said about Guy and the others, they *were* her family, and she was very involved with them, cared about them. She even cared about Guy to a certain extent, even though he did not deserve it.

A sigh of dismay ran through her. He was not very good at reading character, had no insight into people, otherwise he would know better how to deal with his father and Collie and her. His irresponsibility had seemed only to grow as he himself had grown older; she had always known he was weak, but lately she had come to believe he was the most selfish human being she had ever met.

Now her eyes strayed to the other photograph on the desk. It was identical to the one which sat on Gavin's dressing table; even the Tiffany frame was the same. Nell had given each of them one for Christmas years ago and had kept one for herself.

Leaning forward, she peered at Nell's face. How fragile she looked with those finely-chiselled features, shining hair the colour of silver-gilt, and dreamy eyes as blue as a perfect summer sky. Petite, small-boned and delicately made though Nell was, she was strong. The strongest of all of them is how it seemed to her sometimes. Guts of steel and an iron will, that's how she characterized her Little Nell these days.

Smiling out of the picture was their beautiful Sunny, their Golden Girl. She was as fair-haired as Nell, but hers was a golden blonde, and she was taller and more solid in build, very good-looking in a Slavic kind of way: slanted, almond-shaped eyes, prominent cheekbones, a square jawline. Sunny was robust and healthy, her pink and white skin fresh and dewy, the unique amber-coloured eyes flecked with gold – and full of life. Her appearance signalled that she probably came from peasant stock, and this was true, she did; her parents were first-generation Americans of Polish extraction. Poor Sunny. She had turned out to be made of spun glass and just as fragile and as easily shattered. Yes, poor Sunny indeed. Living out her days in that awful place, her mind gone somewhere far away, far away from all of them, and from reality.

Kevin stood next to Gavin. Darkly handsome, black Irish eyes brimming with laughter and mischief. In his own way he was lost to them too, living his life in the belly of the beast, living on the edge, forever running from danger zone to danger zone, caught up in a horrific netherworld that one day might cost him his life.

And there was Mikey, towering over Kevin and Sunny in the picture, another victim of the era they had grown up in, another one they had lost. In this photograph his sandy hair looked almost golden, was like a shining halo around his face; she had always thought Mikey had the nicest of faces, pleasant and friendly. He was handsome in a reserved, quiet way, and he dwarfed them all with his height and broad shoulders.

They did not know where Mikey was. He had disappeared, literally vanished, and try though he might, Gavin had been unable to come up with any valid information about him, or a hint of his whereabouts. Neither had the private detectives Gavin had hired.

She and Nell and Gavin were the three who had turned out all right, who had made it to the top, had fulfilled their youthful dreams: although her brother Kevin might disagree that they were the *only* ones who had succeeded in what they had set out to do. Kevin Madigan had also made it – in his own way. Certainly he was doing what he wanted, and was doing it well, she supposed.

Rosalind reached for the picture and held it up in front of her eyes, studying their faces intently for the longest moment. They had all been so close once, loving and caring, their lives intertwined.

After a while her gaze settled on Gavin's image. How famous it was these days – that bony face, all planes and angles, with its high, sharp cheekbones and deeply clefted chin. His eyes, of a clear grey-blue the colour of slate, were wide apart but deeply set. *Cool eyes*, that was how she thought of them. Long-lashed, they gazed out from under black brows that matched his hair. Appraising, honest and unflinching, they were the kind of eyes the crafty did not care to meet. His mouth was sensitive, tender almost, and the curious, crooked smile she knew so well was now as famous as his face: his trademark, in a sense.

Women the world over had fallen in love with that face, possibly because it was a poetic face, one which seemed touched by heartbreak and suffering, a romantic face. And medieval, perhaps? She pondered that, asked herself if she was getting the actor confused with his most recent role, and she knew she was not. Gavin did have the type of face so often depicted in fifteenth-century paintings – old-world, European. That was no wonder, since he was Scottish on his mother's side, hence his first name, and Italian on his father's, his surname having been Ambrosino until he had altered it ever so slightly for the stage.

Despite his fame, fortune and success, Gavin Ambrose had not changed much deep down inside, that she knew. In countless ways he was still the same young man he had been when they had first met in 1977. She had been seventeen and so had her friend Nell; Gavin had been nineteen, Kevin and Mikey both twenty, and Sunny had been the youngest at sixteen. They had come together as a group for the first time one balmy September evening during the Feast of San Genarro, the Italian festival that took place on Mulberry Street in Little Italy in lower Manhattan.

So very long ago, she thought. Fourteen years, to be exact. In the intervening years so much had happened to them all . . .

Loud knocking startled Rosie, brought her up straighter in the chair, and before she could say a word the door flew open to admit one of her assistants, Fanny Leyland.

'My apologies for not being here when we wrapped!' Fanny exclaimed breezily, flying up to the desk in a flurry of rustling skirts. Small, slender and neat as a new pin, she was smart, talented, a bundle of nervous energy and a genuine workaholic.

Fanny was devoted to Rosalind, and with an apologetic smile she continued, 'I'm afraid I got delayed by a *difficult* actress. You haven't needed me for anything, have you?' She hovered in front of the desk looking slightly worried.

'No, not really, although tomorrow I will,' Rosie answered. 'We're going to have to buckle down and get my research into boxes.'

'No problem. Val and I will pitch in like the devoted slaves we are, and we'll have you all packed up by the end of the day.'

'I'm not so sure about that,' Rosie responded, and began to laugh. 'I'm certainly going to miss your smiling face, your boundless energy and cheerfulness, Fanny. Not to mention that efficiency of yours. I've grown very used to you, and let's face it, you've spoiled me.'

'No, I haven't, and I'll miss you, too. Think of me, Rosalind, *please*, when you do another movie or a play. I'll be there in two shakes of a lamb's tail . . . wherever it is you are. I'll go to the ends of the earth to work with you again!'

Rosie smiled at the younger woman, and nodded her assent. 'Of course you can work on another project with me, Fanny. And Val as well. I'd love that. You two are the best assistants I've ever had.'

'Oh gosh, thanks, that's wonderful to know! Just super! By the way, the reason why I was not loitering around here, waiting to be of service to you when you came back from the set, was Margaret Ellsworth.' Fanny pulled a face and continued, 'She's absolutely *determined* to get that gown, the one she wore for the

Coronation scene in Westminster Abbey. She's ready to *kill* for it.'

Puzzled, Rosie frowned. 'Why would anyone want a medieval dress, for God's sake? It's not even all that beautiful . . . certainly it was never a particular favourite of mine, even if I did design it.'

'Actresses are actresses, a breed apart. Well, at least the difficult ones are,' Fanny muttered, and then she flashed Rosie a bright smile. 'But of course there are those who are very special, and they far outnumber the miserable ones like the Maggie Ellsworths of this world.'

'They do indeed,' Rosie agreed. 'Anyway, you'd better take this matter up with Aida. If Production wants to sell the dress, or give it to Maggie, it's fine with me. I mean, I don't own it, you know, nor do I want it for my archive. Why don't you go and see Aida now? Sort the matter out with her, and then come back as quickly as possible. I'd like to start cataloguing the sketches this afternoon.'

'Okay. I'll be back in a minute, and Val's on her way here from Wardrobe right now, so don't worry, the three of us will make light work of all this.' So saying, Fanny swung around and darted out, carelessly slamming the door behind her so hard the light fixture rattled.

Smiling to herself, Rosie reached for the phone, shaking her head as she did. Fanny was such a character; she really was going to miss her and Val. Opening her address book, she found the number of the Broadway producers who had contacted her about their new musical, and then glanced at her watch.

It was three-thirty in the afternoon here in England. With the five-hour time difference that made it ten-thirty in the morning in New York. The perfect time exactly to make this call.

THREE

Almost three hundred people had been invited to the wrap party, and to Rosie, standing in the doorway, it looked as if everyone had shown up.

The entire unit was present, along with the cast, some of the studio executives, and quite a few civilians. The latter were the people only associated with the movie through their spouses, or nearest and dearest, and whom the producers had included on the invitation list as a courtesy.

Holding drinks in their hands, all were chatting animatedly, mingling together on the biggest sound stage at Shepperton, where the Great Hall of Middleham Castle had been re-created.

Moving forward to join the throng, Rosie saw that the set looked a little different than it had a few hours earlier, when the movie had finally wrapped. The large pieces of medieval-style furniture had been removed, a small combo played popular music in one corner, and the caterers had placed long trestle tables around the sound stage. Covered with starched white cloths, these were laden with food: smoked salmon and poached salmon from Scotland, roast chickens and turkeys, glazed hams, legs of lamb, sides of roast beef, and all manner of salads and vegetables, assorted cheeses, and fancy desserts ranging from French pastries and chocolate mousse with whipped cream to fruit salad and English trifle.

Two similar tables had been set up as bars and were being serviced by a string of bartenders, while dozens of waiters and waitresses were circulating with trays of drinks and appetizers.

A waiter glided past her, and Rosie whisked a glass of champagne off the tray, thanked him, and sallied forth into the crowd in search of Aida, and her assistants, Fanny and Val.

Within seconds she found the producer in conversation with some of the studio brass, and when Aida saw her approaching she excused herself and hurried forward.

Rosie exclaimed, 'This is some wrap party. Congratulations!'

'Oh, but *I* didn't do anything,' the producer demurred quickly, 'except pick up a phone and call the caterers.'

Rosie grinned at her. 'Of course you did something. You planned all this, so don't be so modest. And incidentally, what do you have up your sleeve for later?'

Aida gave her a puzzled look. 'What do you mean?'

'Last week, over lunch, you told me you'd think of something special, something *appropriate*, to celebrate Bonfire Night, as well as the wrap.'

'How about burning an effigy of Margaret

44

Ellsworth?' Fanny muttered in a low voice, as she sidled up to them with Val in tow.

'Naughty, naughty,' Rosie chastised, but her voice was mild and there was an amused glint in her eyes. Glancing at the producer, she went on, 'What happened about the medieval dress? Did you sell it to Maggie?'

Aida shook her head. 'No, I gave it to her. And if I live to be a hundred, I'll never know why on earth she wanted it.'

'Perhaps to play Lady Macbeth,' Fanny suggested. 'It's the ideal role for *her*.'

'Or Vampira,' Val added, rolling her eyes to the ceiling, faking horror. 'She'd be perfect for that part, too.'

'Thanks very much, the three of you!' Rosie said. 'That certainly says a lot for my costumes.'

'Your costumes are never anything but great, *the* greatest,' Gavin said behind her, put his hand on her shoulder and squeezed it. Then he added softly, with a chuckle, 'Look what the cat dragged in.'

'I knew I'd find you somewhere around here, Rosie, swilling champagne and living it up,' an unmistakable English voice said.

Instantly pivoting, her eyes opening wider, Rosie came face to face with Nell, who was beautifully made-up and coiffed and looked band-box smart in a black suit and pearls.

'You made it, Nelly! How wonderful!' Rosie exclaimed in delight.

The two women, such close friends for years, hugged each other fiercely, and when they finally

45

drew apart, Nell said, 'How could I miss *this* wrap party? It's my picture, too, isn't it?'

'Indeed it is,' Aida asserted, and stepping forward she shook Nell's hand. 'Welcome back.'

'Thanks, Aida, and I must say it's nice to see all of you again,' Nell responded, and she smiled warmly at Fanny and Val, including them in this statement.

Rosie's assistants greeted her affectionately, returned her smile, and then quickly slid away.

Aida also made a move to take her leave, explaining, 'I think I'd better go and check on everything. And persuade that combo to play something a bit livelier. Oh, and regarding Bonfire Night, Rosie, I did come up with *something*. But it's a surprise. See you later.' With this comment she hurried off.

Gavin took two glasses of champagne from a passing waitress, handed one to Nell, and immediately the three of them moved into a corner of the sound stage where it was a bit quieter.

Rosie took hold of Nell's arm affectionately. 'It's great to see you. When did you arrive in London?'

'A short while ago. From Paris.'

'*Oh.* What were you doing there?'

'I had a business meeting this morning. I came in last night on the French Concorde from New York . . . with Johnny Fortune. He's in the midst of planning a concert for next spring – the French adore him, you know. Anyway, we had to get together with the impresario involved, but once everything was clarified and the meeting more or less finished, I rushed out to the airport and grabbed the first plane to London.'

'How long are you staying?' Gavin asked.

'Just a few days. Johnny's coming in on Thursday morning. He has a concert at the Albert Hall on Saturday night, so I've got my hands full. After that I'll be heading back to New York, once I've seen Aunt Phyllis. I'll probably go on Monday or Tuesday.'

'I'm glad to hear it,' Rosie murmured. 'I'd have been disappointed if you were away when I'm there. We don't see enough of each other these days, and I was looking forward to spending some time with you.'

'I know; me too, darling, and there's no danger of our not seeing each other, Rosie mine. Oh, and before I forget, here's the spare key to my apartment.' As she spoke, Nell fished around in her handbag, brought out a key and handed it to Rosie. 'You know the house rules – make yourself at home and don't lift a finger. Leave everything to Maria, she'll look after you beautifully.'

'Thanks, Nell,' Rosie said, and put the key in her purse.

The two of them began to make plans for Rosie's trip to New York, and Gavin took a step backward, wanting to give them space and privacy to talk between themselves for a few minutes.

Propping himself up against a wall, he took a sip of his wine, hoping he would be feeling better soon.

Gavin had not wanted to don the surgical collar for the party, because to do so would prevent him from wearing a tie. But at the last minute he had had to put it on when his neck had suddenly begun to bother him. Because of the bulky collar, he had dressed more casually than he normally did for this kind of occasion, selecting a navy silk shirt, worn open at the neck, grey slacks and a navy cashmere jacket. Now he was glad he had chosen these clothes; they were comfortable, and he felt less constricted in them, despite the surgical collar around his neck.

As he continued to sip his drink, he surreptitiously studied Rosalind Madigan, his best friend and only confidante.

Earlier in the day he had thought she looked excessively pale and overtired, which was one of the reasons he had made such a fuss about the new projects she was planning to take on, now that *Kingmaker* was finished. But tonight, surprisingly, she seemed refreshed, and there was a wonderful glow about her. The dark rings under her eyes had disappeared and colour flushed her cheeks to a pretty pink. It pleased him that she unexpectedly looked so much better, and then almost immediately he knew what she had done.

She made a trip to Make-up, he thought, that's the real reason she's acquired such a peachy bloom in the past few hours. Katie Grange, the head make-up artist on the movie, was noted for her very special talent for giving even the most tired-looking actor a healthy and youthful appearance. Undoubtedly Katie had skilfully applied a few cosmetics, and in so doing had instantly camouflaged those tell-tale signs of overwork, long hours, and perpetual worry which had given Rosie's face such a washed-out tinge of late.

And she had also visited Hairdressing, he thought,

leaning forward slightly, peering more closely at
Rosie. She had beautiful hair: it was reddish-brown
and fell to her shoulders in glossy, luxuriant waves,
and he could see that it had been professionally set
and combed by Gil Watts.

No matter, Rosie had benefited from the bit of help
from the professionals, and this pleased him no end.
She looked better than she had in months, although
he had to admit he didn't particularly like the wool
dress she was wearing, mostly because of the colour.
It was dark grey, and although it was superbly cut
and tailored it was far too dull for her. But then this
was something of an old story these days. Rosie was
so busy designing costumes for other people that half
the time she didn't pay too much attention to what
she wore herself. He liked her best in the bright
colours she used to favour when they were kids –
scarlet, yellow, blue, and almost any shade of green,
which enhanced the colour of her large, expressive
green eyes.

Gavin stifled a sigh as he considered Rosie's problems, the burdens she had shouldered in the past
few years. Too many for one person. He was forever
telling her this, but she would not listen to him, and
the stringent response she usually made invariably
ended that particular topic of conversation.

Obscurely, in a remote corner of his mind, there
lurked the nagging thought that he ought to shoulder
her burdens, indeed *must* do so, out of love and
friendship. But she would not let him; she refused
his help, as well as his money. He had made a lot of
that from his movies in the last few years, and what

was the point of having money if you couldn't use it to make life easier for someone you cared about. He wished Rosie would take some of it, since it would free her in so many different ways.

Because of her constant refusal to do this, he harboured a profound and permanent sense of frustration, and deep in his gut there existed a gnawing anger with those irritating people she persisted in calling her family. Bums, the lot of them, he thought, the anger flying to the surface momentarily.

Rosie was too good for them, that was for sure.

Rosalind Madigan was the finest, most decent person he knew, had ever known. She did not have one bad bone in her body, was kind, considerate, and generous to a fault. She never said an unkind word about anyone, and was always trying to help those less fortunate than she was herself.

That's the basic problem, Gavin suddenly thought. She's far too good – for her own good. But she had been like that as a teenager, usually seeing only the best in people, expecting the best of them. He suspected she would never change. A leopard didn't change its spots, did it?

In his mind, Gavin characterized Rosie as the All-American Girl. A long-stemmed American Beauty rose. She *was* beautiful. And vital, friendly, open, honest. In particular, he loved her intelligence and enthusiasm. Because she had such a good mind, he could talk to her about anything, and she always understood what he was getting at; and that enthusiasm of hers was a bonus. She was not a bit jaded; in fact, she was the least jaded person he knew. Even though she was sophisticated in many ways, had been exposed to a great deal and was well travelled, she was neither world-weary nor cynical. He considered that to be an extraordinary accomplishment for someone who lived in their world – the glitzy, glamorous, bitchy, competitive, cruel world of show business.

Suddenly growing conscious that he had been staring too hard and too long at Rosie, Gavin shifted the focus of his eyes to Nell Jeffrey.

Rosie was of average height, about five feet six, but she looked so much taller and bigger-boned when she was with Nell, who was much smaller, and delicately made. To Gavin she was like a little china doll, with her pink and white English complexion and silver-gilt hair. But he was well aware that her porcelain looks belied great tenacity, one of the shrewdest brains he had ever encountered, and an unusual stubbornness which occasionally bordered on pigheadedness.

Yes, she's quite a gal, our Little Nell, he thought, regarding her over the rim of his glass, his expression contemplative.

In the fourteen years since he met her, which was when she first came from London to New York, Nell had carved out quite an extraordinary career for herself, had become one of the most successful and powerful publicists in America. Apart from representing *the* bel canto balladeer of the nineties, the immensely popular singer Johnny Fortune, Rosie, himself and all of his movies, Nell also handled the public relations for a major Hollywood studio, a number of other top movie stars, screenwriters, directors, producers and a handful of best-selling novelists.

After working for several prestigious public relations firms in New York, where she learned her trade and learned it very well, Nell had founded her own company when she was twenty-seven. Over the past four years that it had been in existence it had truly flourished, and now she had a big staff and offices in New York, Los Angeles and London.

Successful though she was in business, Nell's personal life was as unfulfilled and as unrewarding as Rosie's. How he wished the two of them would find a couple of nice guys to settle down with.

Gavin took a long swallow of his wine, genuinely amazed at himself. And he wondered how *he*, of all people, could think a thing like that.

It was Mikey, as far as Nell was concerned, Gavin knew. For a long time now he had been convinced that she had never properly recovered from her youthful romance with Mikey, and then when he had vanished two years ago she had simply switched off. At least as far as men were concerned.

As for Rosie, that was another matter altogether.

In a sense, she was in far deeper trouble with her personal life than either him or Nell. But he did not wish to contemplate that at the moment.

Already an extremely complex woman, because of her very nature Rosie was submerged in any number of other complications, all of which stemmed from the life she had chosen to lead. Consistently, she denied this; equally, she pooh-poohed the idea that she was a complex person. But he knew better.

Nell cut into his thoughts, when she said, 'You're looking awfully pensive, my lad. One is sad, of course, when a movie ends. But under the circumstances, I would have thought you'd be relieved . . . I mean, as executive producer surely you must be thinking thank God it's in the can, there're no more disasters to worry about. That sort of thing. No?' She raised a blonde brow questioningly.

Gavin nodded in agreement. 'I am relieved, Nell, believe me I am. And I'm not pensive, at least not about the movie. To tell you the truth, I was thinking about the two of you, and wishing you'd find a couple of nice guys. Settle down –'

'Bloody hell, perish the thought!' Nell cried, cutting him off, recoiling slightly, looking at him askance. 'I'm perfectly happy the way I am, thank you very much.'

Rosie said, 'And so am I, Gavin, so please don't give us a hard time.'

'Okay, okay,' he said, backing off. 'I was only playing big brother, and there's no need to get all excited and het up.'

Grinning at him, Nell said, 'We know you only have the best of intentions, Gavin, when it comes to us – your favourites. But we can take care of ourselves, you know. We're grown-up girls now. Come on, let's grab ourselves fresh drinks and plunge into that mob.' Winking at him theatrically, mugging, she finished, 'Who knows *who* we might find lurking out there in the madding crowd, eh?'

He laughed and so did Rosie.

Gavin said, 'We *had* better join the party, circulate

a bit. This crew and the entire unit have been really terrific, and I'd like to have a drink with them, spend a bit of time chatting. Anyway, I want to thank all of them personally.'

The surprise Aida had arranged for Bonfire Night was a fireworks display.

It started at nine o'clock, after the buffet supper was over, and took place on the back lot of the studios. Everyone stood outside, watching, cheering, and clapping loudly as different special effects filled the night sky. Catherine wheels, cascades, waterfalls, rockets, starbursts, rainbows and snowfalls were set off one after the other, exploding brilliant colours and delicate, intricate patterns into the darkness and illuminating the studio buildings. It was breathtaking, a magical, fairy-tale show of colour and light that lasted for over twenty minutes.

But the most spectacular part was the finale, when the name of the movie was spelled out in fireworks mounted to a giant frame. And following the title *Kingmaker* came the words, *Thanks, Gavin.*

Once the renewed burst of loud cheering and clapping subsided, a clear baritone voice began to sing, 'For he's a jolly good fellow, for he's a jolly good fellow,' and everyone joined in enthusiastically.

Singing along with them, Rosie knew they meant every word, and so did she.

'Do you think Gavin's marriage is in trouble?' Nell asked, giving Rosie a penetrating look.

So startled was Rosie by the question that she

almost dropped her mug of tea, and she simply stared back at her friend speechlessly. When she eventually found her voice, she said, 'Whatever makes you say a thing like that?'

Now it was Nell's turn to be silent, and she sat back on the sofa, a thoughtful expression settling on her face.

Rosie continued to stare at her, waiting for an answer.

It was late, well after one o'clock in the morning, and the two women were relaxing in Rosie's suite at the Athenaeum Hotel in Piccadilly. She, Gavin, and most of the American contingent on the film had been living there for months, and Nell had checked in earlier in the day, as she invariably did when she came to London.

They had been driven back from the party at Shepperton Studios in Gavin's limousine, and he had come with them to Rosie's suite for a nightcap. But he had left well over an hour ago, claiming total fatigue. There was no denying he had looked exhausted, his face grown pinched and wan all of a sudden, and it was obvious that the surgical collar was bothering him. 'I've got to get this damn thing off, take a pain-killer and go to bed,' he had mumbled to them as he left the suite.

Rosie and Nell had continued to talk for a while longer, catching up on all their news; a few minutes ago, Rosie had gone to the small kitchenette at one end of the sitting room where she had made a pot of tea.

Now she sat nursing the mug in both hands, her

eyes on Nell's face. 'Why would you think a thing like that, Nell? About Gavin's marriage?' she asked again, and repeated, '*Why?*'

Nell looked at her fully, and explained slowly, in a low voice, 'Louise was not here for the wrap party. That's never happened before. I mean, she's *always* been at his wrap parties, whether they've been in New York, LA, or on foreign location.'

'But she had to go back to California,' Rosie replied. 'To get ready for Christmas.'

'Christmas! It's only the beginning of November, for God's sake!'

'Well maybe it was for Thanksgiving, I can't really remember. In any case, she *has* been here a great deal, commuting between London and Los Angeles. So I'm sure everything's all right. Besides, she does have a career of her own.'

'*Career!* What career? Sitting on charity committees, is that what you mean?'

Unable to dismiss the apparent scorn reverberating in Nell's voice, Rosie eyed her friend carefully. 'Do I detect a slightly bitchy note here?' she asked.

'Perhaps you do. I don't like Louise Ambrose, and I never have from the first day I met her, when she came creeping around Gavin. I don't know what he saw in her then, or what he sees in her now – if anything. She is one person who hasn't improved with age and maturity, she's only grown worse. In my opinion, she's perfectly ridiculous, and certainly I'll never understand their relationship. *Never.* In any case, Gavin should have married you.'

'Oh come on, Nelly, don't start *that* at this hour.

You know very well that when Gavin and I had our little thing we were just a couple of kids, for heaven's sake –'

'He's still in love with you.'

Rosie's gaze intensified, then she spluttered, 'Now that *is* pure nonsense! He's no more in love with me than I am with him.'

'Want to bet?'

'No, I don't.'

'Scared to hear the truth, Rosie mine?'

'Not at all. But you're way off on this, Nelly, *way off*. I've worked with Gavin around the clock for the past nine months, so don't you think I'd know if he were in love with me? Anyway, back then in New York we were so young . . . infatuated would be a far better, and more accurate, word to use to explain how we felt about each other.'

'This is Little Nell sitting here, Angel Face. That's what he's always lovingly called you, isn't it? But to continue, it's *me* who's looking you right in the eye, and you can't fool *me*. You *were* in love with him, Rosie Madigan, you told me so at the time, just in case you've forgotten. And I remember very well that you were so smitten with him you couldn't see straight. And Gavin reciprocated those feelings. He *was* in love with you. He's in love with you now.'

'Don't be so ridiculous. I'd *know*.'

'No, you wouldn't, you're too involved with all those bloody Frogs.'

'Please, Nell, not tonight. I'm tired,' Rosie said, a pleading note entering her voice.

'So am I. Listen, getting back to my original point,

I really *do* think Gavin's unhappy with Louise.'

'And I'm absolutely certain he isn't. I've been with them a lot during this picture, more than you have, Nell. He adores Louise, and his behaviour towards her hasn't changed, it's exactly the same as it's always been.'

'So what – he's an actor.'

Rosie frowned but made no comment. After a moment, she said in a firm voice, 'You still haven't given me a valid reason why you suddenly think his marriage is in trouble.' There was a little pause. 'Do you know something I don't?' she demanded.

'No, I don't. Let's forget it, shall we?' Nell said this far too quickly, and then she shrugged, offered Rosie a faint, somewhat regretful smile.

A silence fell between them.

Eventually Nell said: 'Look, it's just a feeling I have, Rosie. As I started to tell you before, it did seem awfully odd to me that she wasn't at the wrap party this evening. God knows – and so do I – the fuss she's made in the past about being present, no matter what it entailed getting her there.' Nell shook her head. 'She was unbelievable! I became aware of her tonight because of her very noticeable *absence*. I also thought it was peculiar that she wasn't cheering him from the sidelines, if not, indeed, from the centre of things. You know her ego. She wants to be perpetually in the limelight. I suppose what I'm trying to say is that one would think she'd want to privately and publicly pat him on the back for pulling this off, wouldn't you? *Kingmaker* is one hell of an achievement.'

Recognizing certain truths in all of this, Rosie nodded her head. She said slowly, 'But, nevertheless, it's not really enough to think they're having problems, is it?'

Nell let out a small sigh, and shook her head. 'I guess not. And as I said a moment ago, let's forget it, Rosie. Perhaps I'm just imagining things.' Nell sprang to her feet purposely, added briskly, 'I'd better let you get to bed.'

'I do have to get up early,' Rosie murmured, placed her mug on the table and also stood up.

Together they walked across the room; Rosie opened the door and turned to Nell. 'Gavin's marriage is not in trouble, honestly it isn't. *I would know.*'

No, you wouldn't, Nell thought, you can't see the wood for the trees. And he would never tell *you* how he feels. How could he?

Leaning closer, Nell kissed Rosie on the cheek. 'Good night. I'll see you tomorrow. I'm going out to Shepperton, to go over the stills the unit photographer took this past week. I'll be there all day, planning some magazine spreads on *Kingmaker* with the unit publicist.'

'Then let's have lunch at the studio.'

'I'd love to, Rosie. See you.'

'Sleep tight, Nell.'

Rosie closed the door and walked slowly back to the bedroom, reflecting on Nell's words. She found them quite extraordinary.

FOUR

It was a glittering day.

The sky was a clear and vivid blue, unblemished by cloud, and although the sun had no warmth on this cold November Saturday it was, nevertheless, a bright golden orb flung high above Park Avenue that added immeasurably to the sparkle and zest of the morning.

Rosie walked at a rapid pace, enjoying being back in New York, and assailed by many memories. Most of them were good memories, and so her present-day problems were lifted, at least temporarily. Certainly she felt less weighed down by them, and the heaviness she had been experiencing of late had miraculously evaporated the moment she had planted her feet on American soil. And she was determined to enjoy her few weeks here; nothing was going to spoil her first visit to her home town in two years.

She had arrived three hours earlier on Concorde from London, an amazingly rapid flight across the Atlantic which had taken only three hours and forty minutes. Her ticket on the supersonic plane was a present from Gavin, one he had forced her to accept.

As usual, she had been reluctant to take anything from him, but now she was glad she had succumbed to his pressure. He had told her that Concorde was not a luxury but a necessity, if you were in their business and under so many different time constraints; she now agreed wholeheartedly with him.

The plane had landed at nine-thirty; she had whizzed through Baggage and Customs, and by eleven-thirty she had already been well ensconced in Nell's apartment on Park Avenue at Eightieth Street, unpacked, freshly made-up and enjoying the cup of tea Nell's housekeeper had made for her, and which Maria insisted she drink before going out into the cold weather.

Because it was such an icy day Rosie had exchanged her black suit and matching coat for a loden-green wool trouser suit worn with a wine-coloured turtle-neck sweater, her favourite Lucchese cowboy boots made of a wonderful dark reddish-brown Cordovan leather, and a long, full, highway-man's cloak cut from Austrian loden cloth. She had bought the cloak in Munich a few years ago, and had it lined with wine cashmere which added extra warmth. But mostly she loved the cape for its dramatic looks, the sense of élan it gave her when she wore it.

Well dressed for the weather, she had left the apartment intending to hail a cab, but the crisp air felt so good after being cooped up in the plane that she decided to walk instead.

Now she paused for a second and stared down Park Avenue.

It was so clear she could see for ever, all the way to the Pan Am building where the tip of the avenue led into Grand Central. Despite the fact that she was based in Paris, and adored that beautiful, graceful, elegant city of light, New York was home to her, and it *was* unique. There was no other city like it anywhere in the world.

Earlier, coming in from Kennedy Airport, the limousine driver had chosen to enter Manhattan by way of the Fifty-ninth Street Bridge. As they had driven over it from Long Island City she had suddenly caught her breath as she gazed out of the car window.

Straight ahead of her, ranged on the other side of the East River, rising up like giant cliffs shimmering in the sunlight, were the towering apartment buildings of the East Side. And behind them floated the gargantuan office blocks of mid-town Manhattan; standing out in particular were the Empire State and the Chrysler buildings, the latter her favourite with its perfect art deco tower and slender spire. Those immense skyscrapers piercing the high-flung azure sky formed formidable canyons of steel and glass and concrete, and to Rosie they had never looked more impressive and awe-inspiring than they did at that moment. In the brilliant, mid-morning sunshine the skyline of Manhattan seemed to have been carved from crystal by some enormous god-like hand; it was so breathtaking it was almost otherworldly.

But then she had always thought this city was beautiful, high-powered, challenging, and the most exciting place to be – if you were talented, ambitious, driven and lucky. Conversely, her brother deemed it to be Sodom and Gomorrah, for Kevin had recognized, at an early age, its dark and decadent side, its seamy, sleazy underbelly, had been aware of the corruption, ruthlessness, cruel poverty and inequities that permeated New York, flourished alongside the excitement, the glamour, the success, the great wealth and privilege.

Now, as she thought of her brother, a flash of anxiety shot through her, and it made her tighten her lips imperceptibly. Kevin's lack of response to her calls was the only thing which marred her gladness at being back in New York. She had phoned him every day for the past week, first leaving her London numbers and then yesterday, knowing she was about to depart, she had repeated Nell's number into the machine.

He had not called her back, as yet, and her anxiety was running high; she had told him so when she had phoned once more, before leaving Nell's apartment this morning, adding, 'Please, Kevin, call me to reassure me you're all right. I'm beginning to worry.' Then she had repeated Nell's number even though she knew that he knew it by heart.

He'll call me today, she told herself, genuinely believing this as she plunged on down Park, her pace increasing, her cape flying out behind her like a proud banner. She made a striking figure in her dramatic outfit, and her mass of coppery hair which caught and held the sunlight was turned into a bright burnished helmet around her creamy-complexioned, heart-shaped face.

Quite a number of men glanced at her covetously, and several women admiringly, as she floated past them, staring straight ahead, intent in her purpose, aiming for her destination.

But Rosie was unaware of the dashing figure she cut, and of her special kind of beauty. Vanity had never been one of her traits, and these days she was so consumed by her work and worry and responsibilities that she never had much time for primping and preening.

Even getting herself 'done up and dusted' – as Fanny called it – for the wrap party had been Fanny's idea, and her two assistants had virtually had to drag her to Make-up and Hair at Shepperton Studios. She had only given in finally to Fanny's entreaties when Val had pointed out how exhausted she looked. Gavin was bound to pounce on *that*, and the last thing she wanted was him nagging her, making snide remarks about Collie and Guy, which he *would* do because, for the most part, he blamed them for her tiredness and worry, and anything troublesome that ever happened to her, in fact.

When she reached Sixty-fifth Street, Rosie swung to her right and strode down the block, passing the Mayfair Regent Hotel, where she loved to go for afternoon tea, and Le Cirque, one of her favourite restaurants in the city, heading in the direction of Madison Avenue.

Just as the Faubourg St-Honoré in Paris, Bond Street in London and Rodeo Drive in Beverly Hills were all special to her, so was Madison. It was lined with the type of elegant shops and boutiques carrying designer clothes and other high-fashion items that appealed to her, and to her sense of aesthetics as a costume designer. However, Rosie only intended to window shop on Madison this morning; her real destination was Bergdorf Goodman, where she planned to do the first of her Christmas shopping.

Today was November the ninth, and Thanksgiving was still two weeks away, but Christmas was already very much in the air. It was in evidence in the store windows, and in the lights which were being strung up on the streets of Manhattan.

Fifth Avenue had been dressed up no end, she noticed, as she turned the corner of Sixty-fifth. She smiled inwardly, hurrying down Fifth towards the department store, remembering how excited she had been as a child when her mother had brought her in from Queens to see the Christmas decorations.

In particular, the store windows had always thrilled her, most especially the windows of Lord & Taylor. They were inventive, fanciful, imaginative; each one had been decorated to depict a specific scene, either religious or from a fairy tale, and was guaranteed to delight the eyes of a child – and the young in heart. She could easily recall how *her* eyes had stood out on stalks, how she had pressed her nose to the plate-glass window, mesmerized by what she saw, drinking everything in.

Every year there had been something different to captivate her, and so much to absorb . . . the Nativity with Mary and Joseph and the baby Jesus . . . Santa Claus coming over the chimney tops in a sledge filled with toys, pulled by trotting reindeer which *actually* trotted . . . Swan Lake with pirouetting ballerinas that *really* moved, these two creations miracles of mechanical ingenuity. And the scenes taken from best-loved fairy tales were equally eye-catching and beautiful . . . Cinderella sitting in her glass coach, Sleeping Beauty in her glass coffin being awakened by a kiss from the Prince, and Hansel and Gretel in the gingerbread house.

How they had enchanted her, those magical windows. It was not very difficult at all for her to cast her mind back to those Christmases of the past. Her mother had always been as excited as she, and once they had thoroughly viewed the windows, and she had feasted her eyes to the limit, her mother had taken her inside the store for lunch. They favoured the Birdcage Restaurant, where she was permitted to choose anything she wanted since it was a special treat. Without fail, as a finale to the lunch, she ordered a banana split for dessert, and, even though her mother was for ever saying she must watch her weight, she would order one too.

Her mother had died when she was fourteen, and the day after the funeral and the wake – it was a Saturday and she remembered it so well, even today – she had gone to the Birdcage for lunch by herself. She had been trying to bring her mother back to life, to recapture the past, she knew that was why she had made the trip into Manhattan. But she had been so choked up she had been unable to eat lunch, even the dessert, and had sat staring at the untouched banana split, tears rolling down her cheeks, aching inside for her mother, filled with the most searing grief.

She thought of her mother frequently, almost every day, even though she had been dead for seventeen years now. Her mother was part of her, residing in a very special corner of her heart, and as long as she was alive her mother would be alive too, for there was no such thing as death in her lexicon. And stored up inside herself were all those wonderful memories of the happiest of childhoods, and the memories gave her great comfort and strength when she felt alone or sad. How lucky she and Kevin were to have been so very loved as children.

Kevin. She wondered what to get him for Christmas, and there was Gavin to think of, too, and Guy and Henri and Kyra, and her dearest friend, Nell. Their names danced around in Rosie's head as she crossed Fifth Avenue at Fifty-ninth Street, skirted the Plaza, walked across the little square in front of the hotel, and into the famous department store.

Coming over on Concorde she had made a few notes, and high on her list of priorities were special gifts for Lisette, Collie and Yvonne, who were stuck in the country and never got to visit exciting shops. After an hour spent browsing in the store she selected a cream silk shawl for Collie. This was trimmed with a gold fringe and embroidered with a peacock, its huge, colourful tail spread out like a fan composed of iridescent blues and greens and golds, and in Costume Jewellery she found an unusual pair of flower-shaped earrings made of pastel-coloured rhinestones for Yvonne.

Once these purchases had been made, she left
Bergdorf's and headed down Fifth Avenue to Saks,
glancing quickly in the store windows but not stopping as she walked at her usual rapid pace. When she
arrived at Saks she went straight up to the children's
department, and within fifteen minutes she had
picked out a party dress for Lisette. Beautifully made
of fir-green velvet and trimmed with an ecru-lace
collar and cuffs, it had a Victorian air about it, and
she knew five-year-old Lisette would look adorable
in it. Expensive though the frock was, Rosie couldn't
resist buying it.

It seemed to Rosie that it was colder than ever
when she finally left the big department store, and
walked back up Fifth. The wind was icy and she
pulled her cape around her more tightly, glad she
had worn it. Passing St Patrick's she paused for a
moment, staring up at the beautiful old cathedral and
its Gothic-style cusps; then she hurried on, wanting
to finish her shopping and get home to the apartment, in case Kevin had called.

The two last stops on her list were Gap and Banana
Republic, not far from each other on Lexington. These
were the best shops in which to pick up T-shirts and
jeans for Collie and Yvonne, who so much admired
hers. She generally donned these typically American
clothes at weekends; in actuality, they had become
something of a uniform for her, worn with the man-
datory white wool socks and highly-polished brown
penny loafers, and Collie and Yvonne both wanted
to emulate this look. Since she wouldn't have time to
go shopping when she returned to Paris, she had

decided to take a supply back with her. Also, the jeans and T-shirts could be gift-wrapped to go under the big Christmas tree which they would put up in the stone hall at Montfleurie.

FIVE

Nothing much had changed in the apartment since she had last been here two years ago, Rosie noticed, as she wandered aimlessly around later that afternoon, waiting for Kevin to call. In fact, it was very much the same as it had always been.

Rosie had first come to this apartment in 1977. She and Nell had met in the spring of that year, and they had taken to each other at once, each, perhaps, recognizing the maverick in the other, and not long after their first meeting she had been invited to Sunday lunch by her new friend.

The instant she had stepped inside the large, somewhat rambling apartment on Park Avenue she had felt at home, and, with her discerning eye, she had recognized that whoever had decorated the place was knowledgeable about antiques, and had considerable decorating expertise, not to mention superlative taste.

The expert turned out to be Nell's Aunt Phyllis, her father's sister, who had lived with them since Nell was ten, which was when her mother Helen Treadles Jeffrey had died of a brain tumour. In

August 1976, when Adam Jeffrey, Nell's father, had been appointed chief American correspondent for his newspaper, the London *Morning News*, and transferred, his sister had rushed over to New York with him. She had found the apartment relatively quickly, and begun decorating it without wasting a single moment of her time. When Nell finally arrived that Christmas, having left her English boarding school for good, the apartment had already been turned into a replica of the gracious flat they had just vacated in London.

On that first visit, Nell had explained to Rosie that most of the lovely English and French antiques she was so busy admiring had been shipped over from their Chelsea home. Nell had added that Aunt Phyllis had zeroed in on some of the top New York fabric and wallpaper houses, had selected only the most handsome wallcoverings, and the finest French silks, English chintzes and brocades in order to create the look for which she was well known in London, where she enjoyed great success as an interior designer.

Suddenly, in 1979, when he was only fifty-two years old, Adam Jeffrey dropped dead of a heart attack. Nell and her aunt had remained in New York, where the latter had already established herself as a decorator of some distinction, and acquired a roster of notable, wealthy clients. It was not until Nell was twenty-three that her Aunt Phyllis finally decided to return to London permanently, leaving her niece behind in New York.

By this time Nell had a good job, most of her friends were in the city, and, not unnaturally, she had no desire to leave Manhattan, where she had lived for six years, and where she was perfectly happy and content. Nell's father had left her the Park Avenue apartment in his will, and she had continued to live in it, had changed very little of the decor over the years, loving it exactly the way it was.

To Rosie, one of the prettiest and cosiest rooms in the apartment was the small library, charmingly decorated all those years ago by Aunt Phyllis. It had striated, apricot-coloured walls, a lime-green-and-black needlepoint carpet, a colourful floral chintz used for balloon shades at the windows and to cover a sofa, and a collection of mellow English antiques. One long wall of white-painted shelves held books intermingled with English Staffordshire animal figures; current magazines and the day's newspapers were arranged on several small tables.

And so it was to this room that Rosie gravitated with her cup of tea around five o'clock, where she turned on the radio and sat down on the sofa to relax with the *New York Times*. Once she had finished reading the newspaper and drinking her tea, she leaned back, closed her eyes and drifted with her thoughts, praying that Kevin would call today. When she had returned earlier from her shopping expedition, the first thing she had done was check Nell's answering machine. There were no messages on it at all, much to her disappointment.

Lulled by the soft music on the radio, Rosie dozed off after a while. But some twenty minutes or so later she awakened suddenly, feeling oddly disoriented, and she sat up with a jerk, wondering where she was, completely at a loss, and it took her a few seconds to realize that she was at Nell's in New York.

Shaking herself awake and rising, Rosie carried the cup and saucer into the kitchen, where she rinsed and dried both, and then put them back in the cupboard.

She stood in the centre of the large blue-and-white kitchen, hesitating for a moment, and then she went to the refrigerator and looked inside, wondering what Maria had left prepared for her. She found a delicious-looking veal casserole with vegetables in a covered glass dish, and there was also a cold roast chicken, as well as a selection of cold cuts, various salads, a cake, and assorted cheeses on the next shelf. Obviously Maria, who had the weekend off, was determined that she would not starve in her absence. It struck Rosie that if she did not hear from her brother she would not fare so badly here; she could at least have a light supper and watch television.

By six-thirty, Rosie was beginning to feel more worried than ever that there had been no word from Kevin, and just as she was on the point of calling him one more time the phone began to ring. She lifted the receiver, hoping to hear his voice, and much to her relief she did.

'Sorry, Rosie, but I couldn't get back to you before now,' he explained, after greeting her affectionately. 'I've been unavailable all week. *Business*. I only just got your many messages, honey.'

'I understand, Kevin,' she said quickly, so happy to talk to him she instantly forgot about her anxiety and frustration of earlier. 'I hope I'm going to see you. Is your . . . *business* finished?'

He hesitated, but only for the barest fraction of a second, before saying, 'Sort of . . . Well, yes, I guess it is, and I'd love to see you too. I can't wait, in fact.'

'So when can we get together, Kev?'

'Tonight? Are you free?'

'Of course I am! Where shall we meet? Or do you want to come over here?'

'No, let's go out. What about meeting at Jimmy's? How does that sound to you?'

'Like old times!' she exclaimed, laughing.

He chuckled into the phone. 'Is seven-thirty too soon for you, honey?'

'No, not at all. I'll see you in an hour at Neary's.' Hanging up the phone, she raced into the bedroom to refresh her make-up and do her hair. Like Gavin, her brother would start chastising her if she looked tired or out of sorts, and this she wanted to avoid.

SIX

Kevin Madigan stood leaning with his back against the bar at Jimmy Neary's Irish pub on East Fifty-seventh Street, his eyes focused on the door.

And so Rosie saw him the moment she walked in, saw the wide grin spreading across his handsome Irish face when she raised her hand in greeting.

She flew into his arms and they held each other tightly, hugging. They had been close from childhood, Kevin forever her protector, she his sage adviser, even when she was a little girl, always telling him what to do and explaining why he should do it. They had drawn even closer after their mother's untimely death, taking comfort from each other's presence, feeling more secure, safer, when they were in close proximity.

Kevin had gone to London – as Gavin's guest – at the start of principal photography on *Kingmaker*, and they had seen a lot of each other during the week he was there. But that had been six months ago and they both suddenly realized how much they had missed each other.

Finally they stood apart, and Kevin looked down

into her upturned face. 'You're a sight for sore eyes, mavourneen.'

'So are you, Kevin.'

'What would you like to drink?'

'A vodka tonic, please,' she answered and took hold of his arm, lovingly smiling up into his happy face. Her relief that he was safe and well so overwhelmed her it knew no bounds. She worried about her brother constantly; she supposed she always would, no matter what. He was her flesh and blood, after all.

They stood at the bar, sipping their drinks and catching up, so happy to be in each other's company the time just flew by. Eventually, Jimmy Neary himself came over to say hello to Rosie, whom he had not seen for several years, and after a minute or two of genial conversation he led them to Kevin's favourite table, situated at the back of the dining room.

Once they were settled and had ordered dinner, Rosie looked at Kevin across the table, fixed her eyes on him intently, and murmured, 'I wish you'd give it up.'

'Give what up?' he asked, breaking his roll in half, spreading butter on it.

'Being a cop.'

Kevin stared at her, his eyes widening in surprise, incredulity registering. 'I never thought I'd hear *you* say a thing like that, Rosalind Mary Frances Madigan. All the Madigan men have been with the New York Police Department.'

'And some of them died because of it,' she pointed out quietly, 'including our Dad.'

'I know, I know, but I'm fourth-generation Irish, fourth-generation cop, and there's no way I can give it up, Rosie. I wouldn't know what else to do. I guess you could say that for me it's bred in the bone.'

'Oh Kevin, I don't think I explained myself very well! I didn't mean you should quit the *force* – I just wish you'd stop working *undercover*. It's so dangerous.'

'*Life* is dangerous, and in a lot of different ways, honey. I could get killed crossing the street, taking a plane trip, driving a car. I could choke on my food, get a fatal disease, or drop dead from a heart attack . . .' He left his sentence unfinished, gave her a long hard stare, and then shrugged his broad shoulders almost nonchalantly. 'People other than undercover cops die every day, Rosie. Especially these days, what with kids toting guns and stray bullets flying around everywhere. I know you love this city, and so do I in my own way, but it's gone to hell on crack and smack and random violence, to name only a few of its ills. But that's another story, I guess.'

'I don't want *you* to get killed the way Dad did,' she persisted.

'I know . . . Funny about Dad, when you think about it. He was just a plain old garden variety detective, doing a standard job at the Seventeenth, minding his own business so to speak, and he went and got himself killed, and at that by accident –'

'By the Mafia you mean,' she cut in.

'Ssssh, keep your voice down,' Kevin said swiftly, warily glancing around, while knowing full well there was no real reason to do so. After all, this was a well-known and respectable mid-town establishment on the East Side, just off First Avenue and a stone's throw away from posh Sutton Place. Still, he couldn't help himself. Being cautious was a habit he had honed to astonishing perfection over the thirteen years he had been with the police; that was the reason he only ever sat with his back to the wall, facing the door, when he was in a public place. He could not afford to be taken by surprise from behind, not ever, not in his job.

Leaning forward, bending over the candle in its red glass container, bringing his head closer to hers, Kevin went on, '*Supposedly* Dad was taken out by the Mafia, but there's never been any real proof, and I've never been absolutely sure of that myself. Nobody has, not even Jerry Shaw, his partner. And let's face it, the Mafiosi don't make a habit of shooting cops, for Christ's sake; it's kinda bad for their business, if you get my drift. Look, they much prefer to neutralize cops, you know, get them on the pad – on the take. Wiseguys feel easier dispensing cash not coffins.'

'I suppose you're right,' she agreed reluctantly. 'A dishonest detective is more valuable to them than a dead one . . . that spells trouble.'

'You betcha it does.'

'Even so, Kevin, I do wish you'd come in from the outside. Couldn't you get yourself a desk job?'

Her brother threw back his head and roared, obviously highly amused by the sheer absurdity of her suggestion.

'Oh Rosie, Rosie,' he gasped at last in a strangled voice, as the laughter began to subside, 'I could, but I won't. You see, I don't want to, honest I don't. What I actually *do* for a living is the centre of my life. Jesus, Rosie, it *is* my life.'

'You take your life in your hands every day of the week, Kev, hunting down murderers, crooks, criminals, and drug-dealers, who are the worst, to my way of thinking. They're certainly the most dangerous – violent, brutal.'

Kevin was silent.

She pressed, 'Well, they are, aren't they?'

'Damned right they are, and you know how I feel about those fucking bastards!' he exclaimed harshly, although he kept his voice contained, trying to be circumspect, having no wish to draw attention to himself.

After a moment's pause, he said, 'Listen to me, Rosie, almost all crime centres around narcotics these days. And I loathe and detest drug-dealers – all cops do. They're the scum of the earth, dealing death around the clock. They're even killing little kids now for profit, selling crack and coke at the school gates, getting seven-year-olds hooked on dope. *Seven-year-olds*, Rosie, and to me that's unconscionable! It's my job to destroy these foul specimens, these . . . these . . . animals. My mission is to nail the sons of bitches to the cross, bring them to justice, get them behind bars, hopefully on a federal rap. That way, they're in for five years *minimum*, usually much, much longer, depending on their crimes. And don't forget, there's no parole in the federal system, thank God.

Personally, I wish we could lock 'em up and throw the keys away. *For ever.*'

His mouth compressed into a grim line, and a hardness settled on his face, making him suddenly look much older than his thirty-four years. 'Doing what I do is very important to me, Rosie. I think, I *hope*, I make a difference in this world, fighting crime the way I do. In any case, it's the only way I know how to keep my sanity,' he finished, reaching out, squeezing her long, slender hand resting on the red tablecloth.

Rosie inclined her head, knowing exactly what he meant. It had been silly of her to think he would ever change his job. He was just like their father. The New York Police Department was the centre of his existence. In any case, Kevin had been on something of a crusade for the past six years – because of Sunny.

Their beautiful Golden Girl was a victim. Bad drugs had scrambled her brains. That's why she lay in a hospital bed in a mental home, catatonic, a lost soul. Lost to herself. Lost to them. Lost to Kevin, who had loved her so.

Sunny would never recover, never be herself again, forever a vegetable, rotting in that place in New Haven, where her two sisters and her brother had been forced to put her out of their own desperation. It was costing them a fortune to keep her in the private home, but they had told Rosie they could not stand the thought of her being locked away in a state mental institution, and neither could she.

She had always believed that Kevin and Sunny would marry, and they would have, if it hadn't been for the drugs that had turned Sunny into a zombie. None of them knew how she got hooked on drugs in the first place, how she slid into such fateful abuse of them, or who had kept on supplying her. Somehow it had just happened. But the seventies and the eighties had been the drug decades, hadn't they? Pot and hash, pills and poppers, uppers and downers, coke and skag, or smack, as Kevin called heroin. Some addicts were stupid enough to compound their habit by mixing drugs with booze, and inevitably that spelled death at some point in their already ruined lives.

Perhaps Sunny Polanski would be better off dead than living the way she is today, Rosie thought, and felt a shiver trickle through her.

Rosie had never been interested in drugs, had only ever once taken a few puffs on a joint years before, had instantly felt sick to her stomach, had wanted to throw up. Gavin had been furious with her for accepting the joint at the party they were attending together, and he had lectured her relentlessly about the danger of drugs for days afterwards. She had not needed to hear his dire warnings; she knew how dangerous drugs were. Poor Sunny hadn't known and that was the tragedy.

'You're thinking about Sunny,' Kevin said softly, breaking the silence, zeroing in on her thoughts as if he could read her mind.

'Yes, I am,' Rosie admitted, hesitated briefly, then asked, 'Have you been to see her recently, Kev?'

'Three months ago.'

'How was she?'

'Just the same. Nothing's changed.'

'I thought I might go to New Haven before I go back to Europe to –'

'Don't!' he exclaimed sharply, and then shook his head, looking chagrined. 'Sorry, I didn't mean to be snappish, but you mustn't go see Sunny. She won't even know you're there, Rosie, and you'll only upset yourself. It's just not worth it.'

Merely nodding, making no response, knowing it was better not to argue with him, Rosie decided that perhaps he was right. Maybe it *would* be better not to visit Sunny as she had planned. What would it mean to *her*, poor thing? Sunny wouldn't even know she was in the same room, and anyway, there was nothing to be gained, nothing she could actually *do* for her old friend to make her existence better. In all truth, she would only create yet another worry for herself, if she saw Sunny in the pitiful state she was in today. It would be another problem she was unable to solve, and she had enough of those as it was.

Taking a sip of water, Rosie straightened up in the chair and gave Kevin a faint smile.

He smiled back. But there was a sadness in his smile and a great deal of pain in his eyes. Rosie knew the pain was a reflection of a deep sorrow that ran through to the very core of him. And it was a sorrow that was almost unendurable. She suppressed a sigh, hurting inside for her brother.

Yet she also knew that Kevin was resilient and courageous and would keep going, no matter what. Continuing to look at him, she realized that his heartache about Sunny had done nothing much to mar his looks, and neither had the life he led as an undercover cop. Her brother was the most handsome of men, with the kind of glamour usually associated with a movie star; he was husky in build, strong and very masculine.

This evening, Kevin's resemblance to their mother was very marked. Moira Madigan, who had come from Dublin to New York as a young girl, had been born a Costello. 'I'm Black Irish,' she had constantly told them as children, sounding very proud of her heritage. According to their mother, the Costellos were descended from one of the Spanish sailors who had been wrecked off the coast of Ireland at the time of Elizabeth I, the Tudor Queen, when King Philip of Spain had sent a great armada of ships to invade England. Some of the Spanish galleons had foundered on the rocky coastline of the Emerald Isle during a violent storm, and the crews had been rescued by Irish fishermen. Many of the survivors had settled in Ireland, and it was a Spanish sailor called José Costello who had been the founding father of the Costello clan. At least, this was the story their mother told, and they had been brought up to believe it was the absolute truth. As far as they were concerned, it was.

And certainly no one could deny that Kevin Madigan was Black Irish since he had Moira's raven hair and sparkling eyes as black as obsidian.

'You're very quiet, Rosie; a penny for your thoughts.'

'I was thinking how much you looked like Mom tonight, Kevin, that's all.'

'Mom would have been so proud of you, proud of your great success as a costume designer, and so would Dad. I remember how Mom used to encourage you with your fashion drawings and sewing when you were still a little kid.'

'Yes, I do too,' Rosie said, 'and they would have been proud of us *both*. I guess we turned out all right . . . we're healthy, sane, doing what we want to do and being successful at it, and that's what they wanted for us. Dad would have been especially proud of *you*. You're carrying on the Madigan tradition as a fourth-generation cop. I wonder, will there be a fifth-generation Madigan to follow in Dad's footsteps and yours?'

'What do you mean?'

Rosie regarded him thoughtfully for a moment, then said, 'Isn't it about time you started thinking about getting married, having kids?'

'Who'll have me?' he shot back, laughter reverberating in his voice. 'I can't offer a woman much, not with my job and living the way I do.'

'Don't you have *any* girl friends, Kevin?'

'No, not really.'

'I wish you did.'

'Look who's talking. What about you? There you are, sitting in that ridiculous situation, and for all these years. Gavin's right, it *is* time you sorted out the mess in France.'

'Is that really what Gavin said?' Rosie asked, staring hard.

He nodded. 'It sure is. Gavin thinks you're wasting your life, and so do I. You'd be better off moving on now, coming back to the States to live. And maybe here at home you might find a decent guy –'

'Talking of France,' she cut in peremptorily, 'are you coming over for Christmas? You promised.'

'I know I did, but I'm not sure that I can . . .' His voice faltered, and fortunately he was saved the trouble of making a string of excuses as the waitress appeared at their table. She carried a tray laden with dishes of the Irish stew they had ordered, and was all set to serve them dinner. Glancing at her, Kevin flashed her a warm smile. 'And if it's not the lovely mavourneen with our food,' he said, radiating his special brand of Irish charm, a charm most women found irresistible.

Watching him, Rosie thought: What a waste of a beautiful man.

SEVEN

The bar was called Ouzo-Ouzo and it was located on the Bowery not far from Houston Street.

The neighbourhood was not particularly salubrious, but then Kevin Madigan had grown accustomed to the disreputable in his four years as an undercover cop. It seemed to him that he spent half his time in murky hideaways such as this, waiting for every kind of lowlife to bring him what he wanted – namely information of some kind or another.

He mused about this situation now as he nursed his beer in a bosky corner of the little Greek hole-in-the-wall on the outer fringes of SoHo and Greenwich Village. He was sick to death of places like this, there was no getting away from that fact. On the other hand, such places were essential to him. Where else could he have his meetings with the sleazy characters he had to do business with?

It was exactly a week ago tonight that Rosie had suggested he come in from the cold, get himself a desk job with NYPD. He had laughed uproariously that night, but now he wondered if she might be right. This thought hardly had time to take hold before he dismissed it. A desk job would bore him. Worse, it would kill his soul.

When he was out on the street his adrenaline pumped like crazy. He was full of vitality and on top of it all, ready to go the whole nine yards, capable of dealing with anyone and anything that came flying at him. He knew that any job other than the one he had would do him irreparable damage, and not even his sister could convince him otherwise.

But maybe some sort of change *was* in order. That was one of the reasons he was sitting here at seven o'clock on Saturday night, already running late for his uptown date with his uptown girl, waiting for Neil O'Connor.

Neil was a special kind of guy, an old buddy, and a former undercover cop. He was still with the NYPD, but was now attached to the police department's Crime Intelligence Division, which specialized in organized crime.

Earlier in the week, Neil had unexpectedly called him, and had asked if he would be interested in transferring over to the Crime Intelligence Division.

Much to his own astonishment, he had found himself saying that he might be, and he had agreed to meet Neil to discuss it. For the past few years he had been part of an NYPD Strike Force working closely with the FBI and the DEA, targeting Colombian and Asian drug-traffickers. He had been highly successful in this job, putting some of the most notorious drug kingpins away for years; they would be very old men before they were out on the street again.

Kevin glanced at his watch; out of the corner of his

eye he saw Neil coming in through the front door, and raised his hand in greeting. Neil responded with a nod, striding forward.

His old friend was tall, well built, sandy-haired, with the brightest of blue eyes and masses of freckles on his wide Irish face.

Kevin stood up when Neil reached the table.

They shook hands, slapped each other on the back with the affection and camaraderie of good old buddies who had been through a lot together.

When they drew apart, Neil glanced at his half-finished glass of beer. 'Want another, Kevin? Or something stronger?'

'A beer's fine, thanks. A Bud Light,' Kevin answered, and sat down.

Neil moved over to the bar, came back a second later carrying a glass in each hand. After putting them on the table he took off his overcoat, threw it on an adjacent chair, and seated himself next to Kevin. Lighting a cigarette, Neil inhaled deeply, then plunged right in, keen to get straight to the point. 'I want you in my unit, Kevin. *Need* you. Badly. And immediately. If you say you're in then I'll get you transferred practically overnight.'

Leaning forward slightly, fixing his eyes on Kevin, Neil continued with sheathed ferocity, 'Destroying the Mob is a worthwhile cause, the kinda challenge you like. And I can sure promise you action, and plenty of it. So, whaddya say?'

For a moment Kevin did not respond.

He simply sat there, staring back at Neil, weighing his words carefully. Bringing his head closer to his friend's, he said, 'You didn't explain much on the phone the other day, Neil.'

'What's there to explain?' Neil eyed him curiously, raised his brows, added succinctly, 'The name of the unit says it all, kid.' He sighed, muttered, 'We're after the Mob, want to get as much on 'em as we can.'

'I realize that. What I meant was, would I be working undercover? And who *specifically* are you zeroing in on? Or aren't you? Are you after the Mob in general?'

'Answering your first question, you don't have to go undercover if you don't want to, but I'd prefer it if you did. You're the best of the very best. To answer your second question, although we're focusing on all the crime families in New York, at this particular time we're making a real effort to bring down the Rudolfos.'

Kevin let out a long, low whistle on hearing this name. There were six organized crime families operating in New York: Gambino, Colombo, Genovese, Lucchese, Bonanno and Rudolfo. The latter organized crime family was the shrewdest and the most powerful organization in the American Mafia. The Don, Salvatore Rudolfo, was considered by police and mobsters alike to be one of the greatest dons there had ever been in the annals of organized crime. He was *capo di tutti capi*, boss of all bosses, the most respected and revered, and apparently the don to whom every other don on the Eastern Seaboard kowtowed.

Kevin exclaimed, 'Jesus, Neil, that's mighty ambitious! The Rudolfo family have proven to be almost impregnable for years now. It's been pretty damned hard to get anything really spectacular on them, anything really incriminating, that's why they're so damned strong. It's going to be pretty tough –'

'Maybe not as tough as you think!' Neil cut in sharply. 'We've made a breakthrough, managed to infiltrate the Rudolfo family. We've put an under-cover cop in there, and that's where you come in, Kev. You're gonna be in the drug business with 'em. Our inside man is gonna introduce you, vouch for you, stick close to you. *If* you'll work undercover, that is.'

'The Rudolfos have always denied they traffic in drugs, and continue to deny it.'

'That's bullshit, Kevin! All Mafiosi deal drugs, whatever their names, and you know it as well as I do. The Rudolfos are no better than any of their . . . their . . . brethren!' Neil exclaimed vehemently in a voice grown suddenly acerbic.

He gave Kevin one of his hard, pointed stares. 'You're an expert in drugs and the drug business, and you've made a lotta busts. I need your expertise, your contacts, your special ability to blend into their scummy world, to move around with ease and con-fidence in it. So, give me an answer, kid.'

Kevin was silent.

Neil pressed, 'I thought you were on a mission to *get* all the dirty bastards in the dirty drug business? This is your chance to strike at a really powerful and lethal purveyor of death, my friend. The Mob do it all, y'know, from smack to crack, you name it, they got it and they *sell* it. Millions of dollars' worth of junk *they* put out on the streets of this city. Billions of dollars' worth, in fact, if you count all the families, and the quantity they deal in a year.'

'I'm in, Neil,' Kevin said, making a decision.

There was a small pause. He lifted his glass, took a swallow of his beer, added, almost as an afterthought, 'And I'll work undercover, since that's what you want.'

'I knew I could count on you.' Neil sounded extremely relieved. He continued, 'I'll talk to Eddie LaSalle on Monday, and start the paperwork immediately. As I told you when I called the other day, Eddie gave me the go-ahead, said I could approach you, so he won't be surprised to hear you've agreed to transfer.'

'No, he won't. I mentioned it myself, told him I was seeing you tonight.'

Neil downed his beer and pushed back his chair. 'How about something stronger to seal our deal?' he suggested, rising and hovering behind his chair.

'Thanks, Neil, but it'll have to be one for the road. I'm running late for my date. And look, let me get it.' As he spoke, Kevin half stood.

Neil shook his head. 'No way, kid, this is on me.' A wide grin spread across his face. 'A date with your uptown girl, I don't doubt. And I guess you'll want a single malt on the rocks?'

'Correct both times.'

A few seconds later they clinked glasses and toasted each other and wished each other great success in their venture together.

There was a short silence.

Neil lit a cigarette, drew on it, sat smoking, his expression contemplative.

Kevin sipped his Scotch, watching the other detective carefully, wondering what he was thinking, what was coming next. Neil had always been full of surprises. He hoped this really *was* going to be the last drink. He was itching to get away, leave this crummy bar, cab it uptown, shed his cop's skin, relax for the weekend, make like a normal human being for once. Life was hard, and his job was tough, more than tough, it was a ball-breaker. *She* was the one bit of sunlight and joy and happiness he had. He hated to keep her waiting, to be late like this, and he always endeavoured to be on time. She worried when he wasn't, her heart in her mouth, thinking he'd bought it at the hands of the criminals he stalked.

A few weeks ago she had talked about breaking it off with him, mostly because her fear for him was difficult to live with. He hadn't said much in response to this announcement, but, surprising himself, inside he had felt a sudden surge of unfamiliar panic. He wasn't sure what he would do if she left him, what he'd do without her . . .

Neil broke the silence between them. He said, 'Maybe you should put it out on the street that you're taking off, goin' on a trip, gonna be outta town, then do a genuine disappearing act from your neck of the woods. It'd be wiser, I think, Kev.'

'You're right. I'm not working on anything special. I just made a big bust, did it with Joe Harvey. Listen, I'll tell Eddie I'd like a week off before I move over to your division. To be honest, Neil, I could use a break.'

'Take it now. You're gonna be awful busy with my unit. I told you, we're hard pressed, we need you, and we're sure as hell gonna make use of you, twenty-four hours a day, if necessary.'

Kevin nodded his understanding. 'And let's just hope we can strike some real blows at the Rudolfos, cripple them once and for all. The Mafia have never been as exposed as they are right now. The Colombo family is in a shambles and falling apart, and the Gambinos are in big trouble. It looks like the Dapper Don's number-two guy is going to be singing quite a few big hits at Gotti's murder and racketeering trial.'

Neil began to chuckle. 'You got it, kid. John Gotti, wearing his two-thousand-dollar suits, is in deep doo-doo. Sammy "The Bull" Gravano is a *star* witness for the prosecution, and there's never been one like him. Think about it, Kevin, a sacred brotherhood consecrated in blood and celebrated with wine has been broken by a little piece of tape – a police recording of a highly incriminating conversation between mobsters.' His grin was huge. 'Gotti's gonna be in the can for years, and I do mean *years*. And years and years.'

'The underworld is reeling from that defection – not to mention the prosecution.'

'You don't have to tell *me*! My unit's been part of it all along. Look, Gravano's co-operation is the highest-ranking Mafia defection ever, especially given the Gambinos' stature as the largest of the Mafia families and Gravano's position in it as Gotti's right-hand guy.' Neil shook his head as if in disbelief. 'And it's really been surprising to me that he broke the oath of *omertà* . . . the oath of silence is taken very seriously by all Mafiosi. But Gravano sure as hell did it, he ratted on his *goombah*, his best buddy. Surprising, eh?'

Not waiting for any comment from Kevin, Neil hurried on, 'After all, they started out together, Gravano and Gotti, were street soldiers together, just a coupla wiseguys packing heat who made it, *unbelievably*, to *capi*.' Neil shrugged. 'But Gravano wanted to save his hide, so he said to hell with the sacred brotherhood and *omertà* and my good old *goombah* Johnny boy, and he sang like a canary.'

Kevin nodded. 'And Gotti's upcoming trial in Brooklyn is going to be some spectacle, mark my words.' Kevin glanced at his watch. 'Hell, Neil, it's later than I realized! I've got to be going.'

'Me too. My old lady's waiting for me. Our first Saturday night out in months and I'm late. She'll kill me.'

They grabbed their coats and left the bar.

EIGHT

Out on the sidewalk, the two detectives stood talking for a moment or two, and then Neil took hold of Kevin's arm. 'Come on, kid, I'll walk you down the block to Houston. You can grab a cab there. Your uptown girl won't be mad at you, will she?'

Kevin shook his head as he fell into step with Neil. 'No, she's used to me showing up hours late. She doesn't like it, but she doesn't take it out on me. Anyway, she'll be pleased, no *relieved*, when I tell her I'm moving to the Crime Intelligence Division.'

Neil threw him an odd look. 'But it's still dangerous work.'

'*You* know that, Neil. *I* know it. But she doesn't. And neither does my sister Rosie. Lately, they've both been on my back, wanting me to make a change, so I'm damn sure they'll be happy to hear that I have. Crime Intelligence Division *does* sound like a desk job, doesn't it?'

'It could mean anything . . . I guess.'

Shivering, Kevin shrugged deeper into his overcoat, pushed his hands into his pockets. 'Shit, it's freezing tonight, and there's never a cab around when you need one.'

'That's what they usually say about cops,' Neil remarked, and let out a hollow laugh.

'Why the hell did you have to pick a crummy bar all the way downtown? On the *Bowery*, for God's sake!'

'Because it's as far removed from Little Colombia as I could get without goin' to New Jersey,' Neil explained, making reference to the Elmhurst section of Queens, where Kevin operated most of the time.

'I can't say I'm sorry to be saying goodbye to that neighbourhood,' Kevin confided as they strode on down the street. 'And thank God I'll never have to darken the doors of Mesón Asturias again. I've grown to detest the place. And to think, thirty years ago that little *cantina* was a typical Irish neighbourhood bar, full of cheerful Micks downing boilermakers and telling tall tales about the *ould sod*. But the Irish fled long ago, moved over to Woodside like we did a few years before Mom died, and Roosevelt Avenue *has* become a little Colombia, and then some, when you really think about it. A jazzy strip where hundred-dollar bills are the normal currency and flashy suits and salsa clubs flourish.'

'And where shootings are as common as they are in Cali, Medellín and Bogotá,' Neil remarked, 'as if *you* didn't know that.' He sighed under his breath. 'It boggles the mind, Kev, New York is a city gone mad on guns and made even crazier by crack.'

'You and me, Neil, we're living in the belly of the beast. We see it all, and every day of the week . . . the homeless, the hungry, the desperate, as well as the demented, the junkies, the crazies, the criminals. And *we* know the score. The majority of folk don't see it, or don't want to see it, or turn a blind eye if they do. Tragic, but that's the way it is, I'm afraid.'

Neil stopped in his tracks, swung to Kevin, grabbed his arm. In the lamplight, the older cop's face was suddenly stark. 'A fifteen-minute drive from Manhattan over the Queensborough Bridge and you're in South America, to all intents and purposes. And you're taking your life in your hands, mingling with drug barons, pushers, users and every kind of sleaze ball there is. I'm sure as hell glad you're moving over to my unit, kid, *real* glad.'

'So am I . . . Let's face it, I've probably just added a few extra years to my life.'

Neil nodded, went on, 'And then there's Bushwick, a hellhole of the damned, if ever I've seen one . . . a shanty town filled with coke and crack heads, and heroin addicts pumping shit into their veins. Broken-down specimens of humanity who'll mug, rob and kill you just to get a fix. It's sickening.'

'Only too true, *compadre*, only too true,' Kevin said quietly, taking Neil by the elbow, forcing him to walk on towards Houston Street.

'And this is America,' Neil said in a bereft voice, 'the richest and most powerful country in the world. It's more than sickening, it's horrific. *Diabolical*. Whatever happened to America the beautiful? And the American dream?'

Kevin did not respond. There was nothing he could add. Neil had just said it all.

*

Kevin let himself into her apartment with his own key.

He stood in the hallway, waiting for her to make an appearance, the way she usually did when he came in. But tonight she did not.

He hung his overcoat in the hall closet, slipped out of his shoulder holster and gun and carefully draped them over a coat hanger in the closet. It was bad enough that she knew he lived in a world of violence, without her seeing blatant evidence of it. Anyway, he preferred to keep his two worlds separate. Then, still puzzled, he cocked his ear, listening, wondering if something was wrong.

It was quiet. Nothing stirred. But as he crossed the small entrance hall, walking through into the apartment, he heard the faint sound of the radio playing in the kitchen, and he knew she was home.

He poked his head into the living room; the lights blazed, but the fire was dying in the grate. It looked to him as if it had been neglected for some time.

Kevin went down the corridor, making for the bedroom. The door stood ajar. Pushing it open, he went inside. The bedside lamps had been dimmed and in the soft, muted light he saw that she was curled up on the bed, dozing; or perhaps she was sleeping soundly, he wasn't sure.

Reaching the bed, he noticed the pile of manila folders fanned out next to her on the eiderdown, some of them spilling their contents. Obviously she had been working, had grown drowsy, and had fallen asleep waiting for him to arrive.

Bending over her, he whispered her name, not

wanting to startle or frighten her, and touched her face lightly with one hand.

Instantly, her eyes flew open. Relief and happiness flooded her face at the sight of him. 'Kevin,' she breathed softly. 'Oh, God, I'm sorry, I must have dozed off.'

'No problem, honey,' he said, kneeling down next to the bed in order to bring his face closer, and to the same level as hers. 'I'm the one who should apologize for being late. I got caught up with Neil O'Connor longer than I'd planned. You remember Neil, you met him last year. Anyway, he needed to talk to me, and tonight was the only time he could make it. It was urgent.'

'It's all right, Kevin, really.'

He gave her a direct look, and explained, 'Neil has asked me to transfer over to his division. I've agreed.'

Startled by this announcement, she blinked several times, half frowned. 'Which division is that?'

'The Crime Intelligence Division.'

'Is it a desk job?'

'Part of the time,' he lied, wanting to make her feel better, more secure about his safety.

'And the rest of the time?' she probed, her vividly intelligent eyes now focusing on him with sudden intensity.

'I *will* have to be out on the street, of course. But this new job is much less dangerous than the one I've been doing. Honestly it is.' Kevin paused, flashed a winning smile, then improvised quickly, 'And listen, I'll have more time off, much more.'

'I'm glad it's a safer job,' she said. Reaching out

she touched his cheek, a smile striking her mouth as she did.

He loved her smile. It was sweet, innocent, like a small child's smile, and it illuminated her face, filled it with radiance. Taking hold of her shoulders, he drew her closer to him, brought his lips to hers and kissed her gently.

Immediately, her arms went around his neck, and she returned his gentle kiss with such ardour it inflamed him. He put both his arms around her, held her closer to him, kissing her more passionately, letting his tongue linger against hers. They kissed this way for a long time, devouring each other's mouths until they were breathless.

It was Kevin who finally drew away. He loosened the top of her peach-satin robe and brought his face down to her breasts. She was wearing a matching peach-satin nightgown with thin shoelace straps, and he had no problem slipping his hand into the lace-trimmed bodice. When a breast sprang free from the nightgown, he took the small magenta-coloured nipple in his mouth and kissed it until she began to moan softly.

Kevin paused in order to untie the robe completely, then he ran his hands down the length of her body, bent over her again and continued to caress and kiss each breast in turn. Eventually he raised his head and looked down at her. Her eyes were closed; her lips slightly parted, she was breathing rapidly. He saw how excited she was becoming.

The expression on her face, one of abandonment mingled with ecstasy, turned him on, as did the feel of the satin nightgown under his hands. Lifting this, he smoothed one hand along her thigh until his fingers came to rest on the silky mound between her legs. As he moved his fingers against the hidden flesh, she parted her legs slightly, and he felt the sudden moistness, the heat flowing out of her.

'Oh Kevin,' she murmured, and opened her eyes.

He raised a dark brow. 'What is it?'

'Don't stop.'

'I won't,' he promised, and bending his head again, he sought the core of her with his mouth, lavishing her with kisses as he slid his fingers inside her. He knew her body well after a year of making love with her, knew she was on the verge, ready to climax, and he wanted her to do so. But exactly when he thought this was going to happen, when he expected her to erupt with pleasure, she unexpectedly sat up.

Grasping hold of his shoulders, she whispered hoarsely, 'Please, Kevin, get undressed and come to bed. I want to feel you inside me.'

'But I want to give you pleasure this way first.'

'I know, and I want you to, and I want to do the same for you, but please, get undressed. *Please.*'

Pushing himself to his feet and tossing his jacket onto a chair, he stepped out of his shoes, unzipped his trousers and stripped.

Meanwhile, she gathered the bunch of manila folders, threw them off the bed and removed her satin robe.

Kevin was across the room in two strides.

Stretching out on the bed next to her, he took her in his arms, murmuring her name, nuzzling her neck.

But after a moment or two he rolled over to his side, groped in the drawer of the bedside table for a condom. Damn things. He hated them. On the other hand, he was well aware of AIDS and what was going on out there. After Sunny had left his life, there had been other women from time to time, although no serious involvement. He was absolutely positive he was all right, but it was best to be careful, to take precautions for her sake. Kevin swallowed a sigh. This was a dangerous age they lived in. Sex and death walked side by side these days.

She stroked his back as he fumbled with the packet, then began to kiss him between his shoulder blades, whispering his name over and over, telling him how excited she was, how much she wanted him. Her words were erotic, tantalizing, and his erection grew harder, and suddenly he had no problem dealing with the rubber sheath.

Turning to her, he kissed her on the mouth. Once again, after a few passionate kisses, he let his lips trail down over her exposed breasts. Her nipples were erect, growing tauter under his mouth, sending a thrill through him. He ran his hands down over her lithe, satin-clad body. The fabric was sensual, just as she was, her body heat increasing as he lowered his head to kiss her stomach and thighs through the thin material.

Impatiently, he pulled at the nightgown, and she sat up, helped him to take it off. Her eyes, impaling his, were full of emotion, her desire naked on her face. She lay down again, and he savoured her beautiful body with his eyes, admiring the tautness of the pale ivory skin, smooth and sleek like the satin nightgown he had just taken off.

He knew she wanted his hands on her, and so he let his fingers explore that tender and secret part of her, at first moving them gently on the fleshy core, gradually increasing the pressure until she was trembling under his touch. Crouching over her, Kevin brought his mouth down to her thighs, began to kiss her, slipped his fingers into her. Within seconds she stiffened; a deep spasm ran through her and she climaxed, a moan trickling out of her throat, her body throbbing with intense pleasure.

'Kevin,' she said at last, her voice so low he could hardly hear it. 'Oh, Kevin, darling.'

Kevin threw himself up along the bed, in order to rest his head against hers on the pillow. He murmured, 'Did I please you?'

'You always do. And you always have, from the very first time. There's never been anyone like you.' She sat up, adopted a kneeling position, stared down into his dark eyes, smoothing one finger over his black eyebrows, and then his lips, and with a small smile of pleasure she lowered her mouth to his, kissing him tenderly.

Wanting her so much he could hardly stand it, Kevin pulled her on top of him almost roughly, continuing to kiss her and fondle her breasts. As always, she met his kisses with equal fervour, but suddenly she leaned back on her haunches, bent over him, began to kiss his chest and his belly, running the tip of her tongue over his body until he thought he was going to explode.

Swiftly he drew her up to rest beside him, lay on top of her and, bracing his hands on either side of her, he entered her with some force, moving against her, wanting to satisfy her. Wrapping her legs around his back, she clung to him, moving in rhythm with him, but he was aware she was holding back.

'Come to me,' he breathed against her face.

'No,' she whispered back, 'I'm waiting for you.' Yet as she was speaking a deep trembling seized her, the heat flowed out of her, enveloping him, and she cried, 'Kevin!'

Her reaction to him never failed to excite him, and as she continued to move against him he could no longer control himself. 'Oh God, Nell, I'm coming,' he gasped. 'Oh, Nell! Oh, Nell!'

She lay within the circle of his arms, her head resting on his chest, her eyes closed, her breathing light and even.

Kevin glanced down at her, half smiling to himself. With her he enjoyed the aftermath of lovemaking as much as the sexual act itself. He was as relaxed as she was, and at ease with her, and with himself, was always comfortable in her presence. Perhaps this was because he had known her since she was seventeen. Like his sister Rosie, her best friend, she was thirty-one now, but at this particular moment she looked much younger, more like a woman in her early twenties, her figure girlish, her skin youthful, her face without a line.

Nell Jeffrey had become very special to him, and whenever he was with her he felt renewed. Every day the city claimed a little bit more of him, but when he was with Nell she somehow managed to claim part of him back, or so it seemed to him, and without even knowing she was doing so. She was restoring him to himself, in a way.

To a certain extent, Kevin was able to lose himself in Nell, and when he did some of the pain went away, and his heartache and sadness about Sunny dimmed. In any case, it was as if Sunny was dead, considering her terrible condition, and life *was* for the living, wasn't it? Certainly he had come to understand this very well during the past year, especially since Nell had become such an essential part of his life.

These days he found himself thinking less and less about Sunny; six years was a long time, after all. And anyway, about nine months ago he had started to cut back on his visits, although this was her sister Elena's idea, not his. It would be easier on Sunny if he didn't come quite so frequently, Elena had said to him one Sunday afternoon at the mental home, since she appeared to grow more agitated whenever he was present. It was as if vaguely, somewhere in her demented and damaged brain, Sunny recalled that they had had something together once, and that this knowledge disturbed her. At least, so Elena had said to him that day.

Finally, three months ago, he had stopped going to New Haven altogether. Her family seemed to be relieved that he had made this decision; he discovered that he was, too.

But occasionally he wondered if he was being a moral coward, shirking his duty. When he had voiced this thought to Nell she had been vociferous in her insistence that he was not only doing the right thing, but the *only* thing he *could* do.

'You can't help her,' Nell had said. 'All you're doing is rubbing salt into your wounds. Not only that, she's an albatross around your neck, weighing you down. You've got to let Sunny go – for your own sake. You've got a life to live, for God's sake.' Her strong words had helped him, and lately he had come to realize that a burden had been lifted. Nell was right, Sunny was a part of his past, and he had to let go of certain parts of his past in order to move forward.

Now his memories of Sunny were of the early years when they were kids. He supposed it was easier to remember her before she had become a junkie craving dope, willing to do anything to get it. And he had begun to admit to himself that he felt better than he had in years. Thanks again, in no small measure, to his friend Nell.

Kevin buried his face in her hair. It was soft and silky, fragrant with the scent of lemon verbena, just as every part of her was sweet-smelling and fresh. Deeply, he breathed in the perfume of her; it helped to kill the stench of the city that forever filled his nostrils.

Nell was such a part of his life now he couldn't imagine what it would be like without her. But it was odd how they had become lovers so suddenly, a year ago, and after knowing each other for fourteen years.

Gavin had come to New York last October to see Nell on business. He was en route to London for meetings about *Kingmaker*, which at last he had managed to get under way. His old friend had phoned him, had invited him to join the two of them for dinner, and since he was taking a few days of R&R he was able to accept. He had not seen either of them for well over a year, and it had been a marvellous evening, full of good humour and laughter, shared reminiscences and lots of genuine affection.

They had eaten in Gavin's suite at the Carlyle Hotel, and when he and Nell left, long after midnight, he had insisted on taking her home. Even though it had been a cold night, they had walked to her apartment, and when they reached the building on Park Avenue where she lived she had invited him in for a nightcap.

While she had filled two brandy balloons with Remy Martin, he had set a match to the logs and paper in the grate, and then they had sat on the sofa together, savouring the aged cognac, chatting about their present lives as well as old times.

As long as he lived, he would never know how it had happened. All of a sudden, she was in his arms and he was kissing her, and she was responding ardently. And they ended up making passionate love on the rug in front of the blazing fire.

It had been a Friday night, and because he was off duty he had been able to spend the weekend with her. Cosseted in the warmth and comfort of her beautiful apartment, and smitten with each other, they had forgotten the everyday world they lived in, their pain and their worries for the next forty-eight hours.

At one point, during the weekend, they had talked about Mikey, who had vanished the year before. Everyone was troubled by his mysterious disappearance, and most especially Nell. After their youthful romance had ended, they had remained good friends, drawing even closer over the ensuing years, sharing confidences as old pals so frequently do.

That night when she and Kevin had first made love, Nell had told him that this was one of the reasons she was so concerned about Mikey; it was simply inconceivable to her that he had chosen to leave New York without telling her he was going away. Or where he was heading.

What Kevin had thought but not said that night was that perhaps Mikey hadn't had a chance to tell her. No one really knew what had happened to him, not even his room mate. He had simply vanished.

Kevin had often thought that Mikey might easily have been the victim of foul play. Being a cop, he was only too well aware of the frightening statistics – every year hundreds of thousands of Americans disappeared without a trace. Few were ever found, or showed up again to pick up their lives. The Missing Persons List at his own precinct was dismaying, miles long.

Nell stirred in his arms.

Kevin glanced down at her.

She opened her eyes and looked up at him, returning his steady gaze. 'That's a mighty serious face you're wearing, Kevin mine. Is something troubling you?'

Although there was no subterfuge between them, only honesty and straightforwardness, he chose not to mention Mikey at this moment. It was inappropriate. And so he said, 'I was thinking about us, Nell, how we've been seeing each other for a year now. Yet nobody knows about us.'

'Neil O'Connor certainly does,' she said, and laughed.

'I was talking about our nearest and dearest.'

'You mean you haven't mentioned it to Gavin?'

'I've not seen him this year, except for those few days when I came to London during filming. Besides, you should know I'm not the sort of guy to kiss and tell. And I know you haven't confided in Rosie, or she would have mentioned it.'

'I don't know why I've never told her, Kev, or why we've kept it a secret, and we have done that, you know.' Nell moved closer to him, put her arms around him, held him tightly. After a moment, she added, 'I suppose I should say something to her. We are best friends.'

'It'll please her . . . that we're seeing each other, I mean.'

'Oh, yes, she'll be approving!' Nell exclaimed, leaning her head back, looking up at him, eyeing him a bit coquettishly. 'Of that I can assure you, my darling. Oh yes, she'll give us her blessing all right.'

'When is she coming back from LA?'

'Good God, Kevin, she only left last night. But I expect she'll return with me.'

'What do you mean?'

'I'm going to the West Coast myself –'

109

'*When?*' he cut in somewhat sharply, staring down at her in surprise.

'On Tuesday or Wednesday.'

'And I was just about to take a week off, before transferring over to the Crime Intelligence Division. I was hoping to spend a bit of time with you, honey.'

Nell bit her lip, looking chagrined. 'I wish I'd known, Kevin, it would have been great. But I've made all the arrangements now, and it'd be really difficult to change my plans. I have a meeting scheduled with Gavin, who's flying in to LA from London on Monday for a week. And I also have meetings set with other clients.'

'I see.'

'I'm sorry, really sorry. Look, I've got a great idea! Why don't you come out to the coast? That'd be fabulous, like old home week, me and you and Rosie and Gavin.' Her face lit up at the thought of this, and she exclaimed excitedly, 'Oh come on, say yes, Kev! Please say yes.'

He hesitated. 'I just don't know . . .' He let his sentence trail off, not sure what to do, wondering whether to commit himself or not.

Nell sat up, kissed him playfully on the nose and slipped off the bed, heading in the direction of the bathroom. From the doorway she said, 'Well, at least think about it.'

'I have. It's better I don't come.'

'But *why?*'

'I'd be at a loose end, since you'd all be busy during the day. And I've got a lot of things to attend to here,

Nelly. You know, personal stuff that always gets neglected because of my job.'

She nodded, and went into the bathroom.

When she came out a moment later she was wrapped in a terry robe and carrying another one. 'Here, put this on, and let's go and eat something. Dinner's cooking in the kitchen.'

'I was planning on taking you out, lady.'

She grinned at him. 'Allow me to have my moment of domesticity, please. I made a chicken casserole earlier. Mind you, it's been in the oven for ages, and I just hope it's not ruined. Otherwise, you may well be taking me to the local hamburger joint, or eating scrambled eggs here.'

He followed her out of the bedroom, pulling on the robe as he did, and laughing with her. 'I'm not all *that* hungry, Nelly,' he said. 'But I wouldn't mind a glass of wine.'

The casserole was delicious, and they ate it at the kitchen table, sipping a good Beaujolais Villages, which Kevin had opened earlier.

At one moment he touched his glass of red wine to hers. 'Who'd have thought that our Little Nell would become such a high-powered businesswoman with a brilliant career . . . travelling the world and running her own international company.'

'Me,' she answered, and winked at him, her eyes twinkling with amusement.

He gave her the benefit of an admiring smile. 'I'm proud of you, you know, and of Rosie, too.'

'You *should* be proud of your sister,' Nell

murmured, her voice growing serious. 'Her costumes for *Kingmaker* are quite extraordinary. They'll knock your socks off – wait until you see the film. She'll be winning another Oscar in the not too distant future.'

'No kidding! That's great! She said something to me about Gavin's next movie. Is she going to do it?'

'I don't know.' Nell lifted her shoulders in a small shrug, shook her head. 'He hasn't told her, or me, what it is. Perhaps he doesn't know himself yet. Mind you, whatever he decides to make, it's bound to be a humdinger.'

'I must've misunderstood her. I thought that was why she went to Los Angeles.'

'Not really. She went to see Garry Marshall. To discuss his next picture. It's a contemporary romantic comedy. He's a big fan of hers.'

'I don't blame him,' Kevin said. 'And listen, a guy who directs such great pictures as *Beaches* and *Pretty Woman* is certainly worth being associated with, so I hope Rosie takes it. She'd be a fool not to, *I* think.' He took a sip of the wine, and asked, 'And how long are you both planning to stay out there?'

'A few days, a week at the most. It depends on Johnny Fortune.'

'Oh.' Kevin threw her a quizzical look.

'He and I have meetings about his New York concert for next spring or summer. It's going to be at Madison Square Garden again. We've a lot of ground to cover.'

'You've made him into a big star, Nelly.'

She shook her head. 'Not true, Kev. He did that

himself. With his voice. And his looks and his charm and the way he makes women swoon.'

Kevin looked amused, and after a moment he remarked, 'You and Rosie are so alike. Neither of you ever want to take credit for anything great that you do. Believe me, you certainly *helped* to make him a star.'

'You're just prejudiced, my darling.'

'He's a bit of a mystery man, isn't he?'

'Who? Johnny? Not at all.' She frowned. 'What do you mean by mystery?'

'He comes out of nowhere, makes a couple of records, takes women by storm, and boom, he's on his way. Then you come along, take over his public relations, and almost overnight turn him into this giant superstar. No, megastar.'

'If only it were so easy. It's a bit more complicated than that. Johnny worked the small rooms in Vegas and Atlantic City for years, not to mention the night-club circuit. Until he was blue in the face. He did Los Angeles, Chicago, Boston, New Jersey, Philadelphia, New York, year after year . . . you name the club, however obscure, and I'll bet you Johnny's sung there.'

'Whatever you say, you *have* made him into America's answer to Julio.'

Nell burst out laughing and shook her head again. 'No way. There will only ever be *one* Julio Iglesias. Now there's a *real* megastar. He's also one of the nicest guys I've ever met. As for Johnny Fortune, I think there's a little bit of everybody in him . . . Perry Como, Vic Damone, Little Ole Blue Eyes himself, *and*

Julio. That's why everybody loves Johnny – he reminds them all of their favourite crooner.'

Kevin chuckled. 'There's nobody like you, Nell. You call it exactly the way it is every time, but I'm not too sure that Johnny would like to hear those words . . . you're suggesting he's derivative.'

'Well, he is. But he's special in his own way, of course, and he is *the* bel canto balladeer of the nineties.'

'To coin a phrase.'

'Which *I* did,' she shot back, leaned forward and kissed him on the cheek. 'At least I'll admit to that, Kev.'

NINE

The house stood on a high, densely-wooded hillside in Benedict Canyon, overlooking Bel-Air.

It was an old house, dating back to the 1930s and Hollywood in its heyday. Although Spanish Colonial in style, the interiors had been considerably remodelled in the 1950s by a legendary producer and his movie-star wife. To this sprawling, comfortable dwelling they had brought their unique taste, adding fine wood panelling, handsome fireplaces and vast floor-to-ceiling windows that drew the lovely surroundings into the house to become part of the decor.

Shaded terraces, flower-filled gardens with fountains and statuary, and an unusual pool house were the other elements that helped to underscore the beauty of the bucolic setting.

To Johnny Fortune, the house on the hill, as he always referred to it, was a magical place, and he loved it in a way he had not loved any other material thing, except for the guitar his uncle had given him when he was a boy. The house had great distinction and elegance, and not one ounce of pretension whatsoever. The spacious rooms were beautifully proportioned, airy and filled with light, and almost all of them boasted a fireplace – even the pool house had one.

One of the most important things about the house was that it had not been tampered with since its remodelling in the fifties. It had therefore retained the purity of design imposed on it by the producer and his wife. Everything they had done had been in impeccable taste, and subsequent owners had had the good sense not to touch the beautiful interiors and exteriors.

Whenever he was in the house on the hill, Johnny experienced a great sense of well being; it was the nearest he ever came to feeling happy. Many things contributed to this emotion – the obvious beauty of the place, its intrinsic comfort and luxury, its grand history, the fame and importance of its past owners, including, at one point, Greta Garbo. And, not the least by any means, just the prestige of owning the house gave him a great deal of satisfaction.

Johnny had never thought he would live in a house like this, not even in his wildest dreams; it was as far removed from his beginnings as anything could ever be.

Johnny Fortune, born Gianni Fortunato in 1953, had grown up on the crowded streets of Lower Manhattan, and his home had been a cramped and dismal apartment on Mulberry Street, where he had lived with his uncle and aunt, Vito and Angelina Carmello.

His father, Roberto Fortunato, he had never known; his mother, Gina, he could barely remember. After his aunt died, when he was five years old, his

Uncle Vito, who was his mother's brother, had been both father and mother to him until he was fifteen. It was then he had dropped out of school, knowing he would never make it to college anyway.

And so the streets of New York became his university, just as they had, in a sense, been his kindergarten. At an early age he had learned to take care of himself, was street-smart, forever wary and on guard, conscious of everyone and everything going on around him.

But Johnny had never been a typical street kid, full of sass, with a cheeky mouth and a belligerent manner; nor had he been a tough and dangerous young punk, constantly making trouble, or in trouble with the law. Uncle Vito had seen to that.

Also, Johnny was lucky in that he had something special, something which made him different from the other kids, lifted him out of the ordinary, and, in a peculiar way, even protected him. That something special was a voice. It was a sweet and melodious voice, one so pure it was breathtaking, and it caused his uncle's colleagues and male friends to listen to him rapt, almost in awe, applaud loudly when he had finished and generously shower him with dollar bills.

Without exception, each one of them told him he sang like an angel. Uncle Vito said his voice was a gift from God, and that he should treat it with respect and be forever thankful for his great gift. He was.

For a while, the young Gianni toyed with the idea of calling himself Johnny Angel, after the popular song of that title. But in the end he decided to use

Johnny Fortune, the anglicization of his own name, hoping that it presaged things to come. And ultimately it did, although it took Johnny many years to make that fortune.

Now, on this cool November evening, his past was the last thing on his mind. Johnny was thinking about the future – next year to be exact. It seemed to him that 1992 had all but disappeared before it had even begun, what with the foreign concert tours which had been planned, plus the lengthy recording sessions for his new disc, which his manager had already set up with the recording studio in New York. Once Christmas was over he realized his time was no longer going to be his own; the next twelve months were spoken for.

It struck Johnny that the more successful he became, the less time he had for himself. But he would rather be overworked, overtired and pressured, with no social or private life to speak of, *and* rich and famous, than the reverse. He had achieved what he had set out to achieve; he had everything he had always wanted.

Sighing lightly under his breath, a wry smile touching his mouth, Johnny allowed his long, elegant fingers to drift over the keys of the Steinway baby grand, playing his favourite song, one he had long made his own and which had become his signature tune. It was *You and Me (We Wanted It All)*, words and music by Carole Bayer Sager and Peter Allen.

Abruptly, he stopped playing, slowly swung around on the piano stool, sat perfectly still, staring out into the living room. His eyes roamed around.

As usual, he could not help but admire it; even after four years of living in the hillside house he continued to derive immense pleasure from merely *looking* and *appreciating*.

Some of his possessions he continued to regard with awe. Not the least of this awe and admiration was directed at his collection of paintings, which he had been acquiring since he moved into the house.

The room Johnny was staring at *was* beautiful, its overall design graciously executed. A mixture of creams and dark wood tones predominated, with the vivid colour coming from the art, the book bindings, and the lush, freshly cut flowers arranged in crystal vases and bowls.

A pale-cream rug on the dark polished floor centred the room in front of the fireplace, with two cream sofas, deep and luxurious, facing each other across an antique Chinese coffee table of carved mahogany. French bergères from the Louis XV period, upholstered in striped cream silk, flanked the fireplace, and there were antique occasional tables, as well as a long sofa table holding a small sculpture by Brancusi and a black basalt urn overflowing with branches and flowers. The whole was bathed in soft light emanating from the many silk-shaded porcelain lamps.

But it was the paintings which caught the eye and commanded attention – the Sisley landscape over the fireplace, the Rouault and the Cézanne on the far wall, and the two early Van Goghs hanging on the wall behind the piano.

Even though Johnny said it himself, the room was

in perfect taste. He had not created it, nor, indeed, *any* part of the house. It was all Nell's handiwork, with the help of an interior designer. Nell had found the house, picked the designer and created the look, the mood, the very special ambience that permeated throughout.

Everything Johnny looked at had Nell's stamp on it, since she had chosen everything with him. The whole house represented Nell's taste, but he didn't mind; he loved her taste. In fact, he had made her taste his own.

It pleased Johnny that he could now recognize what was excellent and what was inferior. He had come to appreciate quality and style, not only in art and furniture but in everything else, and he was proud of his newly-acquired knowledge.

Even his clothes had undergone an overhaul since Nell had become part of his business entourage. He liked the way he looked these days – more conservative and well tailored than he had ever been. Nell had given him an image.

Rising, Johnny walked across the room and stood with his back to the fireplace, admitting to himself that the only really good taste he had had before meeting Nell Jeffrey was in his music. And everyone acknowledged that his musical taste *was* impeccable. He never put a foot wrong with that.

It was not surprising that he had not known much about art and antiques. After all he had not had much exposure to them. His Aunt Angelina had filled the little apartment on Mulberry Street with gaudy pictures of Jesus and the Saints, crucifixes, and religious plaster statues in improbable colours, and after she had died Uncle Vito had not touched anything, perhaps out of love and respect for his dead wife.

Once Johnny had escaped the dreary little space he and the old man occupied, his years on the road had been spent in cheap motel rooms or garish hotels in Hollywood, Vegas, Chicago, Atlantic City and Manhattan, and they were hardly the ideal places to get an education about art and precious objects.

Johnny chuckled to himself as he walked across the floor and out into the large entrance foyer, heading in the direction of the dining room. He was thinking of Uncle Vito, who he knew would flee this elegant house if he ever set eyes on it, running to the nearest motel out of sheer embarrassment.

He had invited Vito to the coast four years ago, when he had first moved in, but the old man had declined. He had not pressed him to come, nor had he repeated the invitation at a later date. His uncle did not fit in here, very simply because the house would make him feel ill at ease, and the last thing Johnny wanted was to cause him discomfort. Uncle Vito might not have been the greatest parent, but he had done the best he knew how, and Johnny was very well aware that the old man had always loved him as if he were the son he had never had.

The dining room where Johnny hovered in the doorway was in shades of apricot and cream, with touches of bright raspberry. It was simplicity itself, with an old yew-wood dining table from the south of France, surrounded by chairs with high backs of carved cherry. An elegant armoire and a buffet, also made of cherry, were set against different walls, while paintings by the great English watercolourist Sir William Russell Flint hung above the buffet.

Tonight the mellow wood table gleamed with antique English silver, the finest of porcelain and crystal. Pale, champagne-coloured roses in full bloom, their perfume heady and sweet, filled the silver rose bowl resting between the four silver candlesticks holding cream candles, and a pair of dessert stands flanked the latter on each side.

There were three place settings at the table, and as he gazed at it Johnny discovered he was annoyed. He would have preferred it if Nell were coming alone tonight, as they had originally planned. Instead she was dragging a friend along with her. There was so much he still wanted to talk to her about, not to mention going over the coming year's agenda again, and with a stranger present he would certainly have to curtail his conversation – at least to some extent.

Now the prospect of meeting Nell's friend put a sudden damper on his buoyant spirits. But at lunch yesterday he had agreed when Nell had asked if she could bring someone, so it was his own fault. Nothing to do but put up a good front.

Turning away from the doorway, Johnny crossed the vast hall and ran lightly up the staircase to his bedroom, taking the steps two at a time. Like the rooms on the lower floor, the bedroom was large, full of light, with a huge plate-glass window running from the ceiling to the floor, making the wooded landscape outside an integral part of the interior decoration.

The room was furnished with French provincial antiques made of cherry and other fruit woods, and the colour scheme was similar to those in the rooms downstairs. Shades of cream, coffee and buttery-yellow mingled with pale-celadon and rose, all of them taken from the handsome Aubusson rug on the floor, the inspiration for the colour theme in the bedroom.

Taking off his blue jeans, T-shirt and brown suede loafers, Johnny went through into the bathroom to take a shower. A few minutes later, he stepped out of the steaming shower stall, grabbed a bath towel, wrapped it around himself, and reached for a smaller towel to dry his hair.

Johnny Fortune was thirty-eight years old. His body was lean, lithe and in perfect condition. He swam a lot, went to the gym whenever he could, and watched what he ate and drank. In consequence, he was in good physical shape. He had a finely-boned, sensitive face that showed fatigue very quickly, and when he was tired he could look older than his years. At this moment, regarding himself intently in the mirror, he thought that in spite of his tan he looked lousy.

After thoroughly drying his blond-streaked brown hair with the blow dryer, he brushed it back, leaned closer to the mirror and grimaced. The ravages of the night before really showed. He had faint bluish smudges under his eyes that resembled light bruises, and he certainly looked as if he was in need of sleep. He was. For the first time in years he had stupidly hung one on, drinking far too much red wine over dinner at La Dolce Vita on Little Santa Monica with his friend Harry Paloma.

What was even more stupid, he had taken one of the groupies who forever trailed him to the local hotel where he kept a permanent suite, and had bedded down with her. He never brought girls here to the house. The house was sacrosanct. That was why he kept the hotel suite on a permanent lease; it was ideal for his sexual encounters, which, as it so happened, were infrequent these days. Well, he had done one intelligent thing last night; he *had* remembered, at the last minute, to wear some protection. His arranger, Gordy Lanahan, had recently died of AIDS and that deadly disease was a spectre that haunted him.

Dropping the towel, Johnny walked through into the bedroom and went on into the large dressing room which adjoined it. This was actually the same size as his bedroom; the dressing room was full of racks holding expensive, beautifully-made clothes from the best tailors in London, Paris and Rome; Plexiglas-fronted drawers contained the finest of shirts, plus wool, silk and cashmere sweaters and pullovers for all occasions. Highly-polished shoes made of the best leathers, others of suede, were arranged on other racks which rested underneath the suits and sports jackets; silk ties were suspended from smaller racks attached to one of the walls.

After a few seconds spent going through some of his more casual clothes, Johnny made his selections, choosing a pair of dark-grey slacks and a black cashmere blazer, a pale-blue Swiss-voile shirt and a blue silk tie. He dressed rapidly in these clothes, then stepped into a pair of black leather loafers and went to select a silk handkerchief for his breast pocket.

A moment or two later, Johnny Fortune was running back down the staircase, having realized that Nell Jeffrey was due to arrive any minute.

TEN

Johnny Fortune did not like Nell's friend.

Try though he might to push aside his antipathy for her, he discovered he could not. There was something about her which disturbed him, filled him with irritation, and whenever she spoke he had a terrible compulsion to contradict whatever she said. Not only that, he had to make a supreme effort to be civil to her.

In all truth, Rosalind Madigan brought out the worst in Johnny. This was mainly because he was a man filled with innumerable insecurities about himself, although he did not comprehend that this was the actual reason for his aversion. He had not, as yet, attempted to analyse his reaction to Rosie. He was far too preoccupied thinking the worst about her – how plain she was, how superior of manner, how snobbish.

Rosie was none of these things. But the instant Johnny had set eyes on her he had instinctively sensed that she was different from the girls who normally crossed his path, and very simply he did not know how to cope with a woman who was so classy.

And so in his mind he put her down, turning her attributes into faults, seeing her as he wanted to see her and not as she truly was. Rosie was not plain, only conservative in her mode of dressing; she was not superior, but good-mannered; and certainly she was not snobbish, merely shy with him.

Looking at her now, through the corner of his eye, Johnny thought how dreary she was in appearance. He could not stand drab women; they turned him off. Flashy looks, brilliant plumage, lots of pizzazz and glamour were what he went for. He had a weakness for glamorous girls, in fact, which was one of the reasons Nell Jeffrey so appealed to him. Even though their relationship was strictly business, he took immense delight in her striking blonde beauty. Nell was loaded with glamour, in his opinion, and he thought she was a gorgeous specimen of young womanhood. He was proud that she was part of his entourage.

He was sipping his wine, listening to the two women chatting about their mutual friend, Gavin Ambrose, the mega movie star, when he had an unexpected, and rare, flash of insight into himself. Suddenly he realized what it was that disturbed him about the Madigan woman. It was her intelligence.

Brainy women frightened Johnny Fortune, made him feel like a dunce, and inferior, because he had not finished school.

Nell was also intelligent, but she was so well endowed with good looks and feminine attributes that Johnny never really noticed her brains until she was gone from his presence. Then it always hit him how clever she had been, usually on his behalf, and in his best interest. Nell Jeffrey was much more than his public relations representative, more like a business adviser, and he fully appreciated her talents, which he thought were considerable. She had changed his life in many fundamental ways since she had represented him.

Understanding the cause of his discomfort with Rosie, a feeling that had assailed him when she first walked in, made Johnny feel much better, and he picked up his fork, twisted spaghetti onto it.

Nell, Rosie and Johnny were seated at the dining table, eating the first course of the dinner Johnny's cook, Giovanni, had prepared. Sophia, Giovanni's wife, had just served the pasta primavera, while Arthur, his English-trained American butler, had poured chilled white wine into the fine crystal goblets.

There was silence in the room for a few seconds as the three of them ate, savouring the flavourful pasta. It was Nell who broke it, exclaiming, 'This is superb, Johnny, the most delicious pasta I've eaten in ages. Isn't it good, Rosie?'

'Delectable,' Rosie agreed, and looked across at Johnny. 'It's better than anything I ever had at Alfredo's . . . Alfredo's in Rome.'

'Giovanni's a genius in the kitchen,' Johnny said almost snappishly, and turning to Nell, excluding Rosie, he softened his voice, as he asked, 'So, how're we gonna do all these concerts next year? I think I'll need a stretcher at the end of the tour.'

Nell gave him a very direct look and decided to

say what had been on the tip of her tongue since yesterday, when they had done more brainstorming on his proposed world tour.

'I don't think you should do the whole tour, Johnny,' she announced carefully. 'It's just too much for anybody. Too many cities in too many far-flung countries. It'd be a killer. In my opinion you should restrict the tour to Los Angeles, New York, London, Paris and Madrid, some of which have been more or less set. Skip the rest.'

Johnny was taken aback by her statement, and his surprise showed on his face. He gaped at her. 'Hell, honey, I think that's a terrific idea, but I don't know that my agent'll agree with me. Anyway, he's already started the ball rolling around the world.'

'But he hasn't made *all* of your bookings, or closed all of the foreign deals with the theatres and auditoriums. I know that for a fact, and –'

'How do you know?' Johnny interrupted, frowning.

'I asked him just before I left yesterday. You were on the phone in the other office. You see, during our brainstorming session, it struck me that the tour was far too strenuous, perhaps even a bit ill-conceived. The distances you would have to cover are tremendous, continents apart. You'd be on that tour for almost the entire year, virtually living on your plane, as *you* well know, I'm sure. In any case, Johnny, this particular kind of tour spreads the artist too thin. I really do believe you should stick to the States and Europe this coming year. You can do Japan, the Far East and Australia the year after – in 1993.'

'It don't sound half bad to me.' Johnny beamed at her. 'I just hope Jeff'll go for it.'

'I am quite certain he will, if you broach it in the right way. Better still, why not let *me* bring it up at the meeting tomorrow afternoon? I could make the points I've just made to you. Also, let's not forget the recording sessions for the new disc. Those sessions are going to take several months, and put a great strain on you. You know what a perfectionist you are. Maybe I should mention that too, don't you think?'

An admiring look flickered in Johnny's eyes. He nodded. 'You're the smartest, the brightest, Nell. I love it when you do my thinking for me. Okay, it's agreed. You drop the bombshell on Jeff. I'll duck. You take his fire. And when the dust settles I'll take us all out to dinner.' Johnny grinned. 'I like it, I like it. And Jeff admires you, darlin'. You can certainly make some good points with him. Listen, he'll take it from you.'

'Thanks for your confidence in me, Johnny, and for those kind words. But –' she stopped abruptly, cutting off her sentence.

'But what?' he probed, leaning closer to her.

'Oh nothing really,' she hedged, not wanting to voice the thought that lately he seemed to be intimidated by his agent, Jeff Smailes. Instead, she said, 'I was going to say that I think it's important, at this particular stage in your career, that you're not over-exposed.'

'But the live concerts help boost my record sales!'

'I know they do. However, I think you can hold a little of yourself back, not give so much to your public. And without damaging your position. It will be better for you, in the long run.'

'Mmmmm.' He fell silent, looked thoughtful as he gazed into his wine glass. Lifting his head a moment later, he remarked, 'Julio just did a world concert tour. In fact, he's done several in the past few years, and they haven't damaged him. Not at all.'

'True, very true. On the other hand, Streisand hasn't sung live in concert for six years, and her record sales haven't slumped at all.'

'Barbra makes movies, though,' Johnny pointed out swiftly.

'But she doesn't always sing in them,' Nell countered, and laughed. 'We'll discuss more about this tomorrow. We can even have another meeting on Saturday, if you want, since I'm not leaving LA until Sunday.'

'That's great.'

Wanting to change the subject, to get Johnny away from his preoccupation and worries about his career, which were eternal, Nell now continued in a different vein. 'Rosie's costumes for Gavin's new picture *Kingmaker* are out of this world, Johnny. I wish you could see them. Anyway, you will. You'll come to the opening next year I hope, and I predict my dear old friend Rosie is going to win another Oscar.'

A flush spread up from Rosie's neck to flood her face, and she exclaimed, 'Honestly, Nell, you're too much. I'm sure I won't get an Oscar . . .' Her voice trailed off in embarrassment.

For once Johnny looked directly at Rosie, and said in a somewhat cold voice, 'Take it from me, Nell's predictions usually come true. It doesn't do to contradict her.'

Rosie made no response to this remark. She picked up her glass of water and took a sip, wondering why this man disliked her so much. It had been apparent from the moment she walked into his house that he resented her presence, and he had been curt to the point of rudeness. She wished Nell hadn't persuaded her to come; she would have been much better off having room service and watching television in her suite at the hotel.

Nell was also silent. She had not failed to notice Johnny's cold tone, and, like Rosie, she too was perplexed. His behaviour towards her friend had been odd, and his apparent dislike of her was illogical.

Wanting to smooth things over, and break the stony silence that had settled in the room, Nell took a deep breath. She was about to touch on the subject of Johnny's new compact disc; it had just been released and was already hitting the top of the charts. But she was saved the trouble. The door opened and Sophia entered. The housekeeper began to clear away their plates; Arthur followed closely on her heels, placing clean ones in front of them. A moment or two later they were serving the sea bass, which had been baked in herbs, and a selection of steamed fresh vegetables.

Johnny took a sip of his wine, said to Nell, 'And what will you be doing at this time *next* Thursday? For Thanksgiving, I mean?'

'I'll be cooking for Kevin,' Nell blurted out,

surprising herself, and quickly added, 'And Rosie, of course.'

'Kevin? Who's Kevin?' Johnny asked, a brow lifting.

'My boyfriend,' Nell said, deciding it was best to tell the truth, 'and Rosie's brother.' She met Rosie's startled look with a warning glance, her eyes narrowing slightly. 'We'll be back on the East Coast by then,' she went on, 'and I plan to cook for my two closest friends, give them a good old-fashioned Thanksgiving dinner. Turkey, cranberry sauce, sweet potatoes with marshmallows, corn bread, the whole works, in fact. I do a great Thanksgiving, Johnny, even though I am English.'

'More American than apple pie these days,' Johnny answered with a laugh, adding in a somewhat wistful voice, 'It sounds great.'

'Why don't you come, too?' Nell said. 'You'll be in New York, and I'd love to cook for you.'

'I can't. I've promised my uncle I'd spend it with him and his er . . . friends. But thanks for the invite.' Pushing his fork into the fish, Johnny murmured, 'A boyfriend, eh? Well, whaddya know. You've certainly kept it a secret from me.'

And me, Rosie thought, and her eyes telegraphed this message to Nell, who was sitting across the table from her.

Nell bit her lip, understanding only too well Rosie's astonishment and confusion, and averted her face. Her only response to Johnny's remark was a light laugh. Then she concentrated her entire attention on the food on her plate.

After a short while Johnny started to talk to Nell about his career again, touching on his worries, the commitments he had made for the coming year. She knew he was unable to let go, and would be obsessed until everything was settled. And so she gave him her full attention and tried, to the best of her ability, to offer him good advice.

For her part, Rosie was lost in her thoughts, which were centred on Nell and Kevin. Naturally, she was consumed with curiosity about them, but she knew she would have to bide her time until they were back at the hotel to ask Nell about this new development in their lives. If it *was* new. Perhaps the two of them had been involved for a long time, and if this was so why hadn't either of them mentioned it to her? She was baffled; yet her bafflement was overshadowed by her intense pleasure. It was great that they were involved, and she was quite certain they made each other happy. She was especially glad for Kevin. Her brother's life was so fraught with danger, he needed the comfort of a good relationship.

Rosie sank deeper into herself, making plans for Christmas at Montfleurie, thinking of the decorations, the menus, mentally ticking off the presents she had bought, those she still had to find.

Eventually her mind turned back to the immediate, the rest of the time she had in Los Angeles, and, most importantly, her meeting with Gavin tomorrow. They were going to lunch at his house and discuss his next movie. He had not told her what this was going to be, but whatever it was she knew she would design the clothes.

Garry Marshall and she had had a very successful meeting earlier in the week, and he had more or less indicated he would like her to work on his new project. If Gavin hadn't been hovering in the background she would have accepted the job, and with alacrity. As it was, she had been non-committal with Garry, had told him the truth about her prior commitment to Gavin, and said she would get back to him.

However, Rosie knew that Gavin's films would always come first with her. Not only because of his extraordinary talent as an actor, and the unusual subject matters he chose, but because he meant so much to her.

Nell said something, and Rosie roused herself, looked across at her, frowning slightly, pushing aside her thoughts about Gavin.

'So, if you'll both excuse me, I'll go and make the call now, get it over with,' Nell was murmuring as she pushed back the chair and stood up.

'Okay,' Johnny said. 'Use the phone in my den.'

'Thanks,' Nell said and whirled out of the dining room.

Johnny sat back in his chair, picked up his glass of wine and sipped it, patently ignoring Rosie.

Rosie's eyes rested on him for a moment, and then she glanced away, not knowing what to say to him. His antipathy towards her transmitted itself so strongly she was at a loss to find a topic of conversation, a common ground between them.

A deadly silence descended on the room.

ELEVEN

Rosie was mortified.

She sat perfectly still, staring ahead. Not an eyelash flickered and she scarcely seemed to breathe. She was wondering what she should do.

Since Nell's sudden departure to make a phone call, the silence in the dining room had become overwhelming – and very dismaying to Rosie. There were no two ways about it, Johnny was behaving oddly, and try though she did to find an excuse for him, she could not.

It occurred to her that there was only *one* thing to do: she must excuse herself, leave the table, find Nell and tell her that she was going back to the Regent Beverly Wilshire. Nell would understand. They had already exchanged several pointed looks earlier in the evening, and Nell's troubled expression had indicated that she, too, was totally baffled by Johnny's extraordinary behaviour.

Rosie's eyes shifted, rested again, for a brief moment, on the pair of dessert stands which stood on either side of the candlesticks. She had been eyeing them all evening, on and off. They were the most exquisite she had ever seen. Each one was composed of two puttis standing on a raised base on either side of a leopard, their plump young arms upstretched to support a silver bowl with a crystal liner. The silver had an extraordinary patina, and every inch of each stand was beautifully detailed. She knew they had been made by a master silversmith, that they were one of a kind, and undoubtedly very costly.

Rosie pulled her gaze away from the antique silver pieces, and turned to Johnny, fully intending to thank him and then depart. But instead of excusing herself, she said, 'The dessert stands are absolutely exquisite. They're English Regency, aren't they? And unless I'm mistaken, they're by Paul Storr.'

Startled, Johnny gaped at her for the longest moment. Finally, he nodded. 'I just bought them. In London.' Although he was completely taken by surprise that she knew the name of the silversmith who had made them, it pleased him that she admired them. They meant a lot to him. They were his pride and joy. Of all the things in the house, the English silver had, for the most part, been chosen by him. Nell had not even been with him when he had gone to his favourite shop on Bond Street earlier in the month to see these particular treasures. Francis and Toni Raeymaekers, the owners, had been holding the stands for him, certain he would want them.

'How did you know they were by Paul Storr?' Johnny asked, shifting slightly in the chair so that he was now looking directly at her.

'I have a friend who's an expert on silver,' Rosie

replied. 'And especially the English Georgian and Regency periods. She used to be a dealer.'

'Isn't she any more?'

'No, she's not.'

'That's a pity, I'm always on the look-out for interesting pieces, and it's good to know a few reputable and knowledgeable dealers.' Johnny cleared his throat. 'Listen, even dealers who are no longer in the business often continue to dabble. So if your friend ever comes across a really unusual piece I'd –'

'She won't,' Rosie cut in abruptly. 'She really doesn't work any longer.'

'Retired, is that it?'

'Sort of . . .' Rosie paused and looked away, thinking of her dearest Collie and wishing that she *could* work. If only she were able to, it would help her; of that she was sure. Sudden sadness trickled through Rosie, but she instantly shook it off, brought her eyes back to his, and then, much to her astonishment, she found herself confiding: 'Collie, my very dear friend, has had a lot of trouble in the last few years. Her husband was killed in a terrible car crash, and she fell ill just after that. She wasn't able to work for a long time. When she did finally go back to her business, she discovered she really wasn't up to it any more. It was too exhausting really, and she's given it up. At least for the moment.' Rosie forced a smile onto her face. 'Who knows, she might be able to start again, when she's stronger. She *is* passionate about antique silver, and used to derive a great deal of satisfaction from finding good pieces, and from dealing. Collie thought buying and selling was very exciting.'

'I'm sorry . . . about your friend being sick,' Johnny murmured, having noticed the hint of sorrow lurking at the back of her eyes. 'Is she living in New York?'

Rosie shook her head. 'No, she lives in France. She's French.'

'You learned a lot about silver from her, did you?'

'Oh yes. She used to take me to auctions in London . . .' Rosie's voice trailed off as memories enveloped her. Those were the really good years we both had, Rosie thought, before everything started to fall apart for her. And for me. She sighed under her breath, remembering those happier times at Montfleurie, and then she blinked rapidly as another unexpected rush of sadness rose up in her throat.

Swiftly composing herself, Rosie said as brightly as possible, 'Paul Storr was an amazing silversmith, wasn't he? He's Collie's favourite, and mine. If she saw these dessert stands, she'd go crazy. They take my breath away, they're so incredible, just gorgeous.'

Johnny nodded. 'It was Nell who got me interested in English silver. She helped me buy my first candlesticks and a coffee service. But most of the things I've acquired in the past two years I managed to find myself.' He half smiled. 'What I should say is that I found them with the help of some friends who own a shop in London, Toni and Francis Raeymaekers. They have great taste, and I've learned a lot about antique silver from them.'

He paused, feeling a bit more relaxed with Rosie, filled with gratification that she was so admiring of his taste. He also realized he was beginning to dislike her less, and suddenly, unexpectedly, he was ashamed that he had been so cold and brusque with her. After a swallow of wine, he murmured, 'Nell says I have a good eye.'

'For *what* exactly?' Nell asked from the doorway.

'Silver,' Johnny said, and chuckled. 'Rosie's been going on about the Paul Storr dessert stands, raving about them.'

'Well, they are very beautiful,' Nell said, and sat down.

'Is everything all right?' Rosie asked, looking across at her. 'You were gone for ages.'

'I know, and I'm sorry. I do apologize to you, Rosie, and to you, Johnny.'

'It's okay, darlin',' Johnny said.

'I think things are under control,' Nell continued, 'but I'm afraid I will have to make a couple of calls later. When we've finished dinner. It's a blinking nuisance, but what can one do.' Nell shrugged philosophically, and shook her head. A regretful expression settled on her face. 'When you're a press representative, you're a press representative. Always on duty. Always on call. So if you don't mind, Johnny, I'll have to make sure I've got the lid on this particular situation.'

'No problem. You can go to my den and dial to your heart's content,' Johnny told her. 'You know you're at home here, there's no formality with me. But in the meantime, how about dessert? Giovanni's prepared *crostata di mele alla crema*.'

'Good Lord!' Nell exclaimed, raising her brows. 'It sounds positively indecent. And I'll bet it's fattening!'

Johnny said, 'Oh come on, for God's sake, you don't have to worry about your weight. And what's one little dessert now and then?'

'Twenty-five pounds on the thighs,' Nell sighed, rolling her eyes to the ceiling and laughing.

'Anyway, what exactly is it?' Rosie inquired.

'An apple-custard tart. You'll love it.' He glanced at her fleetingly, before adding, 'And *you* don't have to worry about your weight either.'

After dinner, Nell hurried off to Johnny's den to make her phone calls, and Johnny escorted Rosie to the library at the back of the house.

As he pushed open the door, he said, 'I thought we'd have the espresso in here. I'd like to show you some of my other finds . . . the silver I've been buying in London.'

'I'd love to see it,' Rosie said, genuinely meaning this. She was amazed at the difference in his demeanour, and relieved that he was being more friendly towards her. He was speaking to her so pleasantly, in fact, the change in him was radical, and she could not help wondering what had caused it. Unless it was her interest in his silver. Was that possible? Could such a small thing make all that much difference to him?

'These are George III candlesticks, also by Paul Storr, dated about 1815,' Johnny explained, ushering her up to the long library table positioned behind the sofa facing the fireplace. 'I got them at the same shop in Bond Street. I've had some great luck there, thanks to Toni and Francis.'

Rosie stood looking at the candlesticks, nodding her head, her expression admiring. Then she turned her attention to a large silver bowl in the centre of the table. 'This is also beautiful. But it's not by Storr, is it?'

He shook his head. 'It's much earlier than Storr – by about a century. It's a Queen Anne monteith, dated 1702, and it's by another great English silversmith, William Denny.'

'You have some lovely things. In fact, the whole house is beautiful,' Rosie said, and then moving forward swiftly, she walked into the room, and took a seat on the sofa.

'Thanks,' Johnny said and followed her. He seated himself in a chair near the huge stone fireplace. 'Would you like a drink? A liqueur? A cognac?' he asked, glancing in her direction.

'Just the coffee, that'll be fine, thank you.'

At this moment, Arthur hurried in carrying the coffee service on a tray; Sophia was right behind him with the cups and saucers, and after they had served them they quietly disappeared.

Rosie and Johnny sipped their espresso.

Neither of them spoke, but this time the silence between them was not fraught with undercurrents; Johnny's antipathy towards Rosie had by now completely evaporated. It had been replaced by a mild curiosity about her. Johnny felt like a jerk for behaving the way he had earlier, and he was irritated with himself. Known for his charm the world over, and especially with women, he wondered why it had fled the minute Rosie had walked into the house.

'Who is that painting by?' Rosie asked, looking up at the landscape hanging over the fireplace. It depicted two farm workers in a field of wheat rippling under the wind; Rosie thought it was lovely, and she felt suddenly homesick for Montfleurie.

Johnny sat up straighter, following her glance. 'It's by Pascal. She's a local artist, and a favourite of mine. I have more of her paintings upstairs.'

'I love modern impressionists . . . that field looks as if it might be in France,' Rosie murmured, still eyeing the painting, thinking of the land surrounding the château.

'That's exactly where it is. Pascal paints there a lot,' Johnny explained, his interest in her increasing. He stared at her.

Rosie stared back, frowning slightly, her expression questioning.

It was Johnny who broke off the prolonged stare. Putting down his coffee cup, he got up, walked over and sat next to Rosie on the sofa.

On principle, Johnny Fortune never apologized to anyone for anything. But now he found himself apologizing to Rosalind Madigan. He said hurriedly, in a slightly embarrassed voice, 'Listen, I'm sorry, I guess I was rude before, I didn't mean to be.' He paused, shook his head. 'Yeah, I'm sorry. I shouldn't have taken it out on you.' There was a tiny pause. 'I've had a bad day, a lotta business problems to deal with,' he improvised adroitly, trying to excuse his inexcusable behaviour, to show himself in a better light.

'I know what you mean,' Rosie answered, 'I have days like that too sometimes.'

'Am I forgiven?'

'Of course.' Rosie smiled at him. It was a smile that filled her face with radiance, touched her mouth with sudden sweetness and brought a glow to her eyes. She smiled again, and he felt as if something had reached inside to touch him. This puzzled him, and he simply sat there, still staring at her.

Rosie gazed back, looking into the brightest, bluest eyes she had ever seen. She shifted her position on the sofa, tilted her head to one side, gave him a much more quizzical look than before, deciding that without doubt he was the strangest man she had met in her entire life.

As Rosie moved the light fell across her face.

Instantly aware of the compelling greenness of her eyes, the burnished copper tone of her hair, Johnny was struck by the beauty of this woman. And she *was* beautiful. He asked himself how he ever could have thought of her as plain and drab. If the truth be known, Rosalind Madigan was stunning.

Still baffled by this man, and confused by the peculiar expression crossing his face, Rosie reached out and touched his hand. 'It's really all right, you know. I *do* understand, and you are forgiven.' A smile touched Rosie's mouth again. She was liking him, and already forgetting his rudeness of earlier, seeing the best in him, which was always her way with everyone.

Johnny nodded, and although he did not know it yet, he was undone.

TWELVE

Long after the two women had left, Johnny was still staggered by his extraordinary reaction to Rosie. There was no question that she had unnerved him.

Having hated her on sight, he was nothing if not amazed at his one-hundred-and-eighty-degree turn. He did not understand himself, and he lay on top of the bed in his pyjamas, worriedly attempting to analyse exactly what was going on inside him.

The shrill ringing of his private line interrupted this process, and as he reached for the receiver he glanced at the clock on the bedside table, wondering who it could be at this hour. It was well after eleven. It had to be one of his entourage, or someone close to him, since only a few special people in his life had this particular number.

Nevertheless, there was a certain wariness in his tone as he said, 'Hello?'

'Johnny, how are ya?' a gravelly voice asked in a gruff manner.

'Uncle Vito! For God's sake, what're you doing up so late? It's after two in New York.'

'Yeah. Is this a bad time, kid? I ain't interrupting nothing?'

Johnny chuckled. 'No, I'm alone.'

'Pity,' the old man sighed. 'What do I keep telling ya? Find a nice girl, a nice Italian girl, marry her, have plenty nice bambinos, settle down to a happy life. Why doan ya do what I say, Johnny?'

'One day, Uncle Vito, one day.'

'Promise?'

'I promise.'

'I been on the island. For the family dinner. Always on Thursdays, ya know that. Anyways, the big man, he's sending his love, you're his favourite, and doan forget that. He's expecting us Thanksgiving. It's still on, ain't it, Johnny?'

'Sure it is. Don't I always come in for that little family reunion? I'd never disappoint you. Or the big man. Listen, where're you calling from?'

'Doan worry . . . a pay phone.'

'Please, go home to bed. You don't need anything? You're okay?'

'I'm great, kid. Never better.' Far away in New York, standing on the sidewalk, shivering slightly in the cold night air, Vito Carmello began to laugh. 'Others 'round here not doin' so good, Johnny. Too many loud mouths . . . talkin' too much. A bad thing. Bad for business, *capisci*?'

'Yes,' Johnny answered and laughed with his uncle. 'Now, do me a favour, go home to bed. I'll see you next week. I'm coming in late Wednesday night.'

'Where're ya gonna be staying?'

'The Waldorf.'

Once again, from far away, Vito's laughter echoed down the long-distance wire. 'Good night, Johnny.'

'Good night, Uncle Vito.'

Johnny's thoughts stayed with his uncle, and for a while he reflected on him. Vito was in his late seventies, seventy-nine to be exact, and getting too old to be doing what he was doing. It was time he retired. But the old man was stubborn, and wouldn't listen to him; nor would he take any money from him. 'I doan need it, kid. I got plenty. More'n I can spend. Keep it for when the pipes dry up,' he would mutter whenever Johnny offered it.

His uncle was a proud Sicilian, and also deeply loyal to his old *goombah*, Salvatore Rudolfo, the big man, as he was called by many, and that was why he would not retire. 'Not until the *Don* hands over his power,' Vito was forever saying to Johnny. 'When he retires, I retire. We start out together, we end together.'

And so it was that Vito Carmello was still a *caporegime*, a captain, in the Rudolfo organization, as he had been all of his adult life.

Vito and Salvatore had been friends since childhood. They were from Palermo, and their families had come over from the Old Country on the boat together, when the boys were eight years old. That had been in 1920, and the two families had settled in the same neighbourhood in Lower Manhattan, living as close to each other as possible, which they had done all of their lives in Sicily.

Johnny had heard many stories from his uncle

about those early days, when the Carmellos and the Rudolfos had first arrived in the great metropolis that was New York.

Times had been hard for the new immigrants, and the parents of the boys soon discovered they were no richer, no more successful and certainly no happier than they had been in Palermo, and very frequently they wished themselves back in their homeland.

There were occasions, especially family get-togethers, when Guido Carmello and Angelo Rudolfo would commiserate with each other and wonder out loud why they had ever been foolish enough to come to America, the land of plenty, where the streets were paved with gold. Except that they weren't, and the 'plenty' they had heard so much about was for others, not for them. The two men, who had grown up together and were best friends, worked hard at their trade as furniture-makers, but life was not easy; for the most part, it was a struggle for Guido and Angelo to pay the rent and put food on the table for their families.

But the boys loved the city, and once they had mastered English they made the streets of Manhattan their own, became addicted to the excitement, the noise, the bustle, all of it so different from sleepy Palermo. School bored them; the streets brought innumerable thrills, adventure – and eventually money.

By the time they were thirteen the boys had formed their own street gang, or *borgata* as it was called in Italian. To start a gang was Salvatore's idea; he was the stronger, the tougher and shrewder of the two, and a born leader. Inevitably, petty crime became their business, their way of life, and they flourished, robbing street merchants with stalls, and factory lofts, stealing in a variety of different ways, including rolling drunks, and also running errands for the local Mafiosi, often bringing home more money than their honest, hardworking fathers.

With his quick wits and drive, Salvatore eventually moved on from gang leader to become a low-level Mafia hood, having attached himself to a *capo* who had taken a shine to the young Sicilian, recognizing his natural talents – astuteness, nerves of steel and brute force. Salvatore dragged Vito along with him, singing his praises to the *capo*, and so creating a niche for his *goombah* in the family. Within no time at all, Salvatore rose in the ranks of the organization, despite his youth, and became a formally inducted member of the Mafia, as did Vito.

Along the way, Salvatore Rudolfo had developed a reputation as a hard-headed young mobster to be reckoned with, and one who was heading nowhere if not to the very top. Apart from being street-smart, Salvatore had a brilliant business sense, a chilling ruthlessness, instinctive treachery, plus a unique ability to inspire unswerving loyalty in others. Aside from Vito, he gathered around him a staunchly loyal cadre of *goombata*, who would literally do anything for him, including go out and kill for him, if he asked. Which he did quite frequently.

The time came when Salvatore, propelled by greed, ambition and the lust for power, tried to break away from the crime family who had employed him, and, with Vito in tow, he attempted to start his own organization.

That these two succeeded was due more to their timing, and luck, than anything else. The breakaway took place in 1930, when they were eighteen, and when a particular, and for them fortuitous, situation was developing in the New York Mafia.

A group of young Turks, feeling their oats and frustrated with the ruling dons – known derisively as 'Moustache Petes' – revolted against their old-time, old-style leaders.

Once the revolution was over in 1931, most of the elderly dons had been pushed to one side, or murdered. The Old World style of management they had favoured was abandoned; the modern American Mafia as it is today came into being. And so did the Rudolfo crime family. Because Salvatore and Vito had helped to bring about the coup, the young Turks who were now in positions of power gave them the nod to go ahead with their own plans, or, more correctly, Salvatore's plans.

The Rudolfo family quickly grew in size and stature, and over the years became a dominant player in the 'honoured society', the brotherhood of the Mafia, also known as *La Cosa Nostra*, which translated means *this thing of ours*. Salvatore was the boss, his brother Charlie the underboss, his cousin Anthony the *consigliere*, or councillor, and Vito a captain, as well as being Salvatore's closest confidant.

As a child, Johnny Fortune had not known exactly what his Uncle Vito did, except that he worked in the family business with his uncles – Salvatore, Charlie and Tony. When he was older, he came to understand that all of his uncles were hoods, and part of the Mob. But this did not worry him unduly since he had grown up in a strictly Italian neighbourhood, in which the Mafiosi were commonplace. He knew very little about what went on beyond this insular world where the *amici*, the men of the 'honoured society', were spoken of in awed tones of respect. Or fear.

In accordance with traditional Mafia rules, business was never discussed at home, and so he knew nothing of Uncle Vito's daily routine, or what his job was. Nor did he really care. The only thing that mattered to the young Gianni was that the four men loved him, protected him, and made sure he never wanted for the basic essentials of life.

Whenever Vito needed extra money for him, for new clothes and shoes, the doctor, the dentist, music lessons or a special treat, it was always forthcoming from Uncle Salvatore. And although the apartment on Mulberry Street was cramped and dreary, Johnny was well taken care of, was always well fed and clothed.

It was Uncle Salvatore who first recognized Johnny's talent, and who one day pronounced that he sang like an angel, then gave him a five-dollar bill as a gift. Once he started out on his singing career professionally, Salvatore bought him his first tuxedo, and saw that he got regular bookings in the nightclubs around the country, which were owned by his friends.

Ever since then, in a somewhat loose, undefined way, Johnny had been watched over by Salvatore Rudolfo, who considered Vito's talented, good-looking nephew to be his protégé.

Although he had grown up in the shadow of the Sicilian Mafia in New York, Johnny had never been a part of it, nor had he ever wanted to be. His music was his life. Uncle Vito and Uncle Salvatore had been pleased about this, and they had encouraged him, and helped him to build his career – and had kept him at arm's length, not wanting him to be tainted in any way because of them.

As far as they were aware, no one knew of Johnny's close, familial connection to them, and that was exactly how they wanted it to be. Nothing must tarnish his image. And so far nothing had.

For his patronage over the years, Salvatore had asked nothing of Johnny in return. Except an appearance at the annual Thanksgiving dinner. It was then that he was expected to come to Uncle Salvatore's house on Staten Island, and in the middle of the evening's celebrations he was requested to sing some of the Don's favourite songs. It was all very casual, easy-going, and they usually had a great time.

Johnny thought of the dinner now, wondering what Uncle Salvatore would like to hear. The old favourites, of course, such as *Sorrento*, and *O Sole Mio*. But Johnny knew he must also select a few current, popular songs, favourites of the younger members of the family. He had to please the crowd as well as the big man himself, hold their interest for the half hour or so that he sang.

Johnny smiled inwardly, thinking of Salvatore with affection. There was a very special bond between them. It was unspoken but it was there, had always been there, in fact, ever since he had been a little boy in short trousers. He felt closer to him than he did to his Uncle Vito in certain ways, and he loved and revered him. Though the term godfather was rarely, if ever, used in the Mafia, that was how Johnny thought of Salvatore. He *was* his godfather, in the best sense. And he considered Salvatore to be a great man in his own way. That he was the tsar of a vast criminal empire, not to mention *capo di tutti capi* of all the Eastern Seaboard Mafia families, never occurred to Johnny. Salvatore Rudolfo was, very simply, his uncle to whom he owed so much.

Glancing at the clock a little while later, and sighing under his breath when he saw the time, Johnny reached for the remote control. He flicked off the television set, which had been on without sound for the past half hour or so, then slipped between the sheets and attempted to go to sleep.

But sleep turned out to be a fugitive tonight.

Johnny Fortune lay in the darkness for a long time, his thoughts moving away from Salvatore and Vito, focusing instead on Rosalind Madigan. He was discovering he could not get her out of his head.

Now, visualizing her face in his mind's eye, he felt a sudden lightness of being, a lifting of his perpetual worries. Then an unexpected feeling of warmth spread through him, and he experienced such a profound sense of happiness it almost took his breath away. He was amazed. He, who had hardly ever experienced that emotion in his entire life, was actually *happy*, and it was because of her. It seemed to Johnny that this was something akin to a miracle.

He didn't know anything about her . . . if she was single, married, divorced, or what. And he didn't really care. Rosalind Madigan was the first woman, the *only* woman, who had ever made him feel like this, and it was a feeling he never wanted to go away. This thought dominated his mind for the longest time until he finally began to doze off.

I *hope* I see her again.

I *want* to see her again.

I *must* see her again.

I *will* see her again.

154

THIRTEEN

'So, come on, 'fess up, Rosie mine. What exactly did you do to him to turn him into the docile little lamb?'

'What do you mean?' Rosie cried, her voice rising slightly as she turned to stare at Nell in the dim light of the foyer.

Nell laughed, tucked her arm through Rosie's, and led her through into the sitting room of the suite they were sharing at the Regent Beverly Wilshire Hotel.

'You know very well what I mean, my darling, so don't pretend otherwise. When I first went out to make my phone call, Johnny was acting as if you weren't there, or even worse, as if you were his greatest enemy . . . whichever, take your pick. Then when I come back I see he's a bit friendlier. At least, his sour expression had disappeared. The second time around, I come across the two of you in the library, all cosied up together on the sofa. What's more, he's eating out of your hand. If not indeed slobbering all over you. Now come on, Rosie, *something* must have happened. The change in our bel canto balladeer was so radical it was positively mind-blowing.'

Rosie had to smile, and then she extracted her arm

and swung to Nell, shot back swiftly, 'Nothing happened. The only thing I did was talk to him about his antique silver. You're just challenging me because you're embarrassed. About your relationship with Kevin and the fact that you haven't told me. Now it's your turn, Nelly. *You* 'fess up. When did all of this start with my brother?'

Throwing her wool cape on a chair, Nell crossed the room without answering. Lifting the phone, she dialled room service, looked over at Rosie, and asked, 'How about a nice cuppa, before we go to bed?'

Rosie nodded. 'Good idea, I'd love it.'

After Nell had ordered the tea, she slopped down on the sofa, and sighed heavily. 'We didn't mean to keep it a secret from you, honestly we didn't. In fact, Kevin and I were just discussing this the other night.' She shrugged, shook her head. 'We haven't told *anybody*, actually, and I'm not sure why. That's not true . . . that cop friend of Kevin's, Neil O'Connor, knows about us, but he's the only one.'

Having shed her own coat, Rosie joined Nell on the sofa, and murmured, 'I'm not mad at you, or upset, Nelly darling. Really I'm not. Quite the opposite. I'm thrilled that you and Kevin are involved.' She smiled as she said this and reached out, touched her friend's arm affectionately. 'Is it serious between you and Kev?'

Nell stared at Rosie for a long moment. Finally, a faint smile crossed her mouth. 'I don't know . . . and perhaps that's the reason we never told you, or Gavin, or anyone. Maybe we just didn't want to have to explain ourselves, or analyse our own feelings, or, most important of all, have any pressure put upon us.'

Rosie gaped at her. 'Good Lord, Nell, I'd never put pressure on you and Kevin! Please don't ever think such a thing. I was just being nosey. I love you, and I love my brother, and of course it would be wonderful if you were serious about each other, planned a long-term relationship. But in all truth, it's none of my business.'

'I wasn't chastising you, just attempting to explain. I guess we haven't seen much of you or Gavin . . .' Nell left this sentence unfinished, turned away, looked out of the window for a minute. Then, turning back to Rosie, she added, 'That's such a silly thing to say. Of course we've seen both of you. On the movie, for one thing. And even though Kevin was only on the set once, *I* have been there off and on over these past few months, and I *should* have told you. I didn't because . . . well, because I didn't want to be pinned down, I guess. I'm sure Kevin felt the same way. We just wanted this to be a private thing between us, not a topic open for discussion.'

'I understand,' Rosie said, squeezing her arm.

'Oh I hope you do, my darling. I wasn't excluding you. *We* weren't excluding you. As I just told you, we never even discussed it with each other until the other night.' Nell cleared her throat, continued quietly, 'I adore Kevin. He's the most wonderful man. We're the best of friends, get on well, like the same things. And that's it.'

'You don't have to explain. I'm just glad you and he are giving each other a bit of comfort and happiness.'

'So am I. And I do care for him you know, even if I don't want to marry him.'

Rosie was silent, digesting this remark, and then she asked, 'Does Kevin want to marry you?'

'I don't think so.' Nell made a *moue* with her mouth. 'Actually I don't really know. He's never mentioned marriage, and neither have I. I don't suppose it's ever crossed our minds. He's so caught up in being an undercover cop, and then I have my business, the company to run.'

'When did it happen? What I mean is, when did you first get involved?'

'About a year ago. That night Gavin was in New York en route to London to start talks on *Kingmaker*. Don't you remember? I told you on the phone that we'd all had dinner together at the Carlyle. Kevin took me home. I asked him in for a nightcap. And bingo! Suddenly we were in a hot clinch.'

'How wonderful!' Rosie said. 'Here's a bit of advice from me. Take what you can while you can, and to hell with the consequences. That's my new motto.'

'Is it really!' Nell's brows lifted in astonishment. 'Well, well, that's the biggest surprise of the evening, except for Johnny's quite extraordinary about-face. Now, let's talk about him for a minute. How on earth did you get on to his silver?'

Rosie grinned. 'I was appalled at his behaviour, and I was just about to come looking for you, to tell you I was returning here. But instead of politely taking my leave, I actually started to compliment him on the dessert stands. The Paul Storr dessert stands.'

'Aha! *That* explains it! You couldn't have chosen a

better subject. Those stands are, quite literally, his greatest pride and joy. His friends in London, the Raeymaekers, found them for him, and he kind of went ballistic when he saw them earlier this month.'

'I was surprised that he knows so much about antique silver. Odd, isn't it?'

'Yes, quite curious, in a way. He was a poor boy, raised in the Bronx or Brooklyn, somewhere like that. Not much formal education to speak of, except musically, and he had little exposure to the world of art and antiques. He was too busy climbing the show business ladder most of his life to indulge himself in anything. Johnny has always been very driven, from what I understand. But he has a good eye, and he seems to have developed this affinity for priceless silver. I guess he's read a lot about it lately, and he truly cares about it, which is the secret of being a good collector.'

Rosie nodded, then got up, walked over to the window, stood staring out. The suite overlooked Rodeo Drive, which already glittered with Christmas lights and decorations even though it was only November. Her thoughts were on Johnny, and before she could stop herself, she asked, 'Is he involved with anyone?'

'Not that I know of,' Nell answered, her interest piqued by this question, watching Rosie from her position on the sofa. 'In fact, I'm sure he's not.'

At this moment there was a knock on the door, and Nell went to open it for the waiter, who came in bearing the tray of tea.

A few seconds later, when they were alone again,

Nell poured the tea, and continued, 'I don't believe there's ever been anybody special in Johnny's life. At least, from what I can gather. Certainly not in the last few years, not since I've been around. Oh yes, there's been the occasional show girl, the odd groupie, and sometimes he's had a bimbo in tow. But they haven't meant anything. One-night stands, that's all.'

'Why do you think that is . . . that he's never married?'

Nell shook her head. 'God knows, and he won't split. Come and sit down and have this cup of tea. As for Johnny Fortune, I can't even hazard a guess why he's not married, or why he's not been involved with anyone on a permanent basis. Now that I think about it, there have been a few rumours at different times, about his involvement with a couple of women. But they were not serious relationships.' After taking a sip of her tea, Nell said in a slightly surprised tone, 'It's just struck me, perhaps he's never been in love. Perhaps that's the reason.'

'It's possible.' There was a tiny pause, before Rosie asked, 'What's he *really* like?'

Nell's brow shot up, and she gave Rosie a very direct, questioning look. 'I'm not sure, to tell you the honest truth. He doesn't let anyone get too close to him, you know, holds most people at arm's length . . . at least, on a personal level.'

'But he seems very close to you.'

'On a *business* level, yes. He's a perpetual worrier about his career, as you no doubt noticed tonight, and I seem able to reassure him. As a matter of fact, he's a chronic worrier about almost everything. But he's quite a nice man, and he's always been kind and considerate to me. Of course, he's riddled with all kinds of insecurities. He's also a bit of an egomaniac and terribly self-involved, but then he's an entertainer. You know better than anyone how nutsy performers can be.'

'Not Gavin!' Rosie exclaimed.

'No, not Gavin, but he's the exception to the rule. Getting back to Johnny, he *is* a decent person, and nice, as I just said. And yet . . .'

'Yet *what*?'

Nell sighed. 'I'm not sure . . . there's just something about him, something I can't quite put my finger on, Rosie. He's remote for one thing, distant most of the time, and not very forthcoming about his family. Sort of mysterious.'

'Does he have any?'

'There's an old uncle somewhere. I think he lives in Florida. The aunt is dead. It was this aunt and uncle who raised him. He told me once that his mother died when he was very young. There are no brothers or sisters. No family at all, actually, other than the uncle. I think he probably had a somewhat lonely, dismal childhood, and certainly it was impoverished. Although I believe the uncle started to do quite well at one point. He's never told me too much. Johnny's not big on intimacy, or sharing confidences with anyone. Mind you, I've never asked him very many questions. Perhaps because he has always been cagey about himself, his past, and his personal life. He doesn't have too many friends, keeps himself to himself.'

'I like him, Nell.'

'I know you do.'

'You *do*?'

'Sure.'

'*How*?'

Nell laughed. 'Because you never showed such interest in any of the men I've introduced you to in the past few years. The fact that you've questioned me about Johnny is very indicative of your feelings. I think you're intrigued by him.' Nell grinned at her dearest friend. 'And I must admit, I'm absolutely delighted that you fancy somebody.'

Rosie flushed. 'I don't fancy him!'

Nell burst out laughing. 'Of course you do, Rosie. Don't deny it. And I'll tell you something else. Johnny Fortune fancies you.'

'Don't be so ridiculous!'

'You always say that when I hit the mark. And it's *not* ridiculous. Know what?' Nell stared at Rosie, her eyes grown suddenly merry, almost mischievous.

'No, I don't,' Rosie muttered.

'I'm going to fix you up with him, arrange a date –'

'Nell, no! Please don't do that!' Rosie cried, her eyes opening wide.

'Yes, I *am* going to do it!' Nell pressed on determinedly, 'I shall make a date for the day after Thanksgiving. He's going to be in New York, on business, and for Thanksgiving dinner with his uncle. He told us that. I think it's a great idea. *Inspired*, even if I do say so myself. I'll make it a foursome. Me and Kevin, you and Johnny. It'll be wonderful.'

'I'm leaving that day for Paris,' Rosie announced.

'Change your flight. Go on Saturday. Don't pass this up, Rosie,' Nell pleaded.

'I can't change my flight. I've been away too long. I spoke to Yvonne today, and Collie hasn't been feeling well. I must get back. In any case, Collie aside, there's so much to do at Montfleurie for Christmas.'

'You and Montfleurie!' Nell exclaimed in exasperation, and although she did not want to upset Rosie, she could not help adding, 'Oh botheration! Why am I so foolish to think *you* could ever be interested in a man, when you're in love with a bloody house!'

Rosie gaped at her. 'You *are* foolish, Nell, for saying such a rotten thing. I'm not in love with a house. That's so far-fetched it hardly behoves me to respond to you. But I do love Collie, Lisette and Yvonne. They love me and need me, and I certainly have obligations to them. I can't let them down.'

Nell was silent, sipping her tea, her face suddenly clouding over. Inside she was seething. There were times when Rosie tried her patience, most especially when she put the people at Montfleurie first, often thinking of their well being before her own. She was too good in so many ways, and Nell believed there were those who took advantage of Rosie's goodness, the French family in particular.

Rosie said, 'Please don't let's quarrel, darling. We spend so little time together these days, and I do miss you so. The last thing I want is to fight with you, Nell. You're my best friend, I love you.'

Nell gazed at her silently, nodded, and offered her a faint, conciliatory smile. Without saying a word she pushed herself to her feet and went into the bedroom.

Rosie watched her go, full of sudden regrets that she had ever mentioned Johnny Fortune. She was about to follow Nell into the bedroom, to make peace with her, when Nell appeared in the doorway, waving a tape at her. Returning to the sofa, she handed the tape to Rosie, again without saying anything.

Rosie examined the tape. It was Johnny's latest recording, just released, and it was already a big hit, she knew that. It was called *Fortune's Child*, and there was a colour photograph of him on the front. There was no question about it, he was very good-looking. She studied the sensitive face for a moment, then, lifting her head, Rosie gave Nell a quizzical look.

Nell said, 'Johnny's handsome, talented, rich, and basically a pretty decent man, quite a catch in his own way, I would say. So listen to me. I know that he *is* interested in you, Rosie, because I noticed the way he was acting when we were having coffee. I've never seen him like that.'

'Like what?'

'For one thing, he was hanging on to your every word, and practically purring. For another, he couldn't take his eyes off you. And he certainly didn't want us to leave when we did. I bet if I hadn't been there he'd have made his intentions more obvious. I bet if you'd been alone with him, he'd have tried to seduce you.'

'God, what an imagination you have!'

'I *know* what I saw!' Nell answered somewhat fiercely. 'Why won't you give it half a chance? Let me arrange dinner, or even lunch before you leave for France. For the four of us, the day after Thanksgiving.'

'I just can't, Nell, I really can't. I mustn't disappoint Collie. She's so anxious for me to get there. I've been away so much because of the movie, and then coming here to the States has delayed my return.'

She's afraid, Nell thought. Afraid of getting involved with a man because of what happened the last time she did. That's what this is all about. She hides out in that ridiculous house, because at Montfleurie she feels safe. But she's not at all safe there. It's the most dangerous place in the world for her to be. I must convince her to leave that house once and for all, before it's too late. Before something terrible happens.

FOURTEEN

'I've been here for over twenty minutes and you haven't mentioned the movie, or told me anything about it,' Rosie complained, glancing at Gavin.

The two of them were sitting on the terrace overlooking the gardens of his Bel-Air house, enjoying a glass of white wine before lunch on this cool but sunny morning.

He chuckled. 'Just listen to the girl. You haven't stopped talking since you arrived. I haven't been able to get a word in edgeways, what with your report on your meeting with Garry Marshall, and the news about Nell and Kevin. Now that's the most interesting titbit of all.'

Rosie agreed with him, then added, 'It was the last thing I ever expected to hear.'

'Me too. I was astonished, to tell you the truth. For a long time I thought that Nell was still carrying a torch for Mikey, but I guess not.'

'And I thought Kevin was hung up on Sunny. Just goes to show you how wrong we both were,' Rosie pointed out, and laughed.

'Is it serious?' Gavin asked, shifting his position in the chair, crossing his legs.

'I don't know. I asked Nell that question myself, and she was sort of . . . well, evasive. I think that's the best way to describe her attitude.'

'They certainly managed to keep their affair a big secret from us.'

'I explained that, Gavin. I told you, they didn't want us prying, or putting pressure on them.'

'I guess they wouldn't. And who does need that?'

'About the movie, Gavin, I –'

'You'll love it, and you'll certainly want to do the clothes,' he cut in.

'That goes without saying, doesn't it?'

'I hope so, darling,' he answered, grinning at her. Then he got up, walked across the terrace, stood leaning against the railings, facing her, his eyes focused on hers. 'It's about a great man,' he began, and paused.

'Who else!' Rosie laughed. 'You have a fascination for great men . . . the great men in history. I presume he's an historical figure?'

'But of course he is. There certainly aren't any great men around today to speak of . . . maybe Gorbachev, but we'll see about him when the dust settles. Anyway, as you well know by now, in my opinion Winston Churchill was the *truly* great man of this century. He stands side by side with the giants of history, and –'

She interrupted him, asked quickly, 'You mean your new film is going to be about Winston Churchill?'

Gavin shook his head. 'It's about a man who was around a bit before Churchill's time, a man who has had over two hundred thousand books written about him, and who was the most dominant figure in the world in his own time.'

'Who?'

'Napoleon.'

This was the last name she had expected to hear and Rosie was flabbergasted. She stared at Gavin in utter amazement, incredulity registering on her face. 'Gavin, it's insane to attempt to make the life of Napoleon!' she cried heatedly. 'It's biting off more than even *you* can chew. Why, it's an impossible task, and a far greater challenge than *Kingmaker* was.'

'Yes, it is, you're quite right about that. But I'm not going to do his *life* as such. I'm not *that* stupid. I'm going to make a portion of his life. Obviously, to attempt to do a full, biographical film about him would cost too much money, and it would end up being far too long. My aim is to film a particular *period* in his life.'

'Which period? His rise to power?'

'No, the period when he was already in power, when he had gone from great general to First Consul to Emperor. When he was at his happiest, to my way of thinking anyway, and when he was at the apex of his life. And it's going to be more of a love story, a family story, than one about his colossal achievements and his world-shaking successes as a general. I want to tell the story of . . . a man and a woman actually . . . Napoleon and Josephine. It starts just before he had himself crowned Emperor, and Josephine crowned Empress, and shows their closeness, their togetherness, the great love they had for each other. Naturally, I have to jump time, in order to bring the story up to the point where Napoleon decides he must divorce Josephine. For his country, for France. I want to show the terrible internal struggle he had with himself, once he concluded he must give up the woman he loved in order to protect his country. It was very much a political move. He needed to cement his alliance with Russia, and what better way to do it than with a marriage. He sought the hand of Tsar Alexander's sister, Anna. He wanted this marriage to be the way to permanent peace, a guarantee of peace, in fact. The Tsar was for it, but the Empress Mother was against it, and Napoleon was rejected in the end. But he needed to build peace, and he also needed an ally among the great European powers. There was another thing, Rosie: he had thought often about an heir, and longed for a son, one to whom he could bequeath his power, his glory, his throne. In the end he married the Austrian princess, as I'm sure you know.'

Rosie said, 'Yes, Marie Louise of Austria, daughter of Emperor Francis, who did bear him that son he so wanted. She was very young, though, wasn't she? And Josephine was six years older than he.'

Gavin nodded, and moved away from the railings. 'Come on, let's go inside. I want to go over a few things with you.'

Taking her arm, he led her through the dining room and into the long hallway which in turn led to his favourite room in the house. This was his study, where he did all of his work. It was a huge, airy room, with a high-flung cathedral ceiling, walls of books, and many windows overlooking a manicured green lawn that rolled down to a small lily pond. A huge antique mahogany table, the type used in board-rooms, served as a desk, and there were groupings of comfortable chairs and sofas upholstered in soft coffee-coloured leather.

Gavin pulled up a chair for Rosie, and they sat down next to each other at the table. He found his notebook, flipped it open, and explained: 'I have a theory. I believe that leaving Josephine was the begin-ning of Napoleon's downfall. It was then that his luck seemed to change. Giving up Josephine, the truest love of his life, was the single biggest *mistake* of his life. It seems to me that without her nothing was ever really the same again for him.'

'There's something so sad about their story,' Rosie murmured. 'I've always thought that, Gavin.'

'I agree.' Gavin glanced down at his notebook. 'Now, consider this for a great scene, Rosie. It's a cold day, November thirtieth, 1809. We're at the palace – the Tuileries – with Napoleon and Josephine. He tells her he is going to have their marriage annulled. This is what he says to her: "I still love you, but in politics there is no heart, only head." Josephine faints, then pleads, then breaks down completely and weeps, her sorrow overwhelming her. But he is adamant. He has to be. And he has to do it.'

'Oh Gavin, how terrible. What happened next?'

'She went to Malmaison, the house he had bought for her years before, and where they had led such a peaceful existence, been so happy. That was on December fifteenth, when Josephine left his life for ever, after being with him for some fourteen years. But he never stopped loving her; there's loads of documentation to prove that. In fact, only a month later he was writing to her, saying that he wanted to see her. Their parting broke her heart, of course. And his. At least, that's what I believe, and that's what the movie's partially about – a man and a woman, not just a great man.'

Gavin paused, glanced down at the notebook again, turned the pages. 'Just listen to this. It's a letter he wrote to her when he was twenty-six, after he had made love to her for the first time. She was thirty-two, and at that moment not quite as besotted with him as he was with her. She fell in love with him later; but listen, Rosie.'

'Go ahead, I *am* listening.'

It was obvious to Rosie that Gavin knew the words by heart. He didn't even look in the notebook as he began to speak.

'*I have woken up full of you. Your portrait and the memory of yesterday's intoxicating evening have given my senses no rest. Sweet and incomparable Josephine, what an odd effect you have on my heart! Are you displeased? Do I see you sad? Are you worried? Then my soul is grief-stricken, and your friend cannot rest . . . But I cannot rest either when I yield to the deep feeling that overpowers me and I draw from your lips and heart a flame that burns in me. Ah! last night I clearly realized that the portrait I had of you is quite different from the real you! You are leaving at noon, and in three hours I shall see you. Until then,* mio dolce amor, *thousands of kisses; but don't kiss me, for your kisses sear my blood.'*

Rosie sat gazing at Gavin, for a moment unable to speak. He had held her mesmerized, had spoken the words beautifully, as only he could, and she felt as though he had become Napoleon in those few moments. Now she couldn't wait to see him in that role.

Frowning slightly, he asked, 'Well, what do you think? You're not saying a word, and I thought that was a wonderful love letter from a man the world forever thinks of as an ambitious general out to conquer the world, when he wasn't that at all. At least he was much more than that.'

'I was moved, Gavin, that's why I'm silent.' She gave him a direct look. 'You have the script already, don't you?'

'Ah, you're too sharp, Angel Face, I can never pull the wool over your eyes. Yes, I do have a script and it's more or less finished. It just needs a final polish.'

'It's by Vivienne Citrine, isn't it?'

'You got it.'

'I'm glad she's written the script. There's nobody better, and she works so well with you.'

'You're going to enjoy being on this movie. For one thing, I'm going to be shooting in your favourite country, France. I'll be based in Paris, at Billancourt Studios, and I'll be doing a lot of shooting in and around Paris, and at Malmaison. If the French Government will give me permission to shoot exteriors there, that is.'

'It's such a beautiful house, Gavin, and I'm sure

they will. They might even let you shoot inside too. The French Government are usually very co-operative when it comes to this kind of historical film-making.'

'I know. Anyway, my people are working on all that, and I hope you'll start your research for the clothes after Christmas. Can you?'

'You bet I can.'

Gavin laughed. 'I knew I could count on you, and by the way, even though you'll want to design some of those flimsy gowns Josephine and the women wore, I'd like to point out that Napoleon disapproved of them.'

'He did?'

'Sure. Once, he had the fires stoked so high at Malmaison everyone was sweating. The place was like an oven, and he kept exclaiming, very pointedly, that he wanted the women to be warm in their *nakedness*.'

Rosie laughed. 'He had great wit, I think. Anyway, this is going to be an exciting project . . . I'm *already* excited. I can't wait to get cracking on the clothes.'

'I knew you'd say that.'

'When can I have a copy of the script?'

'Early in January. I'll bring it to you myself. I'm going to be in Paris at the end of that month, since I'll have finished postproduction on *Kingmaker* by then.'

'Good. I can't wait to read it.'

The phone at the far end of the table rang, and Gavin got up, went to answer it. Rosie's eyes strayed around the table. It was piled with books, manila folders, and maps. She saw that there were many volumes on Napoleon, Josephine, French politics of the period, and Napoleon's military campaigns. There were also books on his contemporaries, from Barras to Talleyrand, both of whom she knew turned out to be his enemies. It was obvious that Gavin, as usual, had done his homework and had done it well.

When Gavin hung up, he said, 'Let's go and have lunch, Angel Face. Miri is going to serve it out on the terrace.'

Later that afternoon, long after Rosie had left, Gavin was working on the script in his study when the door flew open unexpectedly.

Annoyed that he was being disturbed, he glanced up to see his wife Louise standing in the doorway.

He stared at her, his irritation barely concealed.

Louise, a petite, dark-haired beauty, was elegantly dressed in couture clothes, as usual. She glared back at him, detecting his displeasure immediately, so finely tuned had she become to his moods of late.

'I'm going,' she announced in a clipped tone.

When no response was forthcoming, she added, 'To Washington.'

'But naturally,' Gavin said finally, his voice full of acerbity. 'Where else do you go these days?'

Kicking the door shut with an elegantly-shod foot, wanting privacy from Miri, Louise stepped forward into the room, still glaring at him. Then a flush rose up from her neck to flood her face as she exclaimed, 'At least I'm made to feel welcome by my friends there. Which is more than I can say about being in this house.'

'This house, as you term it, is *your* home, Louise. Stop playing drama, please. It doesn't impress me, or affect me. I'm the actor in the family, remember. Anyway, when are you coming back?'

'Showing some interest in me at last, I see. I don't *know* when I'll be back.'

Gavin's brow furrowed. 'What about Thanksgiving?'

'What about it?'

'Won't you be here?'

'Why should I be?'

'For David's sake.'

'David only has eyes for his father, and you know that only too well, since you're the one who has turned him against me.'

'You're being stupid, Louise!' Gavin exclaimed furiously, his voice rising almost to a shout. 'Damn stupid! Why would I turn our son against his own mother, for God's sake?' Gavin shook his head. He was honestly puzzled by her last statement. He found it difficult to believe that she really thought he had driven a wedge between her and their son.

Changing the subject, knowing she was losing ground, Louise said, 'And how long are *you* staying? How long are we going to have the pleasure of *your* company in LA?'

'I have to go back to London at the end of November. I'm in postproduction on *Kingmaker*, as you well know.'

'And will you be coming home for Christmas?'

'Yes. Why wouldn't I be here?'

'I thought you would be starting your new movie almost immediately. That's what you seem to do these days, make movies back to back. And all of them on foreign location, I might add. You've made it pretty obvious these last few years that the movies come before me and David.'

'That's not true, Louise, and you know it isn't. And while you might hate my movies, which is what you keep announcing to me and anyone else who'll listen, you certainly don't hate spending the money they make.'

Louise looked at him coldly, but she made no comment.

Gavin said, 'I'll be starting preproduction on the movie in February or March.'

'Bully for you.'

'Oh, Louise, *please*. Stop it, will you?'

Stepping closer to the long work table, she eyed the books piled up. '*Napoleon!* Good God, I ought to have known you'd get around to *him* one day. Another little man with grandiose ideas,' she intoned sarcastically, her eyes steely blue daggers in her pale face.

Choosing to ignore this pointed dig, Gavin said, 'I'll be out of your hair, since I'll be living and working in France for the next six months or so.'

'That figures,' she cried. 'I might have guessed you'd end up there!'

'What's that supposed to mean?'

'Your precious Rosalind lives and works in France, and you just can't bear to be away from her, can you?'

'Oh come on, cut it out,' he exclaimed. 'Your

congenital jealousy clouds your judgement constantly. That's what's ruined our marriage.'

'Hah! Don't give me that bullshit, Gavin Ambrose. I haven't done anything to our marriage. You have. You and all your women.'

Gavin knew that they would end up having one of their horrendous rows if he did not curtail this particular topic of conversation, and he must do it right now. Adopting a softer, quieter voice, he said, 'Please, Louise, let's stop this. Immediately. I'm working, and I have a deadline on this script. And you have a flight to make. Have a good time in Washington, and give Allan my best.'

Louise drew back slightly. 'I'm not going to Washington to see Allan. I'm going to see the Merciers. It's Alicia's birthday. They're having a party, and I'm staying with them.'

Like hell you're not going to see Allan Turner, he thought, but said, 'Then give the *Merciers* my best. Enjoy yourself. I'll see you before I leave for London, I suppose.'

'I suppose,' she mumbled, and turning on her heels she walked out imperiously, slamming the door behind her.

Gavin stared at the door for a few moments, and then he dropped his eyes to the script. It was the final draft, but it was so complete it was almost a shooting script.

Just a few more changes, he thought, picking up his pencil. I must get the nuances right in a few more places.

A short while later, Gavin realized he was not able

to concentrate. Louise's words were still echoing in his head. She had implied – no, she had said quite pointedly – that he wanted to work in France because Rosie lived there. And that wasn't true.

Or was it?

He sat pondering this for a long time, the script suddenly forgotten.

PART TWO

Sacred Friendships

FIFTEEN

Although the traffic in Paris was heavy, it moved along at a rapid pace, and much to Rosie's relief she was leaving the centre of the city behind within half an hour.

But it was only when she hit the motorway and headed her Peugeot sedan in the direction of Orléans that she began to relax. Settling back behind the wheel, she let out a sigh of relief. It was the sixth of December, and after a week in Paris, mostly spent clearing her desk, attending to her affairs, and doing a little business for Gavin, she was at last on her way to her beloved Montfleurie.

Since it was Friday, there was additional traffic on the motorway as people headed to their country homes. But it was still early afternoon, and there was not enough, as yet, to cause congestion. She was able to move along at a steady speed, and as she drove her thoughts turned to Johnny Fortune.

Automatically, she reached for the tape Nell had given her in Beverly Hills, and which she had dropped into her canvas carry-all before leaving her apartment on the rue de l'Université in the seventh *arrondissement* a short while ago. Having played only a portion of the tape in her apartment earlier in the week, she was not entirely familiar with all of it. And so, as his voice filled the confines of the car, she was suddenly struck by the poignancy of his voice and of the words he was singing, from *You and Me (We Wanted It All)*.

To her surprise she discovered that the words of the song touched her quite deeply; more than she had thought a popular song ever could.

And as she listened to him singing, a strange sorrow enveloped her, and inexplicably tears pricked the back of her eyes. She felt an acute sense of loss, thought then of what might have been, what her life might have been like, how it could have turned out differently. The words he was singing were hauntingly, profoundly sad. And how prophetic they sounded to her . . . it *was* so easy to break someone's heart, and to have your own heart broken. She knew that only too well.

Johnny moved on to another number, his melodious voice still surrounding her, and not unnaturally her thoughts stayed with him and the evening they had so recently spent together at his house. At this moment it seemed far away to her. And yet it was only a little over a week ago that she had been in Beverly Hills with Nell and Gavin, her two dearest friends; had met the famous Johnny Fortune for the first time, and had found herself curiously drawn to him. Now she was driving into the heart of France, and to another life altogether. How different those two worlds were, thousands of miles apart, and in more senses than one. Everything was much more structured in Europe than it was in California, and there was no question that moving from the free-wheeling style and hoopla of Hollywood celebrity to the formality of the French aristocracy was quite a leap. Nell was forever saying this to her, teasing her about her two wholly different existences, although her girlhood friend was the first to acknowledge that she had managed the leap with infinite dexterity and skill.

Nell had called her from New York yesterday, to tell her that various Christmas gifts would be winging their way to her by courier later in the week, and then she had chuckled, sounding very mischievous. 'Johnny's been pestering me for your phone number. I wasn't sure what you'd want me to do, so I gave him the studio number in London. Then I faxed Aida at the studio and told her she mustn't give out your number to anyone. *But no one.*' Nell had laughed again, wickedly, and added, in a conspiratorial voice, 'Naturally, I said I was acting on your instructions, and that you didn't want to talk to anyone for a few weeks, that you wanted a rest at Montfleurie. But *listen* to me, Rosie mine, I *was* right, you know. Johnny's got it bad. He's quite smitten with you, my darling, oh yes, quite smitten.'

Rosie smiled to herself, thinking of how she had pooh-poohed such an idea to Nell. But she had to admit that she had been flattered yesterday when Neil had told her about his interest in her. She thought there was something truly special about Johnny, and she liked him; quite a lot, in fact. He

183

was totally unlike any of the men she had known in the past, and she had recognized many lovely qualities in him. There was no doubt in her mind that she would have enjoyed seeing him again, but there was no way she could do that. And she wasn't entitled to think about him either . . . at least, not in *that* way. After all, there was an impediment.

I won't even permit myself to indulge in daydreaming, Rosie thought, and punched the stop button on the tape deck in the dashboard. Instantly, his voice was stilled, and the interior of the car was silent.

She drove on for a while, the word *impediment* rolling around in her head. It was a funny word for her to use, and her mind flicked back to her youth and the remembrance of an old movie she had seen on television. It was *Jane Eyre*, a great favourite of hers, both as a book and a movie.

One scene remained forever imprinted on her brain: Jane and Mr Rochester in the village church, the vicar asking if there was any *impediment* to their marriage, and then shock and pandemonium when a man stepped forward to reveal that there was indeed an impediment. A wife. And a mad wife at that . . . the wife Mr Rochester had married when he was a young man, who was locked away in a padded room at the top of his house, the crazy woman Grace Poole looked after, the one who had set the fires.

Well, there are all kinds of impediments, I suppose, Rosie thought, some worse than others.

She was pulled out of her reverie by the crack of thunder and flashes of lightning as a sudden storm erupted. Turning on the windscreen wipers, Rosie peered ahead, concentrating on the road. Everything else was forgotten as she coped with the heavy downpour, handling the car with adroitness on the motorway, which was growing slick with rain, and dangerous.

Stretching more than six hundred miles, from its source in the Cévennes to its estuary into the Atlantic just west of Nantes, the Loire is the longest river in France. Although part of its course runs through land now blighted by pylons and power stations – the French frequently refer to it as the *fleuve nucléaire* – there is a two-hundred-mile stretch that is still stunningly, breathtakingly beautiful.

This particular band of the Loire river runs from Orléans to Tours, and flows through a verdant landscape known as the Valley of Kings.

For it is here that the most magnificent of the famous three hundred châteaux of the Loire are located: Langeais, Amboise, Azay-le-Rideau, Close-Lucé, Chaumont, Chambord, Chiverny, Chinon and Chenonceaux, to name only a few of them.

Even in winter, this section of the Loire is different from any other place in France, softer, gentler and infinitely lovely in all of its green peacefulness. At least, so it seemed to Rosie. It was her most favourite spot in the entire world, and only an hour and a half after leaving Paris she was about to enter the heart of it, the best part of it really, in her opinion.

As she glanced out of the car window, her face instantly lit up with pleasure. The rain had stopped ages ago, and the light was crystal-clear, the skies a delicate blue, filled with wintry sunshine, floating above the deeper blue of the flowing Loire whose sandbanks gleamed pale and silvery in the soft, serene air.

I'll be home soon, she thought, her mood changing from happiness to spiralling excitement, an excitement that knew no bounds. Soon I'll be where I truly belong. That place was Montfleurie, another great château of the Loire, the most magical of all of them to Rosalind Madigan.

Situated exactly in the centre of the long valley between Orléans and Tours, Montfleurie lies close to the legendary Chenonceaux, once the home of Henry II, his mistress Diane de Poitiers, his wife Catherine de Medici, their son Francis II, and *his* wife, Mary Stuart, the *petite Reinette d'Écosse*, as she was always called – the little Queen of Scotland.

Montfleurie began its life as a medieval castle, a fortress stronghold built by Fulk Nerra, Comte d'Anjou, the formidable eleventh-century warrior known as the Black Hawk, ruler of the area, founder of the Angevin line and the Plantagenet dynasty which subsequently came to the throne of England.

Twice destroyed by fire and twice rebuilt, the château changed hands innumerable times over a span of three hundred years. Finally, in the sixteenth century, it was bought by the powerful Comte de Montfleurie, who wished to expand his lands in the Loire. Also, its closeness to Chenonceaux was vitally important to him.

Philippe de Montfleurie, *grand seigneur*, magnate and landowner, held various ministerial positions in the government and was a popular courtier during the brief reign of Francis II and his consort, Mary Stuart. Closely allied to the young queen's Guisard uncles, he was an influential figure, very much enmeshed in the politics of the day, and he never failed to profit from his political and royal connections.

It was in 1575 that the Comte laid the château's present foundations, and eventually, over the years, created the great stone edifice which still soars upward on a hill overlooking the valley. He spared no cost and built his Renaissance pleasure palace on a scale of great extravagance. He is entirely responsible for the château as it stands today, for its great beauty inside and out, and the extraordinary furnishings throughout the impressive rooms.

Earlier, Rosie had left the motorway at the exit to Tours, and as she rounded the corner of the secondary road, which she had taken at Amboise, she slowed the car. Coming to a standstill, she sat for a moment, as she usually did when she had been away, enjoying her first sight of the château, savouring its ancient and impressive elegance, its timelessness, the sense of the past which it always invoked in her.

Sitting on an enchanting bend in the Cher river, a tributary of the Loire, Montfleurie was built of local Loire stone, a stone that slowly changes colour over the years until it becomes almost white. It rose up ahead, dominating the top of the hill in the same way that it had for centuries, its pale stone gleaming luminously in the bright afternoon sunlight, the clustering conical rooftops and spires of its cylindrical towers dark outlines against the azure sky.

Her heart was beating that much faster and her excitement soared when, a few minutes later, she rolled over the drawbridge and into the interior courtyard at the front of the château. Even before she braked, the great oak door was wrenched open and Gaston, the house man, came running down the front steps.

As Rosie alighted from the car, he rushed forward to greet her, a wide smile on his face. '*Madame de Montfleurie!* Hello! Hello! It's wonderful to see you!' he exclaimed, extending his hand, grasping hers, shaking it with some vigour.

'And it's good to see you,' Rosie answered, her smile as wide as his. 'And great to be back here at last. You look well, Gaston . . . and how is Annie?'

'Very well, *Madame*, and she will be happier now that you've arrived, *bien sûr*.' He frowned, shook his head. 'But you are early. *Monsieur le comte* did not expect you until five. I am sorry, he is not here. He is still out, at lunch –'

'It's perfectly all right,' Rosie cut in. Out of the corner of her eye she caught sight of a small figure dressed in red running down the steps, coming towards her. Excusing herself, Rosie hurried forward and caught Lisette in her arms as the child flung herself against her body.

'*Tante* Rosie! *Tante* Rosie! I thought you were never coming!'

Rosie hugged the five-year-old girl fiercely, loving her so very much. She stroked her head, then tilted the child's chin, stared down into the bright little face upturned to hers.

'I've missed you, *ma petite*,' she murmured softly, and kissed Lisette on her cheek. 'But now I'm here and we're going to have a wonderful Christmas.'

'I know, I know,' Lisette cried excitedly.

Yvonne was hovering in the background, her own face wreathed in smiles. How she's grown in the three months I've been away, Rosie thought, *and* grown up all of a sudden. Swiftly she took in the eighteen-year-old girl's new look: the bright red hair upswept into curls on top of her head, the touch of pink lipstick on the vulnerable young mouth, the dusting of powder on the freckled face.

'Hello, Yvonne darling,' Rosie said, her eyes admiring as she walked towards her, holding Lisette by the hand. 'And you look very smart. Did you make the dress yourself?'

Yvonne grabbed hold of Rosie's arm and hugged her hard, then gave her a resounding kiss on each cheek. 'I can't believe you've finally come home, Rosie. It's been so sad here without you, we all miss you when you're away. And yes, I made the dress myself, and of course I copied it from one of yours.'

'So I noticed,' Rosie laughed, 'and you've done a good job. I'll make a dress designer of you yet.'

'Oh, do you think so? That would be wonderful, my dream come true! But come on, let us go inside. Collie is waiting for you, she's longing to see you. Why, Rosie, she's just been counting the days.'

'So have I. Let me get my bag, I won't be a minute.' Rosie strode back to the car and, after taking her canvas carry-all off the front seat, she turned to Gaston who was unloading her suitcases and packages

189

out of the trunk. 'Everything can go up to my room, thank you, Gaston.'

'De rien, Madame de Montfleurie, de rien.'

Rosie caught up with Yvonne and Lisette, and the three of them went into the château together, Lisette chattering away non-stop. They were half way across the vast marble entrance hall when Rosie happened to glance up.

At the top of the staircase, dressed in riding clothes, stood Guy de Montfleurie. He was watching them closely.

For a moment Rosie was paralysed, and she stood stock-still, unable to move, her heart sinking. The last person she had wanted to see at Montfleurie was among the first she had set eyes on.

He was down the stairs and standing in front of her before she had a chance to collect herself.

He stared at her.

She stared back at him, trying to keep her face neutral, displaying no emotion.

He said: 'We didn't expect you until late this afternoon or early evening, Rosalind.'

'So Gaston said.'

Guy took a step closer, peering into her face. 'And how are you, my dear?'

'I'm well, thank you. And you?'

'The same.'

There was a short pause during which neither of them spoke. Then he half smiled, and a brow lifted somewhat sardonically. 'No wifely kiss then?'

Rosie was silent.

He laughed. 'What a shame. But no doubt I will

survive your coldness. I always have.' Laughing again, he stepped around her, sauntered across the hall, slapping his riding crop against his leather boot. At the door he stopped, swung around, called out, 'I will see you later, my dear. I presume we *will* be dining together.'

Rosie sucked in her breath. 'Where else would I be having dinner but here with your father and the girls,' she exclaimed, somewhat impatiently for her, and, putting her arm around Lisette, she ushered the child up the staircase; Yvonne followed quickly on their heels.

As the three of them climbed the central staircase, Rosie glanced around at all the familiar things . . . the huge, ancient crystal chandelier dropping down from the ceiling, the seventeenth-century tapestries on the walls, the portraits of the de Montfleurie ancestors lining other walls, and she thought of Guy with some sadness. What a shame it was that he was not a different kind of man, the kind of man his father would have liked his only son to be, the kind of man who would have taken his responsibilities at Montfleurie seriously. But Guy was weak, ineffectual, selfish and a wastrel. He had bitterly disappointed his father. And he had disappointed her.

Eight years ago she had come to this great château as a young bride: his bride. She had been full of love and admiration for Guy de Montfleurie, the future count. But everything between them had deteriorated, so very quickly. They had become estranged within a few years of their marriage. Today she felt nothing for him except perhaps a touch of pity.

SIXTEEN

Rosie looked across at Collie, and said quietly, 'I was so surprised to see Guy just now. I thought he was away.'

'He was,' Collie replied. 'He showed up unexpectedly, and unannounced, this morning. Like the proverbial bad penny, I might add.' There was a slight pause. 'Maybe I shouldn't say that,' she sighed, 'it is a little unkind, I think. After all, Guy *is* my brother, and I am fond of him. He can be the most aggravating person, though.'

'I know, but he doesn't mean to be, he just can't help himself,' Rosie murmured, giving her sister-in-law a loving smile, reaching out, taking her hand, squeezing it affectionately. The two women sat together in Collie's upstairs study, enjoying a private chat now that the girls had left them alone.

Collie smiled back at Rosie, then she shook her head almost in bemusement, and said, 'You always see the best in everyone . . . make excuses for everyone, but I'm afraid I cannot, and I certainly can't excuse Guy. He's impossible. The problem is that we've all spoiled him for years and years. My father, me, even Claude when he was alive, and my mother until the day *she* died. And you too, Rosie, since the very moment you met him with me in Paris, all those years ago. Guy has been over-indulged, you know. *Always*. And by everyone.'

'What you say is true, Collie, but he really isn't a bad person, is he?' Not waiting for a response, Rosie said in a rush of words, 'He's like a little boy who's never grown up. He wants instant gratification, his own way in everything. He has absolutely no sense of responsibility, or commitment to anything –'

'Or anyone,' Collie interjected, giving Rosie a very knowing, penetrating look.

'Maybe the failure of our marriage is partially my fault,' Rosie replied swiftly, honestly meaning this. 'As my mother used to say, there are always two sides to every story.'

'And mine used to say something to the effect that there's her side, his side, and the *truth*,' Collie shot back.

Rosie simply laughed, made no comment, not wanting to delve into her marriage, which had gone so wrong, and all of its inherent problems; certainly not at this particular moment.

Collie went on, 'Anyway, I was not only referring to you when I said Guy couldn't make a commitment. I was also thinking of Father. He really needs help with this place, and Guy . . . well . . . he doesn't give a damn about Montfleurie, that's perfectly obvious, isn't it? The costs of running it are crippling, and the work is backbreaking for my father, even though he does have François Graingier to help him these days.

And some extra money coming in at long last, because he finally took *your* advice and opened the château to the public. If only Guy would pull his weight even a little bit, things would be so much easier for Father, and for everyone else here. I don't understand my brother.'

'I know, darling, and he baffles me most of the time,' Rosie admitted, adding quietly, 'I really don't profess to understand him either. And I certainly don't understand his lack of interest in Montfleurie, when you consider that it's his birthright, his heritage, and will one day be his . . .' Rosie's voice trailed off into silence, and she turned away, stared into the fire, her face growing reflective and just a little sad.

Collie did not respond. She leaned back against the faded dark-green brocade of the Louis XVI sofa and closed her eyes, feeling exhausted all of a sudden. And silently she condemned her brother for his behaviour. Over the past few years he had become worse than ever, had grown more selfish and self-indulgent, headstrong and impulsive. She wondered what his life was all about, and how he actually spent his time when he was away. She knew some of the things he did: he devoted weeks to those quasi-religious men in India and the Far East – his gurus, he called them – and was forever trotting off to meditate with them in some godforsaken ashram on a mountaintop. She thought of them as charlatans who had taken his money, and still continued to take what little bit he had left. And when he came down from his mountain perch he hung around Hong Kong and other parts of the Far East for months on end.

It was odd, the fascination the Orient held for him; what was even odder was his ridiculous behaviour towards Rosie. It was unforgivable; *she* could never forgive him.

'Why did you marry Guy?' Collie blurted out, surprising herself with her words, sitting up with a jerk, staring at Rosie.

Rosie gazed back at her and blinked, startled by the sudden question, for a moment rendered speechless. Then she said slowly, 'I was in love with him . . . I admired him . . . and I suppose he swept me off my feet.' She hesitated briefly, and then continued in a very low tone, 'You know how captivating your brother is when he wants to be . . . effortlessly charming, warm, amusing, flirtatious. I guess he sort of . . . overpowered me, or perhaps *overwhelmed me* is a better way of saying it.' There were other reasons why she had married him, and Rosie was well aware of them, but she had no wish to elucidate further.

'Yes, he is all of those things,' Collie agreed, 'and certainly women always did find him quite irresistible, even when he was very young – sixteen or seventeen. My God, all those conquests before you! Well, I suppose he was not so selfish, or so strange, when you married him.' Collie looked Rosie right in the eye, and exclaimed, 'Why don't you divorce him?'

'I don't know.' Rosie laughed, a trifle self-consciously, and then asked with a small frown, 'Are you trying to get rid of me? Throw me out of the family?'

'Oh Rosie, no! *Never!*' Collie cried, her eyes widening in horror at the mere idea of such a thing. She moved closer to Rosie on the sofa, caught hold of her, hugged her. 'How can you say such a terrible thing? Or even think it. I love you. We all love you. And I am entirely on your side. Guy is a fool.'

Collie drew away, and peered into her sister-in-law's face, her feelings of affection, loyalty and devotion transparent in her light-blue eyes, in the tender expression on her small, piquante face. 'When you've gone away, Montfleurie is like a morgue, it really is, darling. Father is terribly affected by your absence, we all are. It's as if the sunshine has gone out of our lives. You're such an important part of our lives, Rosie, and a very special member of the family, the sister I never had, another daughter to Father. Surely you must know that?'

'Yes, I do, I suppose. And I feel the same way about you, Collie, and I love all of you . . . you're *my* family, too, and Montfleurie is my home. Why, my life just wouldn't be the same without you, and I couldn't bear it if I didn't live here part of the time.'

Rosie shook her head, gave Collie a faint smile. 'But look here, don't let's talk about Guy any more. He's a law unto himself, as *you* well know, and in any case, he isn't here very often these days, so we don't see very much of him, do we?'

Collie nodded her agreement, leaned back against the sofa again, gazed at the burning logs in the fireplace for a few seconds, wishing her brother had not come back at this *particular* time of year. Lately, and for some odd, unfathomable reason, he seemed to blame her and Rosie for all of his problems, and she hoped and prayed he wasn't going to put a damper on Christmas, with his demands and impatience and bad temper. Yvonne and Lisette were so looking forward to the holidays.

Almost as if she had read Collie's mind, Rosie said, 'Let's try to make Christmas work for the girls.'

'I was thinking exactly that!' Collie exclaimed. 'And of course we must.'

Now wanting to change the subject entirely, and move on, Rosie confided, 'When I arrived earlier this afternoon, I couldn't help thinking how grown up Yvonne looked. And all of a sudden.'

'Yes, she does, she bloomed overnight, after you left at the end of August.' Collie's light-coloured eyes drifted to the skirted table at one side of the fireplace, her glance resting on the silver-framed photograph of her late husband, Claude Duvalier, and his only sister Yvonne, whom he had raised. 'She has such a strong look of Claude these days, don't you agree?'

'Why yes, she does, now that you mention it,' Rosie answered. 'And her personality's similar to his – she's outgoing and fun. Full of energy, as he was.'

'Yes.' There was a sorrowful little silence before Collie said, 'It's so sweet of you to send her a cheque every month, for the bit of work she does for you. But it's not necessary, Rosie, really it isn't. She's happy to do it, and to learn about designing from you. Nor do you have to keep sending *me* money either. It's lovely of you, but I can manage on what Claude left me, truly.'

'I want to do it, Collie, want to make your life easier, if I possibly can. God knows, running this place eats up all of your father's income, and there's

not much left for him or you at the end of the day.
So let me help out when I can. Goodness, I don't
give either you or Yvonne very much. It's only pin
money.'

'You're so good to us, such an angel,' Collie murmured, and looked away as tears unexpectedly
welled.

SEVENTEEN

'Mademoiselle Colette looks so much better, *n'est-ce pas?*' the housekeeper said, without looking up, continuing to unpack the last of Rosie's four suitcases as she spoke.

'She certainly has a good colour, and her eyes are very bright and sparkling, Annie,' Rosie replied, placing several sweaters in the drawer of a chest and closing it. 'But she's awfully thin.'

'*Mais oui, c'est vrai.*' Annie looked up and glanced across at Rosie, nodding her grey head vigorously, a thoughtful look settling on her face as she took Rosie's dressing gown out of the case and placed it on the bed.

Annie, like her husband Gaston, had been born in the village and had worked at the château all of her life. She had started out as a kitchen maid at fifteen, worked her way up to become housekeeper and now, at fifty-five, was part of the family after forty years in their employ. She knew each one of them intimately, coped with all of their idiosyncrasies without batting an eyelash, and never broke a confidence. She would take their secrets to the grave with her, they were convinced of that, and they were correct in this assumption.

Closing the empty suitcase, Annie glanced across at Rosie once more, and volunteered, 'Collie has always been slender. When she was a little girl, I used to call her the *épouvantail* . . . how do you say in English? The crow scare?'

'No, the scarecrow,' Rosie corrected, and smiled in amusement. From their very first meeting, she had appreciated Annie, who ran the château like an admiral on the bridge of a battleship, absolutely confident of herself and her judgement, and totally in control of her vessel. She ran a tight ship, at that. She was not only hardworking and devoted to the count and his family but compassionate and perceptive, being a good judge of character and human nature. Rosie considered her to be a miracle-worker, and she often wondered what they would do without her.

Annie exclaimed, 'That is right! She was the *scarecrow*! So thin, nothing but arms and legs, and the body of a boy. Ah well, not much has changed, has it? But it does not matter, it is her nature to be skinny the way she is. *Madame la comtesse*, her late mother –' Annie broke off, crossed herself, muttered, 'God rest her soul, poor woman,' cleared her throat and continued, '*Madame la comtesse* was also slender and very boyish. That look – ah, it runs in the family of her mother, the great Caron-Bougivals.' Shaking her head in the energetic manner she had, Annie added, in an even more emphatic voice, '*C'est pas important*, her weight. *You* have known Colette for years, you must recall that she has always been like a stick of asparagus.'

'Yes, she has,' Rosie agreed, knowing that Annie was correct. Nevertheless, she was still worried. A short while ago, when she had first arrived and went to see Collie in her study, she had been shocked. How easily she had felt the bones of her body through her sweater when she hugged her; it had seemed to Rosie that there was very little flesh on that small, delicate frame.

Picking up the empty suitcase, Annie carried it over to the door which opened into the adjoining sitting room, where she had already stacked the others. Then she swung to face Rosie. 'Is there anything else I can help you with, Madame de Montfleurie?'

Rosie shook her head. '*Non, merci beaucoup.*'

Annie gave her the benefit of a warm smile. 'I am glad you are home, and so are Gaston, Dominique, Marcel and Fannie. Everybody at the château is happy, and because you are here, everything will now be all right, *bien sûr.*'

Wondering what exactly she meant by this statement, a repetition of what Gaston had said earlier, Rosie frowned, and asked, 'Have there been lots of problems then, Annie?'

'*Non, non, Madame.* Well – not exactly. *Monsieur le comte* . . .' She shook her head. 'He is so grave, so serious these days, he hardly ever smiles any more, and looks perpetually worried. And Mademoiselle Collie is still grieving for her husband, I am sure of that. But when you arrive, ah, then it is so different.

La famille joyeuse, très gaie. C'est vrai, Madame. Oh yes, this is very true, what I say.'

'I'm glad to hear that, Annie. But I want to ask you something else. When I was in California a couple of weeks ago, Yvonne told me that Collie wasn't feeling well. Was that so?'

'Yes. But I do not believe she was ill. She was – how shall I put it? Full of her terrible sorrow, I think. She has her moments of intense grief. They come unexpectedly, I know this, but eventually they do go away. How she loved Monsieur Duvalier, and oh how she misses him. That accident! So bad, so bad. *Oh mon Dieu!*' Annie made the sign of the cross and shivered involuntarily.

'I understand,' Rosie murmured. 'So *you* think it was grief that made her unwell a few weeks ago?'

'*Oui.* And please, *Madame*, don't worry so much about her. She will be all right. I know her since before she was born. She is strong, that one. Now, I had better go downstairs to the kitchens. I must help Dominique make preparations for the dinner. I will send Marcel to take away the empty cases.'

'Thanks, Annie. And thank you so much for helping me to unpack.'

'It's nothing, Madame de Montfleurie. It's always my pleasure to do anything for you.'

Left alone, Rosie busied herself in her bedroom for the next ten minutes or so, putting the rest of her things away, and then she walked through into the adjoining sitting room.

This was a graceful room, large, airy in feeling, with

a high ceiling, and many tall windows overlooking the gardens and the Cher river beyond. The windows were so high and wide, the sky was virtually pulled inside the room, and the vistas visible through them were panoramic.

Decorated in soft shades of sky-blue and cream, with touches of greyish-pink and a pale mustardy-yellow, the room had a certain kind of faded elegance that bespoke ancient lineage and impoverished aristocracy, but at the same time it was an eminently comfortable room, one Rosie loved.

Many of the silk, taffeta and brocade fabrics used in the room were old, had long since lost their true colour, and the Aubusson carpet, dating back to the eighteenth century, was worn in spots. But it was a genuine treasure. The wood pieces were handsome, and most notable of these was a Louis XVI *bureau plat*, made of yew wood and decorated with ormolu. This stood between two windows at the far end of the room, and it was a desk of museum quality. So was a marble-topped console table, its base intricately carved with cherubs. Comfortable sofas and chairs, and several occasional tables of fruit wood inlaid with marquetry, rounded out the furnishings, and the whole was pleasing to the eye.

Over the years the count had been obliged to sell off many of the less valuable possessions, in order to preserve the rest of them, to maintain the château and its grounds properly, and to make ends meet. This was because the income from investments, inherited from his father, was not sufficient to meet the basic needs of Montfleurie; also, although the

French Government gave monetary support to historic seats such as the château, the amount the count received was small, nominal really.

However, in the past three years his finances had begun to improve, and the steady drain of beautiful objects to auction houses in Paris and antique dealers on the Quai Voltaire had finally stopped, to his considerable relief.

This was because he had opened the château to the public, and begun to sell all manner of souvenirs, the most popular being a series of replica medieval toys and dolls which Rosie had designed, using as models an antique collection she had found in the attics.

While this new venture had not made him a rich man, the money earned from entrance fees, brochures, the toys and other products was becoming quite substantial. In fact, the revenues collected this past spring and summer were enough to keep the place running efficiently for the next six months. Also, the little family industry, mostly created by Rosie's ingenuity, ensured that the count would not get further into debt.

As he was forever saying to her, 'Thanks to your talent, practicality and persuasiveness, I can balance the books these days, and, *finally*, I am able to keep the bankers at bay.'

Rosie thought of money now as she noticed several ugly damp spots on the ceiling, in a corner just above a window. They had not been there in August. But she doubted there was a single spare franc readily available for repairs and a paint job. Certainly not this month, with Christmas coming, and so many responsibilities and commitments for Henri de Montfleurie to handle.

Never mind, she thought, I'll do it myself, after the plumber has fixed the leak, and once the holidays are over. Gaston and his brother will help me. All we need is plaster and white paint. Not too hard to come by, I'm sure. Rosie prided herself on her do-it-yourself decorating ability, a skill she had picked up from studio carpenters, other craftsmen and set designers who worked on movies. And whatever costs were involved she would take care of.

Reaching for her canvas carry-all, she placed it on an upholstered bench, and began to take out manila folders of the research she had started for Gavin's film of Napoleon, as well as the grey briefcase from Concorde, in which she had stowed her personal papers, along with various other items.

Included among these was the silver-framed photograph of the group, taken in New York so long ago. It always travelled with her wherever she went. She placed it next to those already arranged on top of an antique chest of drawers, and Nell, Gavin, Kevin, Sunny and Mikey were suddenly gazing out at her, their faces smiling.

How young and beautiful they looked, so untouched by life. And how innocent.

But we lost our innocence long ago, she murmured to herself. Life got at us, changed us, toughened us, disappointed us, destroyed our illusions, and even some of our hopes and dreams. Perhaps irrevocably. And we all took the wrong roads.

'The roads we didn't take, where would they have

led?' she said aloud to the empty room, remembering the words of a song in *Follies*, that marvellous Sondheim musical of the early seventies. It had starred Alexis Smith, John McMartin, Yvonne de Carlo and Gene Nelson, and whenever she listened to the Broadway album she was entranced by the words and music, as well as entertained.

Then she thought: Perhaps we didn't take the wrong roads. Maybe they were the right roads for each of us. Perhaps what we are living now *is* our destiny . . . what is meant to be is meant to be.

Certainly she and Gavin, Nell and Kevin had pursued their professional dreams, had been successful in their given careers, if not in their personal lives. For, according to Nell, Gavin was no better off in that area than they were.

Sighing under her breath, she straightened the frame and paused for a moment to study the photograph of Colette and Claude, taken here on the terrace at Montfleurie several summers ago.

It was a colour photograph and very true to life.

How beautiful Collie looked, her face tanned, her dark curls ruffled by the breeze, her generous mouth ripe with laughter, her eyes radiantly blue, the colour of the sky above. And Claude, youthful, handsome, *his* eyes full of adoration for his young wife. And how thin Collie looked in this picture – and of course Annie was right, she *had* been like a stick most of her life.

But something troubled Rosie about Collie's extreme slenderness now; it was somehow dismaying to her. She's so frail, Rosie thought. That's what it *is* about her that is so different. She's become terribly, terribly frail since I've been gone these past three months. Her worry about her sister-in-law flared as she turned away, continuing to put her many possessions where they belonged.

At one moment, as she hovered over the *bureau plat*, filling its drawers with papers, she glanced out of the window and caught her breath in delight.

The high-flung sky was vividly blue, filled with gauzy clouds, and there was a sheen on the river like the glaze on ancient porcelain. The late-afternoon sunlight was glorious, the gardens spread out before her burnished, almost molten, and they looked as though they had been brushstroked with gold. It seemed to Rosie that everything outside appeared to shimmer in the extraordinary light.

For Rosalind, there was nowhere else on earth like Montfleurie, and, unable to resist the pull of her beloved gardens, she grabbed her loden cape off the sofa, where she had thrown it earlier, and hurried out. Flinging the cape over her shoulders, she flew down the long corridor in the direction of the back stairs, having no wish, at this moment, to meet anyone coming up the main staircase.

EIGHTEEN

Within the space of a few seconds, Rosie was slamming the door of the back porch behind her and speeding along the stone-flagged path towards the river. Her cape billowed out behind her like a sail as she covered the ground almost at a run.

Rosie was heading for one of her favourite spots in the vast and endless gardens, a tumbledown pile of stones known as Black Hawk's Keep, so named because it had been built by Fulk Nerra, the Black Hawk.

The ancient, crumbling building, reduced to a pile of stones by the passing of the centuries, had been a watch tower once. Strategically placed on high ground, above a bend in the river Cher, it was the perfect spot for keeping watch over Montfleurie, keeping marauders at bay in the Middle Ages.

In the eighteenth century, trees had been planted around the ruins, and its stones were overgrown with moss and lichen; in summer all kinds of pretty flowers sprouted up through cracks and crevices. It was a unique little corner, with a strange and captivating beauty all of its own, and it was redolent of the past, and of the history of France.

The ancient and decrepit battlements, decaying though they were, plus the profusion of trees, served to create a sheltered spot, and often in the summer months the family enjoyed having picnics here. For years Rosie had used it as a place to work and sketch, or to read and relax, or simply daydream.

She was out of breath as she reached the half-demolished archway that had once been the main doorway into the tower. But she did not slow her pace until she was on the far side of the ruins and out of sight of the château, hidden from view.

Here she sat down on the stone bench which one of the de Montfleurie ancestors had placed there hundreds of years earlier, and gazed out across the winding, flowing waters of the Cher. Everything was quiet, absolutely still. The only sound was the thudding of her heart. Slowly, the pounding in her chest lessened; her breathing became more normal, and she began to relax.

Wrapping the cloak around her for warmth, she leaned her body against the trunk of the tree behind her, and let herself be soothed by the gentleness of her surroundings, the beauty of nature in all its abundance.

How peaceful it was, this spot where once violent battles had raged when Fulk Nerra, warlord, predator and ruler of the area, had stalked this valley. The dust of the battlegrounds had settled long, long ago, and to Rosie it was now a most gentle place, a place to be alone, a place to think.

Her thoughts were concentrated on Guy, her husband of the past eight years. She was wondering what would become of them both. They rarely saw each other these days, and when they did there were disturbing undercurrents between them. And certainly there was no chance of making the marriage work, not after five years of estrangement, plus a lot of ill will on his part.

Aware that Guy harboured bad feelings towards her, Rosie had discussed this problem time and again with Collie. And Collie had invariably pointed out that Guy was hostile to everyone, not only to her, and eventually she had come to agree with her sister-in-law. But the situation in which she was sitting was growing more ridiculous with the passing of the years; not only that, it was unhealthy, in Rosie's opinion, but she was unable to do anything to change it.

The unexpected snapping of a twig, the rustling of footsteps through fallen leaves, made Rosie sit up straighter. At once she was alerted, and realized that someone was approaching.

Swinging her head, she peered about, hoping that it was not Guy who had followed her here. She was not in the right frame of mind to be alone with him. Not yet, at any rate. She had to adjust to his presence, to arm herself against him, to be in readiness for his verbal onslaughts, to be on her guard, before she could confront him head on.

Much to her relief, it was not him. She leapt to her feet, a smile breaking through her glumness, as Henri, Count de Montfleurie, came into view, raising

210

his hand in greeting, his expression loving, his eyes warm, welcoming.

Rosie ran to him, and they embraced affectionately, hugging each other hard. Finally he held her away from him, looking into her face intently, his wise brown eyes searching, quizzical. After kissing her on both cheeks, he asked, 'Are you all right? You're not upset, are you? Guy's not upset you, has he, Rosie?'

'No, he hasn't, Henri. Anyway, I only saw him briefly, when I first arrived. We bumped into each other in the entrance hall as he was heading for the stables. Naturally, he was a bit sardonic, which seems to be his usual way with me these days.'

'I know exactly what you mean. He is the same with me, and with Collie, unfortunately. I do not know why he can't be kinder to his sister. God knows, she's been through so much these last few years. Ah well.' He sighed, before remarking, 'That is Guy, I'm afraid. Eternally self-involved, and with no thought for others and their feelings.'

Henri took hold of Rosie's arm and together they walked towards the stone bench.

The count was a slender man of medium height, about five feet seven inches tall, with greying black hair, a pleasant, rather attractive, craggy face, and the slightly weather-beaten complexion of a man who spends a good deal of time outdoors, which he did. He was sixty-three years old, and had spent most of his life at the château, except for the years he had attended the Sorbonne in Paris.

Immediately after he had finished university, he had returned to the Loire Valley, which he loved with a passion, and had learned more about running the estate from his father, who had started training him when he was a boy. The only son, he inherited Montfleurie upon his father's death, when he was only twenty-four; a year later, at the age of twenty-five, he married Laure Caron-Bougival, his childhood sweetheart. His son Guy was born when Henri was twenty-seven, and Colette came along four years later. A widower for the past twelve years, he had not seen fit to remarry, despite the urging of Colette.

Henri was bundled up in a shabby tweed overcoat, a little threadbare and worn, and, shivering, he pulled this around him as he and Rosie sat down on the bench together. Taking hold of her hand he squeezed it. 'I'm so happy to have you home, Rosie. It does my heart good to see you, darling.'

'That's how I feel. I'm glad to be here. It's been quite a year for me, because of the filming. In so many different ways I've hated being away from Montfleurie as much as I have, but it couldn't be helped.'

He nodded, then looked deeply into her eyes once again, and asked, 'But tell me, how are you *really*? And I want the truth, you know. Nothing less will do.'

'I'm not bad,' Rosie answered, meaning this, but she laughed unexpectedly, a small, hollow laugh. She went on, 'At least I'm okay when I'm working. I suppose I'm too busy to be anything else. But I don't know –' Breaking off, pausing thoughtfully, she shook her head and her mouth suddenly drooped dejectedly.

He did not miss this. 'What is it?' he asked, frowning.

'When I'm at a loose end I seem to be so weepy,' Rosie confided. 'The least little thing sets me off, and I'm always filling up with tears, on the verge of crying. And that's not like me, feeling sad all the time. You ask me what's the matter with me, and I can't answer you. I don't really know.'

'I do,' he murmured, tightening his hold on her hand. 'You're very unhappy, Rosalind. And the life you live is most unnatural for a young woman of thirty-one, if you don't mind me saying so. You're not married and you're not divorced. It seems to me that you're in . . . a kind of limbo. I truly believe you should do something about the situation which exists between you and Guy.'

'Oh, but there's no chance of a reconciliation!' Rosie exclaimed. 'Not now. We've grown too far apart.'

'But of course you have! I wasn't talking about the two of you getting back together. I was talking about your separating. Permanently. I was talking about *divorce*.'

Rosie gaped at him speechlessly.

'Don't look so thunderstruck, Rosie, people do get divorced, you know. Catholic though you both are, I think the time has come for you to take legal steps to dissolve your marriage to my son.' When she remained silent, he thought to ask, 'It hasn't been a marriage for the past five years, has it?'

'No . . . perhaps even a bit before that.'

'Then what's your problem?'

213

There was a very long silence, and Rosie confessed in a whisper, 'I'm afraid.'

The count drew back slightly, staring, his eyes filling with puzzlement. '*Afraid! You!* I can hardly believe such a thing. What are you afraid of?'

Rosie bit her lip, and looked down at their clasped hands, wondering how to explain what she felt. When she finally lifted her head she saw such concern in his kindly eyes, she knew she had no alternative but to tell him the truth. He would understand.

Swallowing, she said in a low, almost inaudible voice, 'I'm afraid of losing you and Collie and the girls. You're the only real family I have, have had for years, and I love you all very much. I couldn't bear it if I had to go away, if I couldn't call Montfleurie my home, if I couldn't ever come back to be with you all.'

'That's not likely to happen, my dear,' he said swiftly, wanting to reassure her.

'But if I am divorced from Guy, I won't be part of the family any longer.' Much to her own irritation, tears sprang into her eyes and trickled down her cheeks before she could check them.

Henri fumbled in his suit pocket for a handkerchief, gave it to her silently, and waited until she had dried her eyes.

Once she had composed herself, he said, 'We all *love* you, Rosie. And I always have, right from the beginning, when you first came here with Collie, long before you married Guy. And you will always be another daughter to me, whether you're married to him or not. Even if you marry someone else, my feelings for you won't change. How could they? I don't love you because you're my son's wife, I love you because of all the things you are, the wonderful person you are, Rosie. I love you for *you yourself*. And remember this: Montfleurie is your home, no matter what happens, for the rest of your life. I wouldn't have it any other way.'

He put his arm around her and drew her closer to him. 'I don't know what's wrong with Guy, I won't even attempt to analyse him.'

Henri de Montfleurie stopped and shook his head, and then added in a saddened voice, 'All I know is that I fathered an idiot. Yes, I admit it, I have a fool for a son. How he could behave towards you the way he has is quite beyond me. I'll never understand it. Nor will I ever understand his total disregard for Montfleurie, which one day will be his, God forbid! I hope I live a very long time, so that I can make it safe for the next generation, because God knows what will happen to it once he inherits. It will go to rack and ruin, I've no doubt, unless I take steps to forestall that in advance, make some sort of provision for the future. It worries me considerably these days, in view of his behaviour.'

'But why can't you leave Montfleurie to Collie?'

'I could under the Civil Code – the Napoleonic Code, the law created by him – *if* she were my only child. A girl can inherit under French law. However, I cannot bypass my son in favour of my daughter. That's most assuredly *against* the law. If Guy dies without an heir, the estate and the title would pass to Collie then, or to her offspring, Lisette. But

215

forgive me, my dear, for digressing in this manner, discussing my worries like this. Now, just let me reinforce what I said a moment ago. You are like a daughter to me, and nothing will ever change that fact.' He drew away to look into her face. 'Will you do something for me?'

Rosie nodded.

'Will you go to see Maître Hervé Berthier when you return to Paris? You've met him you know, he was here several years ago for dinner. He's an excellent lawyer, one of the best in France, and a good friend. We go back for years. Please, Rosie, go and talk to him, and finally make a move to free yourself from Guy. He does you no good. For my part, I promise you my total support, and my love.'

'All right, I will. I'll go and see the lawyer. I suppose there's nothing else left to do really, and thank you, Henri, for the lovely things you've said. You're like a father to me, and I couldn't bear it if . . . if . . . if you and Collie stopped being part of my life.'

'We'll always be your family, my dear, and by the way, that brings me to Kevin. How is he? And is he joining us for Christmas as he promised?'

'I don't think so. I did ask him again, but he's started a new job with the New York Police Department, something to do with the Crime Intelligence Division, which investigates the Mafia. I understand they're targeting the Rudolfo family, one of the most powerful crime empires in New York, and he's caught up with that.'

'Dangerous work,' Henri murmured. 'But then

Kevin seems to thrive on danger. It's a pity though, since it's so worrying for you.'

'I wish he'd get a desk job, or do something else to earn a living, but he won't. He once wanted to be a lawyer . . .' Rosie left her sentence unfinished and made a small grimace.

Henri smiled at her. 'Kevin's stubborn, like you, Rosie, and we all know a leopard doesn't change its spots very easily. But what about Nell Jeffrey? You told me on the phone that they had become involved with each other. Cannot she influence him?'

Rosie laughed and shook her head. 'I doubt it. I had hoped she might be able to persuade Kevin to come for the holidays, that they would *both* come to France to be with us here. But I guess he has to work, from what she says anyway.'

'What a shame, but never mind. Perhaps you will be able to inveigle them into coming for a visit at Easter. That's always such a nice time of year in the Loire Valley.'

'Yes, it is, and I'll speak to Nell again. Perhaps she can talk Kevin into it. I hope so.'

A silence fell between them and they sat staring ahead, enjoying these few moments.

A flock of birds rose up in flight, wheeling and turning against the white clouds, a graceful, moving band, resembling a black velvet ribbon flung high into the pale sky. They flew on, higher and higher, up above the slate-grey turrets of Montfleurie, then they suddenly wheeled away, formed a great arc above the rooftops of the house, heading south for hotter climes.

Clouds scudded across the remote and fading sky, which seemed suddenly full of movement and changing colours: blue turning into grey tinted with amethyst, lilac bleeding into burnt saffron, and along the rim of the far horizon, scarlet and orange streamers of light glowed like distant fire. Across the river the trees clustered on the bank were suddenly dark, inchoate shapes, bluish-green and hazy with evening mist as the light changed once more and twilight finally descended.

'How beautiful it is out here, Rosie, so very tranquil,' Henri said.

'My mother used to call this time of day the gloaming.'

He smiled and patted her hand, and helped her to her feet. 'I'm glad we had this little chat. When I saw you disappearing down the path a while ago, I thought it was a good opportunity to talk to you alone. But now we had better go in; it's turned unexpectedly very chilly, icy almost.'

Together, hand in hand, Rosie and the count walked back to the great château poised on top of the hill.

They were in step and in tune with each other, understanding each other as they always had, and as they always would. The silence between them was easy, comfortable, companionable.

Just before they reached the château, Henri came to a standstill and turning to her, asked, 'Have you still not met some nice man?'

'No, of course I haven't!'

'What a pity! I hate to see you alone, and lonely.

And so unhappy, my dear. Don't you think *I* know what that's like? To live as you do?'

'I know you do, Henri,' Rosie responded. She hesitated uncertainly, then asked, 'How is Kyra?'

She felt him stiffen next to her, and even though the light was dim and fading rapidly she noticed the sudden tightening of his jaw. 'She's well,' he said at last. 'At least, I believe she is. She's away.'

'Oh,' Rosie said, surprised. 'But she's coming back for Christmas, isn't she?'

'I don't know,' he replied in a muffled, unhappy voice, and increased his pace up the hill.

Rosie decided to leave well alone, and so she asked no further questions, hurrying to keep up with him.

Suddenly he began to chuckle and he stopped again, and remarked in a teasing tone, 'I think it's about time you went out and found yourself a gentleman friend. Otherwise I'll have to do it for you.'

Rosie laughed. 'You're incorrigible!'

'No, I'm a Frenchman, remember? And even though I'm old, I'm eternally romantic, like most of my countrymen.'

'You're not old! You're special. And no other woman I know has ever had a father-in-law like you.'

'I trust you mean those words to be complimentary, Rosalind de Montfleurie.'

'*Bien sûr!*' she exclaimed. And she was relieved that his good humour was restored. But as they walked on she could not help wondering if something had gone wrong between him and Kyra, the Russian woman. Perhaps Collie would tell her later *if* this was

219

so, for she was bound to know. Kyra was her friend and shared many confidences.

A short while later, Rosie and the count went into the château, still hand in hand, and she felt better than she had in a long time. Somehow the future no longer looked quite so bleak.

NINETEEN

Much later, after she had bathed, redone her make-up and put on her favourite red wool dress in readiness for dinner, Rosie took a small hatbox out of the armoire and left her suite of rooms.

Walking to the far end of the long, carpeted corridor, she stopped in front of Lisette's bedroom door, knocked, called out, 'It's Auntie Rosie,' and went in.

Yvonne, who was kneeling on the floor buttoning the back of Lisette's brown velvet frock, glanced up. 'Hello, Rosie. We were just about to come looking for you.'

'I beat you to it!' Rosie laughed, and crossed the room, holding the hatbox behind her back so that Lisette would not see it. 'I thought we'd all go down to dinner together.'

'But we must wait for *Maman*,' Lisette said, her face puckering up worriedly. 'We can't go down without her. She won't be long, Auntie Rosie, she's gone to change her dress and comb her hair.'

'Of course we'll wait, darling,' Rosie replied. 'I wouldn't dream of going downstairs without her.'

She smiled at her niece as she leaned towards her. 'I have a present for you, honey.'

The child's bright smile lit up her small round angelic face, brought a sparkle to her dark-brown eyes which were so like her grandfather's. They grew larger in her face as excitement and anticipation took hold. 'What is it?' she cried. 'What is the present? Oh please tell me, *Tante*.'

'I'll give you three guesses.'

'Did you bring it from America?'

Rosie nodded.

'*Un chapeau!* It must be a hat!'

'Goodness me, however did you guess so quickly? You *are* a clever little girl,' Rosie exclaimed, then said in a teasing tone, 'Somebody must have told you about it. A little bird, perhaps?'

'Oh nobody told me, Auntie Rosie. Really they didn't,' Lisette said, suddenly looking solemn. 'But *you* promised me you'd bring me a hat from America. Don't you remember? You promised me in August.'

'That's so, I did promise, and here it is.' Rosie brought her hands from behind her back and offered the hatbox to the child.

Lisette stepped forward and took it from her. '*Merci beaucoup! Merci beaucoup!*' She opened the hatbox swiftly, her plump little hands fumbling with the strings, and took out a small perky hat made of dark-green felt, banded in red-and-green plaid ribbon and sporting a bunch of bright-red cherries on one side. '*Très joli!*' she exclaimed, and hugged her aunt, then dashed across to the armoire and opened the door. After placing the hat on her head, she stood back, admiring it in the armoire mirror for a few seconds.

'It's so beautiful I'm going to wear it to dinner,' Lisette announced, and beamed at her aunt and Yvonne.

Yvonne exclaimed, 'It is beautiful, but you can't wear it to dinner.'

'Why not?' the five-year-old demanded, giving Yvonne a piercing look.

'You know very well we never wear hats indoors,' Yvonne answered.

'I do,' Lisette countered.

'That's not true!' Yvonne exclaimed, her voice rising an octave.

'But it is, too! In a café I've worn my hat.'

'The dining room at Montfleurie is not a café,' Yvonne pointed out, and shook her head. 'And you know very well it isn't, Lisette. Don't be such a silly girl.'

'But we eat food there,' Lisette argued.

Repressing her laughter, Rosie interjected, 'Yvonne is right, darling. You can't wear a hat indoors.'

'But I did in the hospital, didn't I? *Maman* told me I did.'

Rosie and Yvonne exchanged glances, and Rosie said, 'Yes, and you look very pretty in this hat, it really suits you, Lisette. But I do think you must put it away now. You can wear it tomorrow. I'll take you with me when I drive down to the village, and we'll go to the café for an ice cream. You'd like that, wouldn't you?'

The child nodded and smiled. But, none the less, the hat remained firmly planted on her dark curls, and by the look on her face she had no intention of removing it.

Rosie said, 'Come on, Lisette, let's go and put the hat with the rest of your collection. Do you have any other new ones you want to show me? If you do, I'd love to see them.'

'I have two new ones. Come on then!' Lisette, still wearing the green felt hat, ran into the adjoining playroom where her toys and books were kept. It was here that her large and unique collection of hats was arranged on a series of long shelves lining a wall.

Lisette had always adored hats and rarely went outdoors without one, not even when she was simply playing on the grounds of the château.

Long ago, her mother and Rosie had concluded that this love of hats had started just after her birth. She had been a premature baby and had been in an incubator for eight weeks in the Paris hospital where she had been born. While she was in the incubator she had worn a tiny wool cap to keep her head warm. When Claude and Collie had brought their little daughter home to their Paris apartment they had removed the cap. Immediately the baby had begun to shriek, and had continued to do so for over an hour. Eventually it had struck Collie that she was obviously unhappy at being deprived of the wool bonnet. And so Collie had finally put it back on her head, and Lisette had stopped crying immediately.

Even as a toddler she had wanted a cap or bonnet on her head, and this predilection had not diminished as she had grown. Very simply, she felt happier when she wore a hat, and everyone in the family had indulged her, hence the large collection now displayed in her room.

'Grandpapa gave me this one,' Lisette told Rosie, taking a small, beaded Juliet cap off one of the lower shelves. 'He found it in a trunk in the attic and he said that it once belonged to my Grandmama Laure. It's too big for me now, but Grandpapa said I'd grow into it.'

'It's charming,' Rosie said. 'And obviously very, very old, so you must treat it gently.'

'Yes, I will,' Lisette answered, placed the cap back with care, and at last removed her new hat which Rosie had given her. She put this next to the Juliet cap, and reached for a beige wool hood. Proceeding to tie this under her chin, she then added a circle of brown fur, worn like a wreath around her head. 'This is my other new one, *Tante* Rosie. Can you guess who gave it to me?'

Rosie cocked her head on one side, and pretended to think hard, at the same time adopting a puzzled air. 'Well, let me see . . . it reminds me of . . . Cossacks . . . no, of the Boyars of Russia. Ah, that's a clue, isn't it? Did Kyra give it to you?'

'Yes, she did. You're very clever, *Tante* Rosie.'

'Now come along, darling, let's take this off,' Rosie coaxed, untying the hood as she spoke. 'And Yvonne can brush your hair again before we go downstairs.'

Lisette nodded, and then, as she spotted her mother entering the bedroom next door, she grabbed her new hat off the shelf and ran to show it to her.

'It's adorable,' Collie was saying, as Rosie and Yvonne followed Lisette into the bedroom. 'Now, please go and brush your hair.' She gave Rosie a loving glance. 'You're so sweet, always remembering to bring a hat for her.'

'It's my pleasure. The only thing is, she's grown so used to getting one, it's not a surprise for her any more,' Rosie murmured in a low voice.

Colette nodded. 'I know. We all spoil her when it comes to the hats, but she's such a good little girl, so obedient and loving and never any trouble to me.'

'Like Yvonne, she's really shot up,' Rosie remarked. 'She looks so much older than five. More like seven or eight.'

'It's not only her height and her grown-up manner, but also her intelligence,' Collie explained. 'She's smart, very bright really, and doing so well at school, far outstripping the others in her class. And she's fearless you know: nothing fazes her.'

'Just like her mother,' Rosie said.

'Oh, I don't know about that. I haven't been doing very well lately, have I?'

The smile slipped off Rosie's face. 'Are you feeling sick, Collie?' she asked, going to her sister-in-law, looking at her with sudden concern, putting an arm around her.

'I'm all right. Really, I am. And I'm feeling so much better in certain ways. But I tire quickly, and I haven't the strength to go back to work.'

'Don't even think about that right now. You can always open the silver gallery next spring. In any case, the tourist season is over, and the château's closed to the public until April.'

'Yes, what you say is true, it's just that . . . well, I

miss it. You know how much I love antique silver, how much I've enjoyed dealing in it over the years.'

'Yes, I do. I met Johnny Fortune, the singer, when I was in Hollywood with Nell. We went to his house for dinner, and he has a wonderful collection. There were two Paul Storr dessert stands you would have gone crazy over.'

'I'm ready, *Maman*,' Lisette announced, running out of the bathroom, where Yvonne had been brushing her hair.

'Come along, I'm sure Grandpapa is waiting for us,' Colette said, ushering her daughter out of the room. Turning to Rosie she said, 'Well, you know that Paul Storr is my favourite English silversmith . . . what were the dessert stands like?'

As they went down the grand staircase, Rosie told her about them, and about the rest of Johnny Fortune's extraordinary collection.

TWENTY

'What happened between your father and Kyra? Did they quarrel?' Rosie asked, drawing Collie away from Lisette and Yvonne.

'Quarrel is perhaps too strong a word,' Collie said, as they moved towards the fireplace in the small family sitting room. They were alone, except for the girls, who now went and seated themselves in front of the television set at the far end of the room.

Collie continued quietly, after a moment's thought, 'I think *disagreement* might be a better word to use. Why do you ask? Did Father say something to you earlier?'

'I asked him how she was, and he was a bit abrupt with me. He told me she was away, and to be honest, Collie, he didn't *really* seem to know if she would be coming back for Christmas or not.'

'I hope she is. Father's always happier when she's around . . .'

'What's the problem between them?' Rosie probed.

'I'm honestly not sure. Unless it's to do with . . . *Alexandre*.' Collie had dropped her voice, said the name in a whisper.

The two women gave each other knowing looks. Nothing more was said for a few seconds, until Collie drew closer to Rosie and murmured *sotto voce*, 'There're *always* problems about Alexandre. But neither of them actually confided in me, so I truly can't enlighten you. Very frankly, I wish they'd get married, Rosie. Kyra loves Father, loves him a lot, you know that as well as I do. I've been encouraging the idea for months – promoting marriage – and I really thought I'd got him to the point of proposing to her.'

'You can lead a horse to water but you can't make it drink, to fall back on a cliché,' Rosie said. 'And *I* wish they'd get married too.'

'*Who?* Who do you wish would get married?' Guy asked from the doorway.

Knowing how jealous he was of Kyra, and not wanting to inflame him, Rosie glanced over her shoulder, and said swiftly, 'Kevin and Nell. They're involved, and have been for the past year. I was just saying to Collie that I hope they'll marry.'

'Do you really! *That* would certainly prove to be an interesting union, the heiress and the cop,' Guy said with a cold laugh, and walked over to a console table where a tray of drinks was kept. Lifting the bottle of white wine out of the ice bucket, he poured himself a glass.

Rosie watched him surreptitiously, thinking that he looked tired, and there were new lines around his eyes, deep scores down each side of his face, running from his nose to his mouth, and touches of grey in his black hair. Although he was only thirty-six he looked older; yet, for all that, he was still a handsome man, and there was not an ounce of spare fat on his tall, athletic frame.

It was obvious to her that he kept himself in good shape, as he always had, in fact – at least where his body was concerned. She knew that mentally he was confused and lost, and emotionally adrift. To her he was the eternal little boy, the Peter Pan who had never grown up, indulged by everyone. His growth had been stunted. Because he had never had to fend for himself, he had never developed any inner resources; he therefore had nothing to draw on or fall back on in times of trouble or difficulty.

Yes, he *was* childish and spoilt; he was also lazy, did not want to work for a living, or help his father to run Montfleurie, which was a big job for one man. She had long thought it unfortunate that his mother had left him her money in a trust fund; because he had a small income of his own, he was enabled to do as he wished. What he had done was drop out. And he had been taken in by Eastern religion, renowned as a lure for the weak and the lost.

Gavin had always said Guy was out of sync, and that was true. He was like a left-over from the sixties, out of step with the times; out of step with what was required of a man in the problematical nineties, a period of dramatic changes and trouble in the world.

Walking towards the fireplace, Guy raised his glass to the two women. '*Santé.*'

'*Santé,*' Rosie responded.

Collie did not bother to answer him. Instead she lowered herself into a chair near the fireplace, put her glass on a small table before holding her hands out to the flames.

'Are you cold?' Rosie asked. 'Shall I run up and get you a shawl?'

'No, no, I'm fine, thank you, Rosie.'

'Ah, so you're all here already,' Henri said as he came striding into the sitting room and headed for the console, where he poured himself a straight Scotch. Taking a quick sip, he savoured it, then joined the others grouped around the fireplace.

Looking across at his father, who had propped himself against the mantelpiece, Guy said, 'But that's not quite true, Father. We're *not* all here. Kyra is missing. *For once.*'

There was dead silence.

Neither Rosie nor Collie dared to say a word, and they avoided looking at each other. Rosie cringed inside, and held her breath, waiting for the explosion.

But it did not come. Henri pointedly ignored his son, not deigning to comment, and merely took another sip of his drink.

'So where *is* the beautiful Kyra?' Guy went on, the same acerbic edge to his voice. 'I had begun to think she was a permanent fixture in this house.'

Another silence followed before Henri finally spoke. 'Kyra had to go to Strasbourg. To see her sister. Anastasia has not been well.'

'What are you going to do about her?' Guy asked, his black eyes pinned on his father intently.

'I don't understand . . . what do you mean?' Henri's voice hardened slightly, and the look he gave his son held a warning.

Either Guy did not see this, or he wilfully chose to ignore it. He said, 'You know very well what I mean, Father. Are you going to *marry* the lady?'

'I don't believe that is any of your business!' Henri exclaimed, the gleam in his eye suddenly irate.

'Oh, but it is,' Guy retorted, and smiled.

'Now look here, Guy, I won't –'

'Father, just *listen* to me for a moment,' Guy cut in. This was so rudely said that Rosie gasped.

Collie sat back in the chair and gaped at her brother. She was also horrified by his behaviour, knowing that their father, who was a stickler about manners, was affronted. Why doesn't Guy see this? she asked herself, baffled by his stupidity, his denseness.

Undeterred, Guy foolishly pressed on: 'She's young, Madame Kyra Arnaud, only thirty-five, and therefore still able to bear children. *Presumably*. It's unlikely that I will ever have any.' A smirk glanced across his mouth as he threw a look at Rosie, and continued, 'Inasmuch as my wife and I have been estranged for years. Oh, but do let me correct myself – it is unlikely that I will have any *legitimate* children, given the circumstances. And since that's the case, I would have thought you would want to ensure the continuation of the de Montfleurie line by marrying again and begetting another son. Hopefully it *would* be a son.'

Henri was furious. 'Really, Guy, you are out of order and quite preposterous! This is neither the time nor the place for such a discussion!' Despite his anger, the count spoke in a steady voice and was in absolute control of himself. 'Furthermore, as I said a moment ago, what *I* do is none of *your* business,' he finished icily.

Blithely unaware of his own rashness, Guy plunged on. 'Oh but it is, Father. If I die childless, the de Montfleurie line will become extinct.'

'Not exactly!' Collie cried angrily, rousing herself, sitting up straighter in the chair, glaring at her brother. 'Have you suddenly forgotten your little sister? Under French law, I can inherit, as indeed can my child.'

'I'm not dead yet!' Henri snapped, appalled at what he was hearing, and he downed his Scotch in a gulp. Abruptly turning on his heels, he marched across the floor to pour himself another, larger one, seething inside.

In an effort to break the tension in the room, and to change the subject as quickly as possible, Rosie said, to no one in particular, 'I'm going to be working in France this coming year.'

Instantly catching on, Collie exclaimed, 'Oh that's wonderful, darling. What's the movie you'll be making? Or is it a play?'

'No, it's a movie. For Gavin.'

'*Naturellement*,' Guy said, and sat down in the chair opposite Collie.

Paying no attention whatsoever to her brother, Collie asked Rosie, 'What's the movie about? Do tell us.'

'Napoleon,' Rosie answered. 'Gavin's going –'

'*Mon Dieu!* What a nerve! An *American* making a film about *Napoleon*. That's perfectly ridiculous.

Absurd. How dare he! And don't tell me he's thinking of playing the emperor himself?'

'Of course he is,' Rosie said quietly. She was already annoyed with Guy for the way he had spoken to his father; now his disdainful tone and bitter manner further irritated her. But at the same time she was relieved she had managed to divert him from the subject of Kyra, and so wisely she held her tongue.

Guy began to chuckle. 'At least Gavin Ambrose has *one* thing in common with Napoleon.'

When no one bothered to ask what this was, Guy felt impelled to explain: 'It's shortness of stature. Napoleon was a small man, and so is the great megastar.' Once again he laughed, apparently amused by this.

No one else was. Collie said in a cold little voice, 'Napoleon was five foot six, that's not so short, and it was certainly average height in those days. We've only had giant-sized men in the twentieth century.'

'Gavin happens to be five feet nine,' Rosie could not help pointing out.

'*You* would know *that*,' Guy retorted, picked up his wine glass and took a long swallow.

Having calmed himself, Henri returned to the fireside. He paid scant attention to his son, sat down next to Rosie on the sofa, and said, 'It's good to know that you won't be travelling so much next year, my dear. When does filming start?'

'Not for a good six months or so. There's a lot of preproduction to be done first, a lot of planning. But I'll start to work immediately after the New Year, doing my research for the costumes. Actually, I've already started.'

'Where will you be filming?' Collie asked, also glad that Rosie and she had successfully deflected Guy away from his discussion about the extinction of the Montfleurie line. This was not a new subject with him of late; he seemed preoccupied with it, if not indeed obsessed.

'We'll start the movie in Paris,' Rosie told Collie. 'At the studios, and also, hopefully, at Malmaison. If the Government gives permission, of course, and we'll shoot in other parts of France. Actually, I'm waiting for the script. I'll know more, once I've read it.'

'Rather a big undertaking, even for the great Gavin Ambrose, isn't it?' Guy asked in his usual sarcastic way.

'Not at all.' Rosie's voice was strong, assured. 'Gavin is a brilliant film-maker, as well as being one of the greatest screen actors alive today. He can tackle *anything* and succeed, I'm absolutely certain of that. But as it so happens he's not making Napoleon's *life*, merely a segment of it.'

'Oh really, which part?' Henri asked with genuine interest.

'The period just before and after he was crowned emperor.'

'You mean crowned himself emperor, Rosie,' Guy interjected.

'It was the will of the French *people*,' Collie declared, and threw Guy a scathing look. It seemed to her that her brother was determined to upset her father tonight, and she could not understand why. Actually, he was managing to upset them all, whether he intended this or not.

'Don't be such a fool, Collie,' Guy shot back, and stood up, strode across the room. As he proceeded to refill his glass, he announced, 'Napoleon was a tyrant, no better than Stalin or Hitler.'

Turning to Rosie, Henri explained in a reflective, rather scholarly tone, 'There are two schools of thought about Napoleon Bonaparte, Rosie. Some of us love, respect and admire him, and admire his achievements, think of him as the great saviour of France at a time when she might well have gone down. Others abhor him, somewhat irrationally in my opinion, and consider him to have been a despot and a war-monger. But if one studies the history of that period very carefully, one sees that, for the most part, he did nothing but good for France and the French.'

'You call all those wars *good*!' Guy interrupted, his tone still argumentative.

'They were mostly *defensive* wars,' Henri remarked evenly, holding in check his anger with his son. 'Wars Napoleon had to fight to make France safe.'

'That's not so,' Guy began, 'Napoleon –'

'Oh, but I am correct,' Henri said calmly, cutting across his son, sweeping his arguments aside. 'Please go to the library and dig out one of the many history books, if you don't believe me. You've obviously forgotten your school lessons.' Glancing again at Rosie, the count proceeded to elucidate further. 'England was at France's throat during that period in history, and so was most of Continental Europe. Napoleon had little choice *but* to go to war, in order to defend France from invasion. And from defeat, I might add.'

'Father is quite an expert on Napoleon,' Collie said, jumping into the conversation before Guy could say anything more. 'One of our great ancestors, Jean-Manuel de Montfleurie, fought with Napoleon in the Egyptian campaign, and for his great courage Napoleon made him a brigadier-general. Later Jean-Manuel, who was one of the younger sons of the house, was promoted to full general by Napoleon, after the battle of Austerlitz.'

'How interesting,' Rosie said. 'I never knew.'

Henri smiled at her. 'But why would you know, my dear? We don't go around talking about our ancestors, and we haven't exactly given you a history lesson on the family.' He laughed, and so did she, and there was a lessening of the tension in the room, and the atmosphere became lighter, calmer.

The count continued talking to Rosie. 'Somewhere, tucked away in that vast library of ours, there is a whole collection of books on Napoleon and on the Empire period of French history. Tomorrow, I will ask Marcel to bring a ladder from the barn and get the books down for you. You'll find them interesting, I'm sure, and perhaps they will prove useful to you – for your costume designs.'

'Thank you, Henri, I'd really appreciate that,' Rosie murmured, smiling at him. 'And they certainly would help me.'

'Father,' Guy said. 'I wish to ask you something.'

'Yes?' Henri looked across at his son, who was seated in a chair near the fire.

'Is Kyra's child yours? Is Alexandre Arnaud really *your* son?'

Rosie froze on the sofa. She felt the count stiffen next to her, and stifle a gasp. She could not look at him. Her courage failed her.

Collie was equally stunned, and she held herself perfectly still, hardly daring to breathe. She stared into the flames, waiting, her throat dry with apprehension. Her brother had gone too far tonight.

Henri opened his mouth and closed it again, simply stared at Guy in total silence. The shocked expression on his face spoke volumes. Worriedly he glanced down the room, saw at once that Lisette and Yvonne were absorbed in a game show on television, and for once he was glad they were staring, mesmerized, at the set. He experienced a flicker of profound relief that they had not heard Guy's words.

Placing his glass on an end table, Henri de Montfleurie pushed himself to his feet and walked over to Guy, who appeared to shrink back in the chair as his father approached.

Henri's face was deathly pale, his dark eyes blazing with anger. 'Stand up,' he ordered as he drew to a standstill in front of the chair.

Guy did so nervously.

Henri took a step forward and looked directly into his son's face. His eyes were steely, his voice hard and very low: 'Listen to me, and listen to me very carefully. Never, ever again, are you to impugn the honour and reputation of a woman in this house, whether it's Kyra Arnaud you are speaking of, or any other woman. Never, ever again, are you to speak of adult matters when there are children present. And never, ever again, are you to attempt to make trouble in this family. If you cannot abide by these rules, which are actually matters of common courtesy and good manners, then you can leave this house once and for all. And right now. I will not tolerate your behaviour any longer. You were born an aristocrat, born a gentleman. Kindly act like one, or get out.'

'But Father, *please* . . . I didn't mean to upset you, or anyone else. I'm not trying to make trouble, I'm merely having a discussion with you. Look, I simply want to ensure the future of the de Montfleurie line, in case anything ever happens to me. Which it well might, all the travelling abroad I do. I was only trying to help you –'

Guy stopped at the sound of sharp knocking on the door. All eyes swung to it.

As it opened slowly Gaston's face appeared, and he stepped into the sitting room.

Inclining his head slightly, he said, '*Monsieur le comte . . . le dîner est servi.*'

'*Merci*, Gaston,' Henri responded. 'We'll be right in.'

TWENTY-ONE

Kyra Arnaud came back to the Loire Valley a week later.

It was Rosie who discovered her presence, quite by accident. She had gone to the village to do some errands for Collie early on Friday morning, and was driving back to Montfleurie when she saw Kyra standing on the terrace of her house.

Although the small, grey-stone manor was set well back from the road, it stood on a slight rise and was therefore entirely visible through the copse of trees partially encircling it. Also, Kyra had naturally red hair, a very bright auburn cascade that was quite unmistakable. The woman on the terrace had to be Kyra, there was no question in Rosie's mind about her identity. The hair gave her away.

She drove on without stopping, not wishing to intrude on Kyra, to stop by at the house unannounced, and the minute she got back to the château she ran upstairs to find Collie.

Bundled up in a black sweater, grey trousers and black blazer, the latter was seated at her desk near the fireplace, working on cards for Christmas gifts.

She raised her eyes when the door flew open, and her face lit up at the sight of Rosie.

'You've been quick! Did you manage to find the glue and the ribbon?' she asked.

Rosie nodded. 'I also found something else – or, rather, someone else.'

Looking puzzled, Collie asked, 'Who?'

'*Kyra Arnaud*. She's back!'

'Did you run into her in the village?'

'No, I didn't. I saw her on the terrace of her house as I was driving back here.'

'Are you sure it was her? She does have a new housekeeper, you know, and the housekeeper has a daughter who lives there too.'

'Oh it was Kyra all right,' Rosie answered quickly, taking off her loden cape, laying it on a chair, walking over to the fireplace, standing with her back to it. 'There's no mistaking her. All that flaming red hair.' Rosie looked across at Collie and grinned. 'Unless, of course, the housekeeper and her daughter also have the same auburn hair.'

'No, they don't,' Collie replied. 'So it has to be Kyra. I wonder if Father knows that she's come back?'

Rosie shrugged, then shook her head. 'I doubt it. If they were squabbling when she left, why would they be friendly now?'

'They could have made up on the phone,' Collie pointed out. 'How would we know? Obviously, he wouldn't discuss it with us, and I haven't dared mention her name since last Friday.'

'Neither have I, it would be like a red rag to a bull.

I'm not surprised Guy skedaddled on Saturday. He really put his foot in it this time.'

'*Both* feet you mean.' Collie sighed heavily. 'I still haven't recovered, not really, and I know you haven't. I'm even surprised that Father's behaving with such equanimity . . .' She smiled suddenly at Rosie, and added, 'On the other hand, he's always in a good mood when you're here. As for my brother, he has to be the most stupid person on this planet. I still shudder when I think of what he said.'

'I know. But listen, Collie darling, let's go over and see Kyra, talk to her, see if we can't put matters right between your father and her. Negotiate a reconciliation, so to speak.'

'I'm not sure –' Collie stopped, hesitating for a moment. 'She might resent the interference, she can be rather touchy, you know. Temperamental. More to the point, Father might be annoyed if we get in the middle of his business.'

'When I was here in August you told me you couldn't get over how much little Alexandre resembled Lisette,' Rosie remarked. 'I'd noticed that myself, and I was pretty certain that he was a Montfleurie.'

'You'd have to be blind not to see that! So, what are you getting at?' Collie raised a brow.

'Your father appears to care for Kyra, and care for her a great deal, I might add. You and I both think that Alexandre's his son, and now that Jacques Arnaud has divorced Kyra there seems to be no earthly reason why they can't marry. Am I correct?'

'Yes. And I've been promoting marriage for a long time. I told you that the other day.'

'Okay, so what's the . . . the . . . *impediment*?'

Collie shook her head. 'I've absolutely no idea.'

'Could it be that your father doesn't want to marry her?'

'I'm not certain, honestly I'm not, Rosie.'

'Fair enough. Do you think that maybe Kyra herself is the impediment? That perhaps she doesn't want to marry Henri?'

Collie pursed her lips and remained silent, thinking and staring into space for a few seconds. 'I just don't know.' She sighed. 'My father is much older than she is, of course.'

'Not *that* much older. He's sixty-three, and she's thirty-five. Not bad really, and he looks young, acts young, is very fit and energetic.'

'Everything you say is true, Rosie. However, I'm not sure I understand what you're getting at.'

'Listen, Collie, you and I are attempting to ascertain what's preventing them from marrying. Also, for days we've been trying to guess what they had a disagreement about, and we're not coming up with any answers. That's because we *can't*. We're not a party to their conversations, we're not involved with them in their involvement with each other.'

'What you're saying is that we're not a couple of flies on the bedroom wall.'

'That's right. So the only way we'll know what this is all about is to talk to one of the principals.'

Collie groaned.

Rosie said: 'We can't talk to your father. *I* wouldn't dare . . . at least I don't think I would. Can *you* talk to him?'

'Not on your life. Oh no, not me!'

'Okay, so there's only one thing for it, we've got to talk to Kyra, the other principal in the affair.' Rosie paused, stared at Collie. 'Why are you looking at me like that? I've always thought that Kyra was quite approachable, very friendly in fact. And in any case, you and she have always been good friends, haven't you?'

'Yes.'

'So why the peculiar look?'

'I suppose I'm a bit shy about talking to her about my *father*. I feel a little awkward, discussing their relationship, his love life, his *sex* life, for Heaven's sake.'

'That's understandable, I guess. But she's the only person who can enlighten us, except for Henri, and we've both ruled him out.'

Collie nodded, remained silent.

Rosie walked over to the window, stood looking out towards the Cher river, her eyes thoughtful. After a moment or two she swung around and returned to the fireplace. Leaning against the antique desk, she said to Collie, 'I'll talk to her. But would you come with me? Keep me company?'

'Of course!' Collie exclaimed. 'But we must telephone her first. To arrange a rendezvous.'

'I wasn't intending to barge in on her unannounced,' Rosie said with a faint smile. 'You can call her and make a date, and then we'll drive over. The sooner the better. Why not this afternoon?'

'Why not indeed!' Without wasting any more time, Collie picked up the phone and dialled.

TWENTY-TWO

There was something quite majestic about Kyra
Arnaud, Rosie decided, realizing this was the most
appropriate word to describe her bearing and her
manner.

There was a regality about the Russian woman
which manifested itself in the proud tilt of her head,
the straightness of her back, and the way she moved.
Kyra was slender but taller than average, around five
foot nine, and, although she was not beautiful in the
classical sense, her face was so arresting most people
usually glanced at her twice, completely taken in by
its elegance and distinction.

She had a narrow face, with high, slanted cheekbones, a smooth, rather broad brow, thinly arched
brows above large eyes which were grey, luminous
and set wide apart.

It was her hair, of course, which was her most
striking feature – thick, luxuriant and bright auburn
in colour: naturally curly, today she wore it loose,
and it spread out around her face like a fiery halo.
Dressed in an oversized sweater-tunic knitted in a
mixture of autumnal colours, brown leggings and

245

matching suede boots, she moved around the coffee table in her drawing room with infinite grace and self-confidence, the epitome of an assured, sophisticated woman.

It was Saturday afternoon, and Kyra was serving hot lemon tea to Rosie and Collie, who had arrived just a short while before. As she poured the tea into tall glasses contained in silver filigree holders, she chatted to them about her sister Anastasia who had been ill.

'She had an appendicectomy,' Kyra explained. 'But thank God she is now all right. When she first came out of the hospital she wasn't feeling too well, and that's why I went to visit her.'

'So Father said,' Collie murmured, her expression sympathetic. 'I'm so glad she's better now.'

'So am I.'

Kyra and Collie continued to chat for a few minutes about Anastasia and her family, and about Olga, Kyra's other sister, who had recently moved to New York.

Rosie sat back in the chair; she was only half listening to them, trying to think of a way to broach the subject of Henri, which was the reason they had come here. Collie had made the date yesterday, but had not given a reason for their wish to see her; nor, apparently, had Kyra asked for one.

Last night, Rosie had pointed out to Collie that, even though they were going to ask Kyra what had gone wrong in her relationship with Henri, she might not tell them the truth. Collie had disagreed, explaining that Kyra was scrupulously honest, frequently quite blunt, and would indeed tell them the truth.

The music playing softly in the background was a Rachmaninov concerto, one she was familiar with, and it created a soothing mood in the sun-filled room. The latter was of medium size, with French windows opening onto the terrace and the garden. Somewhat haphazardly decorated with a mixture of French and English antiques, flea-market finds, odd bits and pieces Kyra had picked up along the way, it had a certain kind of bohemian charm, and it was a comfortable room despite its off-beat appearance.

Rosie had always liked Kyra Arnaud, and she found this feeling being reinforced at this moment as the woman spoke lovingly about her two sisters. The three of them were the daughters of a Russian diplomat who had defected to the West in 1971, when Kyra was fifteen years old. Her father had been an attaché at the Russian Embassy in Washington when he had asked for political asylum for himself, his wife, and three young daughters, which the United States had granted. The US Government had immediately placed them in a protection programme, and they had gone to live in the Midwest under an assumed name.

After her father's death from natural causes in 1976, Kyra, her two sisters and her mother had come to live in France, where their mother had relatives. At the age of twenty-seven Kyra had married Jacques Arnaud, the noted modern impressionist painter, but the union had foundered two years later and she had soon vacated Paris for the Loire, buying the old stone manor house in 1986.

Some of Kyra's story Rosie had learned from Collie, the rest of it from Kyra herself, and although Rosie had not spent much time with the Russian woman, she had never felt anything but warmth for her.

'Anyway, I came back here on Thursday afternoon,' Kyra was saying as Rosie roused herself from her thoughts, and sat up a little straighter in her chair, focusing on her.

Kyra went on hesitantly, 'I'm not sure how long I will be staying. But certainly it won't be for long.'

'Why not?' Collie exclaimed in surprise, her face full of questions.

Kyra did not answer.

Rosie said, 'Do you mean you won't be in the Loire for Christmas?'

'That's correct,' Kyra responded. 'There's not much here for me, or for Alexandre either. I'm better off going back to Strasbourg, to be with my sister and her family. My mother will be there and Olga is going to come over from New York.'

'You say there's nothing here for you at Christmas, but that's not true,' Collie said, leaning forward, putting her hand on Kyra's arm affectionately. 'You could come to us. The same way you've been coming to us for the past few years.'

Kyra shook her head. 'I don't think so.'

There was a little silence.

Rosie decided to plunge in. 'Is there a problem, Kyra? I mean between you and Henri?'

Again, the strained silence.

Rosie pressed, 'Is that why you're *really* going back to Strasbourg?'

'More or less,' Kyra finally admitted with a weak smile.

'Can we help to sort it out?' Rosie asked.

Kyra shook her head.

Collie said, 'That's the reason we wanted to see you. Rosie and I decided that there was something wrong, and that we'd be the United Nations negotiators, so to speak. We wanted to try and bring about a truce between you and Father. We both sensed something was amiss, and yet we know you care deeply for each other.'

'That's true, we do, but I don't think there's anything to be done.'

'Why not?' Rosie pinned her eyes on her. 'When you love someone and he loves you, there's always a way to work things out.'

'Rosie's correct,' Collie interjected. 'Father cares for you, *loves* you, Kyra, I just know that. In fact, I thought I'd got him to the point of proposing. Now I realize I was wrong, and it's obvious my efforts went to waste.'

'Not really.' Kyra said this softly, looking across at Collie, her eyes filled with absolute candour. 'Your father did propose . . . sort of . . .'

Collie stared at her. 'What does that mean *exactly*?'

'He said he thought we ought to consider making our relationship permanent, but he didn't actually get down on his knees and propose to me in the traditional way, nor did he actually use the word *marriage*.'

'But you knew what he meant, surely?' Collie murmured.

'Of course, I'm not trying to split hairs. But when I didn't say *yes* immediately, or jump at the idea, he backed off. He muttered something about being too old for me, that twenty-eight years was too big a difference between us, and that it had been foolish of him to think I would want to attach myself to an old man. He hurried out of this room, still muttering under his breath that he was an old fool.'

'You should have gone after him, Kyra,' Rosie admonished softly. 'And told him that you would marry him, that the age difference didn't matter. Weren't those the answers he was looking for?'

'I think so, now that I look back.' Kyra seemed suddenly morose and she bit her lip.

'When did this actually happen?' Collie asked.

'Just a short while before I went to Strasbourg.'

'And that's the reason you went there, isn't it?' Rosie said.

'*Partly*. Anastasia *did* want me to be with her, of course, but my mother was there anyway. Still, it was a good excuse to leave here. I felt I had to be on my own, to think, and I wanted to put distance between myself and Henri.'

'But why didn't you phone Father from Strasbourg? Why didn't you tell him you wanted to marry him?'

Kyra glanced at Collie and shook her head. Her face became closed, emotionless, and she leaned back on the sofa, closing her eyes for a moment or two, breathing deeply. And then she rose and walked across the floor to the window, where she stood looking out at her garden, her eyes suddenly misty. She saw a blur of trees through her tears. They were leafless and stark and the grass was frost-bitten, the plants in the borders dried out. Her garden in winter always looked bereft. That was how she felt. Bereft, grieving and sad. She thought of Henri de Mont-fleurie and her throat closed; her emotions were too near the surface these days. She knew that Henri was suffering just as much as she was, because they *did* love each other, but there was nothing she could do. She could not help him. Or help herself.

A deep sigh trickled through her and she wiped the tears from her face with the tips of her fingers and then turned, came back to the fireplace where Collie and Rosie were sitting. 'I didn't phone him because I don't want to marry Henri,' she lied.

Collie was so taken aback she was speechless for a second. Then she found her voice and cried, 'I find that very hard to believe, Kyra! *Very hard*. You love Father, you've admitted that much.'

'Yes,' Kyra said, 'I *do* love him. But sometimes love alone is not enough to overcome great obstacles.'

'Are you referring to the age difference?' Rosie said. 'No.'

'Well then, is there some sort of . . . *impediment* . . . a reason why you can't marry Henri de Montfleurie?' Rosie asked, looking at Kyra intently.

'If you mean legally, no there isn't. I am divorced from Jacques.'

'But there *is* an impediment,' Rosie exclaimed, eyeing her closely. 'At least, that's what you've just implied.'

Kyra shook her head, as if denying something to herself, and then she pushed herself up onto her feet and walked over to the window once more. But she did not pause to look out as she had before; instead she walked back towards the fireplace, then returned to the window. She began to pace up and down in this manner, her face perfectly still, calm almost, but there was a look of great agitation in her grey eyes.

At last she stopped and stood staring at Collie and Rosie. She took a deep breath and said rapidly, in staccato bursts, 'All right, I'll tell you the truth. I do want to marry Henri. But I can't. I'm afraid of Guy. There is something he knows about me. A secret. If I marry Henri he will tell him. In order to hurt him. I couldn't bear that. So I must go away.'

Collie and Rosie were both on the edge of their seats, staring back at her.

Collie said urgently, 'What kind of secret? What is it that Guy knows about you, Kyra?'

Kyra wanted to confide in them, but she could not. She had lost her nerve.

TWENTY-THREE

Two pairs of eyes, one set blue, the other green, were riveted on her in the most disconcerting way, and Kyra flinched under their fixed and intense scrutiny.

For a brief moment she stared back at Collie and Rosie, and then she swung around and walked over to the fireplace, where she stood looking down into its bright flames, her hand resting on the mantelpiece.

Her mind was floundering now; she could not understand why she had ever been foolish enough to mention her secret to them. It would have been far better not to have said a word; or to have thought up a bunch of lies; anything would have been better than admitting that there was an impediment, as Rosie called it.

'Your secret can't be all *that* bad,' Rosie said.

Startled, Kyra almost jumped out of her skin, and then, brought out of her reverie by Rosie's voice, she tried to gather her swimming senses, to pull herself together.

After a moment she turned, very slowly, and looked across at Rosie, who was seated on the sofa.

The two women exchanged a long look, and then Kyra said, in a low voice, 'It *is* bad.'

'Please tell us what it is that Guy knows about you, Kyra,' Collie implored. 'Nothing you could say will change the way we feel about you. Rosie and I like you, care about you, and I know that my father *loves* you.'

Kyra was silent, thinking hard, wondering what to do, and, more importantly, what to say to them. *Lies.* That was the answer. She must tell them a lot of lies; she certainly couldn't tell them the truth.

Rosie leaned forward, her elbows on her knees. 'The family is aware that Guy is a troublemaker. Nobody pays too much attention to him, or to what he says, you know.'

'I think Henri would pay attention to this particular thing,' Kyra responded swiftly.

'In any case, how does *Guy* know about this secret of yours?' Collie shook her head. 'I mean, how did he find out?'

'He is part of it,' Kyra said, and could have instantly bitten off her tongue. She had already said far too much, and she shrank back against the stone fireplace, endeavouring to still her limbs, which had begun to shake.

Rosie was fully aware that Kyra was dreadfully upset, and she said in the gentlest voice, 'If it were me, I would forestall Guy by telling Henri myself. Why don't you do that?'

'I couldn't possibly!' Kyra cried, her grey eyes flaring.

'Then why don't you take a chance with us? Collie

and I are not here to judge you, only to listen, to help if we can. And you can trust us. Why not tell *us* your secret, Kyra, test it on us, and then we'll all decide *together* what action you should take. Three minds are better than one.'

'Oh yes, that's a terrific idea,' Collie agreed, and added, 'Guy is not in Father's good graces, and he hasn't been for a long time, but surely you know that yourself. My father doesn't listen to his opinions any more. He lost respect for him years ago.'

Kyra stood by the fireplace, saying nothing, weighing their words.

'Well, we know you didn't *murder* somebody, so how bad can it be?' Rosie exclaimed. 'Come on, Kyra, confide in us, and perhaps we can help. Maybe we can find a solution to your problem.'

Kyra looked from Rosie to Collie, and then before she could stop herself she said, 'It might be upsetting to you, Rosie. You see –' and then she stopped abruptly.

Rosie gave her a hard stare. 'What do you mean?'

I'm undone, Kyra thought. I shouldn't have started this. But I've got to go on, there's no turning back. And perhaps it's for the best. Maybe it should be out in the open.

She said slowly, carefully, 'When I came to live in the Loire in 1986, one of the first people I met was your aunt, Sophie Roland, Collie. Anyway, she took me under her wing a bit, and that September, about four months after I'd met her, she introduced me to Guy. We were at the same dinner party in Monte Carlo.'

Kyra felt her mouth go dry with apprehension and she swallowed, cleared her throat, looked directly at Rosie. 'He told me that evening that you and he were estranged. Actually, he said you were separated, that you had left him, and had moved back to the States –'

'I was working on a movie in Canada,' Rosie interrupted.

'I found that out later.' Kyra seemed suddenly acutely embarrassed, and she said rapidly, 'I honestly mean this . . . I do hope what I'm going to tell you won't upset you, Rosie.'

'It won't, Kyra, really it won't, and in September of 1986 Guy and I *were* estranged. That part of his story was true.'

Kyra nodded. 'To continue, Guy asked me for my number in the Loire that night, and I gave it to him. A week later, when we were both back from the south of France, he phoned me. We began to see each other. It started out harmlessly enough, at least on my part. I was separated from Jacques, preparing to divorce, and I was lonely. I was glad to make new friends like Sophie and Guy. Also, Guy had made it clear to me that he was on his own, as he put it. I believed him, of course. Why wouldn't I? But inevitably we became entangled with each other over the next few months.'

'He never brought you to Montfleurie,' Collie murmured. 'But of course he wouldn't have dared.'

Kyra nodded. 'I understand that now, knowing how much everyone loves Rosie. But at the time I thought it was odd, inasmuch as he had said he was a man on his own, whose wife had left him. When I mentioned this, he explained that his father was rather old-fashioned, and that he couldn't possibly take me to the château until he had sorted out his marital mess.'

Rosie and Collie exchanged knowing looks but made no comment.

Kyra glanced at them, then averted her eyes, gazed down the length of the room. After a moment or two, she swallowed and said, 'We became involved and it got a bit complicated –'

'You slept with him,' Rosie said in an even voice. 'That's what you're trying so hard to say, isn't it, Kyra? You had an affair with Guy.'

Kyra bit her lip. 'Yes. But it was short-lived, and we only slept with each other a couple of times.'

A small puzzled frown knitted Rosie's brows. 'Is *that* the big secret?'

'Yes.'

Collie began to chuckle. 'I don't think that's such a terrible thing,' she said. 'I'm sure my father won't be perturbed by it.'

'Yes, he will,' Kyra insisted.

'Well, I'm not and I was married to Guy. *Am* married to him, if only in name,' Rosie pointed out, smiling at Kyra encouragingly, wanting to make her feel better. 'And how long did the affair last?' she asked, although she was not particularly interested in the answer.

'Not long, about three months altogether. Guy soon lost interest in me, once we'd . . . made love. He went off to India, as you both know.'

'And he only came back once for a week, was gone

257

for two years,' Collie remarked. 'And in that time you met my father.'

'Yes. Our relationship started out as a very nice friendship, if you remember, Collie. We shared a lot of common interests, got on so well together, and the friendship grew, and changed, became terribly important to us both, and suddenly we realized we had fallen in love with each other. I knew then that I should have told him about Guy right from the start, but I hadn't, and frankly, I didn't have the courage to say anything once we'd become so involved. I suppose I was afraid of losing him.'

'You can tell him now. *Today*. And I absolutely guarantee that you won't lose him, Kyra,' Collie assured her. 'I know my father, and he is intelligent, compassionate and understanding. He's a sophisticated man, who's seen a lot, done a lot, and he has great wisdom and humanity. Truly, he *will* understand. And after all, you didn't know Father when you met Guy.'

'I don't know what to do . . . I'm afraid . . .' Kyra stared at Collie and shook her head, looking helpless.

Rosie murmured thoughtfully, 'You're assuming Guy will tell his father about this old relationship once you marry Henri, but he might not.'

'Oh come on, Rosie, I bet you he will!' Collie cried heatedly. 'I know my brother. He loves to stir. So don't give him the benefit of the doubt. *Please*.'

'Collie is right, Rosie,' Kyra told her. 'You see, although Guy dropped *me*, when he came back from India and found out about Henri he started to pursue me again. That's the way he is, and you must know that, since you were married to him. Guy always wants what he can't have, and the grass is always greener at the other side of the street. Perhaps that's why he's such a terrible womanizer. He's easily and quickly bored, has to constantly move on.'

Rosie nodded her agreement. 'Oh I've come to realize that now. And I think that's what happened when we were first married. Within a year he was tired of me, wanted to sleep with other women. I needed to continue my career, because I loved it, but also because we needed the money. Anyway, my being away so much gave him ample opportunity to play around.'

'I'm afraid so.' Kyra shook her head. 'Guy is strange, unfathomable in so many ways. But I do know this, he loves the chase more than the conquest, and therefore he'll never be happy with one woman.'

'All right,' Collie said firmly. 'Let's move on. We're all agreed that Guy *will* tell Father, just to be spiteful – after all that's his nature. So, Kyra, you must beat him to it.'

'What do you mean?'

'You have to go to Father and tell him yourself. What do you have to lose? You've already given my father up because of your secret.'

'That's true.'

'Then let's go!' Collie stood up.

'Come on, Kyra, get your coat!' Rosie exclaimed.

'*Now?* You want me to tell him *now*?'

'Oh yes, let's get it over with. Rosie and I will be there to give you moral support,' Collie said.

'I don't want to run into Guy,' Kyra muttered.

'He's not at Montfleurie. There was a bit of an altercation last week and he went to Paris,' Collie explained.

Rosie also stood up. 'We'll drive you over to Montfleurie with us, and drive you back. So let's do this before you have a change of heart, or lose your nerve.'

They hurried her out of the sitting room, and, although she was protesting, her protestations were weak.

The three women ran into Henri de Montfleurie in the grand entrance hall of the château. He was startled to see Kyra with them, believing her to be in Strasbourg, but the look of surprise on his face was immediately brightened by the pleasure flooding into his eyes.

'Kyra, my dear,' he said warmly, and came to greet her, taking hold of her hands, kissing her on both cheeks.

'Hello, Henri,' she said.

'Kyra wants to tell you something, Father,' Collie announced, taking command, determined to see this through. 'She wants to explain why she *really* went to Strasbourg. We'll leave you alone, and perhaps we can all have a drink later.' She focused on Kyra. 'And perhaps you'd like to stay for supper, Kyra.'

Not waiting for Kyra's response, Rosie grabbed Collie by the arm. 'I need to discuss the holiday menus with you. Come on.'

'Yes, let's do that now,' Collie said, and the two of them fled.

*

Henri led Kyra across the hall and into his study at the back of the château. Drawing her towards the fireplace, he indicated a chair, and said, 'Why don't you sit here. You look chilled to the bone, my dear, and very tired.'

Without a word she sank into the chair gratefully. He was always so kind, the kindest man she had ever known. Her eyes never left his face as he took the chair opposite her, leaned back and crossed his legs.

'Now, my dear, what's this all about? Collie and Rosie looked like a couple of genuine conspirators, and they certainly exuded an air of great excitement.'

Kyra recognized that for her there was only one way to handle the situation, and this was to tell him quickly, get it over with before she lost her nerve. And so she did exactly this, explained everything in the same way she had to Collie and Rosie, leaving nothing out, sparing no detail, even though some of the things she had to say were hard for her to articulate.

Finally coming to a close, she took a deep breath and finished, 'And so you see I ran away to Strasbourg, using Anastasia's illness as an excuse, because I knew that if I married you, Guy would tell you about our affair, just to hurt you. And I couldn't have borne that, Henri. Nor could I stand the idea that you'd think ill of me.'

'But I already knew. I've always known, Kyra darling,' Henri said gently, smiling at her. 'Guy told me four years ago, when he came back, very briefly, from India, and discovered we had a warm and loving relationship. Just before he went back there for another year he told me everything, in great detail. He couldn't resist telling me.'

Kyra was dumbfounded. 'But . . . but . . . you never said anything to me,' she stammered.

'What was the point?' Henri asked, leaning forward, reaching out, taking her hand in his. 'He told me you and he had had an affair, and I discovered I didn't care, that it didn't really matter to me. All that mattered was *you*. *Us*. A man knows when a woman truly loves him, Kyra, and I knew without a shadow of a doubt that you loved me. That was all I wanted, and all I needed.'

'I don't understand Guy . . . he's so . . . mean . . .' Her voice faltered.

'He can't bear other people to be happy,' Henri said. 'He's become a spoiler. I don't know why I say *become*. He's always been like that – jealous, envious, angry, bitter, although he has no reason to be any of those things. I've been thinking about him a lot this past week, and looking back I realize that he was always a poor specimen.' Henri sighed and shook his head sadly. 'The breeding's there but there's no character, no stamina. He's always been jealous of Collie, and he was jealous of my relationship with his mother. That's why there has always been this great rivalry in him, rivalry with me, I mean.'

'I believe you're right, Henri.' She paused, then said quietly, 'I'm sorry I caused you hurt. Please forgive me.'

'There's nothing to forgive. And I never thought badly of you.'

Kyra stared at Henri for the longest moment. 'Whatever you say, I know that I should have told you about Guy when we first met, first became friends. It was wrong of me, it placed you in a false position. And not to tell you I'd had a relationship with your son was lying . . . by omission.'

Henri de Montfleurie made no comment, sat gazing at Kyra Arnaud, studying her face. He saw her love for him reflected in her eyes, and he thought of the anguish he had suffered these past few weeks because she had left him, and he knew she had suffered too. Now the time had come to stop the pain. He loved this woman; he wanted her with him for the rest of his life. And so he rose and went to her.

Bending over her chair, he kissed the face looking up at him so yearningly.

'Will you marry me, Kyra? Will you become my wife?'

'Oh yes, Henri, yes.'

A smile struck his face, and he kissed her again before pulling her to her feet. 'Let us go and find those two wonderfully meddlesome young women, and tell them the good news.'

Rosie and Collie were in the small family sitting room, and when Henri and Kyra walked in they looked up expectantly. And they instantly knew from their smiles that everything was all right between them.

'It's settled!' Rosie cried. 'I can see it written all over your faces.'

'You're going to get married!' Collie exclaimed, beaming at them.

263

'Yes, we are, thank God!' Henri said, laughing, the tension that had ringed his face for the last few weeks finally disappearing altogether.

'He knew,' Kyra said, looking from Collie to Rosie. 'Guy told Henri about us four years ago.'

Rosie and Collie gaped at her, stunned to hear this, and Collie said angrily, 'And so all this heartache was for nothing.'

'Ssssh, darling,' Henri admonished gently. 'Don't upset yourself about Guy. He's not worth it. And I have something to tell you and Rosie. Little Alexandre is my son. Once Kyra and I are married I will adopt him legally, give him my name, make everything right and proper.'

Collie went to her father and hugged him.

Henri hugged her back. 'My darling daughter,' he murmured against her hair. 'Always thinking of me, and of my happiness.'

She looked at him and smiled. 'Rosie and I knew Alexandre was your son, Father. Even though he's only two, he looks exactly like you. He's a de Montfleurie through and through.'

TWENTY-FOUR

Tiredness overwhelmed Collie.

She felt weak all of a sudden and she put her pen down on the desk, leaned back in the chair, hoping the feeling of exhaustion would soon pass.

It was Friday morning, just five days before Christmas, and she still had so many things to do for the *fête de Noël*, the very special holiday period that meant so much to everyone at Montfleurie.

As always, Annie had everything under control, and was forever shooing her away whenever she tried to help; she wanted to pull her weight, though, needed to do so, because the meagre staff was always overburdened; the château was vast, and difficult to run. But at this moment she did not have the strength to go downstairs and join in the decorating of the château. It was a grand tradition, something she had enjoyed doing ever since she was a child; today the spirit was more than willing but unfortunately the flesh was far too weak.

Gaston and his brother Marcel, who also worked at the château, had already been busy for hours, she knew, potting the giant-sized pine tree for the hall, which everyone would help to decorate on Sunday, cutting holly branches, other evergreens, and mistletoe for vases, and making sprigs to put on the tops of the paintings in various rooms.

Wishing she felt better, and making an enormous effort, Collie pushed herself to her feet, and moved slowly across the floor towards the sofa in front of the blazing fire.

Unexpectedly, an excruciating pain, like nothing she had ever experienced, shot up her back, and she gasped out loud, gripped the edge of the sofa and doubled over. She leaned against it, waiting for the pain to pass. Eventually it began to subside, and she sat down on the sofa, and rested her head against the soft cushions, taking small gulps of air. She had never had a pain in her back like this before, and it frightened her.

Sudden panic flared. Had the cancer come back? No, it couldn't have. In August, the doctors in Paris had assured her that they had got it all, that it had been arrested, stopped in its tracks. After treatment for cancer of the uterus they had given her a clean bill of health, and she had felt so much better, more like her old self. But lately she *had* found herself feeling constantly fatigued, debilitated, as if all her energy had been sapped out of her, and she had lost so much weight even she was worried. Now this sudden pain. It alarmed her. What was causing it? The mere thought of going through chemotherapy once again made her shudder. I won't, I can't, she thought desperately.

Oh yes, you *can*, and you *will*, a small voice inside

her whispered. You'll go through anything for Lisette, you'll do anything for your child. Your child needs you. She has no father.

Her darling Lisette, her sweet little girl.

Collie's eyes settled on the photograph of her five-year-old daughter on the skirted table near the fireplace. She was a beautiful child, so chic, so bright, and full of so many endearing characteristics. She was a strong little personality. An old soul, that was the way Annie liked to describe her. An apt description, Collie had always thought.

What will become of her without me? Collie wondered worriedly, and immediately she shoved this frightening thought away from her, not wanting to face it. She wasn't going to die. She was going to fight to live for her little girl if the cancer had come back.

But if anything *should* happen to her, there *was* Kyra now, who would soon be her father's wife and part of the family, and this thought brought her a great measure of comfort.

Collie had made a tremendous effort to bring about a reconciliation between these two, and she was relieved and happy that everything had worked out so well. But her efforts, most especially last Saturday, had taken their toll on her, and she felt exhausted, weakened by them.

It was worth it though, Collie whispered to herself. My father is happy at last; Kyra is happy; little Alexandre will be made legitimate, and he will finally have a father, his real father.

And my father will have another male heir to

continue the de Montfleurie line, should anything happen to Guy. Collie realized this was another reason for her vast relief this past week. She had never wanted Lisette to inherit the château and the lands, to be burdened with all of its inherent problems.

Not unnaturally, her thoughts turned to her brother.

What a dismal person Guy had turned out to be. For years her disappointment and irritation with him had been acute; none the less, she had tried to be fair to him, and, indeed, had somehow managed to retain a certain fondness for him. Sadly, even that had finally fled completely, leaving her devoid of any feeling for him whatsoever. In fact, she quite actively disliked him, hoped that he wouldn't have the audacity to show up for Christmas. Surely not, after his hideous behaviour two weeks ago. On the other hand, he well might. You just never knew with Guy. He was unpredictable. And thick-skinned. And very stupid.

Beautiful and dumb, she said under her breath, thinking that this term could be applied to men as well as women.

Certainly Guy had been very beautiful when young, and had grown into an excessively handsome man. And oh how horribly spoiled he had been by women, because of those devastating looks, that fatal charm, which he could turn on and off like tap water. And the family had spoiled him too, always making excuses and allowances for him. We're guilty. We helped to create the monster he has become. Uncharitable though it was, she hoped he would never darken the doors of Montfleurie ever again.

Collie wished that Rosie had not married him, then she would not have been hurt by him. On the other hand, if Rosie hadn't married Guy, she and her father would not have had the benefit of Rosie as part of the family. I'm being selfish, she told herself, thinking only of myself and Father, and not of her. And thank God for Rosalind Madigan, who has given us so much love and devotion and support, and is forever loyal and concerned for our well being. There is no one else like Rosie in the whole world. She's an angel.

And she'll be here at Montfleurie most of the time when she's not working on a film, Collie reminded herself. She will be very actively involved in bringing up Lisette if anything happens to me.

I'm not going to die.

I won't let myself die.

I'm going to get better.

She leaned her head against the soft cushion once more, and closed her eyes, drifting with her thoughts. After Christmas she would go to Paris to see the doctors who had treated her this past summer. They would know what to do. They would help her. They would cure her *if* the cancer had flared again.

Eventually Collie realized that some of her strength was finally returning, and she managed to get up and go over to the skirted table, where she picked up the photograph of Claude in its silver frame. Taking it back to the sofa, she sat staring at his face for a long,

long time, loving him so much. He was deep in her heart, part of her very essence.

He had been killed two years ago, when he was only thirty, exactly the same age as her. What a senseless accident. He had been driving to Montfleurie from Paris when the crash had occurred. It had not been his fault, and yet he was the one who had been killed. Cut down in his prime. The cruelty and irony of it was that he had been a war correspondent for *Paris Match*, and yet he had never suffered so much as a scratch in all the years he was thrust into the centre of danger as a journalist.

As she continued to look down at the photograph in her hands, her heart squeezed and squeezed. *Oh Claude, Claude, I miss you so much. I can't go on without you. You were my life, the very best part of me. There's nothing without you, only a left-over life to live.*

Tears welled up in her and she could not stop their flow; in a way it was a relief to let go of some of her grief.

He was the only man she had ever loved, and he *had* been her entire life; try though she did to put aside her sorrow, to move on as best she could without him, she had discovered that most of the time she could not. Claude haunted her. She wanted to be haunted by him.

Everyone had told her it would get better with the passing of time, but it hadn't, and she knew it wouldn't, even if she lived to be ninety. But *I'm not going to live that long. I'm not going to see old age.*

Collie was well aware that many people did survive cancer, and frequently they lived long and fruitful lives. And yet recently, deep down within herself, a new knowledge had begun to grow: it was the terrible knowledge that her life was drawing to its close. Though not understanding why this knowledge insinuated itself into her thoughts, in her innermost heart she had come to accept it. There were times when she denied it, fought it, as she was doing now, but it always returned.

Without understanding why, a sudden and unexpected calmness came over Collie, suffused her, and she relaxed, feeling at ease with herself. It was as if someone was stroking her hair, comforting her, giving her unbounded love, and she did not want the feeling to go away. She closed her eyes. She was at peace.

They say the good die young, Collie thought. My mother was young when *she* died of cancer; Claude was young when he was so tragically killed in that ball of fire. If it is my destiny to leave this earth sooner than expected, then so be it. I do accept my fate, because I know, without a shadow of a doubt, that I cannot change it. I am in God's hands, and He is the one who created everything, made the Grand Design.

Each one of us comes to this earth for a reason, with a purpose, and when we have fulfilled our purpose, that task He gave us to do, He takes us to Him. Whatever happens to me, to all of us, *is* God's will . . .

'*Maman*, are you coming down to see the tree?'

Swiftly, Collie wiped her damp cheeks with her fingers and pushed a smile onto her face as Lisette flew into the room. When she saw her daughter she

271

smiled again and it was a smile that came from the heart.

How adorable Lisette looked, dressed in the quilted snowsuit Rosie had brought from New York. It was vivid yellow, trimmed with red bows, and she was a little picture in it.

'My sweet yellow bird,' Collie said, smiling at her again, loving her so much.

'Gaston has the tree *up*! It's so big, *Maman*! The *tallest* tree in the whole wide world, Gaston says.' She noticed the photograph of Claude, which lay on the sofa next to Collie, and she picked it up. 'Why is this picture of Papa here?'

'Because I like to look at him when I'm talking to him.'

'Does he talk back to you, *Maman*?' Lisette asked, leaning against Collie's knee, looking up into her face.

'Yes, he does, darling.'

'But Papa's not here. He's in Heaven being an angel with God.'

'That's true, Lisette, but he does speak to me . . . in the deepest, innermost part of my heart.'

'But Heaven is far, far away. How can you hear Papa when he's way, way *way* up there?' Lisette lifted her eyes to the ceiling for a moment, then looked at her mother questioningly, her black eyes huge in her small face.

'Because of love. It's Papa's love for you and for me that brings his voice into my heart, and because of my love and your love for him, I can hear him, and he can hear me, too.'

'Oh.' Lisette held her head to one side, trying to understand this, frowning slightly.

'Love is the most powerful thing in the world, Lisette, always remember that, my darling. It can move mountains.'

The five-year-old nodded, then said, 'I didn't want Papa to go to Heaven. Why did he have to leave us?'

'Because it's God's will,' Collie said softly.

The child pondered, endeavouring to comprehend her mother's words. After a moment, she asked, 'Was it God's will when Annie's little cat went to be a cat angel?'

'Yes, I believe it was.'

'I don't like God's will!' Lisette announced in a shrill voice, and her eyes were suddenly angry.

'Neither do I,' Collie murmured, and reached out, touched her daughter's face gently. 'But that is the way it is, I'm afraid, my darling.'

There was a second or two of silence, and then in the casual, abrupt way that children have, Lisette changed the subject. 'I'm going to be a bridesmaid with Yvonne at Kyra's wedding to Grandpapa. *Tante* Rosie's going to make cherry-red velvet dresses for us.'

'Is she now?'

'Oh yes, *Maman*, and we'll have red velvet Juliet caps trimmed with bunches of red cherries. *Tante* Rosie told me just now when we were cutting up the mistletoe in the kitchen. She's making the caps because of *me*. What will you wear for Grandpapa's wedding? A cherry-red dress too?'

'I don't really know.' Collie smoothed her daughter's hair away from her face, and continued, 'But let's go downstairs and ask Rosie about it, shall we?'

'Oh yes, let's. But you talk to her. I'm going to help Marcel and Gaston with the yule logs.'

'All right. But do me a favour please, Lisette. Put the photograph of Papa back on the table, in its special place.'

'Yes, Mama,' the child said, and went to do this, carrying the picture carefully in both hands.

As Collie tried to get up she felt the pain stabbing at her again, crippling her, and she fell back on the sofa, a look of agony creasing her face.

Lisette was turning around at this precise moment and she saw her mother's expression. Her own little face was washed over with anxiety as she rushed to her. *'Maman! Maman!* What is it? Does something hurt? What is it?'

'Nothing, darling. Nothing. I had a twinge of backache.' Collie forced a bright laugh. 'I must be getting old . . . it's a bit of rheumatism, I think.'

Lisette clutched at her mother, buried her face against Collie's sweater. 'I don't want you to hurt, *Maman*, I don't want you to hurt,' she cried, on the verge of tears.

'The pain is going away, darling. Just give me a minute,' Collie said, and closing her eyes she held her child tightly in her arms, rocking her to and fro. And she said a silent prayer: *Please God, don't take me away from her just yet. Please let me stay with her a little longer.*

Rosie stood on a step ladder in front of the fireplace in the family sitting room. For the last ten minutes she had been endeavouring to anchor two large sprigs of holly on top of the mirror over the mantelpiece.

Earlier she had twisted them together, and tied them with fine wire, and now she struggled to arrange the long spray effectively, but it wouldn't sit quite right. As she leaned back slightly, to view the spray, the phone began to ring. It went on ringing and ringing, and when nobody else picked it up she came down from the ladder, muttering under her breath, and grabbed it.

'*Château de Montfleurie, bonjour,*' she said a bit breathlessly.

There was a good deal of static, and from far away a masculine voice said, 'Miss Rosalind Madigan, please.'

'This is she.' It was a voice she did not recognize.

'Rosie! Hi! It's me, Johnny. Johnny Fortune.'

'Goodness, Johnny! How are you?' she exclaimed, startled to hear from him.

'Doing great, Rosie. How're you?'

'I'm fine, getting ready for Christmas. Where are you calling from? You sound as though you're on another planet.'

'I guess you could say I am – I'm in Vegas.'

'But it must be the middle of the night –'

'Sure it is, honey. It's three in the morning. I just finished my late show. I thought I'd call you before I went to bed. I wanted to wish you a merry Christmas, and tell you that I'm coming to Europe. In January. Do you think we can meet? Have dinner? Or something?'

She hesitated, and instantly wondered why she

was doing so. She was about to divorce Guy, so he wasn't an impediment any more. He never really had been. 'I'd like that, Johnny,' she said at last. 'I'd love to see you.'

'Hey, that's great! *Just great*. I'm going to be in Paris. Will you be there? Or where you are now?'

'I'll be in Paris.'

'Can I have your number?'

'Of course. Incidentally, how did you find me? I mean, how did you get this number?'

'It wasn't easy, believe you me.' He chuckled. 'Yesterday, Nell told me you were in London, and she gave me the studio number. *Again*. She'd already given me that. Anyway, I spoke to some nice lady, Aida Young. She said you weren't in London. Or in Paris. When I pressed her hard she told me she thought you'd gone to Montfleurie, but she wasn't sure how I could reach you. I got the feeling I was being stonewalled by her, and by Nell, to tell you the truth. Armed with that name, I called Francis Raeymaekers at his shop in London, you know, the guy I buy antique silver from. I asked him if he'd ever heard of a place called Montfleurie, and what was it? A hotel? A town? Or what? He knew it all right, explained that it was one of the great châteaux of the Loire. He got the number for me, and here I am talking to you at last.'

'I'm sorry you had so much trouble. Really sorry.'

'Why were Nell and Aida Young stonewalling me, Rosie?'

'I don't think they were.'

'You married or something?' Johnny asked, his voice suddenly sharp.

Rosie took a deep breath. 'I was. I'm separated. I'm getting a divorce.'

'I see. What's your Paris number?'

Rosie gave it to him, then said, 'When *exactly* do you think you'll be in Paris?'

'I'm not sure. About the middle of January, I guess. I hope. I'll let you know. Have a nice Christmas, honey, and I sure am glad I found you.'

'And *you* have a happy Christmas. Thanks for calling, Johnny.'

Rosie put the phone down, and stood with her hand on it for a moment, her face reflective.

From the door of the sitting room, Collie said, 'I wasn't eavesdropping, but I couldn't help hearing, Rosie. Are you *really* going to divorce Guy?'

Swinging around, Rosie stared at Collie for a long moment, and then she slowly nodded her head. 'Your father and I discussed it the day I arrived. He brought it up, and I realized, as we talked, that he was making a lot of sense.'

'All *I* can say is thank God!' Collie came into the sitting room and embraced Rosie. 'It's about time you had your freedom. I'm so glad you're going to take this step. It's long overdue.'

'You don't think Guy will come for Christmas, do you?' Rosie asked worriedly.

Collie shook her head with some vehemence. 'I doubt it. I don't think even he would be that crass, I really don't. He must know he put his foot in it once and for all, and that he's not welcome.'

'I guess you're right, I hope you are.' Rosie sounded doubtful.

'He won't come,' Collie reassured her in a firm voice.

'I suppose I will have to see Guy at some point, tell him I'm going to divorce him,' Rosie murmured, heading towards the ladder.

'I don't know *why*. My brother doesn't deserve any kind of consideration from you, in my opinion, anyway. *He* hasn't treated *you* in a nice way. Not at all.'

'That's true. I guess I won't see him then. But I will start the divorce proceedings.'

Collie gave Rosie a hard stare, and a small smile pulled at the corners of her mouth, as she said, 'Was that Johnny the famous singer who just telephoned you?'

'Yes. He's coming to Paris in the new year. He wants me to have dinner with him.'

'I think that's wonderful, Rosie darling. *Toujours l'amour . . . toujours l'amour.*'

Rosie stared back at her sister-in-law, and she felt herself blushing; she opened her mouth to say something as Annie hurried into the room.

'Madame de Montfleurie, this package just came for you. By special courier. From California. I signed for it.'

'Thank you, Annie,' Rosie murmured as she took the package from her.

Annie turned to leave, then stopped and peered at Collie. 'You look pale, tired. Dominique has made a wonderful soup for lunch. *Des légumes, un poulet . . .*

un grand potage, très bon.' With these words Annie disappeared.

As she opened the package, Rosie exclaimed to Collie, 'It's from Gavin in Los Angeles! Oh great, it's the script of *Napoleon and Josephine*! And there's something else.' Rosie placed the screenplay on the step ladder, and examined the other item – a box, obviously a gift, wrapped in heavy blue paper and tied with gold ribbon. Attached to the box was a small envelope. Taking the card out, she read it aloud to Collie: *'Thank you, Rosie, for the most beautiful costumes ever, for being such a great trouper, and for being my friend. Happy Christmas and much love, Gavin.'*

'How nice of him,' Collie said. 'Open the gift, Rosie.'

'Maybe I should wait, put it under the tree and open it on Christmas Eve when we give out all the presents to everyone.'

'Don't be silly. I'm dying to see what he's sent you. Let's look at it now.'

Rosie tore off the paper, and held a dark-blue cardboard box with the initials HW in the bottom right-hand corner. Inside the box was a leather case with the same initials stamped in gold. 'It's from Harry Winston,' Rosie said, awestruck, and lifted the lid. She gasped when she saw what was inside. 'Oh Collie, look! The most beautiful South Sea pearls I've ever seen.' As she spoke she lifted them out, showed them to Collie, whose eyes also widened.

'They're *real*,' Collie exclaimed. 'They must be real if they're from Harry Winston.'

Rosie nodded. 'Gavin always gives me something

very special when we finish a movie, but never anything quite like these pearls before. Look how beautiful they are in the light.' She held them up in front of the window, then passed them to Collie.

'They're fabulous,' Collie murmured, her voice also awed. 'And obviously very valuable.'

'Yes, they must be. I must call Gavin later, to thank him. It's still the middle of the night in Los Angeles, three o'clock, actually. I'll put through a call this evening around six our time. It'll be nine in the morning there.'

'Here you are,' Collie said, handing the string of pearls back to Rosie. 'Now, if you've got five minutes, can we discuss what I'm going to wear for Father's wedding? I understand from Lisette that she and Yvonne will be dressed in cherry-red velvet. But not I – I hope.'

Rosie laughed. 'No. Two bridesmaids only, no matrons of honour, I said that to Kyra last night. I thought you and I could wear something we already owned. To tell you the truth, it's going to be tough enough for me to make the two dresses for the girls in time.'

'Perhaps Yvonne can help you.'

'She volunteered, and certainly she can sew the Juliet caps. I've already ordered the fabric from Madame Solange in Paris, and she's sending it by overnight courier. It should arrive tomorrow, and I'll start the dresses at once.'

'You'll have your hands full,' Collie murmured, sitting down on the sofa, watching Rosie as she climbed back onto the ladder. 'Their marriage is only ten days away.'

'I know.' Rosie straightened the holly spray, and eyed it, then she said over her shoulder to Collie, 'I'll get the dresses done, even if I have to stay up all night, every night, to finish.'

'I know that, Rosie. There's nobody like you . . . you're quite amazing.'

TWENTY-FIVE

The skies of Paris were an etching in *grisaille*, a monochrome of sombre greys. Overcast, they seemed to threaten rain.

Gavin Ambrose stood at the sitting-room window of his suite in the Ritz Hotel, morosely gazing out. The weather was bleak, dreary, on this Sunday morning and not a bit inviting.

The day and evening loomed ahead before he caught the Concorde to New York on Monday. It seemed like an endless expanse of time to him; he didn't know what to do with himself until then.

Unfortunately, Rosie was noticeably absent, gone to the Loire for Christmas. Apart from her, the only people he knew in Paris were a couple of executives from Billancourt Studios. He had seen them on Friday and Saturday; now, today, he was at a loose end.

The prospect of being alone alarmed and depressed Gavin.

This was unusual for him. He was known as a loner, enjoyed his own company, had never minded solitude in the past. But lately he had come to dread it. When he was alone he had time to think; for months his thoughts had been disturbing.

His life was a mess. His marriage was in shreds. All he had was his work. At least he loved that. It was the essence of him, his entire reason for being. One of the reasons he went from film to film without a break was to keep busy. That way he was able to avoid dealing with his personal problems; nor did he have to confront his private demons.

He had begun to acknowledge, if only to himself, what a terrible sham his marriage was. There was nothing there. Only a black hole. Gaping. Bottomless. There was no emotion. Not even hatred. Only indifference. Louise and he had nothing between them, not even the semblance of a relationship. He wondered now if there had *ever* been one.

Louise was a self-important, self-involved little bitch, with very few brains and absolutely no understanding of him, his work, his demanding career, his life in general. Or any understanding of anybody else. She was singularly dim-witted in that respect.

His fame didn't mean all that much to him, it was merely a by-product of what he did – his acting. But his fame had gone to *her* head. Also, for a long time she had had no interest in him as a man. Greener pastures beckoned. Not that he cared. He was guilty, too, in one sense, because he had no real interest in her either.

Hundreds of times he had asked himself why he had ever married Louise. Foolish question that; he knew the answer only too well. He had married her because she was pregnant. Her pregnancy had turned into a horror: a terrible, heartbreaking tragedy.

He had stayed with Louise because of this. To see her through it all, to see her through her physical and psychic pain. Sincerely wanting to help her to heal, he had also realized he would heal himself just by helping *her*.

Inevitably, she became pregnant again, and when David was born, almost eight years ago, he had fallen in love with his son. He had stayed in a bad marriage because of his child.

Through her infidelities, Louise had elected to betray their marriage when David was still a toddler. He had never tried to stop her, having ceased to care what she did, and anyway they were no longer sharing a bed by then.

He wondered, suddenly, what would happen to David if they got a divorce. Would the child become the victim of a virulent tug of war? Gavin's mind closed down on him. He simply couldn't cope with that thought. Not now. Not today. Not ever.

You'll wait it out, he told himself. Surely, if he waited long enough, Louise would be forced to ask for the divorce. She was on the brink already. He was fully aware how heavily involved she was with the senator she saw in Washington. The widowed senator. The rich senator. The socially-correct senator. Allan Turner was the perfect mate for Louise.

Yes, he *would* wait it out. Then, at least, he might be able to dictate some of the terms. He had no intention of trying to take the child away from her; that would be unconscionable. Ready access to David, and joint custody, that was what he wanted, and he aimed to get it.

Cursing mildly under his breath, Gavin turned away from the window, crossed the floor, went into the bedroom, glancing at his watch as he did. It was almost eleven o'clock.

He needed to get out, to breathe fresh air, to walk in order to shed these dismaying thoughts. But going out presented something of a problem. One of the disadvantages of his kind of fame as an actor was high visibility and an all-too-recognizable face.

He put on a scarf, a felt fedora, and shrugged himself into his cashmere overcoat, added dark glasses and peered in the nearest mirror. He grinned. He didn't even recognize himself. Nor was he recognized by anyone else when he went through the lobby and out into the Place Vendôme.

Paris was not a city Gavin knew well, but since he always stayed at the Ritz, the area surrounding the hotel was familiar to him, and he set off in the direction of the Place de la Concorde. Once he was outside, walking briskly, his dourness and discontent with himself began to evaporate.

Gavin soon found he was focusing his thoughts on *Napoleon and Josephine*. He was seeing Paris through the eyes of a film-maker, and also through the eyes of Napoleon, who had done so much to change the architectural face of Paris and make it look the way it did today.

Gavin knew from his research that Napoleon had wanted to subsidize French architecture for ten years,

French sculpture for twenty years. To do so he had planned to build four triumphal arches, celebrating the battles of Marengo and Austerlitz, peace and religion.

But in the end he had built only two, the smaller one commemorating Austerlitz, the larger one the *Grande Armée*, 'the army I have the honour to command', he had said to his architect.

Now, standing at the bottom of the Champs-Élysées, Gavin stared up the long and elegant boulevard, his eyes trained on that great arch built by Napoleon and dedicated to his beloved army. The Arc de Triomphe de l'Etoile looked just the way he had wanted it to look, the Emperor having remarked that 'a monument dedicated to the *Grande Armée* must be large, simple, majestic and borrow nothing from antiquity'.

And that is exactly what his architect Chalgrin gave him, Gavin decided, as he continued to walk up the Champs-Élysées, heading towards it, absently glancing at the Christmas decorations decking the street as he walked.

For Gavin, making this particular film was the fulfilment of a childhood dream. Even when he was a teenager he had been intrigued by men of achievement and great deeds, and especially by Napoleon.

As a kid growing up in New York he had been drawn to history books, wanting to know more about the men who had put their inimitable and indelible stamp on the world. His fascination had known no bounds. What had made them tick? Why were they different from other men? What had their emotional lives been like? Why had they loved the women they had loved? Or bonded with the men they had bonded with? What inner force had motivated them, driven them to such heights? What was the secret ingredient within their make-up that had lifted them out of the norm? Very simply, why had *they* been greater than their contemporaries?

One thing he had discovered, much to his amazement, was that the men who had been giants in their lifetimes and become immortal after death had been only too human and remarkably flawed.

But it was these men of historical greatness who had been *his* heroes, not football players, baseball stars or rock musicians, whom his friends had constantly put on pedestals. He *had* admired a few actors, of course, being an aspiring actor himself. Paul Newman and Spencer Tracy were a couple of the very special ones who were in a league of their own.

Tracy in *Bad Day at Black Rock* was hard to top; so was Newman in *Fort Apache, the Bronx*. The latter had been released in 1981, and he had seen it four times in as many days, gripped by Newman's performance. The movie, about a precinct in the Bronx and the cops who ran it, had had an immense impact on him from an acting point of view.

The Bronx. What memories that name conjured up for him. He had grown up in the Belmont section of the Bronx, not half so tough or rough as the South Bronx, where the movie was set. But what a far cry his childhood and teenage years in Belmont were from Paris and his life today and his immense fame.

Sometimes he wondered how it had all happened.

One moment he had been unknown, a struggling actor, counting himself lucky when he got any kind of job, whether off-Broadway or in television. The next he was a star of the Broadway stage at the age of twenty-five, being hailed as the greatest talent to hit the boards since Brando had immortalized the role of Stanley Kowalski in *Streetcar* in 1947. He had always questioned that comparison, then and now, since his debut had been in that very role. It had been an easy and obvious comparison for the critics. Did he deserve it?

The year had been 1983. An eventful year. His son had been born, Hollywood had beckoned, and he had gone. And for several years thereafter he had rushed back and forth between the two coasts until he had finally settled in Hollywood. But he had always been known as an East Coast 'ethnic' actor, lumped together with Al Pacino, Robert De Niro, Dustin Hoffman and Armand Assante. Not bad company to be in, since they were all great, although it was Pacino whom he admired the most these days. He was brilliant, mesmerizing, heroic, the consummate actor.

The odd thing was, Gavin Ambrose had never expected his breakthrough to happen the way it had, with such suddenness, without warning, and he had been momentarily stunned. It was as if he had been catapulted up, had gone flying higher and higher into the sky, and thank God he had never come down, had never landed on his ass with a thud. At least, not so far. A wry smile slid onto his face at this thought. Success to him could be categorized as ephemeral, in a certain sense. In his business, you were only as good as your last movie, and wasn't that the truth really.

Gavin was glad about his success. He loved the work he did, was so passionate about it he was consumed, and it would have been unnatural not to want the recognition, the applause. The only regret he had was that his mother and grandfather had not lived long enough to see it, to enjoy the fruits of his success with him. By the time he got his first break in *Streetcar*, which had resulted in instant stardom, they were both gone, having died in the same year – 1976 – when he was eighteen years old.

Tony Ambrosini, his father, had passed away after a heart attack when he was only nine, and his mother, Adelia, and he had gone to live with his father's parents. She simply couldn't cut it financially on her own.

The senior Ambrosinis had welcomed them lovingly, but sadly his Grandmother Graziella had died within seven months of her son. His grandfather and his mother had consoled each other in their mutual grief, and had given moral and financial support to each other. He had become the centre and focus of their lives, and they had doted on him.

His mother had worked in the costume-jewellery department of Macy's, his grandfather had been a master cabinetmaker, and they had pooled their resources, shared the responsibility of raising him. As a family they hadn't been rich, but they hadn't been dirt-poor either, and somehow they had managed. There was no bitterness in Gavin, and he remembered his youth with affection.

His mother and his grandfather had given him an enormous amount of love and encouragement. Home had been comfortable if not luxurious, and his Grandfather Giovanni had spoiled him, had enjoyed taking him shopping every Saturday to the huge Italian food market on Arthur Avenue in the Bronx. It was here that Giovanni had purchased favourite delicacies, imported from the Old Country, to share with his grandson and Adelia.

But it was his mother who had taken him to the movies from the time he was very young. This was her special treat to herself twice a week, and it was his, too. It was from the movies that he had learned so much about acting, watching those men up there on the silver screen doing their stuff. Later he became a devotee of Lee Strasberg and a student of his until his death in February of 1982. But it was really those early days at the movies when he was small that had engendered in him the desire to be an actor.

His mother was his confidante, coach, critic and audience, and she encouraged him in his ambitions, forever told him he was handsome enough to be in the movies. But he had never really believed her. In those days, he thought he was too short. She had just laughed, said his height didn't matter, his talent was what counted, and that anyway he would grow taller as he got older. She had been right about this. However, he hadn't grown quite as tall as he would have liked.

Not long after the deaths of his mother and grandfather, Gavin met Kevin, Rosie and Nell, as well as

Mikey and Sunny. Their little group had been formed and they had vowed to be a family, always there for each other, no matter what.

He had been living with relatives of his father's. They let him have a small room in their apartment for a nominal amount, and he worked in a supermarket at weekends in order to pay them. But as soon as he was able to he had left, had taken a room in a small boarding house in Greenwich Village, existing as best he could, doing odd jobs and working as a waiter at a local café. And acting, always acting, grabbing every bit of work he could, mostly in little theatres in the Village.

His mother and grandfather had not left him entirely destitute. There had been money in the bank for him, but he had preferred to leave it there, earning interest. That money was for his lessons at the Actor's Studio, where he learned at the knee of the master, Lee Strasberg, Deity of the Method School of Acting.

The group had been his mainstay in those struggling days, the friendships vitally important to him. It was Gavin who had given everyone their names during the first year of the group's existence. Rosie had been christened Angel Face because she was angelic and adorable. Nell became Little Nell after one of his favourite Charles Dickens characters. Kevin was Gumshoe, the most appropriate name for an aspiring cop. Mikey had been dubbed Professor, a perfect description for the most studious person he knew. Sunny had acquired the name Golden Girl because she was just that – all golden and shimmering and filled with laughter and light.

Not any more, he thought sorrowfully, not any more.

It was Rosie who had decided he must have a special name, too. Without even consulting the others, she had announced one day that he would be called Actor. 'You're a chameleon, Gavin,' she had said. 'You can become anyone you want, play any part. You're a true *actor*. That *is* you. That defines you.'

Rosie and he had always been attracted to each other, from that first evening when he had met her with her brother. And they had become involved a year later when she was eighteen and he was twenty. This was just after she had started a four-year course at the Fashion Institute of Technology in New York, studying fashion design.

A youthful romance, an infatuation, that's all it had been, and they had broken up three years later, over something so silly and petty he could no longer remember what it was. But more than likely it had been his fault. He was selfish, totally committed to his work. He knew that. And he *was* self-involved. He wondered what actor wasn't. All actors were some kind of pain in the ass to somebody.

He had met Louise when he and Rosie were more or less estranged, and had promptly hopped into bed with her. A torrid little affair had started. And before he could blink twice he had made her pregnant. They had married quickly, because Louise was terrified of her socialite parents and what they would do, and because he felt guilty and entirely responsible for her predicament. He had always prided himself on being a man of honour. And dependability.

A year later, when she was twenty-two and had finished her FIT course, Rosie had rushed off to Paris. Here she had met Guy de Montfleurie, through his sister, her friend Colette. Almost immediately they had become involved and had married about a year later.

And that had been that.

Eventually Gavin and Rosie had become great friends again, and she had soon joined his working team. They were at last able to enjoy a very special friendship, and each other's company, while working together on a permanent basis. She helped to make his life with Louise more bearable somehow.

Gavin sighed to himself. A lot of water had gone under the bridge since those early days in New York when they had all been kids. Young, innocent, full of piss and vinegar, courageous and optimistic and a lot of other wonderful things as well. Fourteen years ago. It seemed so much longer to him. Decades past.

Louise had recently implied that he still harboured strong feelings for Rosie. That was true. *He did*. She was his best friend, after all, and his confidante; she worked on every single one of his movies. He wouldn't have it any other way. And yes, he did *love* Rosalind Madigan. But it was platonic. Their romantic feelings for each other had died long ago; even before he had met Louise that infatuation had been over.

Gavin turned up the collar of his coat, shivering in the cold, and came to a standstill in front of the Arc de Triomphe at last.

It was not a good idea to look back in life, it just didn't pay, and it usually spelled unnecessary heartache. Always forward. That was his motto. Onward and upward, he thought, as he gazed at the huge imposing arch, and the tricolour fluttering under it in the wind. The flag of France. Napoleon's flag.

This movie is going to be a hell of a job to make, he thought, and playing Napoleon the biggest challenge I've ever had to meet. But I've got a wonderful production team pulled together; I'll just make sure the cast is equally good.

It was an easier day on the set when you worked with pros.

TWENTY-SIX

Back at his suite in the Ritz, Gavin ordered a chicken sandwich and tea with lemon, and sat back on the sofa, studying the second draft of *Napoleon and Josephine*.

A waiter appeared in no time at all with the food, and once he had eaten he picked up the phone and dialled Rosie's number in the Loire.

'*Château de Montfleurie, bonjour,*' a woman's voice said and he knew at once who it was.

'Hello, Rosie, it's me.'

'Gavin! I've been trying to reach you in LA for days. Since Friday actually! Since the script and your gift arrived. Gavin, thank you so much for the pearls. They're beautiful, just exquisite. But you're far too extravagant.'

'Nothing's too extravagant for you, Angel Face. You deserve them, after all the hard work you did on the picture, and looking after me when I had my accident. I owe you, honey.'

'Gavin, don't be so silly, it's me you're talking to!' Rosie exclaimed, and then asked, 'But where are you?'

'Paris. At the Ritz. I was in London for a few days. Looping my lines. You know what a problem it is when too many ancillary sounds on the film obscure the dialogue. I had to re-record a couple of Warwick's battle scenes, you know, when he's talking to Edward.'

'I wish I'd known you were in Europe. You could have come here for the weekend, instead of sitting in Paris alone. I mean, I'm presuming you're alone,' she finished, making her last few words sound more like a question.

'I'm alone.'

There was a pause at his end, and he cleared his throat. 'And it was pretty stupid of me not to call you, but to tell you the truth, I wasn't really sure how long the looping would take. Also, I had several meetings planned with the guys from Billancourt Studios.'

'How did that go?'

'Great, Rosie, really great! We'll be using the studio facilities starting in February. We'll be headquartering there. Aida's on as producer, by the way, and I think I may have Michael Roddings as the director. How about them apples, kid?'

'I like them apples,' she laughed. 'And it's all sounding wonderful. Especially the news about Aida. As for Michael, I'm a big fan, he's one of the best directors around.'

'I knew you'd approve, honey.' Gavin leaned back against the cushions, propped his feet on the coffee table and asked, 'Have you had a chance to look at the script yet?'

'Look at it! I've read it already. And it's brilliant. I love it, Gavin. It's very touching, extremely moving in parts, and highly dramatic. The pacing is great. But then you and Vivienne have always worked well together. It reads like a final draft to me.'

'Yep. It's pretty good. Another light polish and that should do it. How's it going down there at the château? How's Collie? I know you were worried about her.'

'Collie seems much better, thank God. Very thin, but really much fitter than I thought she'd be. Everyone else is fine, things are just fine here.'

'And what about Guy? How's he?'

At the other end of the phone, Rosie thought that Gavin sounded suddenly sour. Then she dismissed this and said, 'Oh he's not here. A couple of weeks ago he had a row with Henri and disappeared the next day. We haven't seen or heard from him since. Frankly, we all hope he stays away.'

'As my Scottish mother would have said, good riddance to bad rubbish. Right?'

'Spot on! I have some really good news, Gavin. Henri and Kyra are getting married.'

'No kidding! How did that happen?'

Rosie told him the whole story, leaving nothing out, and finished, 'They're getting married a few days after Christmas. Here at Montfleurie, in the private chapel. The village priest will come up to perform the ceremony in the afternoon and then we'll have a little tea party here at the château. Do you want to come?'

'I wish I could, but I can't. And I'm glad it's worked

297

out for Kyra. I always thought she was a nice woman.'

'Yes, she is. So, when are you going back to LA?'

'Tomorrow. Or rather, I'm taking the Concorde to New York tomorrow, and staying the night in New York. I'll go on to the coast the next day. For Christmas with David . . . and Louise.'

'It'll do you good to have some time with your family, to rest and relax,' Rosie said.

'Sure,' he responded laconically.

'I'm going to Paris immediately after the wedding, early in the new year,' Rosie told him. 'I want to get to work on the preliminaries for the costumes. Henri has dug up some wonderful books on the Empire period here at the château, and I've been really inspired.'

'When are you ever not inspired, Rosie?' Gavin asked, meaning this sincerely. To him she was the most talented costume designer in the world.

Rosie simply laughed, brushed aside his compliment, saying quickly, 'When are you coming back to Paris?'

'I'll be going to London first, around the second week of January, to see the edited film again, and to hear the final score. Then I'll hop a plane to gay Paree, and start the ball rolling on *Napoleon and Josephine*. How does that sound?'

'I can't wait to get going on the movie!'

'Neither can I. Anyway, I just called to say Happy Christmas, Angel Face.'

'Happy Christmas, Gavin darling. And God Bless.'

'Take care, Rosie.' He dropped the phone in the

cradle, picked up the script and began to read again, not wanting to face the fact that he missed her. And a lot more than he cared to admit.

TWENTY-SEVEN

'A man who gives a woman pearls of great value is heavily involved with her,' Henri de Montfleurie murmured in a low voice, giving Kyra a pointed look.

Kyra frowned. 'Do you mean emotionally?'

'In every way.'

'Are you suggesting that Gavin Ambrose is in love with Rosie?'

'It's more than likely, I would say.'

Kyra did not at first respond.

Turning slightly, she glanced down the vast entrance hall, focusing on Rosie, who was busily taking pictures of Lisette, Collie and Yvonne.

The three of them stood in front of the giant-sized tree which was heavily laden with all manner of unique decorations and glittering with tiny lights. The two girls were laughing and chattering, and Collie was gently ordering them to stand still, while Rosie fiddled with the camera before taking more snaps.

Filled with the excitement of Christmas Eve, they were having a great deal of fun, especially Collie, Kyra observed, and this pleased her immeasurably.

Like Rosie, she was worried about Colette, who was painfully thin and drawn. She looked like a waif tonight, even though she had obviously made an enormous effort to dress herself up for the Christmas festivities. The dark-green silk dress she had chosen drained what little colour she had from her face, and she seemed excessively pale to Kyra. But maybe it *was* the dress over-emphasizing the whiteness of her skin after all. She hoped so.

As Kyra swung her gaze back to Rosie, a thoughtful expression settled on her face. Rosie, too, had dressed up this evening. She wore a stunning, black-velvet tunic dress, the square patch pockets heavily encrusted with beaded embroidery. And around her neck were the extraordinary South Sea pearls. How lustrous they looked against the black velvet. They must have cost a fortune, Kyra thought. Perhaps seventy-five thousand dollars, maybe more. Henri was right. Costly pearls were not given merely in appreciation of work well done on a movie. Most especially pearls from Harry Winston, the great New York jeweller.

Another thought struck Kyra, and she turned to Henri and said in an undertone, 'We must remember that they are old old friends, darling. They were teenagers in New York, and she's been working on his movies for a long time. It could be that the pearls are a gift for . . . for all those years they've been close friends and colleagues.'

'I doubt it.' Henri took a sip of his champagne. 'I've seen those two together, been in their presence quite frequently, as you well know, and there is something very special between them. They are deeply involved, take my word for it. Whether they realize this –' He paused and shrugged, then added, 'Well, that is another matter.'

'But Gavin is married,' Kyra murmured, leaning closer to him.

'If you can call it that,' Henri countered. 'Gavin seems very removed from his wife, distant. I believe Louise to be a very strange woman, so I can't say I blame him. She is brittle, neurotic, highly strung and not particularly intelligent. And she's thin to the point of starvation.' He shuddered involuntarily and made a face. 'Haven't you ever noticed that her head looks too big for that bird-like body of hers? Why is it that some women are obsessed with their weight? Have the desire to look like victims of Dachau?' He shook his head in obvious distaste. 'There's nothing feminine or womanly or remotely sexual about bone-thin women like Louise, who resemble boys. Not to me, anyway. I think they are grotesque.'

Kyra gave him a broad smile. 'I am glad you prefer a bit of flesh on the bones, otherwise where would I be?' She laughed and picked up her glass, touched it against his. 'I do love you, Henri de Montfleurie.'

'And I you, my dear,' he said with great warmth.

'Louise Ambrose *is* very odd, you're quite right about that,' Kyra murmured, and she couldn't help glancing at Rosie again. 'She and Rosie are as different as chalk and cheese. Just look how beautiful Rosie is tonight. She looks glorious. Like a ripe peach.'

Amused, Henri laughed at this analogy, but he made no comment.

Kyra went on thoughtfully, 'What a pity it is that Gavin is married.'

'What's that got to do with anything?' Henri asked swiftly. 'Whenever did the state of matrimony ever stop anybody? You know as well as I do that most people usually go after what they want in matters of the heart. And the loins. Especially when they are obsessed. And quite regardless of anybody else's feelings, I might add. However, I genuinely believe that Gavin and Rosie don't understand how they truly feel about each other.'

Kyra stared at him. 'I find that hard to believe.'

'Let me correct myself. I don't think Rosie knows how involved she is with Gavin on a personal level. She's been so embroiled with Guy and their problems and their failed marriage. And too involved with all of us for that matter, and for a number of years. But that is all going to change, of course.'

'What do you mean?'

'Now that she has made up her mind to divorce Guy, her life is going to be very different. Radically different.'

'They haven't lived together as man and wife for years, and Guy's hardly been here, so she's not seen very much of him. Do you really think the divorce will make all that much difference to her?'

'Yes, I do. Rosie is very straightforward, and full of integrity. As long as she was bound to Guy legally, she was somehow bound to him in her own head, and therefore not free to do as she wished. At least, this is the way I have analysed her attitude, and the predicament she's been in for a long time. Just deciding to go ahead and get a divorce has already wrought a fundamental change in her.'

'What kind of change?'

Henri reflected for a moment before he said, 'She's free at last of Guy. *In her mind*. And that gives her a sense of liberation. She'll feel even better once the divorce actually comes through.'

'Oh, I do hope so, Henri! I love Rosie, and I want her to be happy . . .' Kyra fell silent, and then she said a little hesitantly, a second or two later, 'I didn't want to broach the subject of Guy . . . but have you heard from him?'

Henri nodded. 'I haven't had a chance to tell you, nor did I wish to upset you, but he telephoned me last night. From Paris. To apologize, if you can believe it. Naturally I accepted his apology. It was the right thing to do, I believe. I also told him we were getting married, and that I was going to legitimize our son by legally adopting him.'

'What did he say to that news?'

'He congratulated me. He said he was glad about our marriage and that I was acknowledging Alexandre.'

'This is extremely difficult for me to accept, Henri.'

'And for me also, even though I heard it with my own ears.' Henri squeezed her arm. 'But oddly enough, I do think he really meant what he said. He's a strange bird, my son. Certainly he's always baffled me.'

'And everyone else. I'm surprised he didn't ask if he could come to Montfleurie for Christmas.'

'He didn't get the opportunity, Kyra. Once I had

accepted his apology, I told him I wasn't quite ready to take him back into the fold. Not just yet, under the circumstances. I added that perhaps next year it would be a different matter.'

'How did he take it?'

'Reasonably well, I'd say. Just before we hung up he asked if he could speak to Rosie, and I went to get her, brought her to the phone. On our way back to my study, I advised her to tell him there and then that she intended to start divorce proceedings in the new year.'

'And did she?'

'Oh, yes, indeed she did. And she was very forthright, extremely firm. She had the presence of mind to ask him how long he would be staying in Paris, so that she could have him served with the legal papers. Guy told her that he would be there until March, and then he was going to Hong Kong before moving on to Indonesia and other parts of the Far East.'

'I suppose he was taken by surprise, wasn't he?'

Henri shook his head. 'No, I don't think so. According to Rosie he took it in his stride, and didn't seem to be upset. Or put out. In fact, she told me after she'd hung up that he was rather cordial, nicer to her than he had been in several years.'

Kyra's face changed. 'Henri, I don't like it! His attitude worries me. He apologizes to you, congratulates you on your forthcoming marriage to me, and accepts, with apparent docility, Rosie's plans to divorce him. He's got something up his sleeve.'

Henri looked at her intently, his eyes narrowing.

'What could he possibly have up his sleeve, as you put it?'

'I don't know. All I know is that I don't like his . . . his easy acceptance of everything . . .' Her voice trailed off. She couldn't quite put her finger on what she meant precisely, but, none the less, she was worried. Concern flicked into her eyes.

Henri noticed this immediately, and he took hold of her arm reassuringly. 'I think your imagination is running away from you, my darling. Forget Guy. He's not going to cause trouble. Come along, we're being rather impolite, I think, standing here chatting together. We'd better join the girls.'

As they approached the others, Henri's eyes veered to the Christmas tree which soared almost to the ceiling of the entrance hall. 'Even though I do say so myself, I think we outdid ourselves this year. The tree is nothing short of magnificent.'

'It's Auntie Rosie's lights she brought from New York, Grandpapa,' Lisette cried. 'They fill the tree with tiny stars just like the sky at night.'

'What a lovely description, Lisette,' Henri said, smiling at his granddaughter with pleasure.

'Please come and join the girls, Henri, so I can take a picture of the whole family,' Rosie said. 'And you too, Kyra, you must be in this shot.'

Henri said, 'But it won't be a family portrait without you, Rosie.' He turned to Yvonne. 'Will you go and fetch Gaston, please, my dear. Tell him I would like him to take a photograph of us.'

'Yes, Uncle Henri.' Yvonne darted off.

'And you, Lisette, can run upstairs and ask Eliane

to bring little Alexandre downstairs. I think he must also be in the photograph.'

'I'll go,' Kyra said, hurrying towards the staircase. 'I'll bring Alexandre down myself.'

'Of course,' Henri said, and went to fill his glass with champagne.

Rosie placed her camera on one of the hall console tables and picked up her glass. Strolling over to join Henri, she confided, 'All of these wonderful smells emanating from the kitchen are making my mouth water. I must confess, I'm ravenous.'

'So am I,' Henri said, and taking her elbow he guided her back towards the tree. 'I understand from Annie that Dominique has prepared a succulent goose, with chestnut stuffing and all the usual trimmings, and I for one can't wait to sample it.'

'And don't forget the *pâté de foie gras* to start with and the chocolate *bûche de Noël* for dessert,' Collie said, seating herself on a tapestry-upholstered bench. 'There's quite a meal in store for us.'

'We'll go in for dinner as soon as Gaston has taken the family portrait,' Henri announced, then addressing Rosie, he asked, 'How are the bridesmaids' dresses coming along?'

'Very well, almost finished, in fact. They're hanging in my studio. If you'd like to walk over tomorrow morning you can see them.'

Henri laughed and shook his head. 'No, no, I want everything to do with my marriage to be a complete surprise.'

Collie said, 'Kyra's dress is lovely, Father, very simple. That's all I'm going to say about it. But I think you ought to give her Mother's antique diamond pin, the de Montfleurie pin, I mean. It would look beautiful on the dress.'

Henri stared at his daughter for the longest moment, then he walked over to the bench and sat down next to her. Putting his arms around her narrow shoulders, he kissed her on the cheek, overwhelmed with love for her. A rush of emotion choked him; after a moment he coughed lightly, and said, 'That's a sweet thought, Collie darling, and only you would suggest something so wonderfully generous. It's a lovely and very loving gesture. Perhaps I _will_ give the pin to Kyra. As a wedding present from the two of us.'

TWENTY-EIGHT

Collie was desperately ill and Henri needed her.

That was all Rosie could think about on this icy morning as she dashed around the bedroom of her Paris flat, throwing a few necessary items into a small suitcase.

It was the middle of January, and for the past two weeks she had been busy working on initial ideas and sketches of the costumes for *Napoleon and Josephine*. She had been alone ever since she had returned from the Loire at the beginning of the new year, and she had enjoyed her solitariness in many ways, had loved concentrating on work to the exclusion of everything else.

Gavin was in London, completing postproduction on *Kingmaker*, and they spoke every day, sometimes about the film they had just finished, sometimes about the new one, which now so preoccupied them both. They spent hours on the phone, usually in the evening after he had returned to the hotel from the studio, and when she had finally laid down her pencil and closed her sketch book for the night.

Rosie thought of Gavin as she snapped the suitcase

shut and put it on the floor. Going to the phone she dialled his direct line at Shepperton Studios in London.

He picked up on the second ring. 'Hello?'

'Gavin, it's me. Is this a bad time? Can you talk for a moment?'

'What's wrong? I know something's wrong, Rosie. I can tell from your voice.'

'It's Collie,' Rosie began, and instantly stopped as her throat closed.

'Oh, Rosie, I'm sorry, so very sorry. Is she terribly ill again?'

Swallowing, Rosie managed to say, 'Henri just called me, a short while ago. She hasn't been feeling well this past week, apparently. In fact, I think she's been quite ill since just after the wedding. He didn't want to worry me unduly, so he didn't say anything before today. Then last night Collie took a turn for the worse. He wants me to go to Montfleurie. Now. Immediately. He said not to waste any time getting there.'

'Is it that serious? You don't think she's –' Gavin couldn't bring himself to mouth what he was thinking, knowing how much Colette meant to Rosie. His heart went out to her.

With a small sob, Rosie said, 'I'm not sure . . . I don't know . . .' Recouping herself, she went on, 'I just wanted to let you know where I'll be for the next few days. In case you were looking for me.'

'I'm glad you did. Can I do anything to help?'

'No, thanks anyway.'

'How are you getting to Montfleurie? By train?'

'No, no, I'm going to drive. It's easier, faster. I know I must get there as quickly as possible.'

'Listen to me, Rosie, drive *carefully*. Please don't take any chances on the road. *Promise*.'

'I promise, Gavin.'

'Okay. And stay in touch, let me know if you need anything. Anything at all.'

'I will, and thanks.'

'Take care, Angel.'

'Yes,' she said and hung up.

In less than three hours Rosie was driving across the drawbridge and pulling into the interior courtyard of the Château de Montfleurie.

Gaston was already hurrying down the front steps before she had even turned off the ignition, and a moment later he was helping her out of the car. His face was sombre, told its own story.

'The Count is waiting for you in the study, Madame de Montfleurie,' Gaston said, after greeting her in a more subdued manner than was normal for him.

'Thanks, Gaston. There's only one bag in the boot,' Rosie murmured and without saying another word she hurried into the château.

That vast entrance hall, which had rung with their laughter during the Christmas festivities, was eerily silent on this chilly afternoon, and she experienced a frightening sense of foreboding as she walked in the direction of Henri's study at the back.

The door stood ajar, and she knocked on it lightly, before pushing it open and going in.

Henri de Montfleurie was sitting on the sofa in

front of the fire. Lifting his head at the sound of her tapping, he got to his feet when he saw her.

'Rosie!' he exclaimed. 'Thank God you're here! Collie's been asking for you for hours.'

As he spoke he hurried to her and took her in his arms; they embraced affectionately and then drew apart, staring at each other, wanting to help each other in their pain.

A great sadness hung in the air, and inside herself Rosie knew that despite her fervent prayers for Collie the end was near for her beloved friend.

As she continued to look into Henri's face Rosie saw the suffering he was enduring reflected in his dark eyes. His face was haggard and he appeared to have lost a lot of sleep; there were bags under his eyes which, she noticed, were red and puffy.

'How . . . how is Collie?' Rosie asked in a strangled voice, dreading to hear what he said, even knowing the answer before he spoke.

He shook his head. 'Not good, I'm afraid.'

'I know she wasn't feeling great over Christmas,' Rosie said, trying to keep her voice even, but it shook unsteadily. 'Still, this is rather sudden, isn't it?'

'Not really. Collie started to get terrible pains in her back just before Christmas, although she kept this to herself. She didn't confide in either of us.' He shook his head sadly. 'The pains became unbearable at the beginning of the year, just after you left, and so she went to see Dr Junot in Tours. He wanted her to go to Paris, to see the specialists who had treated her this summer. You see he was convinced the cancer had spread. Collie agreed to make the trip, and she was preparing for it when she . . . collapsed . . .'

Henri's voice broke, and he turned away, fumbling in his pocket for a handkerchief. After blowing his nose, and calming himself, he swung back to Rosie, murmured, 'But Collie wants to see you, Rosie, let's not waste time needlessly down here.'

'I waited for you, Rosie. I waited for you to come,' Collie said in a faint voice, her eyes riveted on Rosie.

'I'm here now, Collie darling.'

'I'm going far, far away on a long journey.'

Rosie, who sat on a stool next to the bed, could only nod. Reaching out, she took Collie's small, cold hand in hers, held onto it tightly, stroking it occasionally. She longed to comfort Collie.

'There will be a great distance between us in a way, yet I'll always be with you, Rosie. In your heart. And as long as you're alive, I'll be alive because you'll carry the memory of me until the day you die.'

'Oh Collie, I can't bear it. I can't let you go. You must fight to live, to get better.' Tears trickled down Rosie's face and she quickly brushed them away with her other hand. 'Please don't slip away from us.'

'I'm going to be free, Rosie. Free of pain at last. Free of sorrow. And I'll be with Claude. He's waiting for me . . .' Her eyes, always very blue, suddenly became even bluer, and very bright. They fastened on Rosie's face, and held a strange and brilliant radiance as she said, '*I* believe there *is* an after-life, don't you, Rosie?'

'Yes.'

'The spirit *does* live on, doesn't it?'

'Oh, yes, darling.'

A smile struck Collie's tender mouth. 'Once, a long time ago, my mother told me something I've never forgotten. She said that when a thing is good it never dies, that it lives for always. My love for Lisette and Father and you is a good thing, isn't it, Rosie?'

'Oh yes, it is.' Rosie could barely speak, she was so filled with sorrow and emotion.

'Then my love will live, won't it?'

'Yes.'

'Can you promise me something?'

'Anything, Collie.'

'You won't let Lisette forget me, will you?'

'*Never.*'

'I want her to remember me, and to remember Claude. She mustn't forget her father. Please, Rosie, keep the memory of us both alive for her.'

'I promise she'll never forget either of you,' Rosie said, her face crumpling. She brushed away her tears again, tried hard to control herself for Collie's sake, who was being so brave in the face of encroaching death.

'My little girl will be safe with Father and Kyra, but you'll keep an eye on her for me, won't you?'

'You know I will. I love her very much, and I'll see her all the time.'

'Thank you, Rosie, for everything you've always done for us.'

'Please don't say that . . . I haven't done anything.'

'Yes, you have. Too much. I'm glad you're getting free of Guy. You must start a new life. You'll meet

someone nice one day, Rosie. You'll have the kind of
happiness I had with Claude. It's really the only thing
that makes life bearable . . . a deep and enduring
love.'

Rosie nodded.

Collie smiled at her suddenly, and her eyes
widened slightly. 'I'm so *glad* we met, you and I, all
those years ago in Paris, when we were girls . . . that
you became part of my family.' Collie closed her eyes
and her breathing suddenly changed, quickened,
seemed laboured and shallow.

Rosie leaned closer, searching Collie's face
urgently, and then, as if she were aware that Rosie
was anxiously staring at her, Collie opened her
eyes.

'It's all right,' she whispered. 'I'd like the others to
come in . . . my father, Lisette, Yvonne and Kyra.
And Father Longueville. He's been waiting to see me
for ages.'

Again, Rosie only managed a nod.

Collie tightened her grip on Rosie's hand, and gave
it a little tug.

Rosie leaned forward, brought her face closer to
Collie's.

In a faint voice, Collie said, 'Kiss me, Rosie. Kiss
me goodbye.'

Unchecked tears spilled out of Rosie's eyes and ran
down her face as she brought her lips to Collie's
cheek. She kissed her, and put her arms around her
sister-in-law gently, comfortingly. Holding her close,
she murmured softly, against her hair, 'I've always
loved you, Collie, and I always will. I'll never forget

you. *Never*. And you *will* be in my heart always, darling. *Always*.'

'Don't cry, dearest Rosie. I'm going to a safe place. I'll be with Claude. And my mother,' Collie said, and smiled the most radiant of smiles.

Eventually Rosie stood up and went to the bedroom door.

The others had assembled in the corridor outside, waiting to take their farewells of Collie. Rosie beckoned for them to come in.

Slowly they entered the room, Lisette clinging to her grandfather's hand, looking worried and scared; she was still such a little girl. The young priest, who had so recently married Henri and Kyra, was the last, and he stood slightly away from the family, near the door. After Collie had said her goodbyes to her loved ones, he would perform extreme unction. The last rites.

And then Collie will be at peace, Rosie thought. And we will grieve for her always. But she is far too young to die. Only thirty-two. Only a year older than me.

PART THREE

Dangerous Relationships

TWENTY-NINE

'You're making progress, really doin' good, Kevin,'
Neil said. 'You've just gotta keep it up, but stay
cool, for Christ's sake, and don't make any hasty
moves.'

Kevin nodded. 'Don't worry, I'm being as cautious
as I can. And watching my back all right. The guy I
worry about is Tony. His ass is on the line. Hell,
working undercover smack in the middle of the Mob
is nerve-racking for him, for anybody. It's a tough
road to hack, and I'm glad it's not me. At least I'm
on the outside looking in, so to speak.'

'You mean on the *inside* looking in, don't you?'

Kevin half smiled. 'I'm only partially on the inside,
compadre.'

'True, true, but listen, Kev, Tony's okay. When
you're third-generation Italian, you know how to play
their game, know how to handle them. He speaks
their lingo, for one thing, and don't forget he had a
lotta experience with wiseguys when he was growing
up in East New York. That's one helluva fucking savage
neighbourhood, a real dangerous corner of the uni-
verse. The home of Murder Inc. in the days of Albert

Anastasia, and for all the years Tony was growing up it was a wide-open Mob town.'

Neil nodded, as if confirming something to himself, and remarked very quietly, 'Tony's a cool guy, real cool, just like you. He has to be, as do you, or his ass'll fry; and so will yours, if you put as much as one toe wrong.' Neil took a long swig of his beer. 'Know what? There's no way my old buddy Anthony Rigante can be spotted as a cop. He's always worked undercover, ever since he joined the force six years ago. It's become second nature to him now, kid.'

'Yeah, I guess you're right. But it's still a rough road to hack when you're hanging around with mobsters, playing pattycake with them.'

Neil eyed Kevin knowingly but he said nothing.

The two detectives were sitting together at a table in the corner of a small bar in the Thirties, just off First Avenue. The bar was crowded even though it was only five in the afternoon, and the cacophony of sounds, from high-pitched voices and strident laughter to the clatter of glasses and music blaring from the jukebox in the background, made it a perfect place to have a private conversation. No one could hear a word they were saying.

Nevertheless, Kevin drew closer to Neil and dropped his voice when he said, 'It's taken a month or so, but things are starting to break open for me at last. Tony's finally got me worked in with the lower echelon of the Rudolfo family. I'm on back-slapping terms with several soldiers, and one *caporegime*. And I'll tell you this, Neil, you were right about them. The Rudolfos are up to their armpits in drugs, putting millions of dollars' worth of shit out on the street every week, dealing every goddamned thing from smack to crack, just as you said they were.'

'And they're into the unions, loan sharking, prostitution, gambling, bank fraud, and every other kinda scam that's ever been invented. They've gotten away with it all for too many years, those bastards have, and we've just gotta nail 'em, and nail 'em good, and the charges, when they're made, just gotta stick, Kev.' Suddenly looking well pleased with himself, Neil finished with a satisfied grin, 'Just like the Feds' case against Gotti is sticking.'

'I know it has to stick, Neil, and it will. It's going well, so don't worry, but we do need a bit more time. We can't blow it now, not at this stage of the game.'

'Okay, okay, I'll give you time, but not too much. The longer you drag things out the more you're spreading yourself thin. Putting yourself at risk.'

'I'll be all right, so will Tony. Like him, I've been working undercover for too many years to make a slip.'

'I know, I know, just watch your back, okay?'

Kevin nodded. He finished his beer, pushed back his chair and stood up. 'How about another? One for the road? Or something stronger?'

'Another beer's fine, kid. Thanks.'

Neil stubbed out his cigarette and immediately put another one in his mouth, wishing he could quit. But he couldn't. If he didn't buy it with a bullet, he'd probably drop dead of lung cancer or a heart attack. But what the hell, life was a risk whatever you did. He struck a match, brought it to the end of the cigarette. So he might as well go up in flames, right? He laughed, a silent, cynical laugh.

Kevin returned to the table carrying two glasses of beer and sat down. 'Cheers,' he said, and took a long swallow, leaving a fine line of froth on his upper lip. He wiped it away with his hand, and grinned at Neil. 'So, Gotti's up to his ass in trouble . . . *Yea!*'

Neil couldn't help laughing. 'He sure as hell is, did ya see the *Daily News* the other day? They're calling him the Al Capone of the nineties. That's gonna go to his big head.'

'I saw the same story. Funny thing is, he's going to trial in Brooklyn, which happens to be Capone's old stomping ground.'

'And Gotti's as well, don't forget,' Neil answered, leaning across the table. 'What I hear is that most of the underworld think he won't make it this time, that the government will finally nail him. Yeah, it looks as if the Teflon Don's gonna go down. Is that what *you're* hearing out on the street?'

'Sure is. And our division's done a pretty damned good job of it, bringing in as much stuff as we have. I can't believe that Gotti would be so dumb, shooting his mouth off the way he has.'

'Listen, the guy's a nut, in my opinion. On the other hand, how was he to know that the Ravenite Social Club was bugged? Nor did he ever think that his lawyer would get thrown off the case. Let's face it, Bruce Cutler has been his lucky charm, in a way. But a lotta the wiseguys say he's nobody to blame but himself, that he talked about a lotta things a boss shouldn't talk about – murders, *Cosa Nostra*, and he sure as hell shouldn't have talked at the club. His *headquarters*, for God's sake! He should've taken a walk to talk. In the street.'

'I heard he even admitted that he had a guy whacked, that it's on one of the tapes.'

Neil nodded. 'Look, I'm pretty damned sure he'll go down, and that he'll be behind bars for a helluva long time. He'll get life. The racketeering charges against him are gonna stick, Kevin. So, that's Gotti and Gravano the stooly outta the way. And look, the shit's spinning in the fan in the Colombo family. One of their guys just got hit, and there's gonna be a full-blown civil war, I think, with family members pitted against each other.'

'Some are taking the side of Persico, others are backing the acting boss, Little Vic Orena. The talk around my neck of the woods is that Orena's trying to really take over while Persico's in jail.'

'Fucking mobsters! There's gonna be blood in the streets, you'll see.'

'Flowing through Little Italy, and a few other prime spots around town,' Kevin said, and punched Neil on the arm. 'Don't look so miserable. Law and order is winning out. Last week I heard that the two Gambino brothers are about to face charges in another racketeering trial. Apparently old silver-throat Gravano is singing another hit song for the Manhattan district attorney. This time he's nailing the Gambinos. They're purported to have a stranglehold on the trucking business in the garment industry.'

'So I heard,' Neil said. He looked at his watch. 'I

gotta go, kid. I'm glad we had this meet. Same time next week, okay?'

'You're on, Neil. Just let me know where.'

They grabbed their overcoats and left the bar together. Out on the sidewalk, Kevin said, 'I'm going thataway,' and nodded in the direction of Fortieth Street.

'Aha, off to see your uptown girl tonight, eh?' Neil leered wickedly.

'No. She's away. I've got an old buddy in from out of town. We're gonna break bread together.'

'Take it easy, Kev, and remember what I said – watch your back. At all times.'

'You gotta deal, Neil. And you, too. *Watch yourself.*'

'Sure, kid.'

Kevin hailed a cab, got in swiftly and told the driver to head to Lexington and Forty-fifth Street. Once there, he paid, got out and took another taxi across town to Sixth Avenue and Fifty-eighth, where he alighted again. He made it down the street at a rapid pace, went into the Wyndham Hotel, crossed through into Jonathan's, the hotel restaurant, looked around, returned to the lobby and went into the men's room.

Five minutes later he was hailing his third cab outside the popular show business hotel, and told the driver he wanted to go to Park and Fifty-second Street. Within minutes he was paying again and getting out. This time he walked, taking Fifty-second up to Fifth Avenue, and then heading towards Fifty-sixth Street. Several times he glanced behind him, now quite positive that he was not being followed by anyone.

When he arrived at Fifty-sixth Street he went immediately to the entrance of Trump Tower, pushed through the doors and strode over to the security desk.

'Mr Gavin Ambrose please.'

'Your name, sir?'

'Kevin Madigan.'

The guard dialled, spoke into the phone and then replaced the receiver. 'You can go up. Sixtieth floor, sir.'

'Thanks.' Kevin swung away from the desk and headed in the direction of the elevator banks.

'This is one hell of a view!' Kevin exclaimed as he walked around the vast living room of the apartment where Gavin was staying. 'Jesus! New York looks *sensational*! All bright lights and tall sky and buildings shooting to the heavens. Makes me positively dizzy. I've never been so high up in my life.'

'Sure you have. We once went up to the top of the Empire State together.' Gavin smiled as he handed him a glass of wine. 'Come on, come away from all that plate glass. Let's sit down and catch up.'

'Thanks,' Kevin said, taking the wine. He followed Gavin across the room to an arrangement of large white sofas and chairs. These were placed around a huge, antique Chinese coffee table made of black-lacquered wood and inlaid with mother-of-pearl flowers.

He lowered himself onto one of the sofas. 'So, what the hell are *you* doing in a place like this? It looks like an expensive whore's habitat.'

'God, what will you say next!' Gavin exclaimed. 'And how does an expensive whore's habitat *look*, anyway?'

'Overwhelmingly plush, lush, and reeking of dough. Lottsa dough. Hey, who *does* this place belong to, Gav?'

'I'm honestly not sure, I found it through a real-estate agent. But I think it's owned by some European billionaire tycoon, who prefers to stay in Europe, apparently. I'm renting it for a few months.'

'Oh.' Kevin looked across at him, gave him a hard stare and raised a brow. 'Stuff not good back at the old rancho?'

Gavin laughed. 'Not good. Not bad. Nothing. That's where it's at between me and Louise. Nothing new on *that* front. I just happen to have a yen for the East Coast these days. After all, I'm forever dubbed an East Coast "ethnic" actor, so I thought to myself why not come back here for a short while.'

'That's great, Gav, I'm glad you're here. It's like old times. However, what about Paris? Rosie told me you're starting preproduction soon on *Napoleon and Josephine*. And that she's doing the costumes.'

'She is, and I am. Once I've finished the last bit of postproduction here, on *Kingmaker*. We have some looping to do with a couple of actors, and I've moved a small group over to New York. Part of my production team. They'll help to expedite things. We'll work for about two to three weeks. Then I'm going to beat it back across the Atlantic, and take up residence in Paris for at least six months. Maybe longer.'

'And this place?'

'It's yours, if you want it, Kev.'

'You've gotta be kidding!'

'No.'

'What would I do with a place like this?'

'Live in it, I suppose.' Gavin's mouth twitched with hidden laughter. 'I mean, it's certainly an improvement on Ninety-fourth and First, isn't it?'

'I guess,' Kevin replied. 'But I'm not living in my own apartment at the moment. I'm hunkered down in the Village, in a sublet on East Tenth Street. Under a different identity, naturally. I'm working undercover.'

'When are you not?'

Kevin caught the sudden, almost imperceptible change in Gavin's voice. There was just the faintest echo of disapproval; and perhaps that was regret clouding Gavin's cool grey eyes. Gavin had the most honest eyes he'd ever seen. Kevin made no response, sipped his drink, leaned back against the overstuffed white sofa and crossed his long legs.

'It's taking its toll on you, Kev,' Gavin said after a moment, staring at his oldest and closest male friend. 'It's beginning to show, kiddo.'

Always defensive when it came to his job, Kevin was about to say he didn't know what Gavin was talking about, and then he changed his mind. He wasn't going to play stupid games with a guy he loved, who was like a brother to him, and who was always there for him no matter what. Had always been there.

Slowly he nodded his head. 'The hours *have* been rough lately,' Kevin admitted and grimaced. 'And being undercover can get to be a strain at times.'

'That's not surprising. It can also get to be very dangerous.'

'The whole world's dangerous these days, Gav.'

'I know. But you're right in the middle of it all. In the fray. Pitting yourself against criminals. And bullets fly and anybody who's not got his eyes peeled can get hit. And as long as you're with the Crime Intelligence Division you'll be right in the centre of the danger zone. A target. Cannon fodder, as they used to say.'

Kevin shrugged. 'Well, the perks are great,' he shot back, and burst out laughing at his own absurdity. But making fun of the danger made it all easier to handle sometimes.

'Like hell the perks are great!' Gavin scoffed and lifted his wine glass off the table, took a sip, quickly went on, 'Rosie worries about you. Nell worries about you. And yours truly worries about you. Why don't you pack it in, Kevin?'

'Can you stop being an actor?'

'No.'

'There's your answer.'

'But *I'm* not in danger of being killed –'

'Like hell you're not. Turn in a lousy performance and you don't know what might happen to you. There's always some nut out there, some nut ready to commit mayhem.'

Gavin shook his head. 'You're incorrigible. But I suppose you gotta do what you gotta do.'

'Spot on, man.'

Gavin lolled against a mound of white wool pillows

and murmured, 'Come on, Kevin, *quit*. I'll give you a job.'

'Doing what?'

'Being my assistant.'

'Shit, that's a handout, Gavin!' Kevin cried with a flash of momentary anger. 'I don't need your handouts.'

'It's not a handout, Kev. It really isn't. I do need somebody to take care of a vast amount of stuff for me.'

'How about a secretary? That's who guys in your position normally employ.'

'I have a secretary. I need an assistant, somebody to take care of certain things for me, financial and otherwise. Somebody I can trust. And let's face it, you're like family. We *are* family, Kevin, after all the years we've been together.'

'Did Nell put you up to this?'

'No way, man. No way. But she'd be happy to see you come in from the cold.'

'It's not for me. Thanks, Gav, I know you mean well, but a job like that is not my speed.'

'The offer holds. It'll always be open for you.'

Kevin sighed. 'Thanks. I sound rude and ungrateful and churlish. It was a grand offer, honestly it was. But I'm a cop, just like my dad was a cop, and my grandfather and his dad before him, and so on and so forth. And I don't think I'd be happy doing anything else, I really don't.'

'I guess I know that deep down . . . I think I've always known it. Anyway, what's happening with you and Nell? Are you going to make it permanent?'

Kevin fixed his dark eyes on Gavin's lighter ones, and they exchanged a long look; it was the kind of look only old friends can share.

At last Kevin answered. 'I've thought about it a lot lately. I've even asked her to marry me. She's thought about it. But she's never said yes.'

'More's the pity, you're made for each other.'

'Tell Nell.'

'I will, with your permission.'

'Sure, go ahead. Anyway, you were a bit evasive earlier. What's really happening between you and Louise?'

'Nothing much. She lives in my house, spends my money, and screws a senator from Washington.' Gavin shrugged. 'If my grandfather were alive he'd call me a dumb guinea.'

'And mine would say I'm a dumb Mick.'

They grinned at each other, and Kevin said, 'But are you going to stay with Louise? Seriously, what *are* you going to do?'

'I'm not going to do anything to rock any boats right now –'

'Don't you think that moving back East is going to rock *something*?'

'I haven't moved back permanently. I've merely rented an apartment in New York, my home town, while I finish postproduction on a movie. Then I'm proceeding to France to make a movie there. I'm giving her a lot of rope meantime. Miles and miles of it. She'll hang herself eventually. I can wait. I'm in no hurry.'

'So there's nobody special in your life?'

Gavin shook his head. 'No sweet and lovely lady to brighten my days. Just my work. That's enough.'

'You'll meet somebody one day.'

'Maybe.'

Kevin asked, 'Do you have a cook here, or what?'

'No, why?'

'I just wondered where you planned for us to eat? You loathe going out to restaurants . . . that famous sexy mug of yours causes such trouble.'

'So do you hate going out, Kev. Don't blame it entirely on me.'

Kevin said, 'Did you ever think you'd become such a famous actor you couldn't go to dinner in a public place for fear of being recognized and mobbed by half-crazed women? Or that I'd be reluctant to go with you for fear of getting myself and you whacked by gangsters on the prowl for me?'

'No, I didn't,' Gavin answered and a quick smile flashed. 'But as I just pointed out, we're a couple of dumb guys.'

Gavin rose, walked across the room, then swung to face Kevin. 'As a matter of fact, we *are* going out tonight.'

'*Oh*. Where?'

'Downtown. To Bobby De Niro's Tribeca Screening Room. I've rented it for the evening. Just for the two of us. I'm going to screen *Kingmaker* for you, and then we're going to eat at Bobby's Tribeca Grill.'

'That sounds great, and I guess we're both safe there.'

'That's a sure thing. I can guarantee it, Kevin.'

THIRTY

It was icy weather, and the drizzling rain was rapidly turning into snow that coated the car windows with a film of frosty white.

'Bad night, Vito,' the chauffeur said, flipping the switch of the windshield wipers. 'A bad night to be driving all the way to Staten Island.'

'We're dry in here, Carlo,' Vito replied in his gravelly voice, 'and warm. So it's no problem. Why doan ya put a disc in? Johnny's disc. The new one, ya know, *Fortune's Child*.'

'Sure, Vito,' Carlo mumbled, and did as he had been asked.

Immediately Johnny Fortune's golden voice echoed around the close confines of the car, and Vito settled himself in the corner of the back seat, smiling inwardly, filled with pleasure as he listened to Johnny's rendition of *You and Me (We Wanted It All)*.

He was very proud of his nephew. The big star. Johnny was bigger than anybody around today. There had been others before him just as big, but they had had their day in the sun. Now it was his Johnny's turn. At age thirty-eight Johnny Fortune was 'it', at the top of the charts, and everybody's favourite. Not only in America but around the world.

He sighed with pleasure and closed his eyes for a moment, soothed by the sound of that velvet voice. Sighing again, Vito thought: He sings like an angel, my Johnny does.

It was January the twenty-third, nineteen ninety-two, a Thursday, and as always on Thursdays Vito was on his way to join Salvatore for the weekly family dinner. For sixty years they'd had their family dinner every Thursday; it was a ritual which had begun when they were both nineteen and newly married. He to Angelina, God rest her soul, and Salvatore to Theresa.

Such a long time. He wondered how many more dinners they would enjoy on Thursdays. They were both old men. Seventy-nine years old. He didn't feel it, though, just a touch of arthritis in his hip and a bit of extra weight. And he didn't look seventy-nine, he knew that. Neither did Salvatore. Grey hairs they had, yeah, and deep lines scoring their faces, but they were in good shape, everything considered. And neither of them had lost their marbles, thank the good Lord.

His old *goombah* was a wonder, still goin' strong, still holdin' his power, reigning over all the families on the East Coast. *Capo di tutti capi*. How proud he was of Salvatore, just as proud of him as he was of Johnny.

That song Johnny was singing, he liked it.

'*You and me we wanted it all,*' Johnny sang again.

Wasn't that the real truth about the whole world?

He and Salvatore, they had wanted it all, had wanted everything. They had taken it. And by force, whenever that was necessary. Some said he and Salvatore were dangerous, ruthless, evil men. But they weren't. They were just men trying to pull themselves out of the gutter, out of the bitter poverty of the lower East Side where they had come as immigrant boys, speaking no English, half starved most of the time, with no chance of making it. They had had to do what they had done to survive.

Vito smiled to himself. Life had turned out all right for them. A few headaches now and then, a few glitches, but nothing they hadn't been able to handle. And they had managed to avoid trouble with law enforcement most of the time – and for over sixty years. They'd been lucky, perhaps. But crooked cops on the pad helped; Salvatore paid off every week, but pay-offs were meaningless. What did a few envelopes stuffed with cash mean to Salvatore and him? They could afford it. They still paid; they were for ever protected that way.

Nobody's clean, Vito thought, and laughed out loud, a raucous laugh that shook his plump body and filled the car. Everybody could be bought. The only thing that differed was the price. Sometimes it was money; sometimes it was power they wanted, or a special favour. Whores, the lot of 'em. It was only the price they haggled about.

People stank. The world was full of shits. He didn't think much of the human race. The *amici*, the men of the 'honoured society', were blamed for a lot that ailed the world. I doan know why that should be,

Vito thought, frowning. We ain't done worse than nobody else. Graft, theft, crimes of all kinds and even murder were commonplace, part of big business, part of all walks of life, even government. Politicians stink, he added to himself. They're out for themselves, just like cops, just like everybody . . . Everybody but his Johnny. Me and Salvatore, we did it our way, he muttered under his breath. We made our own rules. We followed the code of the Brotherhood, but we did it our way, oh yeah, that we did. He smiled inwardly. He had a few good memories.

Johnny Fortune.

Big star.

His pride and joy.

His nephew.

More like a son than a nephew.

Johnny was in New York this week. He was coming to the family dinner tonight. Driving out from Manhattan in a limo. Salvatore was happy; he was happy. It was gonna be a grand evening.

Salvatore Rudolfo's house was set back from the road, surrounded by a high brick wall, with large iron gates at the front. Electrified gates. And it was guarded like Fort Knox.

Vito knew that there were men everywhere, men packing heat, but they were not visible to the human eye. Except for the two guards at the gate, who appeared as if from nowhere the moment the car came to a standstill outside it.

The gates slowly opened after the guards had checked him out, made sure it was he. Carlo rolled the black Cadillac sedan up the short circular drive to the front door, braked, and came to help him out. Carlo, a soldier in the organization and assigned to him as a driver-bodyguard, then returned to the car and took it around to the back as Vito climbed the front steps.

Once he was inside the hall, shrugging out of his overcoat, Vito realized that something was different here tonight. Usually on Thursdays only Salvatore's closest aides and family were present. He noticed a number of extra *capi* hanging around at the far end of the hall; two more were positioned near the door to Salvatore's study.

The door of this room suddenly opened and Anthony Rudolfo, Salvatore's cousin and the *consigliere*, came out. Walking forward, he kissed Vito on both cheeks, and said, 'The big man's waiting to talk to you before we have dinner, Vito.'

Vito nodded and immediately went into the Don's private sanctuary, frowning, suddenly worried that something was wrong.

Salvatore was sitting in a chair near the fire. He rose when he saw Vito, came to greet him. The two men, friends since their births in Palermo, embraced, kissed each other on each cheek in the Sicilian way, and then they drew apart.

Vito nodded slowly. 'Ah, you look good tonight, Salvatore. For an old man.'

Salvatore laughed. 'And so do you, my old *goombah*.' He shivered slightly. 'It's a cold night, Vito. Cold enough to freeze a witch's tits, turn 'em into icicles.' He laughed again, a deep belly laugh.

'Remember when we were kids, shivering in them cold winters in our thin threads? Remember how we tried to keep each other warm in them rat holes we called homes in lower Manhattan?' He shook his head. 'Them were some days.'

'Sure I remember. I doan forget nothin', Salvatore.'

The Don put his arm around Vito and walked with him to the fireplace. 'Them days are long gone. Just a memory. But we're getting old, you and me, and once again the cold is hard on our bones. Makes 'em creak. So, come, sit, thaw out near the fire.'

As he spoke the Don lifted a bottle of red wine from the small table set between the chairs, poured two wine glasses full to their brims. 'The fire will warm your flesh, the *vino* your blood.'

The two men clinked glasses, said softly, in unison, 'To the Brotherhood.' And then each took a deep swallow of the wine, rolling it around in their mouths, savouring it. It was one of the few pleasures in life left to them. Then they sat back in their chairs and looked at each other for a long time, their old eyes exuding knowledge, wisdom and power. And everlasting friendship.

Eventually, Vito said, 'Why the extra *capos* tonight? You expectin' trouble, or what?'

Shaking his head, Salvatore Rudolfo murmured, 'Just a precaution. I don't want no nasty surprises, or to get caught off guard. That's our old rule, Vito. Why change it?'

'What're ya gettin' at?' Vito asked, his dark eyes narrowing.

'Too many problems in the other families. The

Gambinos are drowning in trouble, Sammy the Bull been doin' too much singing.' He stared at Vito and hissed, '*Shirru*, stool pigeon! He's just a yella canary, that one. Then there's the Colombo family, they're crazy, at each other's throats, killing each other. I hope there ain't gonna be a war between the families. Like in the past.'

'I doan think the violence'll spread.'

'Who knows what'll happen.' Salvatore raised his hands in a helpless gesture and shrugged. 'One of the other families in New York might take advantage of this situation, try to take over the Gambino or Colombo territories. It *could* be a war. Yeah, better we're prepared, protected should trouble come.'

'That's right, Salvatore. Ain't nothin' wrong in protecting ourselves.'

Salvatore leaned forward and his eyes, faded now and rheumy, were suddenly the piercing bright blue of his youth as they focused intently on his oldest friend and confidant. 'Mebbe I'm gonna call a meeting of all the families, bring the bosses together –'

'You mean like in Appalachia in 1957?' Vito exclaimed.

'Yeah, a conference. To decide what to do. There's too much focus on us, Vito. On the Brotherhood. The cops, the Feds, the press are breathin' down our necks. It's dangerous.' He sighed. 'Suddenly we're very visible, and that's bad. *Capisce?*'

'Yeah, I'm with ya all the way.'

'Then there's Joey Fingers,' Salvatore announced.

'What about him?'

'He's gettin' too big-headed, and he's trigger-happy.

He's connected to us . . . so he's a threat to us. *Scrutiny*, Vito, that's what I've always detested. Too much scrutiny is not good for our business.' The Don paused and, even though he was in his own home and was positive it wasn't bugged, he added in a hoarse whisper, 'It's bad for *Cosa Nostra.*'

Vito nodded, reached out, touched Salvatore's hand, signalling his understanding.

After a moment of silence, Vito asked, 'Who's gonna handle Joey Fingers?'

'Nobody. Not yet. We wait. See what he does next.' A deep sigh rippled through the Don and he shook his head sadly. 'It's not the same, my old *goombah*, times have changed.'

Vito did not say a word, lost for a moment in his own thoughts. Salvatore wasn't *capo di tutti* for nothin'. He was a wise man; he spoke the truth and nothin' but. Vito sat studying him for a moment.

Salvatore was a powerfully-built man, tall, broad, with no fat on him. His face was scored and lined and scratched over with wrinkles, and yet it was not an old man's face. It was too strong and powerful to be that. The nose was Roman, slightly hooked, the eyebrows arched prominently, and flecked with white above those extraordinary eyes. Pure blue. Like the Mediterranean Sea that surrounded Sicily. They could be filled with the sunlight and the warmth of the Old Country one minute, as cold and as icy as the Arctic the next.

Salvatore cut into Vito's thoughts. He said, 'Where's Johnny?'

'He'll be here. Any minute now, Salvatore. Doan

worry so much.' Vito rose and ambled over to the window, stood looking out, and after a moment, he exclaimed, 'Ah, here he comes now. He's a good boy.' Vito glanced at his watch. 'He's on time.'

Theresa Rudolfo, Salvatore's wife, sat at the head of the table. She was a tall, thin, stately woman in her seventies, with pure white hair and eyes like chips of jet. As always, she wore a black dress and her three long strands of pearls – real pearls – and she presided with dignity and pride over her table.

This was covered in a starched white cloth, beautifully embroidered, upon which sat the finest china, crystal and silver that money could buy. A silver bowl of flowers, flanked by white candles in silver sticks, graced the centre and the remainder of the table groaned with dishes and bowls of food.

Assembled together around this splendid table, in the formal dining room of the Rudolfo home, were Salvatore's four children, all grown and married: Maria, Sophia, Frankie and Alfredo, and their respective spouses. Also present were Salvatore's brother Charlie, the underboss, and their cousin Anthony, the *consigliere*, and their wives.

Vito sat next to Theresa, on her right.

Johnny was on Salvatore's right, where he was always seated.

It was a typical Thursday dinner: there was a huge salad of lettuce, tomatoes, olives and sliced onions; red peppers sautéed in olive oil; seafood salad; a baked fish; *tagliatelle* with tomato sauce; and several roast chickens. Red wine flowed as Alfredo poured it; home-made Italian bread was passed around by the others; everyone laughed and talked and joked. It had the makings of a convivial evening.

Only Theresa was quiet, quiet as the grave, listening intently, watching them all through eyes which were exceedingly wary.

Occasionally she murmured a word or two to her daughters, as they helped her pass the dishes around the table to the men, or returned to the kitchen to replenish the empty bowls with steaming pasta and rich sauces.

Studying her surreptitiously at one moment, Johnny had an unexpected flash of insight. He thought: she's unhappy because I'm here tonight. She doesn't like me. Then it hit him like a thunderbolt. His Aunt Theresa, whom he had known all of his life, had never liked him. He suddenly knew, with absolute certainty, that she detested him, resented him. He asked himself why. There was only one answer. Because Uncle Salvatore favoured him. *Jealousy*. She was jealous because he was so close to her husband, and because there was such affection between them.

Across the table, Vito was harbouring similar thoughts. But the old man shrugged them off at once. Theresa was an old woman now. Her venom was weak, had lost its power with age. Nobody paid any attention to her any more. Least of all Salvatore, who had never loved her.

After dinner, Salvatore took Johnny and Vito into his private sanctuary, and closed the door behind them.

'Have a strega, Johnny,' the Don said, pouring the golden-coloured Italian liqueur into slender glasses. 'And you, Vito?' he asked, raising a brow. Vito nodded.

'Thanks,' Johnny said, taking the glass.

Salvatore handed another one to Vito, who thanked him.

The three men touched glasses and sat down around the glowing fire.

'Congratulations, Johnny,' Salvatore said, and beamed at the younger man. 'Great concert at Madison Square Garden last Saturday. Sensational. We all enjoyed it.'

'It was a sell-out,' Johnny pointed out. 'My most successful concert so far.'

'We're proud of you, Johnny. You're a big star. The biggest. And you did it yourself.'

'Oh come *on*, Uncle Salvatore! I know how much you and Uncle Vito helped me.'

'We did nothing.'

Johnny gaped at the Don, and then looked across at Vito, who inclined his head, acknowledging Salvatore's words as the truth.

Salvatore said, 'We opened a few doors, that's all, got a number of clubs across the country to book you. Suggested to the guys in Vegas that they give you a few breaks. We wanted you to do it the hard way, the real way, like anybody else.'

His eyes widening in surprise, Johnny asked, 'But why?'

'We wanted to keep you clean, we didn't want you to be associated with us,' Salvatore explained in the softest of voices.

'If we'd done too much we'd have polluted you, Johnny,' Vito added. 'We didn't want to contaminate you. We don't want you linked to the *amici*,' Vito smiled at him, 'to the Brotherhood. We kinda worked behind the scenes a bit, like Salvatore said.'

'Well, thanks anyway,' Johnny replied, and then he grinned at the two older men. 'And I thought I was under your protection.'

'You were,' Salvatore murmured. '*Always*. But we let you make your own way in the business. And we were right to do it our way. And you . . .' He smiled at Johnny. 'You never let us down. But I do have one disappointment.'

Puzzled, Johnny stared at him. 'What's that?'

'You're not married, Johnny. It'd be better if you had a nice Italian wife.' Salvatore nodded sagely. 'A man needs a wife.'

'I agree with you, Uncle Salvatore, but I've never met the right girl.'

'What a pity,' the Don said. 'You're young . . . there's time.' He sipped his strega, and the men fell silent for a short while. Finally, Salvatore broke the silence when he addressed Johnny. 'So you're goin' to Europe. Tell me about the trip, where you're gonna be goin'.'

Johnny began to talk about the short concert tour he was about to embark on, and Salvatore listened acutely, nodding from time to time, asking a few pertinent questions.

Vito was not so attentive, and his thoughts soon began to wander.

Decades fell away.

In his mind's eye, he saw Salvatore Rudolfo as he had been as a young man in his thirties, as he had been at Johnny's age. So handsome, as handsome as Johnny was now. The women had thrown themselves at him; he had not been interested. Salvatore had been strait-laced. Well, most of the time.

Vito sighed. Life was funny, littered with loose ends, not a bit neat, not tidy at all. He liked things neat and tidy. He wished Salvatore felt the same way. Vito closed his eyes, drifted with his thoughts, enjoying the warmth of the fire, the taste of the strega sweet in his throat, the satisfaction of a full belly, the comfort of family. Contented, he dozed.

'I'll be in touch from London, Uncle Salvatore,' Johnny said, and Vito sat up with a start.

'What? What did ya say?' he asked, looking at Johnny, blinking.

Salvatore laughed his deep belly laugh. 'You been sleeping, old man.'

Vito smiled self-consciously and, deciding it would be foolish to protest, he said nothing.

Johnny came over to him, helped him out of the chair, and they kissed each other on both cheeks, embraced.

Moving across the floor swiftly, Johnny kissed the Don, and then he was gone, closing the door quietly behind him.

Left alone, the two old men resumed their seats and sat looking at each other for a long time, comfortable with each other, communicating without words.

At last Vito said, 'I wasn't sleeping.'

Salvatore chuckled.

'I was dreaming.'

'Of what, *goombah*?'

'The past, my old friend.' Vito let out a long breath, and then slowly a smile spread across his round face. 'I remember you when you was Johnny's age, Salvatore. Handsome you were. Just like he is. Same hair, same eyes, same face.'

Salvatore straightened slightly in the chair but he made no comment, merely sipped his strega.

Vito went on, 'There's a picture. In Angelina's album back at my place. Taken in 1946. You, me, Theresa and her. You are thirty-eight. It could be Johnny in that picture.'

Still Salvatore did not speak.

'I don't know why nobody's never spotted the likeness.'

Salvatore merely grunted.

Vito took a deep breath. 'Well, Theresa has.' There was a pause, and Vito added softly, 'She's always known.'

'Mebbe,' Salvatore finally allowed.

'Why have you never told Johnny?'

'It's better this way.'

'Mebbe not. My sister Gina, she loved you, Salvatore. You was her life after Roberto died. She'd want Johnny to know you're his father, his mother'd want him to know the truth.'

'*No*,' Salvatore said in a low but vehement voice, putting his glass down on the table. Leaning closer to Vito, pinning him with his eyes, he hissed, '*He must never know. Nobody must know he's my son.*'

'Why?'

'That's a stupid question, Vito.' Salvatore shook his head. 'It must be old age.'

Vito ignored this pointed remark. 'What harm would it do if *he* knew?'

'No,' Salvatore said, '*it's best my way.*' In a voice so quiet it was scarcely audible, he whispered, 'I want him to be clean. My son Johnny must always be clean.' He gave Vito a hard stare. '*Capisce?*'

346

THIRTY-ONE

Ever since Collie's untimely death in the middle of January and her return to Paris from Montfleurie, Rosie had been working exceptionally long hours.

She had chosen to do so because of her own need to be fully occupied, for she had discovered long ago that work helped to deaden pain for her.

In this instance it helped to keep grief at bay. And she *was* terribly grief-stricken about her beloved Collie, with whom she had enjoyed a special relationship since the first day they had met in 1982.

'Love at first sight' was how Collie had frequently described their initial meeting and Rosie had felt exactly the same way about the woman who was the first friend she had made in Paris, and who would ultimately become her sister-in-law. They had been devoted to each other. Collie had remained steadfast when Rosie's problems with Guy had begun; if anything, the problems had brought them even closer together. Collie had taken Rosie's side, had been a source of consolation and friendship through trying times. It was natural that she missed Collie and she knew she always would.

And so work had been a godsend these past few weeks, and of great solace to her. Also, it pleased Rosie that she had been able to get ahead with the costume designs, and weeks before preproduction on the movie actually began. It gave her a tremendous head start, and for that she was grateful.

Gavin was delayed in New York. Several snags had developed in the postproduction of *Kingmaker*. He had pulled Aida into New York to help and pushed back the date for the move into Billancourt Studios. Aida and the team from London would not be arriving in Paris until March now, when Gavin was also coming.

Nevertheless, Rosie knew she had her work cut out for her even with this lead time. She was facing a monumental task since, once again, she would have to create period costumes which were elaborate and much more complicated to design than contemporary clothing.

Now, on this clear, sunny morning in early February, Rosie stood in the middle of her studio looking at some of her sketches. It was a large, light-filled room with several floor-to-ceiling windows and a skylight overhead, situated at the back of her apartment on the rue de l'Université in the seventh *arrondissement*.

There were six sketches and they were the first group she had finished down to the last detail. Rosie had propped them up at intervals along the viewing shelf she had had built years ago especially for this purpose. The shelf covered the length of a side wall, and once the sketches were lined up and on display it dominated the studio.

All of the sketches were four feet in height, painted in full colour on board. Three were costumes for Napoleon, to be played by Gavin Ambrose; the other three for Josephine, actress unknown as of this moment.

Because they were so sumptuous and complicated to design, Rosie had first tackled the clothes Napoleon had worn when he was crowned emperor. The under robe was of white silk heavily trimmed and embroidered with gold, worn with a full-length red velvet outer robe draped with a white ermine shoulder cape; his crown was a wreath of laurel leaves made of gold. Rosie fully intended to create exact replicas of everything. As usual, she was being a stickler about authenticity.

Her second sketch for Gavin was one of Napoleon's uniforms. This was a pair of white, skin-tight breeches, black boots, a black cutaway coat decorated with gold and a tricorn hat. The third was a civilian suit, composed of knee breeches and a coat, which would be cut from red cloth, worn with white silk stockings and black shoes with gold buckles.

After looking at these drawings for a few minutes, she moved on, studied the sketches for Josephine's clothes. Like Napoleon's robes for his coronation, Josephine's gown for hers was equally sumptuous. Made of yards and yards of white silk, it was embroidered all over with gold thread; with it went exquisite jewellery and a diamond tiara. But this outfit did not concern Rosie for the moment. Her attention was focused on an evening gown which was already in work as a prototype for the seamstresses.

It was draped on the dress form near one of the windows.

Moving away from the sketches, Rosie walked across to the dress form and began to re-drape the fabric. The gown was designed in the Empire style, popularized by Josephine, with a high bustline, a low, scooped-out neck, and short puffed sleeves. Made of silver-coloured silk, it had an over-dress of pale-blue chiffon. The chiffon mounted on the silk bodice and floated down over the skirt, with an opening at the front like a coat. The sleeves were of chiffon, while the gossamer over-skirt was trimmed at the edge with the silver-coloured silk.

Rosie pulled out a few pins, stuck them in the pincushion strapped to her arm, and took hold of the fabric with strong, confident hands. Endeavouring to make it hang correctly on one side, she worked on it for a good ten minutes until she was relatively satisfied with the results.

Draping was an art in fashion design, and Rosie was as accomplished at this as she was at sketching. She had learned to drape in the workrooms of Trigère, the French-born American *couturière*. It was through her father's sister, Aunt Kathleen, who had died two years ago, that this fortuitous situation had come about. Kathleen Madigan had been one of the head fashion-buyers at Bergdorf Goodman, and she had arranged for Rosie to work as an intern during two of her summer vacations from the Fashion Institute of Technology.

Rosie always said that she had learned to drape at the knee of the master, for Pauline Trigère was renowned at this technique. Trigère handled fabric in the way a sculptor moulded clay, designing her clothes with fabric on a dress form rather than with a pencil on paper.

Making a few small gathers along the high waist-band at the back, Rosie expertly inserted the pins carefully, and then stepped back, eyeing the gown, her head to one side. It still wasn't quite right, and so she opened the book containing photographs of this particular gown. It was an art book which Henri de Montfleurie had bought for her. She had found it extremely helpful since it was the history of Napoleon shown through paintings of him, Josephine, his retinue, his battles and the times in which he lived.

Turning to the page where the gown was shown in a beautiful painting of Josephine, Rosie took her time looking at it once more, as always striving for total authenticity. After a short while she started to work with the fabric again.

Half an hour later her concentration was broken by the ringing of the door bell. Momentarily startled, she glanced at the clock on her desk, and saw to her surprise that it was almost one o'clock. Unstrapping the pin-cushion on her wrist and taking off her white designer's coat, she went out to the foyer. She knew it was Nell, who was in Paris and whom she had invited to lunch. The minute she opened the door they fell into each other's arms, hugging affection-ately, and exclaiming how glad they were to see each other.

Rosie drew Nell into the foyer and closed the door, then stood away from her oldest and dearest friend, regarding her appraisingly. 'You look wonderful, Nell. I think my brother agrees with you.'

Nell laughed and nodded. Then she said, 'Well, most of the time.'

Rosie did not pick up on this. Instead she helped Nell off with her dark mink coat and led her into the library. This was a small cosy room, Belle Epoque in style, where a fire burned in the hearth and the scent of mimosa and other spring flowers was so strong it was almost overpowering.

'Good God!' Nell exclaimed, 'where did you find mimosa at this time of year?'

'I didn't,' Rosie answered. 'Johnny Fortune did. At Lachaume. They're the most exclusive florists in Paris and they deal in hot-house blooms and all kinds of out-of-season flowers.'

'Well I never,' Nell said and grinned at Rosie. 'And *I* told him you liked peach roses and violets.'

'Oh, he sent those too. They're in the living room.'

'He doesn't do things by halves, does he?' Nell said, bending over the vase, burying her nose in the mimosa. 'This smells divine.' Straightening, she walked over to the fireplace and watched Rosie opening a bottle of white wine, which she had lifted out of an ice bucket on the small console table. 'I suppose it goes without saying that he's after you, Rosie. Decidedly keen on seducing you, have no fear.'

Rosie merely smiled as she pulled the cork out of the wine bottle. 'I sort of figured that out for myself, Nellie darling. I told you weeks ago that he phoned me at Montfleurie in December, and here last week, to say he'd be coming to Paris via London.'

'Mmmm.' Nell sat down in a chair, leaned back, crossed her legs. 'I'm not disapproving, Rosie mine. Far from it, I think it's a grand idea that you have a little love and romance in your life. Why not? And especially after all those years of starvation with Guy! What's *happening* with your divorce, by the way?'

'It's on its way. Guy has been co-operative, and he's signed all the papers.'

'And how much did that cost you?'

Rosie gaped at her. 'How did you know it cost me anything?'

Nell shook her head. 'Oh, Rosie, Rosie, I was just making a shrewd guess. But it was a good one at that, wasn't it? I *know* what Guy de Montfleurie is only too well. A male whore, for want of a better expression. I figured that he would hit you up for money. So, how much *did* you give him?'

'I bought him his ticket to the Far East and gave him two thousand dollars. He tried to get more out of me, but I refused. I couldn't spare any more, to tell you the truth. He quickly accepted what I offered.'

'I don't know why you gave him anything at all!' Nell exclaimed, sounding cross.

'It was cheap at the price, believe me. I wanted him out of my hair, and out of Henri's hair. I didn't trust him, and I suspected he might be troublesome at Montfleurie. And to everyone. So I bundled him off to Hong Kong the moment he'd signed everything, and at least this way he's not going to rock *anybody's* boat.'

Nell nodded, accepted the glass of wine Rosie offered, and thanked her. The two old friends touched glasses, and Rosie said, 'If you don't mind, Nell, I thought we'd eat here. It's easier for me than going out. I've got tons of work.'

'Fine. How're the costumes coming along?'

'Very well. They're complicated, of course, as I've no doubt you realize. But I've been very focused actually, and the work has helped me to cope with Collie's death.'

'I know what you've gone through. She was so young.' Nell shook her head.

'Thanks for calling me as much as you have, Nell. It's helped, it really has.'

'I know what Collie meant to you.'

Rosie half smiled at her, and changing the subject asked, 'And how's Kevin?'

'Beautiful. Loving. Exciting. And *maddening*.'

'That all sounds great except for the last bit.'

Nell looked into the fire for a moment, her face suddenly sad, her eyes grave, and then she swung her gaze to Rosie and answered very quietly, 'I adore Kev, you know that. But I can't handle that damned job of his, Rosie. You know as well as I do that he's forever in danger. And I literally *live* through it with him, live on the edge of fear night and day. My nerves are really jagged these days.'

'That's because you love him so very much, Nell.'

'I do?'

'Of course. At least *I* think so. If you didn't, you wouldn't care the way you do, and you wouldn't be so worried about him all the time.'

'I guess you're right,' Nell admitted.

'Why don't you two get married?'

Nell simply stared at her, and decided not to answer.

Rosie said, 'I know he's asked you, because he told me he had on the phone last week.'

'Did he now? And yes, it's true. But I . . . well . . . I don't think I'm ready to become domesticated. At least, not just yet. I like things the way they are.'

'Kevin loves you very, very much, Nell. Gavin told me the same thing the other day.'

'My God! All these transatlantic calls! It sounds as if you and the old Gavers are ganging up on me! And you promised me you wouldn't pressure me. I just can't take pressure about Kevin right now. I've enough stress from a variety of other things. And from clients. Which brings me to Johnny Fortune. I'm here with him to finalize details of his concert in Paris this summer, but then I'm going back to London. I have some problems to deal with at my London office. But Johnny's remaining in Paris. He's going to be all over you like chickenpox, I'm warning you.'

Rosie had to laugh. 'Don't make it sound so *ominous*. A few minutes ago you were delighted he was interested in me.'

'I still am. I'm just alerting you to the fact that he's not going back to London with me tomorrow, that –'

'But I knew Johnny was staying. He's called me every day since you both arrived in London from New York. I'm having dinner with him tonight. You *know* that.'

'Yes, *he* told me and *you* told me. But I wasn't sure you realized he was going to be in Paris a few days longer, perhaps even a week.'

'I did.'

Nell stared at her, then grinned. 'As my Aunt Phyllis would say, you look like the cat that's swallowed the canary.'

'No, I don't!' Rosie protested and flushed.

'You do too, Rosalind Mary Frances Madigan!' Nell shot back and then burst out laughing at the embarrassed expression on Rosie's face. 'But it's okay for you to look like that, Rosie mine – so *satisfied*. After all, Johnny Fortune's quite a catch. Actually, I get the impression he's really got it bad for you. And as I told you when we were in California in November, you could do worse. He's intelligent, good-looking, sexy, rich, famous, the idol of millions of women, and a nice man really. Personally I think he'd make a great husband.'

'Hey, not so fast, Nellie!' Rosie cried. 'I haven't had one date with him yet and you're already getting us married!'

'That's not such a bad idea. And I'll be a bridesmaid.'

'And that brings me back to my brother. What are *you* going to do about Kevin? Now come on, tell me truthfully, and don't make silly remarks about not wanting to be *domesticated* just yet.'

Nell bit her lip, and after several moments of reflection she gave Rosie a very direct look, and said in a low, even voice, 'If you must know the truth, I've got it all worked out . . . sort of.'

'So tell me,' Rosie said.

'Very well, I will. Look, Kevin's working on a

special case right now. I'm sure he's mentioned it to you, hasn't he?'

Rosie nodded. 'Yes. The Crime Intelligence Division is zeroing in on the Mafia. A specific family. Kevin's in the middle of it all.'

'*Exactly*. Kevin expects this case to be finished soon. He mentioned that in passing the other day, just before I left New York. He thinks that in a month or two it will be all over bar the shouting . . . that's how he put it to me. I got him to promise that he'll take a vacation with me then. And when we're on vacation I'm going to make him a proposition.'

When Nell did not elucidate further, Rosie pressed, 'What kind of proposition?'

'I'm going to make him an offer he can't refuse, to coin a phrase,' Nell laughed. 'I'm going to propose that I sell my company, that he gets out of the force, and that we start some sort of business together.'

'Would you really sell the company?' Rosie exclaimed in surprise.

'Yes,' Nell answered in a firm voice.

Rosie was silent, knowing full well that her brother might not acquiesce, might not quit the CID. After a second or two, she said, 'Oh Nell, I don't know.' She shook her head worriedly. 'I don't think Kevin will give in so easily, honestly I don't. He's a fourth-generation cop. He loves the NYPD.'

'I'm hoping he loves me more. And if I make a sacrifice for him, by giving up Jeffrey Associates, he ought to be big enough to make one for me.'

Rosie said, 'But, Nell, let's face it, you're an heiress in your own right, through your mother and grandfather. Kevin might not think that selling your company is such a big sacrifice, since you don't have to earn a living if you don't want to.'

'Oh come on, Rosie! I love my business, and I've built it up all by myself. And from *nothing*. It would be a tremendous sacrifice for me.'

'*I* know that.'

'So does Kevin know.'

'He's very proud,' Rosie pointed out.

Nell stood up and paced around the library for a while, and at last exclaimed, 'I don't know what else to do, Rosie! I thought this was a good plan. Now you're throwing cold water on it. Oh hell, why did I have to go and fall in love with an undercover cop!'

'He's not *any* undercover cop. He's Kevin Madigan.'

'I know, that's the problem. He's so wonderful, he's almost too good to be true.'

'Well, you do have one consolation,' Rosie murmured.

'What's that?'

'He will have to retire from the force one day.'

'I'm not sure I can wait that long,' Nell said.

THIRTY-TWO

Johnny Fortune stood in front of the mirror in his bedroom at the Plaza Athénée Hotel, staring at himself through critical eyes. A thoughtful expression washed over his lean, tanned face, and then he abruptly turned away and strode across the room.

This was the third time he had changed this evening and he was not going to do so again. He decided that his choice of dark-grey slacks, black cashmere jacket, white voile shirt and black-and-white polka-dot tie was correct for dinner at Le Voltaire.

This was where Rosie had suggested they go, explaining on the phone that it was a smart but unpretentious restaurant serving wonderful food, located on the Quai Voltaire on the Left Bank. He had told her it sounded great, and she had offered to book a table for them.

Picking up his black cashmere overcoat from the chair in the sitting room, where he had left it earlier, he went out into the corridor and headed for the elevators. A few minutes later he was getting into the car waiting for him outside the hotel on the Avenue Montaigne.

As the driver pulled away from the kerb and headed towards the Left Bank, a half-smile struck Johnny's face. He was amused at himself. He had not paid so much attention to what he wore for years; at least, he had not changed so many times for one occasion. And when he had done so in the past it had only ever been for his shows, concerts and press photographs. Never for a woman. But then there had never been a woman like Rosie in his life.

And he had never been in love before. He most certainly was with Rosie; he had fallen in love with her the night Nell had brought her to dinner at his house in Benedict Canyon.

Quite frequently, when he remembered his initial dislike of her, he chuckled to himself. *That* hadn't lasted very long, had it? And he had thought about her constantly since that first meeting. In fact, she was rarely out of his mind. For two months, her face had haunted him night and day. But now, all of a sudden, as he rode across Paris to see her again *finally*, he was nervous. And very impatient.

Curbing his need to tell Alain, his driver, to put his foot down, Johnny settled back against the seat and held himself in check.

Oh *yes*, he was in love with her.

And oh *yes*, he wanted to make love to her.

And very decidedly *yes*, he wanted to marry her.

Rosalind Madigan was the right woman for him, the only woman. And certainly she was the only woman he had ever thought of as a potential wife.

A week ago, out on Staten Island, he'd really had to restrain himself. When his Uncle Salvatore had started talking about marriage and a wife, he'd wanted to blurt it out, tell him about Rosie. He still didn't know how he'd managed to keep his mouth shut, but somehow he had.

Rosie was going to be a surprise for his uncles, a wonderful surprise. Once he returned to New York, at the beginning of April, he was going to invite them to dinner at a good restaurant in Manhattan. And this was when he would present Rosie to the two of them. They'd fall in love with her just like he had, no question in his mind about that.

He stifled the laugh that rose in his throat as he thought of the two old guys meeting her. They won't be able to resist Rosie. His Rosalind. He repeated her name silently to himself. He liked it. Rosalind Madigan. *Rosalind Fortune*. It sounded pretty good to him.

Unexpectedly, a curious fear gripped him. Mingled with his nervousness it made him panic. He was suddenly balking at the idea of seeing her, of being with her. What if he were disappointed? What if she didn't live up to his expectations? She had been his dream woman for two months. He had fantasized about her in every way; he had had sexual fantasies about her; he had shunned other women because of her. In a way, he had set himself up to be disappointed, hadn't he?

This was a new experience for him, loving a woman, genuinely caring for her. Apart from his Uncle Vito and his Uncle Salvatore, nobody had ever meant anything to him. Not even Aunt Angelina, Vito's wife, who had always treated him nice. He'd loved his mother, that was natural, went without saying. But she'd died when he was a little boy and he hardly remembered her.

Yep, the two old guys were the only human beings he'd ever felt anything for until he met Rosie. As for other women, he'd never felt anything but lust for them.

Frowning, glancing out of the window, he wondered when they would get to the rue de l'Université. He was so anxious he was almost jumping out of his skin.

And then a few seconds later, just as he was about to ask Alain where they were, the car came to a standstill.

'We 'ave arrived, *Monsieur*,' Alain said, glancing over his shoulder and smiling. The young man got out of the car and was opening the back door before Johnny could even respond.

'Thanks, Alain,' Johnny said, and taking a deep breath he walked towards the building where she lived.

The moment she opened the door and smiled at him, Johnny felt his panic dissipating.

He smiled back, a wide, joyous smile.

And then she reached out, took hold of his hand and drew him inside the apartment.

They stood in the foyer staring at each other, still holding hands. Neither of them said a word.

Finally, he stepped forward, at the same time

drawing her towards him; he kissed her first on one cheek, then the other.

'It's great to see you, Rosie,' Johnny said at last.

'And you, too, Johnny,' Rosie responded, laughter bubbling up in her.

His bright blue eyes were fastened on her intently. All manner of emotions were churning inside him. He wanted to kiss her face over and over again, take off her dress, make love to her passionately, tenderly, and for a long, long time.

He wanted to tell her everything he'd ever thought about her since they had met, confess the sexual fantasies he'd had about her, tell her he loved her, ask her to marry him as soon as possible. He wanted to say it *now*. He wanted everything *now*. At once. All of her, every tiny bit of her. He never wanted to be without her ever again. And that was exactly how it was going to be. They were going to be together for the rest of their lives.

But he knew he couldn't do any of these things, or tell her any of this, or explain everything to her at this moment. Slowly, go slowly, he cautioned himself, and he got a grip on his swimming senses, brought his overwhelming emotions under control.

He had waited most of his adult life to find her, to meet this woman of his dreams, his true soul mate. And so he could wait a little bit longer to take her to him, to possess her completely, to make her his. She was going to belong to him.

'Let me take your coat,' Rosie said, extracting her hand.

'Yes,' he muttered, realizing he'd been gaping at

her, and rather foolishly so, at that. He struggled out of his coat, handed it to her silently.

After she had hung it in the hall closet, she smiled at him once again, took his arm and led him into the sitting room straight ahead.

'I have champagne on ice, and white wine too, but perhaps you'd prefer something else?'

'Oh, I don't care,' he said, giving her a faint smile. 'What're you having?'

'A glass of champagne, but you can have anything, Johnny, anything you want.'

Oh honey, I hope so, he thought, staring at her again, devouring her with his eyes. And then feeling self-conscious, aware of the rush of desire rising up in him, he glanced away swiftly. Moving across the floor in the direction of the fireplace, he added, 'Champagne's fine, yeah, why not. I'd like a glass, sure, Rosie.'

'Excuse me, I won't be a moment,' she said, and disappeared before he could offer to open the bottle for her.

Turning around, he stood with his back to the fire-place, glancing at the room, eaten up with curiosity about her.

He saw at once that she had good taste.

The sitting room was quite large, but she had not cluttered it with too much furniture. The walls were cream, the floor made of highly-polished parquet, covered in the centre with a carpet. It was worn in parts and its colours were faded, but he recognized that it was an antique and obviously valuable. There were some handsome antique tables and a console, sofas and chairs covered in yellow silk, and a grouping of attractive paintings on a long wall. He stared at the rest of the sitting room, noticing his flowers everywhere, the fine pieces of porcelain arranged in niches built on either side of the fireplace and the antique crystal lamps shaded in cream silk.

It was a pleasant, comfortable room, and Johnny was at ease in it. He felt at home, and this pleased him. The piano in the window area beckoned. He walked over to it, but paused for a moment to look at a collection of photographs arranged on a skirted table. He wondered who all the people were. He would ask her when she came back. He needed to know everything about Rosalind Madigan.

Seating himself at the baby grand, Johnny lifted the lid, and involuntarily his fingers slid across the keys. He could never resist a piano, and he began to play Cole Porter, one of his favourite composers. Then, as he always did, he started to hum, and in a moment he was crooning softly the opening lines of *You Do Something to Me*.

'Johnny, that's wonderful!' Rosie exclaimed from the doorway.

'Just tinkling,' he said, glancing up. She was carrying a tray laden with a bucket of champagne and glasses. He leapt to his feet and went to help her with it. But she wouldn't let him take it from her.

'I can manage, honestly I can,' she said, walking forward. She put the tray down carefully on the coffee table in front of the fireplace.

Pouring the champagne into crystal flutes, she continued, 'I wish you hadn't stopped singing. I love your voice. And I love listening to you, Johnny. Please, sing something else. Oh, I shouldn't have said that, should I? It's work for you . . . that's what you do all the time. And you're not in Paris to sing, but to have a few days' rest before your British tour.'

Johnny took the glass she was offering him, glowing inside. She had said she loved his voice. That was terribly important to him; he was happy she had paid him this compliment.

He murmured, 'When I see a piano I can't help gravitating to it. And I'll sing for you any time. But no more songs tonight. I want to talk to you instead.'

Raising his glass, he said, 'To you, Rosie, the most beautiful woman in Paris.'

Gazing back at him, feeling herself blush under his intense scrutiny, Rosie shook her head. She wanted to look away, to escape from those vivid blue eyes pinning hers so forcefully, but she found she could not. Shaking her head yet again, and laughing lightly, she said, 'I'm not the most beautiful woman in Paris, but thank you anyway.' She touched her glass against his. 'Welcome to my city, Johnny, welcome to my home.'

'You're the most beautiful woman in the world as far as I'm concerned,' he said softly, looking at her with longing. And then he tore his eyes away from her face, glanced around the room and, changing the subject, went on hurriedly, 'This is a nice place you have, Rosie. Have you lived here long?'

'About five years. I found it by accident and fell in love with it.'

Strolling over to the photographs, Johnny bent over

the velvet-skirted table and peered at them. 'Here you are with Nell, and I recognize a young Gavin Ambrose. But who are the others in the picture?' He straightened and looked at her questioningly.

Rosie walked across the room towards him.

Johnny realized that she had the most beautiful legs. He hadn't noticed them before. But then he had only met her once; he foolishly kept forgetting that. Very simply, he had made love to her so many times in his head, had had such erotic mental sessions with her, he felt he knew her inside out and upside down. But of course he didn't know her at all.

Rosie drew to a standstill next to him, and he smelled the fragrance of her. It was a tantalizing mixture of lilies of the valley, shampoo, soap and water and youthful skin. He was aware that she was going to drive him crazy before the evening was out. She was sexual dynamite to him.

Picking up the photograph in the silver frame, he showed it to her, and said, 'I guess I'm being nosey, but who're these other kids? Who's the luscious blonde girl?'

'That's Sunny. She was one of our group.'

'She's gorgeous. As they say, she oughta be in pictures. *Is* she an actress?'

Rosie shook her head and the expression on her face changed ever so slightly. 'She's in a nursing home in New Haven. She got into drugs a few years ago, and one night she took some bad stuff. It scrambled her brains. She'll be a vegetable for the rest of her life. Poor Sunny.'

'Oh Jesus, that's a rotten thing to happen!' he

exclaimed and shivered. 'I've watched drugs destroy a few people I knew . . .' He left his sentence unfinished.

'This is Mikey,' Rosie continued. 'He was a nice guy, I should say *is* a nice guy. It's just that we don't know what happened to him. He disappeared two years ago, and although Gavin has tried to find Mikey, he hasn't been successful. He even hired private detectives.'

'When somebody wants to stay lost, they usually manage to stay lost,' Johnny remarked, and looked down at the photograph he was still holding. 'And who's the handsome guy with the wonderful Clark Gable smile?'

'That's my brother.'

'Isn't he Nell's boyfriend?' Johnny said.

'Yes, he is.'

'He's a good-looking son of a gun. He oughta be in pictures too. But I guess he ain't, or I'd know it. What does he do?'

'He's an accountant,' Rosie replied. This was the answer she, Nell and Gavin had always been warned to give. Nobody must know that Kevin was an undercover cop with the NYPD, and there were no exceptions to this rule.

'And you were kids together in New York, is that it?' Johnny asked.

'We met about fifteen years ago. And we've been close ever since. You see, we were all orphans at the time, and became a family for each other. Of course, there are only four of us now. Sunny and Mikey are sort of . . . well, lost to us.'

Johnny nodded and put the photograph back in its place. Another one caught his eye, and he gave Rosie a swift look before saying, 'At the risk of being nosey again, I've got to ask you who this cute little girl is?'

'Her name's Lisette, and she's my niece. That's her mother with her. Collie. If you remember I mentioned her to you the night we met. The silver expert.'

'That's right! How is she?'

'She . . . she died,' Rosie said and found she was choking up. Managing to take control of herself, she continued, 'She had been suffering from cancer. We thought she was much better, that it was in remission, but then she got really sick again over Christmas. She died about three weeks ago.'

'Oh God, I'm sorry, I didn't know, and I shouldn't pry like this!' he exclaimed, almost stumbling over his words, feeling embarrassed at his many gaffes in only a few minutes.

'Oh, it's all right, Johnny, really it is,' Rosie reassured him, and reaching out she touched his arm. 'Collie was my sister-in-law, and that's her brother in the photograph. Guy. He was my husband, whom I'm now divorcing.'

Johnny felt a sharp twinge of jealousy, and he wanted to ask her when her divorce would be final, but he lost his nerve. He was afraid of putting his foot in it again, and so he asked, 'And the house in the background? Is that Montfleurie?'

'Yes.'

Relieved to be on safer ground, Johnny said, 'I understand from Francis Raeymaekers that it's one of the great châteaux of the Loire.'

'That's true, and it's also the most extraordinary place in the world to me. I've always loved it. But goodness, Johnny, your glass is empty. Let me fill it up for you.' Immediately she took it from him, and hurried over to the coffee table where the bottle of champagne sat in a bucket of ice.

He followed her, accepted the glass, thanked her. 'You told me on the phone you work at home. So where's your studio?'

'Would you like to see it? Come on, I'll show you! It's at the other end of the apartment.'

Together they went out of the sitting room and crossed the large entrance foyer. As they did he noticed a small library with red walls, lots of books, a sofa and chairs upholstered in a red-and-green fabric, and more of the flowers he'd sent. She led him down a corridor, and when they passed her bedroom he glanced quickly away, not daring to look inside. Instead he kept his eyes straight ahead, walking slowly behind her, keeping his distance.

'Here it is,' Rosie said, opening the door. Turning, she took hold of his arm, drew him into the studio. 'It's perfect for my work because of the natural daylight.'

Johnny immediately went over to the display shelf and stood in front of the drawings propped up on it. 'These are great!' he exclaimed, admiration apparent in his voice. 'What a talent you have. Nell's been telling me that for weeks, and now I know what she means.'

'Those are for Gavin's new movie, *Napoleon and Josephine*,' Rosie explained.

'It sounds interesting. Tell me about it.'

'I'd love to, but I think I'd better do it over dinner at Le Voltaire. It's getting late. I don't want to lose our table.'

'Come on then, let's go,' he said. 'The car's waiting downstairs.'

THIRTY-THREE

In a funny sort of way, Johnny was relieved to be with Rosie in a public place. The entire time they had been at her apartment he had to struggle with his compulsion to grab hold of her, to kiss her passionately, to make love to her.

Now he had no alternative but to behave himself, and so he sat back, enjoying being with her and gratified to see the glances occasionally thrown their way. Even though he said it himself, they made a handsome couple. A fairy-tale couple, in a sense. He was a big star. There was nobody bigger in the entertainment business today. And she was a beautiful woman, whom any man would be proud to have on his arm.

People in the restaurant had obviously recognized him, were discreetly looking his way. They knew how to behave in Europe, always kept their distance and just *looked*.

Rosie did not have a high profile. At least, not here. Back in Hollywood, yes. Most people would recognize her face; after all, she was an Academy

Award-winning costume designer, and constantly photographed with Gavin Ambrose.

Hollywood. What a splash they would make there together. He had never particularly wanted to do that before. Now it was different, because of Rosie. He longed to show her off. Once they were married he would give a party at the house; he'd never done that before either. He realized suddenly that he wanted to show off his house too, as long as Rosie was in it with him.

The waiter came and interrupted his thoughts when he asked what they would like as an aperitif.

Johnny looked across the table at Rosie. 'Champagne?'

She nodded and smiled at him.

'Bring a bottle of Dom Perignon, please,' he said to the waiter, and then brought his eyes back to Rosie. She had picked up the menu the waiter had presented and, head bent, was reading it. He looked around, eyed the dining room where they were sitting. Le Voltaire was charming, intimate, with panelled walls, filled with mellow light, and although it was busy there was a certain calmness about the atmosphere that he liked. It was obviously a place dedicated to good food and wine, since there were no unnecessary folderols and no fancy decor. And the service was excellent.

Lifting her head, Rosie said, 'I never know what to choose here, everything's always so good.'

'I'll let you order for me. I'm only an expert when it comes to Italian food.'

'I'll be happy to, but let's enjoy our drinks first,'

she said as the waiter returned to the table with the bucket of champagne.

Again they toasted each other, and then Johnny put his glass down and sat looking at her. It was impossible for him to keep his eyes away from her for very long.

Rosie wore a purple wool dress with a round neckline and long sleeves. Rather plain, he thought, but expertly tailored, and it accentuated her beautiful figure. The brilliant purple brought out the vivid green of her eyes, which were huge in her face.

'You've been staring at me all evening, Johnny, and right now more than ever,' she said quietly, leaning across the table. 'What's the matter? Do I have a smudge on my face or something?'

'No, no. I was just thinking how great you looked, and admiring those pearls. They're something else.'

'Yes, aren't they beautiful. Gavin gave them to me for Christmas.'

For the second time that evening Johnny experienced a violent stabbing sensation in his gut. He was aware that it was jealousy, even though this was an entirely new emotion for him. He couldn't recall ever having been jealous in the past, not of anyone.

For a long moment Johnny Fortune could not speak, so amazed was he at his reaction: *he was jealous of Gavin Ambrose.* Unbelievable. He was momentarily thrown by this.

And then he worked a weak smile onto his face and said, 'Good choice: they suit you.'

'Thanks. Gavin always gives me a gift at the end of a picture.'

Johnny sipped the champagne and tried to push the jealousy to one side. 'When does the new one start?' he asked at last.

'We go into preproduction in March, and since it's such a big picture, and so costly because of the battle scenes, we'll need about five months' preproduction, perhaps longer. But Gavin hopes to start filming in August. He plans to do the exteriors first, while the weather's good, and most of the interiors he'll do later in the year. Others he'll have to do as they come up. You see sometimes, when we have an actor only for *four weeks*, let's say, we've got to shoot all of his or her stuff within that time frame.' She picked up her glass, and smiled at him over the rim before taking a sip, then added, 'This picture's going to be a long shoot, in my opinion.'

To Johnny this sounded as if she was going to be tied up until the end of the year and his heart sank. He said, 'When will you finish the costumes?'

'I should have most of the designs completed by the end of April, early May at the latest. I'm ahead at the moment, and my two assistants will be coming over from London in a couple of weeks. They'll be a great help to me, and they'll be able to work on the less important costumes.'

'I noticed that dress pinned onto the dummy in your studio. So, who makes all the costumes?'

'Not me, thank God,' she said, laughing. 'Nor my two assistants. I use a number of seamstresses, and right now I'm pulling a pretty good team together here in Paris. A lot of the clothes for the extras, such as the soldiers in Napoleon's army, we'll hire from theatrical costumiers in Paris and London. And the dresses and accessories for the women extras as well. It would take forever if we had to design and make everything for everybody. I just concentrate on creating costumes for the principal characters.'

Although Johnny was somewhat disturbed that she would be involved and working on the movie for months on end, he was still interested enough to hear more. He asked, 'Where will you be shooting?'

'Various parts of France,' she replied. 'And in and around Paris. We'll actually be based at Billancourt Studios here. Brian Ackland-Snow, our art director, will be building some of the sets out at the studios, but we'll use some real houses and châteaux. And naturally we'll film at Malmaison. The French Government's already given permission.'

'Malmaison?' He frowned. 'What's that? Where's that?'

'It's the château Napoleon bought for Josephine, their private home,' she explained. 'It's just outside Paris, in Rueil, on the river Seine, about fifteen kilometres from here. It's a museum now, and very beautiful. Would you like to see it, Johnny?'

Interested in museums he was not; on the other hand he would go anywhere if it meant he could spend time with her. And so he nodded quickly. 'When do you want to take me? Tomorrow?'

'If you'd like.'

'Hey, that's great, Rosie, and we'll have lunch together. Is that okay?'

'Yes. In the meantime, I think that perhaps we'd better order dinner. I'm getting slightly drunk on all this champagne.'

'Anything you say, honey.'

'Shall we start with a country *pâté*, and then have a grilled sole as the main course?'

'You're on, it sounds good.'

Later, as they ate the main course, Rosie remarked, 'Nell told me that you brought quite a few people to Paris with you.'

'Yep, I sure did. My personal assistant, Joe Anton. Kenny Crossland, who plays keyboard for me, and my manager, Jeff Smailes.' He grinned at her. 'There's more of my group in London, but they wanted to stay put.'

'And where are Joe, Kenny and Jeff tonight?'

'Out on the town. Visiting a few of the famous Paris jazz joints.'

'I bet they headed for the rue de la Huchette, there're lots of terrific spots in that street, and in the whole area around the Boul Mich.'

He stared at her. A brow lifted quizzically.

'Boulevard St Michel,' she explained in answer to his unasked question.

Johnny nodded and reached for the glass of Montrachet. 'Talking of the gang, have you ever been to one of my shows, Rosie?'

She shook her head. 'No, I'm afraid not. But I wish I had. I told you earlier, I love your voice, Johnny.'

'How'd you like to come over to London next week? I'm doing a show at Wembley Arena.'

Rosie looked at him, not answering, full of sudden hesitation.

He said swiftly, 'It'll be no hassle. You can come with us on my plane on Monday morning. Or I'll send the jet back for you later in the week. Say yes, Rosie. I'd love it, and so would you. It'll be fun. And quite an experience, if you've never been to that kind of big, splashy concert.'

'Yes, all right then, I'll come,' she said, making up her mind, smiling at him.

It was a smile that dazzled, and, before he could stop himself, he reached out, took hold of her hand resting on the table. 'Don't worry about a thing. Nell's office'll book a suite for you at my hotel. The Dorchester. And I can promise you a wonderful time.'

'I'm sure you can, Johnny,' she said. And then she thought: I'm glad he invited me. I'm glad I'm going. I haven't had any fun in years.

And deep down within herself Rosie knew that she and Johnny were going to become involved.

THIRTY-FOUR

It seemed to Rosie that Johnny Fortune had taken possession of her life. But then she had permitted it. She had been his willing accomplice.

Ever since their dinner at Le Voltaire on Tuesday he had been constantly at her side. After she had taken him out to visit Malmaison on Wednesday afternoon, he asked her to show him the side of Paris he had never seen on other trips he had made in the past. These had always been for his concerts and he had never had time to see the sights.

Rosie had used her imagination and selected places she thought he would enjoy. And they had had a wonderful few days, meandering around her favourite city, which she knew so intimately, eating lunch at a few choice bistros, and dinner at such five-star restaurants as Taillevent and Tour d'Argent. They had laughed together and found quite a lot to talk about. A nice camaraderie had developed between them.

But now on Friday lunchtime, as she sat opposite

him in the Relais Plaza, Rosie could not help wondering what had wrought the change in Johnny. He seemed cool, distant, distracted, even a little morose; he was hardly speaking to her at all.

'Is something wrong?' she asked at last, peering at him, a worried frown knotting her brows.

'No,' he answered in a low voice.

She leaned a little closer and spoke in as low a voice as he had. 'Look, Johnny, I know something's the matter. Please tell me what it is.'

He shook his head but said nothing.

'Have I upset you in some way?'

'Of course not.' He offered her a faint smile, as if to reassure her of this.

'You seem so sad, Johnny.'

Silently, he glanced away.

'You're not eating a thing,' she persisted, trying to draw him out, wanting to force the issue, *needing* to force it, to get to the root of the problem.

'I'm just not hungry, Rosie.'

She glanced down at her plate of scrambled eggs, which she had merely been picking at with a fork, and muttered, 'Neither am I.'

Johnny looked at her plate, saw that she had not eaten much herself. He stared at her for the longest moment, his eyes riveted on her face, which, he suddenly noticed, was unusually pale.

He put his hand over hers resting on the table and held onto it tightly, so tightly his knuckles whitened with the pressure. Slowly, he nodded his head as if something had just dawned on him. He said, 'Shall we go up to my suite . . . for coffee?'

'Yes.' She gazed back at him, returning the pressure of his fingers.

She was carrying her coat and he took it from her the moment they were inside the suite.

Their hands brushed, and they looked at each other swiftly. Johnny threw her coat down on the nearest chair impatiently. Rosie followed suit with her bag and gloves.

Johnny's eyes did not leave hers. 'I can't eat because I can't stand this torture much long –'

'I know why you can't eat, Johnny,' Rosie interrupted in an undertone. 'For the same reason that I can't.'

They exchanged a glance of sudden intimacy, and then they were in each other's arms, clinging to each other.

His mouth found hers at once, and he devoured it, kissing her over and over again. His tongue slid gently in between her lips, to touch her tongue, and it lingered there. Then his hands moved up underneath her sweater. He found the clasp on her bra and unfastened it. Bringing his hands round to the front of her body, he pushed the sweater and the bra up so that her breasts were released. They were full and beautiful. He lowered his head, sucked on one nipple and then the other, pushed her breasts together and nuzzled them before sinking onto his knees in front of her.

Unzipping her skirt, he let it fall to the floor around her feet. She stepped out of it, out of her shoes, and then stood motionless in front of him. She wore only panty hose and the dark V of her hair was visible through the delicate fabric. Resting his head against her stomach, he closed his eyes, breathing in the scent of her, the wonderful sexual scent of woman, a woman growing ripe with desire. He began to kiss her mound through the fabric, stroking her buttocks, then pressing them harder, bringing her body closer to his face. Vaguely, as if from far away, he heard a long sigh escaping from her.

Opening his eyes, Johnny stood up, took her in his arms again and held her close to him. With one hand he reached out, bolted the door, and without letting go of her he walked her towards the bedroom.

They paused in the doorway to kiss. And suddenly, in a swift movement Johnny put his hands under her thighs and lifted her up onto his body. Putting her arms around his neck, she straddled him: and he carried her over to the bed in this way. Placing her on it, he pushed her back against the pillows and reached for the top of her pantyhose, rolling them over her buttocks and pulling them off.

She shed her sweater herself and lay looking up at him as he flung his jacket on a chair and tore off his tie. Striding across the floor, he closed the bedroom door and walked back to her, unbuttoning his white shirt as he did.

Johnny stood looking down at her. She had a slender body which made her smooth, full breasts seem larger; the aureoles were a dark dusky pink around the tight little nipples. They were the most tantalizing breasts he had ever seen. He wanted to sink his face into them, nuzzle them, rest between them for ever.

After shedding the rest of his clothes, Johnny took

hold of her hands and pulled her up into a sitting position, gently easing her off the bed. He drew her towards him, brought her into his arms, smoothing one hand down her spine as he did, moving her against him so that she could feel him. He had an enormous erection, and he wanted her to understand how much he desired her. He was sick with desire, and had been for days. The agony of wanting her had grown unendurable; he was ready to explode. First kissing her mouth and then her neck, he bent his head to suck and fondle her breasts.

Rosie was trembling in his arms, and as Johnny moved his body against hers, stroked her and lavished her with kisses, she felt her legs start to shake. A lovely warmth was spreading through her loins, into the innermost core of her. It was an extraordinary sensation, one she had not experienced for a long time, ever since her marriage had foundered, and she had thought she would never feel this way again. But she did. Here and now with Johnny Fortune. He was handsome, loving and warm, and she wanted him as much as he wanted her, had wanted him ever since their dinner at Le Voltaire. In fact, she had been waiting for him to make a move, longing for him to kiss her, to make love with her.

Johnny was so aroused now, his desire was exciting her more than ever. Running her hands down his back, she let them rest on his buttocks, stroking them, and then increased her pressure. He lifted his head from her breasts and began to kiss her, his tongue slipping in and out of her mouth in the most sensual way. She ran her hands up his back and onto his shoulders, gripped them, let her fingers slide onto the nape of his neck and up into his hair. Their mouths were locked; they were welded together.

A moment later Johnny was pulling the coverlet off the bed and pressing her down onto the sheets. Bending over her, he whispered against her face, 'Don't leave,' and disappeared into the bathroom.

Rosie lay still, her eyes closed, waiting for him to return. Her emotions were running high, all of her senses were clamouring for him. She was aflame.

There was a slight sound.

Opening her eyes, she saw that he was closing the curtains, shutting out the sunlight. As he turned around and walked towards her she saw how big he was and she shivered involuntarily. Then she realized he had gone into the bathroom to put on some protection.

Touching her face lightly, half smiling at her, he lay down on the bed and took her in his arms, covering her face with kisses. His hands were wandering all over her body, stroking, fondling, exploring, learning every bit of her. Slowly, tenderly, his fingers slipped down between her thighs, and he found the core of her and soon was arousing her to fever pitch.

Unexpectedly and without any warning, Johnny pushed himself on top of her and entered her quickly, almost roughly, and she stiffened, nearly exclaimed in pain and managed to stifle the cry in her throat.

Pushing his hands under her, he lifted her body closer to his, plunged deeper into her and still deeper, until she thought he was touching her heart. Clinging to him, she found his rhythm and they moved in unison, relentlessly so, full of longing and need, desperate to satisfy their own desires as well as each other's.

Rosie felt herself growing more moist and soft. Opening to him, she accepted all of him inside her. In a sudden rush of movement against her, as his rhythm accelerated, Johnny cried out her name, urged her to come, to give herself to him. And she did. His name was on her lips as they climaxed together.

He sank down on top of her like a dead weight with his face against her breasts. He lay like this for a while.

Eventually a deep laugh rippled through Johnny. He began to shake.

'What is it?' Rosie asked, sounding baffled, touching his shoulder lightly.

He lifted his face, and still laughing, he explained, 'It's not supposed to be like this, honey. You know, so good the first time.' He shook his head. 'We're supposed to get to know each other, babe . . .'

Rosie also laughed, and smoothed his blondish hair away from his face. But she made no comment.

Johnny pushed himself off her body carefully, muttering half to himself, 'I gotta get rid of this lousy thing,' and disappeared into the bathroom.

Then he was back on the bed, stretching out next to her. Propping himself up on one elbow, he gazed down into her eyes, moved a strand of hair away from her brow and kissed the tip of her nose.

'We're good together, Rosie, really great. I hope you're gonna stick around.'

'Of course I am. You've got to feed me before I leave.'

'I didn't mean *now*. I meant stick around for . . . you know, a while.' He wanted to say for ever, but he did not dare. Not yet, at least. He was aware that he had to go slowly with her. He didn't mind. After all, he was playing for keeps.

Rosie smiled at him. 'Of course I'll stick around. Why not? In the meantime, aren't you going to feed a hungry girl? I'm starving, Johnny.'

'So am I, Rosie. For you.' His face hovered over hers, and he kissed her on the lips, but lightly, and stared deeply into her eyes.

The expression on Johnny's face was one of total adoration, and as he smoothed back her hair again his touch was full of reverence. 'I've never felt like this before, Rosie,' he admitted. 'There's never been anyone like you. I haven't been able to get you out of my mind since we met in November.'

Rosie was silent, but she reached out, touched his cheek, smoothed one finger down it.

'Say something,' he whispered. 'Tell me how you feel.'

'Well and truly loved, satisfied,' she replied.

This pleased him but he wanted more from her, and so he probed, 'Did you think about me at all after we met? Have you thought about me since I started calling you?'

She nodded. 'Yes, I did. And I have.'

'What did you think?'

'That I wanted to see you again. And, more recently, that I was looking forward to it. And . . .'

'And what?'

'And since Tuesday evening I wanted you, wanted you to make love with me. And I . . .'

Again her voice trailed off, and he pressed, 'Come on, don't be shy, talk to me, I want to know.'

A little smile played around her mouth. 'I wanted us to be together like this, in bed. But I was also a little afraid.'

'Why?' he asked, sounding puzzled. 'Why would you be afraid?'

'Perhaps that's the wrong word to use. Nervous might be a better one.'

He frowned but said nothing.

She murmured in the quietest of voices, 'My marriage went on the rocks five years ago. Actually, a while before that. Anyway, I haven't . . . you know, I haven't slept with anyone since then. I guess that's why I felt nervous.'

It pleased him to know that there had been no other men in her life since her husband, and that she had chosen him. He was the first in the five years. It was as though she were a virgin and this both pleased and thrilled him.

'Were you disappointed in me?' he asked.

'That's a foolish question, Johnny, and of course I wasn't. I was only trying to tell you why *I* felt nervous. I mean, I'd been celibate for such a long time really.'

A mischievous glint entered his eyes, and he said with a grin, 'Making love is like riding a bicycle, you never forget.'

Rosie laughed. 'I guess you're right there, Johnny.

But as my mother used to say, practice makes perfect.'

'If you're on a fishing trip, honey, I can only say that you're very perfect and without any recent practice.'

He leaned closer, kissed her on the mouth and then sat up on his knees. Bending over her, he gently traced lines down her body, stroked her breasts, touched every part of her, following every curve of her arms, her legs and her feet, and returning to her breasts. And again his eyes were full of immense tenderness, his expression one of devotion. He was besotted with her.

'You're exciting me too much,' Rosie whispered.

'I want to, and I want to possess all of you, Rosie. Oh God, you don't know what you do to me, how much you turn me on.'

Rosie held him for a moment, and then she sat up, flung her arms around his lean body and hugged him very hard, holding him close to her. 'Let's order some sandwiches,' she said. 'I told you, I'm ravenous.'

'Okay, I will. Just so long as you know that I intend to bring you back to this bed the minute we've eaten.'

THIRTY-FIVE

Johnny was waiting for her in her suite at the Dorchester Hotel when she arrived from Heathrow Airport a week later.

She walked in, followed by the bellboy with her luggage, and he jumped up off the sofa where he sat reading a magazine, and came to greet her.

Hugging her fiercely, he whispered in her ear, 'Jesus, I've missed you!'

After tipping the bellboy, seeing him out, Johnny helped her off with her coat, dropped it on a chair and pulled her down onto the sofa with him. He kissed her deeply. She returned his kisses, as happy to see him as he obviously was to see her.

'It's been a lousy few days without you, Rosie!' he exclaimed as they drew apart. 'I've been miserable.'

'I'm here now,' she said. 'And I'm all yours.'

Beaming, he rose, took hold of her hand and helped her to her feet. 'Come on, I want to show you the suite. It's pretty nifty.'

The moment she walked in Rosie had noticed how beautifully decorated the living room was; she had also seen the many bowls of peach roses placed around the room. 'Thank you for filling the place with my favourite flowers, Johnny,' she murmured as he led her across the floor. 'They're just lovely.'

'So are you, and it's my pleasure,' he responded as he opened the door and drew her into the room beyond. 'This is the bedroom: nice size, eh? And the bathroom's over there. To your right there's a dressing area. You can look at everything later. Do you want me to get the maid in? To unpack for you?'

Rosie shook her head. 'No, that's not necessary, but thanks anyway.' As they walked past the bed she saw the small vase of violets on the bedside table, and she squeezed his arm, leaned into him and kissed his cheek. 'You're so sweet.'

He grinned at her. 'No more kissing. Otherwise we'll be in that bed, and I gotta do a concert tonight . . . I need all my strength. I gotta keep all my juice for the performance.'

They went back to the living room and Johnny walked over to a door on the far wall and opened it. 'That's my suite in there, so if you need me, all you have to do is holler, honey.'

Rosie merely smiled at this remark and sat down on the sofa.

Johnny came over and stood leaning against the mantelpiece, his eyes focused on her.

'You're doing it again, Johnny.'

'What's that?'

'Staring at me.'

'I can't help it. You're so beautiful, Rosie, I just can't get my fill of you, I guess.'

390

'You'll probably be sick of me next week at this time.'

'No way,' he shot back, and went on, 'You *do* know what today is, don't you?'

She frowned. 'Well . . . I er . . . Of course. It's your first concert tonight, the beginning of your British tour.'

'Yep, that's true. But it's also Friday February the fourteenth. Valentine's Day.'

'Oh gosh, I'd forgotten.'

'But I didn't.' He put his hand in his jacket pocket and brought out a small, gift-wrapped package. 'This is for you, Rosie. With my love.'

Rosie stared at him and shook her head slowly, a look of chagrin crossing her face. Smiling weakly, she said, 'And I didn't remember, so I don't have anything for you. I feel awful, Johnny, really awful.'

'Don't. You're here, aren't you? *You're* my Valentine's Day present. But go on, open what I got you.'

She untied the white satin ribbon, tore off the paper, found herself holding a small, red leather box embossed with gold. Lifting the lid, she gasped and her eyes widened. Lying inside on the black velvet was a large diamond ring. Rosie looked across at Johnny, struggling with her emotions.

He stood watching her, waiting for her to say something.

But she didn't say a word. She was speechless.

At last he asked, 'Don't you like the ring? Isn't it nice enough?'

'Johnny, it's beautiful! Gorgeous! But I can't accept it!' she gasped, still reeling from surprise.

'Why not?'

'I just can't take something so valuable.'

'It's not just a ring. It's an *engagement* ring.'

'Oh Johnny . . .'

'I love you, Rosie.'

She gaped at him through startled eyes and bit her inner lip nervously.

He said: 'I want us to be engaged. I want us to get married. I want to spend the rest of my life with you. I told you last weekend, I've never loved a woman before, never wanted to marry anybody 'til I met you.' His extraordinary blue eyes were fixed on her intently and his face was solemn. There was no mistaking his seriousness, nor the genuine sincerity of his words.

'Oh Johnny, I'm so flattered, honoured, but I can't take the ring now, or get engaged to you. I'm still married, darling.'

'You're in the middle of a divorce.'

'Yes, I am, but it's going to take months and months to come through, possibly even a year —'

'I don't care how long it takes,' he cut in fiercely, giving her a hard stare. 'I'll wait. Anyway, we'll be together 'til we can marry.' Taking a deep breath, he said in a softer voice, 'Please, take the ring. Come on, honey, let me put it on your finger.'

He took a step forward, smiling at her.

'No, Johnny, I can't!' she exclaimed, and realized to her regret that she had sounded sharp, almost cold. She said quietly, shaking her head, 'I just can't, Johnny.'

He stopped dead in his tracks.

She said, 'Johnny, please don't look like that.'

'How do I look?'

'*Hurt*. And I don't want to hurt you.'

'But you don't feel the same way I do, do you?' he probed.

'I'm not sure,' she hedged. 'You're going too fast for me.' She forced a light laugh and continued in a gentler tone, 'Look, I'm just a bit slower than you, I guess. I've been badly burned and I don't want to make another mistake. It's far too painful. A failed marriage is a living hell. Take my word for it. I've been there.'

'I'm not like Guy de Montfleurie. You told me he was soon chasing broads, being unfaithful to you, screwing around. I don't want other women, Rosie. Only you.'

'I know how you feel. It's not that . . . I'm not doubting *you*, Johnny. I'm just trying to be . . . *wise*. And for us both. You've never been married, so you don't understand what it feels like, how it is when it falls apart. It's horrendous, really.'

'We're not going to fall apart,' he countered. 'I love you too much.'

Ignoring this comment, Rosie pressed on. She said, 'I married Guy far too quickly. I hardly knew him. And *we* hardly know each other, you can't deny that. We've only been together a week.'

'Ten days, to be exact,' he argued. 'And I do *know* you, very intimately.' He paused and looked at her carefully, his eyes narrowing slightly as he added, 'Listen to me, you can be with somebody for fifty years and never know them, and you can meet somebody and *boom*! You realize at once that you've met your soul mate and that you're experiencing something special . . . it's total recognition. That's how it was with us. *We're* soul mates, honey. I love you. I adore you.'

She didn't speak.

He said, 'Don't you feel *anything* for me?'

'Of course I do!' she cried, sitting up straighter on the sofa. 'I adore you, too. I'm crazy about you, Johnny. You're loving and sweet and kind.'

A smile flitted across his face. He was pleased to hear these words, pleased he was getting somewhere with her at last, and he said, 'So why won't you take the ring?'

'Please, Johnny, let's go one step at a time. And slowly.'

'What's the harm if you wear it on your right hand instead of your left?'

Rosie shook her head. 'Let's not rush this. Let's at least wait until I'm free for symbols of our relationship.' She closed the jewel box and placed it on the table. 'But I want you to know that it's the most magnificent ring I've ever seen, Johnny.'

He came and sat down on the sofa and put his arms around her, pulled her closer to him with urgency, kissed her passionately. Then he gently released her, looked into her eyes. 'I can't get you out of my mind, I want you all the time, Rosie. And I want you for keeps, honey. As my wife. As Mrs Johnny Fortune.'

'Oh Johnny, Johnny darling,' she sighed and let herself completely relax next to him on the sofa, at ease with him again.

He felt the tension slipping away from her, and he suddenly understood that she was as vulnerable to him as he was to her, and this pleased him.

Unable to resist her, Johnny began to kiss her once more, pushing her down into the cushions, running his hands through her hair. She responded ardently, her arms wrapped tightly around him, clinging to him.

Unexpectedly breaking away from her, he said, 'I'm sorry, honey, I shouldn't have started this. We don't have time now.' He sighed under his breath. 'See what you do to me. You drive me nuts.'

'You do the same to me,' she whispered.

Taking her face between his hands, he stared into her eyes. 'Just tell me where we stand,' he demanded.

'Exactly where we did last week and when I walked in here earlier. Nothing's changed since Paris, Johnny. I wouldn't be here if it had. I want to be with you. I just told you, I'm crazy about you.'

'Do I have a chance with you?' He dropped his hands, sat back on the sofa.

'Yes, you do.'

'Will you at least think about marrying me?'

'Yes.'

'Aren't we great in bed together?'

She smiled at him. 'You know the answer to that.'

'Tell me, say it for me.'

'We're great in bed together.'

'And out of it. Say it, Rosie.'

'And we're great out of bed.'

A little smile settled on his mouth, and he said, 'So

we've got everything going for us. Okay then, it's settled. We'll get engaged the day your divorce comes through. And the next day we'll get married.'

Startled again, Rosie looked at him swiftly. 'I didn't say that!'

Paying no attention to her whatsoever, he jumped up off the sofa. 'I gotta go, babe. Nell's coming over soon. She'll bring you out to the concert.' He strode over to the door leading into his adjoining suite.

Rosie grabbed the Cartier jewel box from the coffee table, leapt to her feet and hurried after him. 'Johnny! Wait! The ring!' She held it out to him.

He shook his head. 'I bought it for you. It's yours. You keep it.'

'*I can't*. You *must* take it. I'd be afraid of losing it. *Please*, Johnny, you keep it for me. Lock it up safely.'

'Okay,' he said somewhat reluctantly, dropping it in his jacket pocket. Leaning closer to her, he kissed the tip of her nose. 'You'll marry me, Rosie. It's in the cards. It's our destiny. *Che sarà sarà*.'

She simply stared at him, once again lost for words.

As he opened the door, he explained, 'Oh, there's a couple of guys working in my suite. They'd never come in here, intrude. But lock the door if it makes you feel better.'

'It's fine. I'll just close it.'

He nodded, then said, 'You *are* going on the road with me, aren't you?'

'If you think I'm going to let you loose in the provinces you're out of your mind. Naturally I'm coming with you,' she laughed.

'And don't forget Scotland, Rosie, we're going to

Glasgow and Edinburgh, as well as Manchester, Leeds and Birmingham. See ya later, baby.' He winked at her and stepped into his own suite, closing the door behind him.

THIRTY-SIX

An hour later Rosie stood to attention in front of Nell in the middle of the bedroom, and asked, 'Well, how do I look?'

'*Perfect*,' Nell said. 'Elegant, refined, but terribly glamorous, Rosie mine. Just right for Johnny. We mustn't forget – you're his woman.'

Rosie looked at her quickly, started to laugh. '*His woman*. That's an odd way of putting it.'

'That's how *he* puts it. "Rosie's my woman," he says, and he says it to everybody. He's very proud of you, of having you in his life, you know.' Nell peered at her closely, her brows furrowing. 'Does it bother you?'

Rosie shook her head. 'No, not really, it just sounds funny, that's all.'

'Well, that's our Johnny. He's hardly a Rhodes Scholar.'

'That's a bit mean, Nellie.'

'I didn't intend it as such. I've always cared about Johnny, and you know I have. In fact, I love him in my own way. He's a good guy, a decent guy, which is saying a lot in this day and age and the business we're in.' Nell took a step backward. She regarded Rosie through critical eyes, her head to one side.

'Turn around,' Nell said. 'Let me see the back.'

'Yes ma'am,' Rosie answered and saluted smartly as she turned very slowly, showing off her black velvet ensemble. This was composed of narrowly-cut trousers and an artist's style shirt with long sleeves and a wide collar made of silk patterned in vivid red, orange, purple, yellow and black triangles. Over this she wore a tailored sleeveless coat with no fastenings in the front, which fell to her ankles.

'You *do* look terrific,' Nell pronounced and nodded her head in approval. 'But where's the ring?'

Rosie spun around. 'You *know* about the ring?'

'Of course. *Who* do you think he dragged to Cartier's with him on Tuesday? And I'd just landed in London from New York the night before. I was exhausted.'

'He bought it on Tuesday?'

'Yes, once he'd got my stamp of approval. I gave it, of course. After all it's ten carats, a pure white diamond, Starburst cut. The very best. So come on, Rosie, where is it?'

'I gave it back to Johnny. And you know very well I couldn't accept that ring, Nell. Johnny and I hardly know each other. We've only been involved for a few days. Besides which, I'm not divorced. So how could I get engaged?'

'There's really no reason why not.'

'Come on, Nellie, let's be sensible, grown-up women. Like we usually are.'

Nell laughed and shrugged. 'You could wear it on your right hand.'

'Don't be so silly.'

'It's not silly. This is show business, remember?'

Rosie searched Nell's face, not sure whether she was teasing or not. Nell's expression was unreadable. Rosie murmured, 'You didn't *really* think I'd accept the ring, did you?'

'To be honest, no, I didn't. But he wouldn't listen to me; he was so determined to buy the ring. I just had to let him go ahead and do what he wanted.'

Walking over to the bed, Nell sat down on it and stretched back on her elbows. Her face was thoughtful as she lay there without speaking for a few seconds.

Rosie glanced at her, then went into the dressing area where she put on three narrow gold bracelets and gold hoop earrings. Spraying herself with Bijan, she returned to the bedroom and hovered at the bottom of the bed in front of Nell.

Nell glanced at her. 'I'm glad you're with Johnny. He's just what the doctor ordered, Rosie. He's nice to you, isn't he? What I mean is, he's okay in bed, isn't he?'

'He's fantastic.'

'Not kinky.'

Rosie shook her head and laughed. 'No, thank God. He's straight as a dye. A bit insatiable, though. When I first arrived we almost ended up where you're lying now. I guess you could say there's a lot of chemistry between us.'

Nell smiled. 'I knew you needed Johnny Fortune!

God, I just *knew* it! Look at you, you're positively glowing. Your skin's like peaches and cream, and you've got quite a glint in your eye tonight, my lass.'

'Oh, Nell, there's nobody like you, nobody at all. I do love you. Now, tell me, how was Kevin?'

'Oh Rosie, just great. *Wonderful!* We had a smashing weekend together. But I have to confess, commuting back and forth across the Atlantic this week has been a bit wearing, even on Concorde. Anyway, he sends his love. I thought I'd told you that on the phone.'

'No,' Rosie replied. 'You didn't. We only talked about Johnny last night.'

A dreamy expression now crossed Nell's face and she sighed, raised her eyes to Rosie's. 'I might end up being your sister-in-law yet, my darling.'

'I hope so. By the way, did you tell Kevin about Johnny?'

'No. You didn't say I shouldn't, but then you didn't say I should, so I made no mention of him. After all, I hate playing God. It's your business and nobody else's.' Nell pushed herself up into a sitting position and eyed her dearest friend. 'So, tell me something now. Apart from being sexually turned on by him, how *do* you feel about our bel canto balladeer?'

'I'm crazy about him, Nell. He's all the things you said he was. And very loving and warm. Thoughtful. I guess you could say I'm infatuated.'

'Not in love?' Nell raised a fine blonde brow and threw Rosie a speculative look.

'I'm the cautious one these days, Nellie, after the horrible mistake I made with Guy.'

'Ah, the dreaded Guy. What a son of a bitch he turned out to be, and I guess I can't honestly blame you for your attitude. I think perhaps you're right to go slowly. After all, you have a fabulous career and a life of your own, quite aside from Johnny. And he can be very demanding.'

'What do you mean?'

'He's a star; he's demanding.'

'Gavin's a star, but he's not demanding. *I* don't think he is, anyway.'

'Gavin's an actor, and a New York actor at that. Johnny's a whole different kettle of fish, Rosie. He's a singer, an entertainer, and the biggest star there is in the music world today. And that *is* quite a different world from the world of film and theatre. It's all big flash, big money, big everything. It's crazy in many ways. And Johnny's *the* star attraction. People want to mob him, claw him, touch him, get close to him. Women swoon over him. Groupies crowd him. He's used to being fawned over, catered to, flattered, offered anything and everything he might want. All that sort of ridiculous bullshit. He's used to getting his own way, too. Look, he was impossible about that ring. He simply wouldn't listen to me or respond to reason. Johnny wanted to buy you the engagement ring, and he sure as hell was going to buy it. Over my dead body, if necessary.' Nell sighed. 'I told him you'd never agree to become engaged, but he wouldn't accept that, not even from me. All I'm saying is that Johnny is used to getting what he wants when he wants it.'

'I see.' Rosie turned away, suddenly feeling

concerned about the relationship, not certain that she could cope with Johnny. Wilful people perturbed her. They were usually unreasonable, difficult and frequently temperamental.

Nell said, 'Don't turn away like that, looking suddenly gloomy and dejected. Johnny's fabulous, despite what I just said. I've always told you that, for years, haven't I?'

'Yes, you have.'

'He's generous to a fault, with everyone. He's kind, and although he likes his own way, he doesn't *really* throw his weight around. Not too much. And he lives a clean life.'

'*Oh*. What do you mean?'

'No dope, no drugs of any kind; he doesn't smoke, he hardly drinks, and he sort of keeps himself to himself in Hollywood. Anywhere for that matter. And he's not all over the place, partying, living it up. Actually, he leads a relatively quiet life, I'd say.'

'That's the impression he gave me.' Rosie smiled at Nell. 'And I *wasn't* looking dejected.'

'Whatever you say, Rosie mine.' Nell glanced at her antique diamond watch. 'Hell, *we'd* better get a move on, my darling girl. It's already turned five-thirty.'

'But the concert's not until eight.'

'I know. However, it'll take us an hour to get to Wembley, maybe a bit longer at this time. And Johnny wants us to go to his dressing room before the show starts.'

'I'll get my purse.'

When Rosie came back from the dressing area

adjoining the bedroom, Nell was standing in front of the mirror hanging over the mantel, smoothing her silver-gilt hair into place.

'You look great, Nellie,' Rosie murmured, walking towards her. 'I love you in that red suit. It's very flattering.'

'Thanks, and I'm glad we discussed what we were going to wear. I'd been toying with a black velvet trouser suit myself, instead of this red one. We'd have looked like a vaudeville act if I'd worn it.' She laughed. 'Let's go. We don't want to upset our star, now do we?'

Rosie laughed and linked arms with her. They left the suite.

Walking along the hotel corridor, Nell said, 'The limo's downstairs. And Johnny's given us Butch to look after us.'

'Butch? Who's Butch?'

'One of Johnny's bodyguards. Andy and Jack, the other two, went with Johnny to Wembley.'

'I see. By the way, why did Johnny leave so early?' Rosie asked as they came to a halt in front of the elevators. 'He rushed out at four-thirty.'

'I told you, it takes a good hour to the Wembley Arena. He was probably trying to avoid the tea-time traffic. But, in any case, he always has about an hour of Hair and Make-up, and he likes plenty of time to get himself geared up, revved up for the show.'

'I'm looking forward to seeing him perform.'

'I thought you already had,' Nell shot back and leered at her.

'Nell Jeffrey! You're wicked and provocative!'

'That's exactly what your brother says about you.'

Johnny's dressing room was full of people, and for a moment Rosie could not see him. 'Is it always this crowded?' she asked, turning to Nell.

'Yes, but it'll thin out very shortly. Anyway, this is the outer dressing room. Johnny's hair and make-up people will be through that door over there. Come on, let's head that way.'

They had only taken a few steps when Nell caught hold of her arm and said, 'Johnny's in the corner, talking to Kenny, who plays keyboard, and to Joe, his personal assistant.'

'He's mentioned them to me, but are you sure we should intrude?'

'Are you joking?' Nell laughed, propelling her forward with a firm grip. 'I bet he's bursting to introduce you to his guys. He's done nothing but talk about you this week, and I told you earlier he thinks you're the bee's knees.'

'Nell, honestly, you do have some weird expressions –' Rosie muttered and paused in the middle of her sentence.

Johnny had swung away from Kenny and Joe in such abrupt manner that she was positive he was angry. And when he turned around and she saw his face this was confirmed to her. He was furious, if his expression was anything to judge by. His vivid cornflower eyes blazed and his mouth was set in a rigid line. He turned back to the two men, who looked suitably chastened, she thought. He hissed something at them, then headed to the other side of the room where he entered the make-up area. Even the set of his shoulders told her he was put out.

'He looks angry, upset,' Rosie said quietly to Nell.

'It's probably a storm in a tea cup, all about nothing,' Nell said in an undertone. 'I'm sure he's all right. He's generally nervous, on edge, sometimes irritable, even a bit crazy before a big show like this, before he goes on.'

'Perhaps we ought to leave, give him some privacy.'

'Privacy! With all these guys here! Anyway, are you mad! He's expecting us, Rosie. Come on. I bet Allie is in there finishing his make-up, and Maury will probably be starting on his hair. Then all he has to do is get out of that robe and into his clothes.'

'All right, Nell, you're the boss, and certainly you know him better than I do.'

'Ah, but not in the biblical sense, my dear, certainly not as intimately as you,' Nell teased, and before Rosie could respond she pushed her through the doorway.

'Hi, Johnny!' Nell exclaimed. 'Can we come in? Or do you want to finish getting ready first?'

Johnny was sitting in a high make-up chair in front of a large expanse of mirror surrounded by theatrical make-up lights. He looked into the mirror and saw them, raised his hand in greeting; then he swung his head and looked at them over his shoulder. 'It's okay, Nell,' he murmured, flashing a smile. 'Come on, Rosie, come on over and meet Allie and Maury, who try to make me look half way decent.'

Rosie smiled at him and did as he said. Immediately she saw that he seemed perfectly normal; the anger of a moment ago had passed. After he had introduced her to Allie, Maury and his manager Jeff Smailes, who had just sauntered in, Johnny sat back in the make-up chair; he finally let the professionals finish the job they had started well over an hour ago.

Nell said, 'Take the chair next to Johnny, Rosie, and I'll sit over here.'

'Thanks.' Rosie lowered herself into the chair, accepted the glass of champagne someone offered her and watched Allie working on Johnny's face. A handsome man without make-up, he was even more good-looking when cosmetics had been applied; devastating was the only word she could think of to describe him at this moment. Because he had a California suntan, Allie had used a tan foundation and she had shaded his cheeks before powdering his face. Now she was applying just the merest hint of blue eye shadow, which instantly intensified the colour of his eyes.

At one moment Johnny looked at Rosie in the mirror and gave her a cheeky grin, then let Allie put on his lipstick. Once she had done so he wiped it off with a tissue, licked his lips several times, wiped his mouth yet again, and then peered at himself in the mirror.

Maury said, 'Okay, maestro, let's get to the locks, shall we? Time's a-running out on us.' As he spoke, Maury began to brush Johnny's blond-streaked hair into shape.

'Not too much hair spray, Maury,' Johnny said,

and fifteen minutes later he was jumping out of the chair. 'I gotta go, honey,' he said to Rosie. 'I gotta get my clothes. Wait here.' He glanced at Maury and exclaimed, 'This is my . . . very special lady, ain't she the greatest!' and then he was gone.

Nell came over to her, dragging a chair with her. 'We'll wait until he comes back dressed, spend another five minutes with him, and then I think we'd better go to our seats.'

'If you say so, you know best.'

'It's just that he's going to get awfully tensed up before he goes on Rosie, and –' She broke off as Johnny appeared.

'You're sitting right up front,' Johnny said, walking back into the make-up area. He wore a pair of black trousers, a starched white shirt, open at the neck, and was carrying a black jacket. He came over to Rosie, and squeezed her shoulder, then swung away, looked in the mirror, patted his hair, wiped his mouth with a tissue and took a sip from a glass of water.

Then he turned away from Rosie and Nell and began to pace. He stopped at one moment and handed his coat to Jeff and kept on pacing, his head down, biting his lower lip. He came to a standstill, looked up at the ceiling and closed his eyes, mouthing words to himself without a sound, as if rehearsing silently.

From the other room there was a sudden burst of loud laughter and he snapped his eyes open and said in a harsh voice, 'Jeff, get everybody outta there. I gotta concentrate.'

He began to pace again and a fine film of

perspiration began to appear on his face. He paused, took a sip of water, and went on walking up and down.

It was apparent to Rosie that he was quite oblivious to them, no longer aware of their presence. Always sensitive to performers, and conscious of the emotional stress they suffered, what they went through before a performance, she drew closer to Nell. Touching her arm, she mouthed silently, 'Let's go. He needs to be alone.'

Nell nodded.

Together they slipped out of the make-up area by skirting the edge of the room, leaving the centre of the floor to Johnny. Still pacing, his eyes were half closed, his lips moving as he went over his songs in his mind.

As they passed through the outer dressing room Rosie saw that it had miraculously emptied; Nell took hold of her arm and ushered her outside, where Butch was waiting to take them to their front-row seats.

Once they were in their places and settled, Rosie glanced around. She had never seen so many people gathered together under one roof; the noise was deafening.

'There must be thousands here,' she said to Nell. 'No wonder he's full of tension. Who'd want to get up and sing in front of a huge crowd like this?'

'A star like Johnny. But I agree, it must be nerve-racking for him, for anybody.' Nell's eyes roamed around. 'It's some mob scene tonight.'

'And they're all his fans. My God, Nell, that says something about him, doesn't it?'

'Yes. Johnny's a big draw. By the way, he told me you're going out on the road with him. Up to the Midlands and the North. And then on to Scotland.'

'He was very persuasive last weekend in Paris.'

'I'm coming after all . . . it'll be fun,' Nell said.

'I'm glad you'll be with us. Are you going with him to Australia at the end of the month?'

'Only for a week. The second week of March. Why?'

'Johnny wanted me to do his Australian tour with him,' Rosie told her, 'but I explained why I couldn't. I have too much work. I had to get up at four o'clock every morning this week in order to complete some of the costume designs, just so that I could take these next few days off.'

Nell eyed her carefully. 'He's always on tour part of the year, you know.'

'Yes, I'm aware of that.'

A silence fell between them. They sat back in their seats, each lost in her own thoughts.

Then quite suddenly the lights in the arena dimmed, the orchestra began to play and hundreds of lights were focused on stage; multi-coloured spotlights and searchlights created spectacular special effects.

Ten minutes elapsed.

Johnny walked out onto the stage.

It seemed to Rosie that the entire arena swayed and shifted on its foundations as thousands jumped to their feet, stamping, waving, cheering and screaming his name over and over again. They were crazed.

Rose had never seen anything like it before.

Involuntarily, a shiver ran through her and she clasped her hands together, feeling suddenly anxious. There was something frightening to her about this roaring crowd, and about their adulation of him. What if they ever turned on him for some reason? They could tear him limb from limb. She shivered again and tensed in her seat.

Nell noticed this and looked at her swiftly. 'What's wrong, Rosie? What's the matter?'

'All these people, the way they're behaving. We could get crushed to death if they surged, made any sudden movement.'

'I know what you mean. Actually, that's why we're sitting down here at the front. We're right next to an exit that goes backstage, so don't worry. And that's why Butch is with us, to look after us. About fifteen minutes before the end of the show he'll take us through that door. We'll catch the end of the concert from the wings.'

Rosie nodded, focused her eyes straight ahead.

Johnny was now centre stage.

He walked down to the front, waving and bowing to the crowds, acknowledging them. And then he looked in her direction and blew her a kiss before pivoting, returning to centre stage.

He remained standing with his back to them.

The audience finally sat down.

The noise abated.

The orchestra stopped playing.

Kenny Crossland on keyboard began to play the first few bars of *My Heart Belongs to Me*.

Johnny turned, his head lowered. Slowly, he raised it and began to sing.

Rosie sat watching him, mesmerized. Just as the audience was mesmerized.

He was a slim, slight figure in the middle of that vast stage and somehow oddly vulnerable. And immensely appealing. His good looks, highlighted by the make-up, leapt out at her; she recognized how enormously charismatic he was on stage, so simply dressed in his black suit and white shirt. There was this extraordinary electricity about him: his voice was superb; he held the audience in the palm of his hand. They loved him.

His very stillness commanded total attention.

Johnny did not gyrate. He stood perfectly motionless. The movement of his limbs was spare and he barely stretched a muscle. Occasionally, he swayed his legs in time to the music but his feet were still; sometimes he moved his body, but only fractionally. He lifted a hand once. For the most part he remained rooted to one spot. His power over them was his mellifluous voice and his looks.

When he finished the first song the response was deafening.

Inclining his head, graciously accepting their accolades, he then held up his hand for silence and went straight into the next number. After doing two more with back-up singers he took the microphone and came down to the edge of the stage.

'Thank you,' he said to the audience when the last round of applause died away. 'It's great to be here with you tonight.' There was a short pause. Walking at a rapid pace along the edge of the stage he did not stop until he was immediately in front of Nell and Rosie.

Staring out at the audience, he murmured into the mike, 'This one's for my lady,' and looking directly at her he blew her a kiss.

Rosie smiled up at him.

The audience went wild for a few seconds. After he lifted his arm and began to hum, a hushed silence descended on the arena. Swaying to the music of the orchestra, he dropped his head, still humming, and when he finally lifted his eyes he focused them on her. His voice rang out, pure and clear, as he began to sing *Lost Inside of You*.

He sang only to her and only for her.

Sitting there watching him, listening to him, Rosie could not help but admire him as a great entertainer. And she also finally understood something else: just how truly serious Johnny was about her, how intent he was on possessing her; and completely; for always. Her heart tightened imperceptibly; a sharp sliver of fear pierced it. It dawned on her that he was obsessed with her. And to Rosie any kind of obsession was terrifying.

THIRTY-SEVEN

Morning sunlight streamed in through the huge plate-glass windows. It bounced off the stark white walls, the steel-and-glass furniture, and the collection of glass, marble and metal obelisks arranged on the glass-and-chrome étagère.

Everything in the large dining room of the rented Trump Tower apartment shimmered and glittered, and Gavin was beginning to find this insistent brilliant light irritating.

Pushing himself up from the chair, he went over to the wide expanse of windows at the far end of the room, intending to close the blinds. But he did not. For a brief moment he stood looking out at the skyline of Manhattan, momentarily awed by the extraordinary view. It was dazzling, really. There was nothing like it anywhere in the world. He knew that. The architecture of Manhattan boggled the mind; he thought it was beautiful. Anyway, it was his town.

The dining room was situated on the Fifth Avenue side of the large apartment, and now, as he stood there at the windows, he was looking across Sixth, Seventh, Eighth and Ninth Avenues, all the way to the West Side and the Hudson river. Beyond the skyscrapers gleaming in the bright blue sky, the river looked like a sheet of silver stretching for miles.

He blinked in the glare of the light and tugged on the metal string; the vertical blinds whooshed across the glass, instantly dimming the room, making it more comfortable.

Back at the dining room table he flipped quickly through the *New York Times*, read Frank Rich's review of a new Broadway play, turned to the movie section and then put the paper down as the phone jangled behind him.

Rising, he strode across the floor to the white-lacquered sideboard and picked it up. 'Hello?'

'Gavin?'

'Yes.'

'It's Louise.'

'I know.' He glanced at his watch and frowned. It was nine o'clock. 'You sound as if you're just around the corner.'

'I am.'

'Where?'

'At the Piere Hotel.'

'And where's David?'

'At home. In California –'

'Louise, you know I don't like us both to be away,' he cut in. 'I thought we'd agreed about that.'

'We did. It's all right. My sister's staying for a few days, and anyway he has a nanny, let's not forget that. We also have a housekeeper, a house man and a cook living in. He's fine. Don't worry so much.'

Gavin sighed. 'What're you doing in New York?'

'I came to see you.'

'Oh.'

'Yes. I want to talk to you.'

'Couldn't you have done that on the phone?'

'Not really, I came in last night. And I'm leaving later today.'

'Going to Washington, I've no doubt.'

'No, Gavin, I'm not. I'm going back to the coast. Because you don't like us both to be away from David at the same time,' she pointed out, an edge creeping into her voice.

'When do you want to meet?' he asked.

'How about in an hour?'

'Okay. Will you come here?'

'Yes, that's fine. I'll see you at ten.'

He stood listening to the dial tone; she had hung up on him. Grimacing at the receiver, he replaced it and returned to the table. Gulping down the last of his coffee, he crossed the marble-clad hall and headed in the direction of the bedroom. Like the rest of the apartment, this was decorated with a great abundance of modern furniture, which he loathed, and there was so much white he was beginning to dislike that colour intensely.

Glancing around, he muttered under his breath, 'This place is driving me nuts,' and went through into the white marble bathroom. After he had shaved, he slipped off his robe, took a shower, washed his hair, and stepped out of the stall, groping for a towel.

Fifteen minutes later Gavin was dressed in dark grey slacks, a white shirt and dark navy blazer, heading in the direction of the small library.

Here he sat down at the desk and made several phone calls about his trip to France; then he sat back and dialled his lawyer Ben Stanley, at home in Bel-Air.

'No need to say rise and shine to you, Ben,' he chortled down the phone when the lawyer answered on the second ring. 'Like all the good guys in la-la land, you were up at the crack of dawn, I've no doubt.'

'Hey, Gavin, how're you doing back there in my favourite city, my old home town?'

'Pretty good, Ben. Postproduction's finally finished on *Kingmaker*, and the picture looks great. You're going to love it. My group left a few days ago for London, and we'll be moving into Billancourt Studios in about a week.'

'When are you going to Paris?'

'Tomorrow. Ben, listen. I called you because Louise is in New York. She just phoned me. She's coming over soon, says she wants to talk to me. I'm sure it's about a divorce.'

'I agree. Be careful what you say, Gavin, and don't promise her anything, don't make any commitments. If she's got a lawyer, which you can be damned sure she has, tell her to tell him to be in touch with me. Remember, you've stayed in that marriage because of your child. Don't blow it now.'

'I won't. And I'll get back to you as soon as she leaves. In the meantime, I'll be staying at the Ritz in

Paris, as usual, and you know where to reach me during the day.'

'I have the Billancourt numbers. Your secretary faxed everything to the office yesterday.'

'Whoops, that's the intercom from downstairs. I gotta go, Ben. Talk to you shortly.'

'Be careful, Gavin.'

'I will.'

They said goodbye, hung up, and Gavin grabbed the intercom phone. He told security to send Mrs Ambrose up immediately.

Louise had put on weight. It was very obvious. But this made her look much better. She was pale, nevertheless, and had dark rings under her eyes. Gavin couldn't help but wonder what was going on in her private life. He took her coat, laid it on the hall bench without saying a word. She was silent also.

Ushering her into the living room, Gavin finally spoke. 'Can I get you anything? There's coffee in the kitchen.'

She shook her head and sat down on the sofa.

Gavin took a chair facing her.

'What do you want to talk to me about, Louise?'

Hesitating for a moment, she cleared her throat nervously and shifted on the sofa, adjusted the skirt of her suit.

Gavin was aware that she was suddenly nervous, and so he said, 'Come on, Louise, I'm not going to bite. I'm not really the ogre you've made me out to be these last few years.'

'I want a divorce,' she blurted out, staring at him, twisting her hands in her lap.

'Okay. You can have one.'

'Just like that? No arguments?' She sounded surprised and a look of puzzlement flickered on her face.

Smiling at her, Gavin said, 'No arguments.' He paused for effect. 'But quite a few *conditions*.'

'And what are they? To do with money, I suspect.'

'No, I'm not going to discuss money with you, or community property, or anything like that, Louise. Our lawyers will deal with those things. My conditions are to do with our child.'

'I expected you to pull David right into the middle of this situation,' she snapped.

'Then it won't come as any surprise to you that I want him.'

'You can't have him!' She sounded shrill; her face twisted in annoyance.

'I'll have joint custody, Louise, and with your agreement. Otherwise, no divorce.'

'Were you a bastard when I married you, or have you just become one since you became a big star?'

'Oh, Louise, here we go again! For God's sake, stop being bitchy with me. You want a divorce. You fly to New York. You come here cap in hand, and then you start making nasty cracks. That's no way to get what you want.'

She sighed and leaned back against the sofa, studying him through her ice-cold pale-blue eyes. Deep down she was filled with hatred for him.

Gavin stared back at her and laughed quietly. 'I know you're having an affair with Allan Turner, and that you wish to marry him. So come on, be reasonable.'

When she did not answer, merely glanced at him, he continued: 'I guess you'll be living in Washington. That's all right, since I have every intention of moving back to the East Coast, once this new movie's in the can. That's not a difficult commute for me. Or for David, for that matter. And incidentally, when *do* you plan to pick up stakes in California and move to DC?'

'I never said I was moving to Washington!' Louise exclaimed.

'But you are,' he asserted.

Biting her lip, realizing there was no point in procrastinating, or lying, she nodded. 'Yes, I will be. But not yet.'

'Have you looked into schools for David?'

'No.'

'Don't worry about it. I'll take care of that. There are very good private schools down there, and there'll be no problems getting him placed.'

'Aside from wanting joint custody, what are your other conditions?'

'Are you *agreeing* to joint custody?'

Louise did not answer him. She glanced away, and then brought her eyes back to his. 'Yes,' she said quickly. 'I'm agreeing.'

Gavin breathed a sigh of relief. 'The other conditions are that he spends at least two major school vacations with me, either winter or summer. And that you do not prevent me from taking him out of the country for those vacations.'

She nodded.

'Does that mean you are agreeing to these *two* other conditions?' Gavin asked, wanting to be absolutely clear on everything.

'Yes, I am.'

'Good.'

'Community property has to be split down the middle, Gavin. That's the law. What else are you giving me?'

'Child support, obviously. But I told you, you must talk about finances to Ben Stanley. Or rather, your lawyer must do that. You do have a lawyer, don't you?'

'Yes.'

'Okay then, so it's settled,' Gavin said.

'It's settled.'

Gavin stood up. 'I still don't understand why you made the trip. We could have had this discussion on the phone.'

Louise shrugged as she got to her feet. 'I always believe in doing things face to face. It's a point of honour with me.'

He started to walk out of the room, deciding not to comment. He didn't want a row with her; he just wanted her to leave now that the discussion was over.

Louise followed him swiftly.

In the foyer she said, 'So, when are you going to Paris to start *Napoleon and Josephine*?'

'Tomorrow.'

'Then I just made it in time, didn't I?'

Without a word Gavin lifted her sable coat from the bench and helped her into it. He stared at her intently. After a moment, he said in a kind voice, 'We went through a lot of emotional stress, you and I, when we were younger. In fact, we went through a lot together, really. I'm sorry it didn't work out, Louise.'

Gavin sighed, and there was regret in his voice when he repeated, 'Yes, I'm sorry. For both of us, actually. We've wasted a lot of good years of our lives that shouldn't have been wasted. But at least David hasn't suffered. And I want to be certain he doesn't. Let's try to be amicable about the divorce, Louise. Please. For David's sake.'

'Yes,' she said and opened the front door, stepped out to the elevator. Turning her head, she announced quietly, 'I loved you, you know. And God knows, I wanted it to work. But our marriage didn't stand a chance, because you never loved *me*, Gavin. Never. You only married me because I was pregnant.'

'Louise, I –'

'Please don't deny it. I've always known, ever since that awful tragedy with the first baby, that you'd never be mine, that you'd never commit to me. Not when your passion lay elsewhere.'

'What do you mean?' he asked, momentarily baffled. 'Are you talking about my acting?'

'If you don't know what I'm referring to, then I'm not going to tell you, Gavin Ambrose.' Surprising herself and him, she reached up, kissed him on the cheek. 'So long,' she murmured, and there was no rancour in her voice when she added, 'I'll see you in court.'

The elevator door opened and she stepped inside,

and Gavin noticed again that she looked plumper than he had seen her in years. As he walked back into the apartment it hit him like a bolt of lightning. Louise was pregnant. No doubt about it. Love her though he did not, he nevertheless knew her very well after all these years. Louise would not have another man's child without being married to him. Certainly not after what happened with their first baby. Besides, she more than likely loved Allan Turner. They were well suited. No wonder she had been so co-operative, had agreed to everything about David. Obviously, she was in a hurry to marry her senator.

So be it, he thought. He wanted his freedom now. Just as much as she wanted hers.

THIRTY-EIGHT

Henri de Montfleurie had never presumed to understand women, finding them too complicated to fathom. However, he was a man blessed with insight and an understanding heart, and he did know when someone, be it a man or a woman, was in distress.

And tonight he was well aware that Rosie, whom he loved like a daughter, was troubled. It showed in the paleness of her face, her unusual quietness, and in her distracted manner. Several times she had asked him to repeat something he had said only a split second before. He knew she had not been listening, had been far away, thinking of something else entirely.

Henri was sitting with Rosie in the small red-and-green library in her apartment having an aperitif before going out to dinner. He and Kyra had come to Paris for a few days on family business; at the moment Kyra was visiting an aunt. Later she would go to Le Vieux Bistro on the rue du Cloître-Notre-Dame, where they were to meet her at eight-thirty.

Having talked to Rosie about her beloved Montfleurie, and answered her questions about the staff, Lisette and Yvonne, Henri said, 'I understand from Hervé that your divorce should be final in September.'

'I believe so.'

'I'm so glad, Rosie. It's time now for you to be free, to get on with your life. It pains me when I think of all the wasted years and –'

He stopped as the phone shrilled.

'Excuse me,' Rosie said and went to answer it. 'Oh hello, Fanny dear,' she murmured into the receiver. 'No, it's all right. Just explain the problem to me as quickly as possible. Hopefully, I'll be able to solve it. Otherwise it'll have to wait until tomorrow.' She stood with her ear pressed to the phone, listening attentively to her assistant at the other end of the line.

Henri went to refill his glass with whisky, then strolled over to the window and glanced out. It was almost the end of March and a blustery night. A sudden gust of wind rattled the window panes and there was a crack of thunder in the distance that sounded like gunfire. A bad storm was brewing. This thought had no sooner entered his mind than heavy raindrops began to splash against the glass. He turned away, shivering slightly, and made his way back to the warmth of the fire.

Taking the same chair, he sipped his drink and thought about Rosie. What he wanted for her was – *happiness*, the kind he had with Kyra. He wished he could give it to Rosie, just hand it to her, but he couldn't. Only one man could give her the joy and contentment she deserved. Unfortunately, she didn't know that; perhaps the man didn't either. Henri sighed. Rosie was so blind to her feelings. If she were more in touch with them she might have made a move in the right direction years ago. Oh, the complexities of the human heart.

'Sorry about that,' she said, putting the phone down. 'There's always a problem with the costumes.'

'Come and sit here with me, Rosie. I want to talk to you about something. Something important.'

She hurried to join him, and he was pleased to see that he now had her full attention.

'Is something wrong, Henri? You sound worried.'

'I am.'

'What about?'

'You.'

She had settled back in the chair and picked up her drink. But now she put it down again on the small side table. Leaning forward, her arms on her knees, her attention was riveted on him. 'Why are you worried about *me*?'

'Because I love you like my own child. You don't look at all well, Rosie. You've lost a lot of weight, your face is drawn, pinched almost, and your colour is quite awful – you're ashen. But these physical manifestations of your problems are the least of it. Ever since I arrived this evening you've been a little edgy, preoccupied, lost in thought. You seem depressed, which is most unlike you. It's not in your nature to be gloomy. In short, you are troubled, my dear, terribly troubled, I'd say.'

Rosie made no response, simply looked out into space, her eyes focused on a painting hanging between the windows, her expression reflective. And then, as if she had made up her mind about something, she brought her gaze back to his and said quietly, 'I've made a terrible mistake.'

He nodded and waited. When she was not forthcoming, he asked gently, 'Can I make the assumption that the mistake has to do with a man?'

'Yes.'

'Johnny Fortune?'

'How did you know?'

'It's a deduction, Rosie. You told me at Christmas that Johnny had been calling you from Las Vegas. In fact, I remember that Collie was excited because he had been in touch with you. And you volunteered that he was coming to Paris to see you in the new year. About six weeks later Kyra mentioned that he was in Paris. A few days later she said you had gone to England. Something to do with Johnny's British concert tour. I just presumed you'd become involved with him. You keep forgetting I'm a Frenchman and incurably romantic.'

A small smile struck Rosie's mouth, but it fled instantly. 'Well, you were right. We did become involved. But we shouldn't have, Henri, not really.'

'Why not?'

'Because it can't possibly work between us.'

'Are you sure?'

'Oh yes. Johnny's different . . . he's not like other people, not like you and me, not *normal* really.'

Henri frowned. 'I'm not sure I understand you, Rosie.'

'He's a big star, one of the world's greatest

427

entertainers, and he lives in a totally different world. He lives a different kind of life . . .' Her voice faltered and she looked into the fire.

'I *know* you, Rosie. You must have felt something for him or you would never have gone to London to see him.'

'Oh I did! Johnny's very attractive, warm, loving, generous to a fault. And there was a lot of . . . well . . . sexual chemistry between us.' She cleared her throat. 'I wanted to be with him, to become involved with him. And so I went, and it was wonderful. Actually, the affair transported me for several weeks. I felt reborn.'

'I'm not surprised. You have come out of a sexual wasteland, and once you made up your mind to dissolve that ridiculous marriage to my son, you felt free at last. I understand, Rosie, truly I do. And I told you months ago, you're far too young to be alone, to be without a loving man in your life.'

'But I don't think Johnny's the man for me, Henri. He's away at the moment on his Australian concert tour, but if he had been here I'm sure the sparks would have started to fly between us.'

'What do you mean?'

Dropping her eyes, Rosie played with the edging on her skirt, but eventually she looked up and explained, 'Johnny's very possessive of me.'

'Hasn't it occurred to you that he might be in love with you?'

'Oh I know he is! He asked me to marry him the minute I arrived in London; he even had an engagement ring. Naturally, I couldn't agree to become engaged. Apart from the fact that I'm not divorced, it was all too fast for me. But I handled it gently with him, made him understand I wanted to go a little more slowly, get to know him better, and I pointed out that he should get to know me, too. He accepted that. For about five minutes. And then he was planning our wedding for the day after my divorce becomes final.' Rosie sighed and fiddled with her gold bangles. 'Johnny is very . . . *macho*. I guess that's a good word to describe him. He doesn't understand about my career at all, and wants me to give it up, the sooner the better for him. That way I can be with him all the time, travel with him, go on tour with him.'

'And you don't want that? You don't want to marry Johnny?'

'I don't think so. For one thing, I can't live the day-into-night life that an entertainer of Johnny's magnitude lives. He's eating dinner when I want to go to sleep when he's on tour, and he's on tour for half the year. Those few days in Britain I was coping with Johnny and all of his demands on me, trying to do my job long-distance, being attentive to his needs . . . there were times when I felt as if I was being spun around in a washing machine, to tell you the truth.'

'But didn't you try to talk to him, explain your feelings?'

'No, not then, not when we were touring England and Scotland. I was kind of . . . well, overwhelmed by him, by his love and devotion, and yes, his sexuality. He's very seductive.' She bit her lip and shook her head. 'But I do remember thinking at his London concert that he was obsessed with me, and I found that quite frightening, Henri.'

'Obsession is always worrying. It's not . . .' He paused, seeking a word.

'Normal,' she supplied.

'It seems to me that the only way to rectify this . . . terrible mistake, as you call it, is to break off the relationship with Johnny.'

Rosie threw him such a startled look he was taken aback, and he said quickly, 'Unless of course you feel you want to continue the relationship as lovers. Isn't that possible?'

'Johnny wouldn't agree. Well, that's not true. He would, of course. Until I was divorced and then he would want us to get married immediately. And besides, another problem has developed.'

'Oh, and what is that?' Henri looked at her closely.

Rosie returned his long, probing look and much to her irritation her eyes filled with tears. Averting her face, coughing behind her hand, she tried to get a grip on herself. Swallowing, she managed to say, 'I think there's something wrong with me, Henri.'

'Darling, what do you mean?' he asked in concern.

'I . . . I . . . just don't feel the same way about Johnny.'

'When did you find yourself changing?'

'About two weeks ago, maybe a bit longer actually. Of course, I *was* perturbed about him when we were in Scotland the last week of February. He was a bit weird, so terribly possessive. He wouldn't let me out of his sight and that scared me. And I've realized these past few weeks that I don't really miss him, I don't seem to have that physical need . . . for him . . .'

'I don't think there's anything wrong with you, Rosie. You're a pretty normal woman in my opinion. But you know sometimes an overwhelming sexual passion can burn out quickly. What begins in white heat can end up cold ashes in no time at all. At least that's been my own experience. This happens because it's lust, nothing more. And lust can be so easily slaked.'

'I suppose you're right.'

'At the risk of sounding like an old fuddy-duddy, Rosie, sex is never enough in a relationship. There has to be love as well. You were sexually attracted to Johnny and overwhelmed, from what you've told me. But sex was all it was. And that's why it burnt out.'

Rosie nodded but made no comment.

Henri said, 'We can talk more later if you like, my dear, but I think we must leave in the next few minutes. For the restaurant.' He looked at his watch. 'Yes, we'd better go. I don't want to keep Kyra waiting, and it's pouring with rain. We'll have trouble finding a taxi.'

Rosie got up out of the chair. 'Yes, we will. I'll get my coat.'

Henri rose and came to her, hugged her tightly, wanting to say more; he thought it wiser to keep his own counsel.

'Thank you, Henri,' she murmured against his cheek. 'Thank you for understanding and for caring.'

'But I love you, Rosie. You're my daughter,' he

said, looking into her eyes, smiling with affection.

His words touched her deeply, and because her emotions were close to the surface they got the better of her.

'Don't,' he said gently. 'Don't weep. Everything's going to be all right.'

THIRTY-NINE

Vito Carmello was so pleased he could not keep the smile off his face, and his happiness was evident in his ebullient manner, the jaunty spring of his step. He felt ten years younger and all because of the phone call from Johnny this morning.

His Johnny had called him from Perth and what he had said had given Vito a new lease on life. He knew it would have the same effect on Salvatore, who had not been feeling his best this past week. That was why he had rushed out to Staten Island in the middle of the morning. To give the good news to the Don. His old *goombah* was going to be as surprised as he had been, and just as happy.

Two soldiers in the organization stood at the front door, and both of them greeted him jovially as he climbed the last few steps. He didn't have much time for either of them. *'Gintaloons,'* he muttered in Sicilian under his breath. But despite this derogatory comment to himself he nevertheless bestowed huge smiles on them as he went through the door and into the entrance hall.

The first person he saw was Joey Fingers, who was

loitering near the door to the kitchen. Joey was rarely out here at the house, and he wondered what was going on.

'Hiya, Vito, how're ya doin'?' Joey cried, grabbing him, endeavouring to draw him into an embrace.

'I'm doin' good, Joey, doin' good,' Vito answered, pushing the hit-man away from him. Creep, he thought, as he rolled on through the hall, heading for Salvatore's private room, the one he called his inner sanctum.

Salvatore was sitting behind his desk, talking to Anthony, the *consigliere*, who was in a chair facing him. They both glanced at the door when Vito entered and stood to greet him affectionately. He embraced them both heartily.

'Sit down, sit down,' Salvatore said, waving a hand in the direction of the fire. 'It's not often you come out in the daytime, Vito, and I told Theresa you'd stay to lunch. She's preparing your favourites . . . mozzarella and tomatoes with our own olive oil, and spaghetti bolognaise. Nothing like good Italian food, eh?'

'Thanks, I'll stay, Salvatore. I doan have much to do today. I'll go to the club later. What's Joey Fingers doin' out here?'

'Anthony wanted to talk to him.' Salvatore shook his head. 'Joey's crazy. He don't want to listen. Today, mebbe, he listens good. To the *consigliere* here. Mebbe Anthony scared him.'

'He's getting no more warnings,' Anthony said, looking from Salvatore to Vito. 'The dumb bastard gets worse. Next time that guy screws up, we take him out. He's trouble, boss, real trouble. He talks too much. To too many people. I dunno, he makes me nervous. I think he's on something.'

'You mean the white powder?' Salvatore asked, swinging around to look at Anthony.

'Mebbe.' Anthony shrugged.

'He makes me nervous, too,' the Don said, and sat down in the chair opposite Vito. 'But leave it alone now.' He spread his hands out in front of the flames. 'I want to sit here, talk to my old *goombah*, and have a glass of wine. We'll work this afternoon. When Frankie gets back from New Jersey.' Salvatore shivered, stood up and positioned himself in front of the fire, warming his body now. 'It's cold for March, Vito. Old bones need sun, eh?'

Vito nodded.

Anthony inclined his head in Vito's direction and said to Salvatore, 'I'll see you later, boss.'

'Stay for lunch, Anthony.'

'Thanks, I will,' the *consigliere* said and left the room.

Once they were alone, Salvatore looked at Vito, peering at him intently in the dimly-lit den. 'So, what's got *you* worked up, Vito? What's brought you all this way in the daytime? And why the big smiles?'

Vito chuckled. 'Ah, Salvatore, I have some good news. Wonderful news. Johnny called this morning. From Australia. He's found a girl. The right one.'

Salvatore frowned. 'In Australia? An Australian girl?'

'No, no. Here. I mean she's in Paris. But she'll be here. Johnny told me he's found the girl he's goin' to marry and she'll be here when he gets back in April.'

'A French girl?'

'No, Salvatore. An American girl. A nice American girl. But she's living in Paris.'

'And that's why you're smiling, old friend? He's found a nice Italian-American girl over there and he's bringing her back. Good, good. No wonder you're all smiles. It makes me smile too. What's her name?'

'Rosalind. Rosie he calls her.'

Salvatore frowned. 'It don't sound Italian. What's her last name?'

'Madigan.'

'*Madigan*. She's Irish?'

'Mebbe she is, but she's a Catholic, a good Catholic girl. Johnny told me.'

'Where does she come from?'

'Queens. She grew up in Queens.'

'What's she doin' in Paris?' Salvatore sat down in the chair and stared across at Vito.

'She makes clothes.'

'Oh.'

'I mean, she designs clothes. For movies.'

'So that's why he called? To tell you all this?'

Vito's face was wreathed in smiles as he nodded several times and said, 'He wanted you to know that Rosie's coming over soon. In April, I doan know exactly when, but she's comin'. Johnny said so. He wants us to meet her. Go into Manhattan to a fancy restaurant. Yeah, that's what he wants.'

'He sound happy?'

'Yeah, real happy. On top of the world he says he is, and the tour's goin' good.'

'When's it finished?'

'End of the month. Then he's goin' to fly from Sydney to LA. He'll be comin' to New York in the middle of April.'

'Easter, mebbe. And the girl?'

'Same time,' he said. 'I told you that.'

Salvatore nodded and rose, ambled over to the small corner cupboard at the other side of the room and took out a bottle of red wine. After he had opened it, he filled two glasses and carried them over to the fireplace, handing one to Vito.

'To the Brotherhood,' they said in unison, as they always did, and touched crystal to crystal.

'Johnny is my son, *sangu de ma sangu*, blood of my blood,' Salvatore said. 'I want him to be happy, to marry, to have children. My grandchildren.'

'And he is *sangu de ma sangu*, only son of my only sister, Gina, God rest her soul. I want him to be happy, too.'

'So, what do we know about this girl, this Rosie Madigan? Tell me more.'

'I doan know any more, Salvatore. That's all Johnny told me this morning. I repeated everything to you.'

Salvatore sipped his red wine, his faded blue eyes thoughtful, the expression on his strong face contemplative. At last he lifted his head and looked at his only true friend, the only man he trusted. 'What about her family? Who are they? Where are they? Still in Queens?'

'I doan know,' Vito muttered. 'Johnny doan tell me. But he *is* goin' to marry her. He told me he's bought her a big diamond ring.'

'Then we gotta find out about her, Vito. Put one of the guys on it, one of the *capi*. Let's start asking a few questions. Find out who this woman is that my son wants to marry.'

FORTY

Rosie felt a wave of nausea sweep over her and she got up quickly, startling Aida, Fanny and Gavin. They were holding a meeting in the production offices at Billancourt Studios, and they all stared at her.

Fanny exclaimed, 'Don't you feel well again, Rosie?'

'I'm fine, just a bit queasy,' she said, edging out of the room, fighting sudden dizziness as well as the awful nauseous sensation. At the door she paused and added, 'Maybe I'm coming down with a cold. Excuse me, I'll be back in a minute.'

Hurrying down the corridor, she went into the ladies' room and leaned against one of the wash-basins, waiting for the sickness to pass. She had no idea what was wrong with her; she hadn't been feeling well for days. Perhaps it *was* the 'flu. Another thought struck her. Alarmed, she stiffened and gripped the edge of the sink. What if she were pregnant! Of course she wasn't. There was no way she could be. She dispelled this thought from her head immediately, reminding herself that Johnny had always worn something. And besides, she hadn't seen him since February: Sunday the twenty-third, to be precise. It was already the first week of April and she had had a period since she had last slept with him.

I'm not thinking straight, I'm exhausted, Rosie thought, and looked at herself in the mirror. Her reflection confirmed this. There were dark rings under her eyes and her face was drawn, almost gaunt. Lack of sleep, she told herself, remembering those endless, restless nights of late. And too much work.

Work. She couldn't dawdle around here, feeling rotten. She must get back to the meeting. Pulling herself together, she splashed cold water on her face, patted it dry with a paper towel and headed for the door.

As she walked back to the production office, Rosie realized that her legs were steadier, the queasy feeling less pronounced. 'Now, where were we?' she asked as she opened the door, returning to the meeting. 'What have I missed?'

'Nothing much,' Gavin said. 'We've been talking about you.'

'That's not nice!' she exclaimed and laughed weakly.

'Aida thinks I'm overworking you, and apparently Fanny agrees. They both believe you need a couple of days off; so that's what you're going to get. Along with my apologies, Rosie, for being such a slave-driver.'

'You haven't been a slave-driver!' Rosie protested. 'And I'm all right.' She looked from Gavin to Aida.

'It's not the work that's done me in. It's lack of sleep. I realize that now. I've been a bit of an insomniac lately.' Her eyes shifted to Fanny. '*You* know I haven't been overdoing it.'

'Well . . . you have a bit,' Fanny mumbled.

'Take a couple of days off, Rosie,' Aida interjected. 'We really are in good shape with the costumes, fairly well advanced, and you know that we are. You've put in some excruciatingly long hours these past few weeks. You deserve a break. And Fanny and Val can manage for a day or two.'

'But –'

'No buts,' Gavin said, cutting her off. 'I'm taking you back to your apartment myself. And right now.' He pushed up the sleeve of his sweater and glanced at his watch. 'It's four o'clock already. Let's pack it in here, Aida, call it a day.'

'You go along,' Aida replied. 'I must stay for a couple of hours, go over my new budgets and make a few calculations. That battle scene you've added is not going to be cheap, I can tell you that. Anyway, let me struggle with it, come up with some answers. You go, Gavin, take Rosie home. I'll get your car and driver for you.' As she spoke she lifted the phone.

Fifteen minutes later Rosie and Gavin were settled in the back of the big Mercedes, heading away from Billancourt Studios in the direction of Paris.

'Aida's right, you know, you don't look well,' Gavin muttered, eyeing her. 'Too thin. Face too pale, too strained. And dark shadows under the eyes.' He pursed his lips, shook his head. 'It's my fault, I should have eased up on you. Look, maybe you should see the studio doctor. I ought to have thought of that before we left.'

'Don't be ridiculous! I'm not *ill*. A little tired. Maybe.'

'Aha, so you're finally admitting it. It seems to me that you're exhausted, and it's my doing. I'm responsible. Well, as producer of this here movie, I'm ordering you to take a few days' rest, my girl.'

'It's the middle of the week, Gavin. I can't afford to take any time off, not with our schedule.'

'It's not the middle of the week. It's Thursday. And you're going to do as I say.'

'You always have been bossy.'

He laughed. 'Enjoy a long weekend. You'll feel terrific on Monday.'

'All right,' she finally agreed, lacking the strength to argue with him. The motion of the car was making her drowsy. Her eyelids drooped; she closed her eyes. Ten minutes later she was fast asleep against his shoulder.

Rosie dozed all the way back to Paris.

Gavin did not rouse her until the car was pulling up outside her apartment on the rue de l'Université. And once they were inside, he took charge. He insisted she take a hot bath, swallow three aspirins and drink a mug of hot lemon tea which he had made. And then he tucked her up in bed.

'I want you to get some rest for a few hours,' he said, turning out the bedside lamp. 'Then later we'll go out for something to eat. Some nourishing soup, a plate of fish. It'll do you good. I suspect you're not eating enough. Okay?'

'Whatever you say, Gavin,' she mumbled, and closed her eyes as he went out, shutting the door behind him.

But, once again, sleep did not come.

Within seconds she was wide awake, staring out into the darkened room. Thinking of Johnny. He haunted her. The affair was over for her, and she knew it could never be rekindled. Henri had been right in everything he had said to her last week. He had pointed out that after five lonely, deprived years she had been very vulnerable to Johnny, to his adoration of her, to his powerful sexuality.

It was true. Johnny had made her feel like a woman again, had made her skin tingle, her blood race; he had brought her back to life. He had been exciting; it had been exciting. But it had only been an affair, and a brief one at that.

Desire. Lust. Sex. White-hot heat. Quick burn-out. Only cold ashes left at the end.

Those were Henri's words; how accurate they were. He was such a wise man, and experienced. He knew life; he had lived it to the fullest, had his share of passion and heartbreak; she knew that from Collie. She also knew that Henri had only *her* interests at heart. That was why she was so glad she had talked to him, confided in him when he had been in Paris. As always, Henri de Montfleurie had given her good advice.

'Look into your heart, examine your feelings,' he had told her. 'Ask yourself what *you* want, how you want to live your life. After all, it is *yours*, no one else's. And be honest with yourself,' he had added. 'You must be true to yourself, Rosie. And you must never settle for second best.'

She *had* been looking into her heart. For days. And she had come up with some essential truths. Everything she had thought several weeks ago had been resolved in her mind. She did not love Johnny Fortune. She had only been infatuated with him. There was no way she could spend the rest of her life with him. He wasn't a bad person, only different. And they had so little in common.

She must go to Johnny as soon as possible and tell him that it was over between them. She would go to New York and tell him to his face. There was no other way. He had behaved decently to her; therefore, she must behave decently with him.

She knew she had made the right decision. And yet she dreaded the thought of breaking it to him. He would be so hurt. He was in love with her and wanted to marry her. If it was upsetting to her, then it would be excessively painful to Johnny. After all, he had never felt this way before.

Johnny would be leaving Australia in a week, flying directly to Los Angeles. From the middle of April through the whole month of May, maybe even longer, he would be in New York. He was going to be recording his new disc at the Hit Factory, the well-known recording studios in Manhattan.

He had reminded her of this when he called her

from Perth the other day. 'I've been miserable without you, honey,' he had grumbled, sounding so close he might have been in the other room. 'We can't be apart like this ever again. I can't take it, Rosie. It's a lousy way for me to live, without you. I'm just not going to do it.' He had gone on and on.

Murmuring something soothing, calming him down, she had managed to get off the phone finally. But there was no denying that his words had worried her. It was obvious that his feelings for her had not changed. If anything, they had intensified.

Thinking again of what she had just resolved to do, Rosie shivered. Burying herself in the pillows, she pulled the sheet up and closed her eyes. It took her a long time, but eventually she fell into an exhausted sleep.

She dreamed of her mother and of being a little girl again in Queens.

'Why didn't you wake me up?' Rosie asked from the doorway of the living room.

Startled, Gavin glanced over his shoulder. 'God, you made me jump!' he exclaimed, getting up out of the chair. 'I didn't hear you.'

'I'm sorry,' she said and looked down at the pages of the script which were scattered on the floor around the chair. 'Working again, I see. You're worse than I am.'

'Perhaps. Anyway, you look better. The three hours' sleep did you good.'

'I feel rested actually,' she answered, walking into the room, sitting down on the sofa. She eyed the bottle of white wine he had opened and said, 'I wouldn't mind a glass of that.'

Picking up the bottle, he filled the glass he had put out for her earlier and brought it to her.

'Thanks,' she said, and raising the glass to him she added, 'To you, Gavin, and thanks for being so considerate. Thanks for looking after me.'

'It's my pleasure. You'd have done the same for me. Anyway, it was my fault.' Lifting his goblet, he added, 'And here's to you.' After drinking some of the wine, Gavin put his glass down and began to pick up the pages of the screenplay, saying to Rosie, 'I'm beginning to worry about Josephine. I mean about who's going to play her. Casting has not come up with very many bright suggestions yet.'

'What about Sara Sommerfield?'

Gavin straightened and threw her a withering look. 'Sara Sommerfield,' he repeated. 'Her face is so empty she can't hold a close-up.'

'She's beautiful enough.'

'An eight-by-ten glossy and that's all. We need a bit of character here, Rosie.' He clipped the loose pages inside the cover of the script and put it on the coffee table. 'I'd thought of Jennifer Onslow, she'd be good. But she's not available. That's the problem, there's always something.'

'You'll find the right actress, Gavin; you always do. And there's still time, you know. We have four months before we start shooting.'

'Yep, that's true.' He fell down into his thoughts for a few seconds and then he looked across at her and said, 'How about Miranda English for Josephine?'

Rosie pulled a face. 'No, I don't think so. She's sort of . . . weird. But she's a good actress.'

'What do you mean by weird? That she's on drugs?'

'Is that what they're saying?' Rosie shook her head. 'But no, I didn't mean that actually. I just think she's a bit creepy.'

'Do you ever think about Sunny? What drugs did to her, I mean?'

Rosie nodded and a shadow fell across her face.

Gavin got up and walked over to the skirted table where Rosie kept her collection of photographs. He picked up the famous one of the group and studied it for a moment before putting it back in its place. Glancing at Rosie he said with a faint smile, 'It's funny how we all cart that picture around with us, isn't it? You and me and Nell and Kevin.'

At first Rosie didn't reply. Then she said, 'I wonder if Sunny has her picture with her in the mental home in New Haven? And whether Mikey took his with him when he disappeared?'

Gavin was half way across the floor, and he spun around to face her. There had been the strangest intonation in her voice, and he saw at once that she had the oddest expression in her eyes.

'You sound funny, and you look even more peculiar. What's wrong?' he asked.

'Nothing's wrong, Gavin. It just struck me the other day, quite forcibly, that none of us has behaved very well.'

'What are you referring to, Rosie?'

'The way we've treated each other. I mean, we said we were a family when we were kids – orphans –

and we promised to be there for each other. But we weren't. We broke our promises to each other, and that's the tragedy. We're *all* guilty.'

Gavin was silent. He took a sip of his drink, carried it with him to the chair and sat down. 'Guilty of what?'

'*Neglect*. Of each other. Selfishness. Self-involvement. Pride. Ambition. All of those things somehow got in the way. But *neglect* is the worst of all. We neglected Sunny at one moment, Gavin, when she needed us the most. We let her down. The same with Mikey. We let him down, too.'

'Sunny yes, I agree with you there. We should have noticed she was getting hooked on drugs. But I don't understand what you mean about Mikey.'

'We didn't help him when he was floundering, after he split up with Nell, when he was at odds with himself in every way and not sure about being a lawyer.' She lifted her shoulders slightly, gave a weary shrug and shook her head. 'I sometimes think that Mikey disappeared just to get away from all of us.'

Her words startled Gavin and he exclaimed, 'I don't believe *that*, Rosie! Anyway, *you* have always been wonderful to all of us, so don't knock yourself.'

'I broke my promise to you.'

'Oh come on –'

'No, listen to me, I did,' she interrupted. 'When we were kids, I promised to understand about your acting, the crazy life you led, working as a waiter in the Village, throwing yourself into those off-Broadway plays, doing soaps, studying with Lee

Strasberg. But I didn't understand, not in the end. And I broke my promise to you. After we had that horrible quarrel, which was my fault, I was too proud to come and apologize to you.'

'And I met Louise, had an affair with her, and the next thing I knew I was married to her.' Gavin paused, and held her eyes with his. 'I broke my promise to you too, Rosie. Let's face it, I did. I did say we were going to get married and work together in the theatre and in films, that we were going to be a team.'

She smiled. 'Don't look so woeful. We *do* work together, and we are a team. Sort of.'

'Yes.'

'Anyway, I was pretty stupid. A headstrong girl. So immature. I ran off, came here to Paris and got married to the first man who asked me.'

He smiled at her. 'My mother used to say something that's proven to be very true. Marry in haste, repent at leisure.'

'Mmmm.' Rosie lifted her glass, took a long swallow of the wine. 'I broke my promise to Kevin, you know. I always told him I'd stop him if I thought he was doing something foolish, and yet I let him follow in Dad's footsteps, let him become a cop.'

'Good God, Rosie, you couldn't have stopped him from joining the NYPD! He was hell-bent on it!'

'Yes . . .' Slowly, she twisted the glass in her hands; her eyes were far away; she was turning something over in her mind. 'But there was that *moment* when he was indecisive. I could have talked him out of it, I think. He was always interested in law, had even mentioned becoming a lawyer once.'

'I remember that . . .'

'And then there's Nell.'

'How did we let Nell down?'

Rosie offered him a small smile. 'She's our saving grace. I don't think you've let her down, nor have I, and I'm sure we haven't broken any promises to her. But . . .'

'But what? Finish what you've started, Angel Face.'

'I think that maybe Kevin has let her down.'

'*Oh*. How?'

'Staying with the force, working as an undercover cop. It's killing her, Gavin. She lives with fear on a day-to-day basis. I welcomed their relationship when I first found out about it, but now I'm not so sure that they should continue. Not if he stays undercover. I think Kevin should quit for his own sake as well as Nell's.'

'But you know he won't.'

'I guess not. As he says, he's a fourth-generation cop.'

'We can't interfere, Rosie. People are the authors of their own destinies, and they live with what they themselves create.'

'Yes, that's true. So why did you get ma –' She broke off, flushing, turned her head, straightened one of the frames on the table.

'Go on, finish it,' Gavin said softly.

There was a small silence. Finally Rosie looked him directly in the eye and asked, 'Why did you marry Louise?'

'Because she was pregnant. I felt it was my responsibility. My duty to stand by her.'

'You never told me.'

'You never asked.'

'But the baby died . . .' Rosie discovered she could not continue. She felt awkward suddenly.

'And you're wondering why I stayed with Louise when that happened.'

When she remained silent, Gavin said slowly, in a voice that was profoundly sad: 'I'll tell you what really happened, Rosie. The baby didn't die at birth, as we let everyone think. The baby died inside Louise, about two weeks before it was due to be born. She had to carry the baby full-term. So she walked around with a dead child in her for fourteen days, and it just about did us both in.'

'Oh God, Gavin, how terrible! What a horrifying experience. Poor Louise. And you. It must have been the worst nightmare for you to live through. What a dreadful tragedy.'

'Yes, it was. I stayed with her to help her through it, and to help myself by helping her –' Gavin broke off, sipped some wine. 'But all that was a long time ago.'

'I'm so sorry. I shouldn't have asked those questions, Gavin. I really shouldn't have.'

'It's all right, and don't start chastising yourself. Now, how about dinner? It's a bit late to go out, isn't it?' Before she could answer, he rushed on briskly. 'I know, I'll make us a nice Italian dinner. You have pasta in the cupboard, don't you?'

'I do, and that's where it's going to stay. You

might be a great actor, but you're a rotten cook.'

'You used to tell me I made wonderful meals.'

'I was young then and didn't know any better,' Rosie laughed. 'I think it would be better if we went to the bistro on the corner. Come on, let's get our coats. Make a dash for it before they close.'

FORTY-ONE

Gavin Ambrose sat on the sofa in the sitting room of his suite at the Ritz Hotel, surrounded by casting directories. Sipping a cup of coffee, he turned the pages of the Academy Players Directory of leading ladies.

That's what he was looking for, a leading lady, an actress with heart and soul, to play Josephine to his Napoleon.

Rosie had been right last Thursday when she had said he had plenty of time; on the other hand, a lot of big pictures were on the slate, and the best women were being signed up at a surprising rate. There was another Kevin Costner film in the works; Dustin Hoffman had just announced one; Sean Connery was getting ready to film a mighty epic adventure. All this sudden production activity made him nervous inasmuch as he was a perfectionist about everything, and most especially his cast. Last week he had turned down the three actresses he and Rosie had discussed, for a variety of reasons.

Finishing his coffee, he placed the cup on the tray

and walked across to the window, looking out into the Place Vendôme. It was a sunny Saturday afternoon, a week before Easter, and he wondered what he was doing cooped up in the hotel, looking at photographs of female Hollywood stars. Because it's your job, buster, he reminded himself. But to hell with it. He was going to call Rosie, see what she was up to on this beautiful April day.

She answered on the first ring.

'Are you sitting on top of that phone?' he asked, laughing.

'Sort of. Actually, I was just about to call you, Gavin.'

'Well, here I am, Angel Face! And you didn't even have to spend your quarter. Why were you about to call me?'

'I had a brainwave about ten minutes ago. It suddenly occurred to me that you could use a French or English actress. You don't *have* to have an American star. You're the box-office draw, as usual. I just remembered Annick Thompson. She's French, but her English is good. She's lived in London for a number of years, ever since she married Philip Thomas, the director. Anyway, I think she's very talented and could be just right for Josephine.'

'She's great, you're right, Rosie. Why didn't I think of her? Oh, I know why. She's very tall.'

'*She* could stand in a hole, *you* on a box,' she teased.

'Thanks a lot. With you for a friend, I don't need an enemy.'

'You know very well I'm only joking. But she's not much taller than you, an inch maybe. And there won't be any high-heeled shoes in the movie, only ballet flats, *Empire* style.'

'Annick's a good suggestion,' Gavin said. 'I'll throw the name at Aida, see what she thinks.'

'Why were you calling me, Gavin?'

'I wondered if you had any plans. It's such a fine day, I thought we might do something. We've both been working like dogs.'

'Such as?'

'I don't know. You're the Parisienne. Make a suggestion.'

'We could go for a long walk in the Bois de Boulogne, but I just came in from doing my Saturday chores, and it's colder than you think. Quite nippy, in fact, and very windy.'

'I just want to get out of the hotel. I don't want to be *outside*, necessarily. What about a movie?'

'That's a very original idea. Let's do it,' she laughed.

'And then I'll take you to dinner afterwards. Why don't we go to the bistro on your corner?'

'Okay. It's my favourite place.'

'When shall I pick you up, Angel Face?'

'Don't. Let's meet at Fouquet's on the Champs-Élysées instead. It'll save time. Say in about half an hour?'

'I'll be there.'

In the end they abandoned the movie houses on the Champs-Élysées. Some were full; others had long lines outside. It seemed that half of Paris had had the same idea.

Instead, they took a cab to a cinema Rosie knew on the Left Bank. 'They only play old movies,' she explained to Gavin as they scrambled into the taxi. 'And I've no idea what's on the bill this weekend. But something good is usually playing.' She eyed the felt fedora. 'Do you really have to wear that hat, Gavin? I'm not sure I like you in it.'

He grinned. 'It's my disguise.'

'You've got to be kidding! I'd recognize you anywhere. And those women certainly did at Fouquet's. I *saw* them eyeing you. Drooling, actually.'

'They weren't eyeing me. Look, I'm serious, Rosie, nobody knows who I am when I wear this hat. I think it's sort of nifty. No?'

'It looks moth-eaten to me.'

He laughed and teased her about her loden cape, which he said he was sick of seeing, and they exchanged friendly banter on their way to the Left Bank. Twenty minutes later, they were rushing inside the cinema to see *Casablanca*. They had missed the first ten minutes, but neither of them cared. They each knew the old classic extremely well.

As they settled into their seats, Gavin whispered, 'I can't wait for Bogie to say, "Of all the gin joints in all the towns in all the world, she walks into mine." It's my favourite line in the movie.'

Once the film was over they went to the bistro at the end of Rosie's street. It was crowded, but Rosie was well known there, and a table was miraculously found.

'You've got to take off your hat,' Rosie hissed once

they were seated. 'I'm not going to sit here with you if you persist in keeping it on. It's rude. And everyone's looking at you.'

'They'll look at me even more if I take it off.'

'Nobody's going to bother you here,' Rosie said, then glanced up and smiled sweetly at the waiter, whom she knew. '*Vodka avec des glaçons, s'il vous plaît, Marcel,*' she said and then addressed Gavin. 'Do you want the same?'

He nodded. 'With a twist, *s'il vous plaît.*'

The waiter stared at him curiously, turned to Rosie, muttered, '*Oui, Madame de Montfleurie,*' and hurried away to fill their order.

'*He* recognized me.' Gavin winked at her. 'But I'll take the hat off just to please you.' Removing the felt fedora, he put it under his chair.

'Much better, Gavin. And nobody's going to bother you. This is La Belle France. Civilization and all that jazz.'

The words had hardly left her mouth when a young man came over to the table, excused himself profusely and thrust a scrap of paper at Gavin. In halting English, he said, 'Monsieur Ambrose, can I 'ave your autograph, *s'il vous plaît?*'

Gavin inclined his head graciously, signed his name and flashed the young man a dazzling smile.

The Frenchman departed, looking jubilant, grinning from ear to ear.

Gavin said, 'You see, I –'

'Don't you dare say I told you so, Ambrosini. Or I'll leave!'

He smiled at her beatifically.

She grinned at him, then studied him for a moment, her head to one side, her green eyes quizzical. She was about to ask him something when the waiter arrived with their drinks.

Seeing Gavin without the hat, the waiter exclaimed, *'Ah, oui, Monsieur Ambrose! Bien sûr!'* He added in English, 'I think it was you.'

Gavin nodded, gave the waiter a weak smile, and when they were alone he looked at Rosie through narrowed eyes. 'So much for your judgement.' Then he laughed as he touched his glass against hers. 'Here's looking at you, kid,' he said in his best Bogart imitation.

It was during coffee after dinner that Rosie said, very quietly, 'Can I ask you something, Gavin?'

'Sure, go ahead.'

'Why did you stay with Louise for so many years? She eventually recovered from the loss of the first baby. You both did. So why didn't you leave her if you were so unhappy?'

'Several reasons, Rosie, but the first and foremost was because of my son. I'd grown up without a father. Oh sure, Grandpa loved me, but it's not quite the same. And I wanted David to have a father, to have *me* there for him when he needed me. Then there was my career, my acting. I knew I had to concentrate on it, dedicate myself to it, if I were to succeed the way I wanted to. I was single-minded about my work, you know that, and I just didn't need marital problems, divorce problems, other-women problems. No distractions, that was my rule.'

'Are you saying there have never been other women in your life?' she asked softly, eyeing him curiously.

'There haven't been many, Rosie. I always kept up a good front, as far as my marriage was concerned. Don't you think I did?'

'Yes, very much so. It's only recently that I've come to realize how unhappy you've been all these years. Even last November, when we wrapped *Kingmaker*, I was sure you had a great marriage. I said so to Nell.'

'And what did she say?'

'Nell disagreed with me. She said I shouldn't forget you're an actor.'

'She's a shrewd one, our Miss Jeffrey is.'

'You'd better believe it.'

'Rosie . . .'

'Yes, Gavin?'

'There's another reason why I didn't leave Louise.' A slight pause followed. He held her with his cool grey eyes. 'There didn't seem to be any point, since you were married to someone else.'

Rosie stared at him. She said slowly, 'And that's why I stayed with Guy . . . because *you* were married.'

It was a cold clear night. The sky was a deep pavonine blue and cloudless; there was a full moon.

They did not speak as they walked up the street to the building where she lived; nor did they touch.

Once they were inside, Rosie threw her loden cape on the small wooden seat in the hallway, and Gavin did the same with his overcoat.

Without a word she hurried into the sitting room and stood in the centre of it, her face half turned from him.

He remained in the doorway, watching her. There was only one lamp on; it was quite dark and he could not make out the expression on her face. He longed to go to her, but he found he could not. For an unknown reason he was rooted to the spot.

Eventually she swung around to face him.

They stood staring at each other without speaking.

She took a step towards him.

He took one towards her.

And at that exact moment, as they moved slowly and purposefully into the middle of the room, they both knew with certainty that their lives were about to change. Absolutely and irrevocably. With sudden clarity they understood that nothing would be the same again.

She came into his arms, almost stumbling towards him in the end.

He closed his arms around her, strong and forceful, holding her firmly against his body.

Her arms encircled him; her hands went up into the nape of his neck, her fingers hardening against his skin; he pressed his against her spine.

They kissed at last, a deep, lingering kiss which they discovered they could not bring to an end. It was as if this kiss was meant to cancel out the years of pain. Lips devoured lips, teeth grazed, tongues entwined, and they clung together, as though they were drowning, afraid to let go.

He tasted the well-remembered sweetness of her

mouth, and mingled with it was the salt of her tears. Finally he broke the kiss, touched her cheeks with his fingertips. They were wet.

His eyes were locked to hers.

She returned the intense look. '*Gavin*. Oh Gavin, I love you. I love you so much.'

'And I love you, Rosie. I've never stopped loving you, not for a single day, not for a single moment.'

There, it was out.

It was said at last, after so many years of silence.

The look they exchanged was full of understanding and knowledge, and without another word he took her hand, leading the way.

Only a few seconds later Rosie was wondering how they had gone from the middle of her living room floor to the middle of her bed in such a short time, and when and where they had shed their clothes. Then all thoughts were stilled as Gavin drew her to him, kissing her over and over again.

Rosie returned his kisses without restraint. It was as though they had never been apart. The years tumbled away. They came back to a place they had once known, a place that was familiar and which belonged to them.

Although he had not made love to her for almost eleven years, Gavin still knew every curve and angle of her body as though it were his own. And she knew his.

They touched each other feverishly, revived the old sensations, the sensual feelings, brought each other to the edge of ecstasy. And their memories were sweet, flooding back to engulf them.

She had been his first love, he hers. Now, when they finally came together at last, it was like the first time they had made love.

And yet it was different. They were wiser; they had suffered for each other; and this brought a new tenderness.

The night was like a dream to them both.

They slept after the first time they made love, only to awaken several hours later, reaching for each other anxiously, afraid it had not been real. And Gavin discovered he wanted her again. Once more he took her to him, loving her without constraint. And Rosie felt the same, consumed with a yearning for him. They slept, made love again as dawn broke. Finally they fell into the deepest sleep either of them had had in years.

Rosie turned over in her bed, and reached for Gavin, only to find an empty place.

Sitting up with a start, blinking in the bright morning sunlight, she looked around the room, thinking, as she had last night, that it had all been a dream.

But it hadn't. She knew that from her body. His imprint was all over her. Smiling, she threw back the bedclothes and got up, found her dressing gown and went looking for him.

He was sitting behind her desk in the studio, dressed in his sweater and slacks, his horn-rimmed glasses perched on his nose. Pages of script were spread out in front of him.

'Gavin, my script! Be careful, it's full of my notes in the margin.'

He lifted his head and smiled at her. 'Is that a way to greet your lover, and after all I did for you last night.'

'Oh you . . . you!' she cried, laughing. 'You're impossible, Ambrosini!'

'I love you, by the way.'

'And I love you.' She came around the desk, bent over him and kissed his cheek. He moved his face slightly, in order to kiss her on the mouth, and then he pulled her down onto his lap, buried his head against her shoulder. 'God, how I love you, Rosie. So much, you'll never know.' He held her for a few seconds longer, then released her. 'Don't worry about the script, I only took one page out to make some changes in my dialogue. I'll replace it tomorrow at the studio.'

She got off his lap and walked across the room, saying over her shoulder, 'I smell coffee brewing. That was nice, darling. Do you want another cup?'

'No thanks, Angel.'

The phone rang.

They both stared at it.

Rose said quietly, 'I hope it's not Johnny.'

Gavin stood up. 'I'll leave you alone,' he said, walking around the desk.

She shook her head. 'It's okay, please stay. I have no secrets from you, Gavin. Anyway, the machine's on.'

The phone went on shrilling.

'No, it isn't.'

She grabbed it. 'Hello?' Then her expression brightened. 'Nell, how are you? Where are you?'

A split second later the smile evaporated. 'Oh Nell, no! Oh God!' Rosie's grip tightened on the receiver, and she sat down heavily. 'Oh my God!' she cried again, and the colour drained from her face. 'Yes, yes. I'll be there. As soon as I can.' She paused to listen, staring at Gavin who was standing near the desk, frowning. He saw that her eyes were wide, frightened, and that she was trembling. 'Yes, okay, I'll do that. I'll leave a message on your machine.' She hung up.

'What is it, Rosie? What's wrong?' he demanded, going to her.

She gaped at him, shaking her head, and her voice wobbled when she said, 'It's Kev. He's been shot. He's very badly hurt. The doctors at Bellevue told Nell his chances are poor.' She began to cry. 'They think Kev's going to die.'

FORTY-TWO

On Monday morning Rosie and Gavin went straight from JFK Airport to Bellevue Hospital, where Nell was anxiously waiting for them.

She was ashen-faced and exhausted after her long Sunday, and the moment she saw them she burst into tears. Rosie also began to cry as she went to comfort her. The two women clung to each other for a few seconds, and then stood apart. Gavin took Nell in his arms and hugged her, trying to keep up her hopes, as he had done with Rosie on the trans-Atlantic flight.

'Kevin's tough, and as strong as a horse,' he said to Nell, putting his arm around her and walking with her to a group of chairs at the other end of the waiting room. 'If anybody can pull through it's him.'

'But you don't understand,' Nell said tearfully. 'It's not just one gunshot wound. They peppered him with bullets. He's sustained quite a few injuries and lost a lot of blood.'

Anxiety-ridden though she was, Rosie added, 'Gavin's right, Kev's going to make it. He's just got to. He *can't* die like Dad did.' Sitting down next to

Nell, she went on, 'When can we see Kevin? Where are the doctors?'

Nell said, 'I'll go and talk to the head nurse. She'll page Doctor Morris. He said to do that when you arrived.'

Rosie nodded, and Nell hurried away.

Gavin took hold of Rosie's hand and held it tightly in his. 'If Kevin needs more blood, I'll be glad to give mine, Rosie. As I know you will.'

She stared at him. 'Most blood is safe though, isn't it, these days?'

'Yes. But I just wanted you to know that I'm willing to do that. Kev would do the same for me.'

'Yes he would and thanks for offering. Let's see what the doctor has to say.'

Nell returned a few minutes later with a white-coated man, whom Rosie assumed was one of Kevin's doctors.

Nell introduced them; then Rosie asked when they could see Kevin.

'He's still unconscious, Miss Madigan,' Doctor Morris said. 'And he's in ICU, but you can look in on him now if you wish.'

'We'd like to,' Rosie said and went on, 'What are my brother's chances, Doctor Morris?'

'Slightly better than yesterday. We operated on him again early this morning, removed the last of the four bullets, and he seems to be stabilizing well. Look, he's a young man, Miss Madigan, very strong and extremely fit, in excellent shape. That all works in his favour.'

Rosie nodded. She was close to tears again and

averted her head, clearing her throat, rummaging around in her handbag for a handkerchief.

Gavin said, 'If he needs more blood transfusions, Miss Madigan and I are willing to be donors.'

'We don't need blood for him right now, and I hope we won't. But that's good to know. Thanks. Shall we go?'

The three of them followed Doctor Morris out of the waiting room and down the corridor, walking in the direction of the Intensive Care Unit.

The doctor finally stopped, opened a door and ushered Rosie and Gavin into Kevin's room. He lay in the hospital bed, attached by tubes to all kinds of machines. He was as white as the sheets on the bed. His eyes were closed; his breathing was shallow.

Going over to the bed, Rosie touched his hand, leaned closer to him and kissed his cheek. 'It's me, Kev darling,' she said, swallowing her tears. 'It's Rosie. I'm here for you, and so is Gavin. And Nell. We love you, Kev.'

Kevin lay perfectly still. Not an eyelash flickered. Rosie squeezed his hand again and turned away. The tears ran down her cheeks. To her he looked as though all the strength had ebbed out of him, and her heart constricted in her chest. Suddenly, she understood why the prognosis had been so grave yesterday.

Gavin stepped up to the bed, and took Kevin's hand in his. 'It's Gavin, Kev. We're going to stay here with you until you get better.' Like Rosie had done, Gavin bent over him, kissed his cheek.

Outside in the corridor they ran into Neil

O'Connor, who had come to see Kevin again. Nell introduced the detective to Rosie and Gavin. The doctor excused himself, and Neil walked with them to the waiting room.

'What happened?' Rosie asked, once the doctor had gone.

Neil shook his head. 'I'm sorry, Rosie. I don't know. And we won't know until we can talk to Kev.'

'Nell told us yesterday that Kev's partner had been wounded, too. Hasn't he told you anything yet? Or is he also unconscious?'

Neil shook his head, and the expression on his face was bleak. There was a sudden stillness between the four of them, and Neil said in a low shaky voice, 'Unfortunately, Tony just died.'

'Oh no!' Nell cried and pressed her hand to her mouth, and the tears spurted again.

Rosie clutched Gavin's arm. She had turned deathly pale.

The three friends kept a vigil for four days.

It was Friday, April the seventeenth when Kevin Madigan regained consciousness and finally opened his eyes. It was Good Friday, and the beginning of the Easter weekend.

Nell was sitting next to his bed, and she was the first person he saw. He gave her the faintest of smiles. 'Hi, honey,' he said weakly.

'Oh Kev! Thank God!' she cried, reaching for his hand, holding on to it tightly. Rising, she leaned over him, kissed his cheek, and murmured against his ear, 'I love you.'

'I love you too, Nell,' he whispered, his voice hoarse.

Still holding his hand, she sat down again, her eyes pinned to his face. Tears glistened in them.

'I'm sorry, Nellie.'

'It's all right, don't talk. You're still weak, you've been through a terrible ordeal. But I know you're going to make it.' She tried to extract her hand. He clung to it.

She said, 'Let me go, Kev. Just for a minute. I want to fetch Rosie and Gavin. They're outside in the waiting room.'

FORTY-THREE

Rosie knew that Johnny was in Manhattan.

He had left innumerable messages on her machine at the apartment in Paris and called Jeffrey Associates numerous times, looking for Nell. Her assistant had been instructed to deal with this emergency by explaining to all of Nell's clients that she was on vacation and unavailable.

But now on this Good Friday afternoon, knowing that Kevin was out of danger, Rosie made the decision to see Johnny. She needed to tell him to his face that they had no future together.

After calling the Waldorf Astoria and being passed to the message desk, Rosie hung up. It was obvious he was having his calls screened; she did not want to leave Gavin's number at the Trump Tower apartment. After mulling things over for a few seconds, she decided to go over to the Hit Factory, where he most probably was working on his new disc. Once, while discussing his recording sessions, he had explained that he liked to start early, around eleven, and work through until six or seven. She glanced at her watch. It was just turning three. She would take a taxi there now.

Having returned to Gavin's apartment at the Trump Tower from the hospital only an hour ago, Rosie hurried into the bathroom to take a quick shower. After putting on fresh make-up and doing her hair, she dressed in a grey suit with a matching three-quarter-length overcoat.

Gavin had remained at Bellevue Hospital with Kevin and Nell. She left a note on his desk saying that she would be back in a couple of hours, and, after consulting the Manhattan Yellow Pages, she made a mental note that the Hit Factory was still at the same address on West Fifty-fourth Street.

Ten minutes later, as she was paying off the cab, Rosie saw Kenny Crossland, who played keyboard, out of the corner of her eye. He was standing in the entrance of the building where the Hit Factory was housed.

As she turned around and took a step forward, he grinned at her and called, 'Hi, Rosie! Johnny's gonna be thrilled to see you. He's been driving us all nuts. When he couldn't reach you he got real upset.'

'I've been trying to get in touch with him,' Rosie said. 'And then I was on a plane coming from Paris.' She shrugged, and gave him a small smile. 'Well, I'm here now.'

Kenny put his arm around her shoulders, and together they went into the building. Riding up in the elevator he explained, 'We're recording instruments today, but Johnny's here anyway. He likes to be in on every aspect of the production. He's probably doing a bit of rehearsing right now, or he might even be over-dubbing.'

Rosie merely nodded, not wishing to say too much to Kenny. After all, her business was with Johnny, and she had noticed on the British tour that he and Kenny had frequent spats about all kinds of things. She suddenly felt protective of Johnny, and did not want to give his associates anything to gossip about.

Kenny deposited her in the reception room, asking her to wait while he went to get Johnny. She thanked him; he grinned at her and disappeared.

Sitting down in one of the chairs, suddenly feeling weary and debilitated, Rosie leaned her head back and stared blankly at the walls. Everywhere there were framed platinum and gold records of stars such as Billy Joel, Michael Bolton, Paul Simon, Madonna and Johnny Fortune.

She wondered what was keeping Johnny, then realized he might well be in the middle of a session, and that he couldn't break away until it was finished.

About fifteen minutes later a young man came into reception and introduced himself as one of Johnny's record producers. Chatting to her amiably, he led her out of the reception area and down in the elevator to another floor. Here he ushered her into the control room. Through the large glass window, she saw Johnny on the studio floor, singing into a microphone. His eyes were closed, and he was wearing headphones.

The young man said, 'Johnny won't be long. His

vocal is being over-dubbed onto the track.' As if he thought she needed to know exactly what was happening, he added, 'Johnny's listening to the music track on the headphones and singing what he hears into the mike.'

'It's very interesting,' Rosie murmured, continuing to watch Johnny.

The young man smiled, nodded and left her alone in the control room with the engineer.

Once Johnny finished the track, he opened his eyes and peered out at the engineer in the control room. The engineer nodded enthusiastically and gave the thumbs-up sign, indicating that the session had gone well.

It was then that Johnny saw her.

He appeared to be taken aback for a split second.

Then his face lit up and he waved. Putting the mike down, he took off his headphones and beckoned to her.

Rosie went to join him on the studio floor.

Immediately, he grabbed hold of her, pulled her into his arms and began to kiss her.

After a moment she managed to extricate herself gently, and with a nervous laugh, she said, 'Johnny, the engineer's watching us.'

'So what. Oh honey, it's great to see you! I've missed you so much!' Still holding her by the shoulder, he stood away from her and stared hard at her, grinning from ear to ear. But his bright blue eyes were intense, and she noticed a tiny spark of anger lurking there. His voice rose when he exclaimed, 'Hey, Rosie,

I've been trying to reach you for days! Calling and calling your apartment. I've been going crazy trying to find you. Why didn't you call me back? Where the hell have you been?'

Speechless, she stared at him. Overwrought about her brother, jet-lagged, exhausted from her hospital vigil and extremely anxious about this confrontation, Rosie felt her control slipping. She endeavoured to steady herself.

When she didn't answer him, Johnny rushed on, 'We've gotta change things, honey; I can't live like this. You've gotta be with me all the time.' Peering at her, his expression suddenly questioning, he cried, 'Why didn't you let me know you were coming? How long have you been here?'

His words touched a raw nerve in her. She thought of her brother's fight for his life in the ICU at Bellevue Hospital and she fell apart, tears streaming down her face.

Startled and confused, Johnny put his arm around her and guided her out of the studio, saying, 'Aw, honey, don't cry. I guess I'm just a bit worked up because I've been out of my mind with worry.' Going into an office, he drew her inside with him and closed the door behind them.

Rosie couldn't stop weeping. She sank onto a chair, groped around in her bag for a handkerchief and brought it to her face. Her pent-up emotions, repressed over the last few days, were released, and she continued to sob.

At a loss, Johnny sat down on the chair opposite her; he was baffled. At last, he said in a much gentler tone, 'I shouldn't have railed on at you, Rosie. I didn't mean to upset you so much.'

Taking a deep breath, she said through her sobs, 'It's not you, Johnny.' And then before she could stop herself, she blurted out, 'It's my brother Kevin! He's been shot. He almost died. That's why you haven't heard from me these last few days, Johnny. I've been with him at the hospital.' Once again she had a mental picture of Kevin's ashen face, and fresh tears flowed.

'*Shot*? What happened? Was he mugged or something?' Johnny asked, frowning.

'No, he wasn't mugged. He was shot when he was working. By the Mafia. I'm sure it was the Mafia. They gunned him down like they gunned down my father,' Rosie cried through her sobs.

'*Mafia*,' Johnny said. 'I don't understand . . .'

'My brother's an undercover cop. I'm not supposed to tell anyone, but –'

'*Cop*,' Johnny muttered, staring at her.

'Yes,' Rosie answered, nodding her head. 'He's with the NYPD, has been for years. For months he's been working for the CID, investigating a Mafia family. The Rudolfos. You must have heard of them. Everybody's heard of them. They shot Kevin. The Rudolfos shot my brother.' Pressing the handkerchief to her face she tried to stem her tears.

Johnny stiffened in the chair and his face paled. He continued to stare at Rosie disbelievingly, trying to digest what she had just told him. In Paris, she had said her brother was an accountant; now she was telling him he was an undercover cop. A cop who had been shot by the Rudolfos.

His world turned upside down.

'I didn't come here to tell you about Kevin,' Rosie said slowly. 'That all came out because I've been so upset. I came to see you to explain something, Johnny, something about us.'

'What do you mean?' he asked in a low voice.

Rosie looked directly at him and pushed a smile onto her face. But it faltered instantly. In the most gentle voice she could summon, she said, 'Johnny, it won't work.'

'What won't?'

'You and I.'

In a way, he had known what was coming, what she was going to say, but still he could not accept it. He felt as though all the blood were draining out of him; feeling sick, he sat back in the chair, trembling inside.

Finally, Johnny said, 'Why won't it work? I love you, Rosie. You know I do.'

Taking a deep breath, she reached out to hold his hand and said, 'But I don't love you, Johnny. At least, not in the way you want me to love you.'

'We're wonderful together! Great in bed, great out of it. You said that to me in London.'

'Oh Johnny, you are very special, so loving and generous. But I can't marry you. It would never work. We're so different and in so many ways –'

'What ways? Tell me what ways?'

'The way we live our lives.'

'I don't get it.'

'Listen to me, Johnny. You're one of the world's greatest entertainers; you're a megastar, and you live in a certain manner; you *have* to because of your work. You keep odd hours. Then again, you need the woman you love to be with you all the time. Night and day. On tour. Always at your side. I can't do that, Johnny. I have a career of my own. I adore my work, and I can't give it up. You're possessive, controlling even, while I'm extremely independent. The sparks would be flying all the time.'

'The sparks do fly when we're in bed. We're not so different then, are we?'

'No, we're not. You're a very sensual man, and I found you extremely seductive. But sex is not enough. There has to be more in a marriage.'

'You're not giving it a chance, us a chance,' he argued, pushing aside his shock, focusing on her. 'I've been in Australia for over a month . . . I haven't seen you for *seven weeks*. We just need to be together, Rosie. A few days with me at the Waldorf, and things will be the same. Just the way they were in Paris and London. I know they will be.'

Shaking her head and letting go of his hand, Rosie stood up. 'No they won't, Johnny.'

'You're wrong, honey!' he exclaimed, jumping to his feet. 'You can't tell me you don't feel anything for me, that you don't love me the way I love you! I can remember every minute we've spent together . . . that wasn't an act . . . you meant it, honey.'

She nodded. 'Yes, I did, Johnny. Being with you was special. I was infatuated with you, but I didn't grow to love you. I'm not in love with you, Johnny. That's why there's no future for us.'

He gaped at her. He was so stunned he could not speak.

Every bit of her sympathy, her innate kindness and gentleness rose to the surface. She reached out and touched his arm. In a voice that was sad, full of regret, she whispered, 'I'm sorry, Johnny, so very sorry.'

'Give us a chance,' he pleaded.

She stared at him, biting her lip. She felt so sorry for him, and yet there was nothing she could do to assuage his pain.

Tears glittered in his eyes. 'But I love you, Rosie. What am I going to do without you? Please, stay with me a few days,' he begged. 'Let's try and work this out. There must be a way.'

'There isn't, Johnny darling. And I can't stay. I'm leaving for Paris on Sunday morning. I have to get back to work.' She turned when she got to the door. 'Goodbye, Johnny,' she said.

FORTY-FOUR

Johnny was devastated.

Rosie had left him. His life was in shreds. He couldn't live without her. He wanted her back. He had to find a way to get her back.

He sat in the stretch limousine on his way to Staten Island, turning everything over in his mind. Very simply, he was unable to accept her reasons for breaking up with him. She hadn't made sense; he knew she was lying. The real reason she was dumping him was because her brother had told her he was part of the Rudolfo family. And she believed the Rudolfos had shot Kevin.

This afternoon, after she had left the recording studio, he had called Uncle Salvatore on the spur of the moment. And now he was going to see him, to talk to him, to ask for a special favour. He had never asked for anything before; he was quite sure the Don would not refuse him. When they had spoken earlier, Salvatore had begged him to come to dinner. 'After all, it's Good Friday, Johnny, a special occasion for us.'

But he had declined respectfully, explaining that

he was recording until seven. This was not true. In fact, he had left the studio almost immediately after Rosie, once he had spoken to the Don. He was no longer able to concentrate on his work. Shaken up, he had returned to the hotel knowing he must pull himself together before he went out to the island. He did not want to show weakness in front of Uncle Salvatore.

His thoughts zeroed in on Rosie. And on her brother Kevin.

It was all very obvious to him. In investigating the family, her brother had somehow found out about his connection to the Rudolfos through his Uncle Vito, a *caporegime* in the organization and Salvatore's closest *goombah*. Her brother had warned her off him. Yes, that was it. That was how it had happened.

It wasn't possible that she didn't love him. He knew better than that. After all, he was Johnny Fortune. Women swooned over him. She had called him a megastar; she had said he was seductive, sensual. She was telling him something, wasn't she?

Johnny closed his eyes.

Her face danced in his head.

She was beautiful.

He loved her. She was the only woman he had ever loved. And she loved him. He was certain of that. They were powerful together.

He was going to get her back.

His Uncle Salvatore was going to help him.

They sat together in the inner sanctum.

Salvatore Rudolfo sipped a strega, Johnny a glass

of white wine, and they talked for a short while about Johnny's Australian tour, the new disc he was recording, his career in general.

And then Salvatore sat back in the chair and smiled at Johnny. *Sangu de ma sangu*, he thought. Blood of my blood. My son. Except that Johnny did not know that he was his father. Lately, he had wondered if he had made a mistake in not telling Johnny the truth. Maybe Vito had been right. Perhaps he ought to know. What harm would it do? And Johnny is a big star now, the biggest of them all. Nothing can hurt him. Only Johnny would know, not the whole world. He would think about it some more. Make a decision before Johnny went back to the coast. If he did tell him, it would have to be their secret.

Focusing his penetrating gaze on Johnny, Salvatore said, 'I'm glad you came out to see me, Johnny. Now I can congratulate you in person. Vito tells me you've found the right woman, a good Catholic girl to be your wife. When're we going to meet her?'

Johnny took a deep breath. 'That's why I wanted to see you tonight, Uncle Salvatore. To talk to you about Rosie. There's a problem.'

'Oh. What kind of problem?'

'Rosie's broken off with me.'

Salvatore was flabbergasted. 'That's impossible. Women are crazy about you, Johnny.'

'I'm sure Rosie still loves me.'

'Then why?' Salvatore raised a snowy brow.

'Rosie's brother is a cop. He's been shot, badly wounded –'

'A *cop*, Johnny? Her brother is a cop? And you got engaged to her?'

'I didn't know he was a cop. Not until today. Rosie says her brother was shot by the Rudolfo family. I think he knows about Uncle Vito, my connection to the family, and that he told Rosie. And that's the reason she broke it off.'

'Mebbe. Except that this brother, the cop, was not shot by the Rudolfo family. The Rudolfo family don't go around shooting cops. It's bad for business. *Capisci?*'

Johnny nodded, and a look of relief flooded his face. 'That's what I thought, Uncle Salvatore, and that's why I came to see you. I wanted to be sure that Rosie was wrong.'

'She is, Johnny, very wrong.'

Johnny hesitated slightly, and then said, 'I want you to help me get her back.'

'How can I do that?'

'I want you to put out the word with the other families, Uncle Salvatore, find out who did shoot her brother. I'd like to prove to her that it wasn't the Rudolfos.'

Salvatore looked at him and his blue eyes narrowed slightly. After a brief moment of reflection, the Don inclined his head. 'I'll talk to Anthony. He'll find out everything we need to know. Leave it with me, we'll talk later this weekend.'

Five minutes after Johnny kissed the Don good-night and took his leave, the *consigliere* came into the study.

Without preamble, he said, 'Listen, boss, Joey Fingers is leaving now. He wants to come in and pay his respects. Is that okay?'

'No. I don't want to see him.'

'I told him this is the last warning he's getting. That if he shoots his mouth off again, discusses our business with anyone, he's out.'

'Joey Fingers has become our biggest liability. Get rid of him, Anthony.'

The *consigliere* looked at the Don swiftly. 'You mean hit him?'

'Yeah. Take him out.'

'Consider it done, boss.'

Johnny relaxed in the limousine as it sped across Staten Island heading for the Verrazano Narrows Bridge. His problem with Rosie would soon be solved. Salvatore Rudolfo was *capo di tutti capi*, boss of all bosses, on the Eastern Seaboard. He was the ultimate power. The other families would give Salvatore the information he needed. By tomorrow, Sunday at the latest, the Don would know exactly who had shot Rosie's brother.

He would go to her, even if it meant following her to Paris, and tell her. The Rudolfos would be exonerated.

For the first time in hours, Johnny felt more like his old self. He smiled. Everything was going to be all right. He and Rosie would be married as soon as her divorce was final.

Half an hour later, as the limousine rolled onto the Verrazano Bridge, it came to an abrupt halt. Sitting up straight and leaning forward, Johnny said, 'Hey, Eddie, what's going on?'

Eddie glanced over his shoulder. 'Gee, I don't know, Mr Fortune. It just stopped. Could be it's the transmission. It's happened once before.'

'Oh Jesus!' Johnny exclaimed. 'That's all I need. What do we do now?'

'I'll call the company on the cellular. They'll send another car immediately, Mr Fortune.'

'Okay, make the call. Just get me back to the Waldorf,' Johnny snapped.

Ten minutes later, Joey Fingers came barrelling onto the bridge. The first thing he saw was the limousine pulled to one side, and he slowed as he approached it. Immediately he recognized it as the one Johnny used. It had been standing outside the Rudolfo house for several hours this evening.

Joey slid to a stop behind the stretch, and got out. He walked to the driver's window and tapped on it.

Johnny recognized Joey and said to Eddie, 'I know him. See what he wants.'

Eddie rolled down the window and Joey looked into the limousine, and exclaimed, 'Hiya, Johnny, what's wrong? Why're ya sitting here?'

'The limo's broken down,' Johnny said. 'We're waiting for another car.'

Joey laughed. 'Hey, what kind of a limo service is this?' he said, directing this comment to Eddie. He cackled.

Eddie gave him a cold stare and was silent.

Joey said, 'Do ya really wanna sit here and wait,

Johnny? Come on, kiddo, I'll give ya a lift back into Manhattan. Where're ya staying?'

'The Waldorf,' Johnny answered and opened the car door. 'So long, Eddie.'

Johnny followed Joey back to the sedan, and got into the front seat with him. Within seconds, they were speeding off the Verrazano Bridge, heading for the Brooklyn–Queens Expressway which would take them to the Brooklyn–Battery Tunnel and the southern tip of Manhattan.

Joey talked non-stop as they drove, mostly about women. Johnny soon grew bored, settled back in his seat and closed his eyes.

Turning on the radio, Joey hummed to himself, pushing the car to its limit. Soon they were streaking along the expressway. They reached the Brooklyn–Battery Tunnel in record time, sliding into the city on the West Side. Joey followed the road, making a gentle U-turn to the left, heading south. Very shortly, they entered the underpass which would take them under Battery Park and on to the FDR Drive heading north to mid-town and the Waldorf.

Joey was concentrating on the road; Johnny was dozing.

Neither of them saw the black van pulling closer. It had been on Joey's tail since the entrance to the Brooklyn–Battery Tunnel where it had been waiting for him.

Now it suddenly surged forward, drawing along-side Joey's window. As Joey Fingers became aware of the van and turned his head to look, a spurt of bullets from a Kalashnikov machine gun sprayed into his body. He slumped over the wheel. The hit-man went on firing into the car before speeding away.

Three bullets struck Johnny Fortune. One punctured his brain, the other two sliced through his chest, killing him instantly.

Joey's car, already spinning out of control, bounced off the wall of the underpass.

PART FOUR

Truest Loves

FORTY-FIVE

'When I get out of here, we can go on that vacation of yours, Nell,' Kevin said, smiling up at her.

Nell was straightening the pillows behind his head, and she went on doing so without answering him.

'Where do you want to go?' he asked, catching hold of her hand as she began to smooth the sheet.

Nell sat down in the chair near the bed, and finally said, 'I don't really know, Kevin. You've got to get better first. You're going to be in the hospital for several weeks yet, and then convalescing. I just want you to get well, then we can plan the trip.'

'You don't sound too enthusiastic,' he said, and cleared his throat. His voice was hoarse, but stronger than yesterday when he had first regained consciousness.

Nell gave him the benefit of a smile. 'Maybe we'll go to France when Gavin starts shooting the movie.'

'That's not much of a honeymoon. Too many other people around.'

'Who said anything about a honeymoon!'

'Me. Just now.'

Nell stared at him, surprised by his words.

He said, 'Don't you want to marry me?'

Nell's eyes remained fixed on his face. He was still deathly pale, but he was much better today. It was amazing really, the improvement he'd made in twenty-four hours. For five days he had been on the brink of death; she had suffered with him. She knew that she could never live through anything like this ever again. It would kill her.

'It's my job, Nell, isn't it? That's why you won't marry me.'

She found she was unable to speak. She loved him very much; she wanted to be his wife. But she knew herself, and she understood now that she could never handle the fear that his being an undercover cop entailed.

A small sigh escaped her. 'I just can't cope with it, Kev, I really can't.'

'You won't have to, Nell.'

'What do you mean?' she asked. Her heart missed a beat.

'When Neil O'Connor was here this morning I told him I'm quitting. I'll be putting my resignation in next week.'

'Oh Kev, that's wonderful!' she exclaimed, breaking into a smile. Then the smile slipped. 'But if you're doing that for me, quitting the force because of me, you might end up hating me one day.'

'Never. And I'm not doing it just for you. I'm doing it for both of us. I made a bad mistake on this last case, somewhere, somehow. I haven't deduced what it was yet. I haven't had a chance to think it through. But slip I did, Nellie. And I always said –'

She held up her hand. 'Don't talk so much, you're exhausting yourself. Anyway, I know exactly what you were going to say. You promised yourself you'd get out the day you made your first slip.'

Kevin nodded. 'And Tony's dead . . .' He was unable to finish his sentence. His face clouded over.

'Yes, Kev,' she said. Wanting to pull him out of his moroseness, taking his hand in hers, she repeated, 'Yes, of course I'm going to marry you.' Standing up, she bent over him and kissed his lips. Pulling away, she added, 'And let's do it as soon as possible.'

There was a tap on the door, and Rosie's head appeared around it. She entered, followed closely by Gavin.

'Well, guess what!' Nell exclaimed. 'You're just in time to congratulate us.'

Rosie looked from Nell to Kevin. She saw how happy they both were, and she grinned. 'You're getting married.'

Kevin smiled and eased himself against the pillows, feeling suddenly tired again; he didn't have the strength to speak.

'That we are.' Nell hugged Rosie and then Gavin. 'We've got a bridesmaid and a best man standing right here, haven't we, Kev? How about it? Will you two stand up for us?'

'Nobody else is going to get a chance,' Gavin said, and went and sat down next to Kevin. 'Congratulations to you both.'

'Kev's quitting the force,' Nell announced.

'Thank God!' Rosie looked at her brother. 'That's two wise things you've decided in one day. To save your life and marry the most wonderful girl in the world.'

'That's right,' Kevin murmured. 'She is.'

'Are you okay?' Rosie stood at the bottom of the bed, her eyes searching his face. 'I mean, you sound tired, Kev. Gavin and I were just discussing it coming over here, discussing whether we should leave or not. Perhaps we ought to stay on for a few more days.'

'No, Rosie, it's not necessary. I'll be okay now. And I've got my . . . Little Nell here with me.'

'That you do,' Nell interjected. 'And for the rest of your life.'

FORTY-SIX

Rosie did not notice that they had passed Trump Tower until they were at Seventy-second and Madison.

'Gavin, where are we going? I still have to finish my packing.'

'You've plenty of time. We're not leaving the apartment until eleven tomorrow morning. The plane's not until one. I just want to take you somewhere, to show you something.'

'What do you want to show me?'

He put his arm around her and pulled her to him, kissing the tip of her nose. 'You'll just have to wait and see, Angel.'

A moment or two later, the car was turning on East Eighty-third, heading towards Fifth Avenue. When it drew to a stop outside an apartment building on Fifth, Rosie threw Gavin a quick look and asked, 'Are we going to see somebody?'

'Ask no questions, and you'll get no lies.'

The chauffeur came around and opened the door, helping Rosie out. Gavin followed. The doorman nodded and smiled as Gavin led her into the lobby of the building. As they stood waiting for the elevator she said, 'Come on, Ambrosini, tell me who we're visiting.'

'It's a surprise,' he answered.

They got out on the top floor, and Rosie was startled when Gavin pulled a key out of his pocket and put it in the lock. Opening the front door wide, he ushered her inside the apartment.

She saw at once that it was completely empty, and she turned to him, her eyes full of questions. 'Is this yours, Gavin?'

He nodded. 'It sure is, Angel Face.'

'How long have you had it?'

'I found it some months ago, but the deal only just closed. You know what these co-op boards are like. Anyway, it's mine now; so come on, I want to show you around.'

Taking hold of her hand he walked her forward through the grand entrance foyer, into the large drawing room beyond, on into the dining room and the kitchen opening off it.

Then he walked her back to the entrance foyer.

'Most of the main rooms face Fifth, which is great,' he said. 'I like looking out at the trees in Central Park, don't you?'

'Yes,' she replied. 'What's there?'

'Come on, I'll show you.' As they moved along the main corridor, he threw open a door and explained: 'I thought this room would be perfect for David. It's a good size, and it's somewhat removed from the rest of the apartment. Now here's the library.' He showed it to her, and moving on, he finally stopped in front of large double doors.

Gavin took her into this room saying, 'It's got a fireplace, and it also overlooks the park.' He let go of her hand and strode into the middle of the floor, looking around as he did. 'It's a perfect room for us, Rosie, don't you think?'

'For us?' she repeated, and then found herself stammering, 'What do you mean, Gavin?'

He walked back to her swiftly, and when he reached her he tilted her face to his. 'I'd like this to be our bedroom, Rosie.'

'Oh,' she said.

He leaned into her, kissed her mouth, and drew away from her. He said, 'We've wasted far too many years already. Don't you think it's time we got married? As soon as we're both free.'

She smiled at him. It was a dazzling smile that filled her face with radiance and made her green eyes sparkle.

'Oh yes, Gavin darling. *Yes*,' she said without a moment's hesitation.

Gavin put his arms around her and kissed her deeply, then he released her and said, 'I read something recently, Rosie, and I want to share it with you.'

She nodded.

'The angels keep their ancient places, turn but a stone, and start a wing! 'Tis ye, 'tis your estrangèd faces, that miss the many-splendoured thing.'

As he had been speaking, Gavin's eyes had not left her face. Again, he bent into her and kissed her full on the mouth.

'I'm so glad that we didn't miss our many-splendoured thing, Rosie.'